The Vo

A nove

By
Kevin William Barry

THE VOYAGE

First edition. August 10, 2019.

ISBN: 978-1393811572

Written by Kevin William Barry.

Also by Kevin William Barry

A Murderous Addiction
Innocent Until Proven Deadly
Dead Tropical
A Lethal Odyssey
A Pain In The Arts
Charlotte and the Morthe
Alien Vermin
Murder In The Outback
Murder, Mayhem and Mystery. A Collection of Short Stories
The Rich and The Dead
Fart From the Madding Crowd
The Voyage

Chapter 1

There should have been more blood, lots more blood. It was a statement the young man couldn't make with any real authority or conviction, so he said nothing. After all, a twenty-year old probationary constable with exactly three weeks 'on the job' experience was hardly an expert witness in forensic science. He was correct though. When someone crucifies a young aboriginal woman, bolts her to the wall by screwing coach bolts through her elbows and knees and then slowly lops off her hands and feet with a hacksaw, it was inconceivable there would be so little blood. There should have been more blood. Lots more blood.

The bastard had used cable ties. Those plastic things electricians use to strap lengths of electrical cable together. He had slipped them over her wrists and ankles and pulled them tight, cutting off the blood. After the amputation he had burnt the stumps with a blowtorch which sealed off the blood flow completely. He didn't want her to bleed to death before he had finished having his fun.

Probationary Constable Daniel Yates felt sick and it was little consolation that his partner and mentor, Jacko Hartman, a man with over fifteen years on the force felt sick too.

"What sort of insane fucker does that to another human being?" Daniel asked his superior. Jacko had no answer.

The girl was a local woman. A 'Dero'. A young homeless woman known to the local community as Marlee. A disturbance had been reported by one of the residents of a nearby housing estate. A man had heard screaming coming from the old house and phoned the police. There was a footy match going on at Brisbane's Lang Park football stadium in the next street and anyone else who had heard the noise must have thought it was something to do with the game. Daniel and his cohort had been sent to investigate and had discovered the poor woman's body. She had died of a heart attack before the evil bastard could do any more damage.

Jacko had said, "fuck me drunk" and got on the radio to the superintendent. That was over an hour ago. Now the place was swarming with cops. They had cordoned off the area and were going over the place with a fine toothed comb, scouring the house for evidence.

Then two guys in suits showed up. They told the Super' in no uncertain terms that he and his goons were to piss off. Daniel was sure he heard the word Interpol. One of the suits, the younger one, a tall, ginger haired man who called himself Randall questioned both Daniel and Jacko at length, grilling them about what they knew. After ascertaining that this was very little, he told them they could leave.

More Interpol guys turned up, some in suits, others dressed in those white, disposable overalls, the type of gear the forensic boys wore, and proceeded to systematically take the place apart. They left no stone unturned, no piece of evidence no matter how small undiscovered.

The Superintendent got on the blower to the Police Commissioner and complained bitterly about how the men from Interpol had stolen his case, but his ranting and raving fell on deaf ears. He was ordered to leave the crime scene as directed. Daniel, Jacko and all the other local cops filed out after him.

The following day Daniel Yates phoned in sick. His resignation arrived by e-mail shortly after ten.

Chapter 2

It seemed patently obvious to Iris Richards, that most people simply wasted their lives. They were born, they died and that bit in between, the bit that should have been interesting and exciting or at the very least fun, was spent in the inane pursuit of those things they thought would make them appear cool to their peers. In a world driven mad by consumerism, the Gods of acquisition had convinced most people that the only true measure of success was to be found in ownership. It didn't matter if your life was as boring as watching grass grow as long as you had the latest model car, DVD player, mobile phone or fashion item. Then everyone else could see how successful you were.

Life to Iris Richards, on the other hand was an entirely different cauldron of seafood. Iris had a dream. Of course she was perfectly aware that Martin Luther King had had one first, and if she was honest with herself she had to admit that her simplistic mental meanderings could never honestly compare with that great man's utopic visions. But in a homegrown, hand made, do it yourself kind of way, Iris's dream was a good one. It was worthy, she liked to think, of a curt nod of approval from whatever board, committee or deity made the decision about which dreams were worth pursuing and which should be consigned to the bin marked "Nail gun body piercing and other dumb ideas".

Iris's dream was to go sailing. Not just a quick beat around the harbour on a Sunday afternoon but a genuine ocean passage.

At an after work piss up a few short weeks ago, one of Iris's workmates had mentioned that she had a mate whose sister's uncle's cousin's best friend's mother's next door neighbour's butcher had a mate who was looking for someone to help him sail his boat from Turkey back to Sydney. Alan Tew, for that was the sailor's name, was in Istanbul with his yacht, waiting for the northern winter to pass, before setting out on the return leg home. In a pique of spontaneity, Iris had thrown caution to the wind and had written to Mr Tew asking to join him. Hopefully, in just four days, she was to embark on what could quite possibly be the adventure of a lifetime.

At twenty-eight years of age, Iris Richards had reached an impasse in her life. Five years ago she had finished her Bachelor of Arts degree in Sociology and scored herself a dead end job, as a Human Resources Officer, with a large multinational marketing company. It was a job she hated with a passion. Her loathing for it was mainly due to the fact she seldom felt any joy in telling people the job they had just applied for, the one they had wanted so desperately, had been given to another, 'more suitable' applicant. There was an even greater dislike for the job when she was forced to appoint an applicant she considered second best. A person for whom the best thing to be said, was that he or she wasn't as bad as the rest of the deadbeats. It was little wonder she hated going to work each day. The burden of having control over people's livelihood, the knowledge her decision might have devastating, long-lasting repercussions that could damage a person's very essence, was often more than Iris could bear. The chance of escape, the possibility of finding a life infinitely more worth living, was an opportunity Iris could not let pass.

In the evening of the day she wrote to Mr. Tew, Iris drove to her parent's house to tell them of her plans. In hindsight her revelations were highly premature. She had, after all, only just written to the yachtsman and it would be more than a week before she heard if her application had been successful. However, her eagerness at the prospect of escaping from a life she considered only slightly less full of shit than a dung beetle's autobiography, was enough to make her feel her plans should be discussed with her parents as soon as possible.

Predictably James and Ellen Richards were not at all happy with their daughter's decision. Her eagerness to throw in a perfectly good job and go gallivanting across to the other side of the world in search of some childish dream, did not gel with their hopes, aspirations and expectations for her. Secretly the girl's parents felt that their daughter's discontentment with her current situation was more likely to do with her recent split with her long time boyfriend, than the proffered excuse of being unhappy with her job.

The truth was, Iris was bored. Dreadfully bored. She had been bored with her ex-boyfriend and that was the reason he was ex, and she was bored with her job. Even if the hoped for trip never eventuated, one way or another, the job was going to be ex soon too.

"You're much too impulsive," her mother had told her on innumerable occasions. "I worry myself sick when I think of some of the near scrapes you've got yourself in." Iris had to admit there was some truth in her mother's observations. Her whole life she'd had an unrequited wanderlust, and that had manifested itself as an almost insatiable thirst for adventure. A thirst that cried out to be quenched. Now that she was finally going to act on her desire and go travelling, Iris considered that to be a positive trait. Her parents did not.

"Do you think it's a wise decision, Iris?" asked her mother as they sat in the living room enjoying one of the seemingly endless, cups of tea her mother always pushed on visitors. "The world out there doesn't seem to be as safe as it used to be".

Iris flicked her long, curly, black hair from her face and launched into the speech she had prepared earlier for the occasion. It was a long, eloquent and impassioned speech, delivered with force and great conviction. Predictably, it fell on deaf ears and Iris was forced to fall back on the tried and true practice of making ridiculous promises that everyone knew were impossible to keep.

"I'll phone every day", she pledged. "I'll just see how it works out for a week or so. If I don't feel perfectly safe or if this Tew character seems a bit strange, I'll hop on the next plane home. Besides, I've only just written to the guy. He might turn me down."

Eventually James and Ellen agreed that if Mr Tew should invite her, then Iris could go. It was a conciliatory agreement, made with the full knowledge of all concerned that it didn't matter what they said anyway, if Iris decided she was going then she would go. She was simply not the type of girl to be swayed once she'd made up her mind. For her, after weighing up the pros and cons between her present lifestyle and that of sailing around the world visiting exotic, interesting countries and meeting exciting, unique people, there was simply no contest. If she got the opportunity she would jump at the chance. No one, not even her parents, could make her change her mind once it was made up.

Chapter 3

T he Interpol agent in charge of the investigation into Marlee's death was called Grey. 'Grey by name, Grey by nature' or so the saying went around the halls of head office. He was sixty-two, tall and lanky, English, and with that deathly pale, 'climbed out of a grave and dusted himself down with wood ash', type pallor which many of his countrymen exhibit. He kept his dense, coarse, grey hair in a closely cropped crew cut and always dressed impeccably. Today he wore a dark blue, pinstripe suit with a crisp white shirt and, as always, his regimental tie and black lace up shoes which had been polished to a blinding sheen. His wife called him Edmond, occasionally darling and frequently infuriating. Everyone else called him one eyed.

He and his team had been tracking the person they believed responsible for Marlee's murder for the last eight months. They had started in London, and unless the forensics guys were mistaken, the aboriginal woman was the perpetrator's fifth victim. All had been young women, the oldest just twenty-eight. The two in France had been prostitutes. The one, in Thailand had been a student of divinity on sabbatical from the US, and the woman in Bali, a Japanese tourist. All of them had been somebody's daughter, sister or partner before their death, and the horrendous torture they had endured before they'd had their lives taken from them, was something which kept Edmond Grey awake night after night.

The Medical Examiner assigned to the case, pulled back the sheet which covered Marlee's butchered body and began to explain to Grey the items of importance he had found during the autopsy.

"In my opinion," he said, "there is no doubt the same man is responsible for all five deaths. The manner in which this young woman has been murdered, differs in many ways from the other four, that is to say many of the things the killer has done to her are different from his previous victims, but the way he's used his tools of torture, the cable ties to stop blood loss, the way he's cauterized the wounds with a blow torch for example, leave me in no doubt that we're dealing with the same man."

Grey nodded and made a few pertinent comments before asking, "What else did you find?"

"As with the others, there has been seminal fluid found. Even though conclusive DNA results won't be back from the lab for about a week, I've done a test and ascertained the perpetrators blood type is, as previously, 'A' positive. Also, there are the same stun gun burns at the base of the woman's spine. There's simply no doubt Edmond, we're dealing with the same killer."

So the good news was, Grey knew he was still looking for the same man. The bad news, he still didn't know exactly who the perpetrator was, or more importantly, when and where he would strike next.

The ME finished his comments and promised to have his written report on Grey's desk first thing in the morning. Then the Englishman excused himself and made his way down the hall to the 'Operations room,' a large office inside the British Embassy, which had been made available to Grey and his team for the duration of the investigation in Australia. Dave Randall was waiting for him. He was grinning from ear to ear.

"Major Grey sir, we found a finger print! On the light switch in the main bedroom upstairs. We ran it against the Interpol database and got a hit. We know who the bastard is."

Grey felt a sudden surge of adrenaline. Perhaps this was the break through they had all been praying for. Randall gave him the name, then Grey addressed the five people on his team.

"I want all the accommodation houses, hotels and motels in the greater Brisbane area contacted to ascertain if he's staying with them. From the amount of travelling he's been doing lately, he'll have a bit of money behind him. So I'd be starting at the up market places first."

He turned to an older woman. Like her boss, she too sported a closely cropped helmet of grey hair, but there any similarity ended. Where Grey was always immaculately turned out, Ms Jones was a hatchet faced, hook-nosed, old hag who had all the style of an airline sick-bag. She wore a pink frilly, low cut, puffy sleeved blouse that showed off far too much of her gnarled and wrinkled cleavage, and a beige, tight-fitting skirt which was far too short for someone whose legs had adopted the same colour scheme as a topographical map showing rivers and steams. Her shoes could be described as 'comfortable knock abouts' by a kinder person, but in truth they were just cheep crap. They were scuffed and worn, dark brown pumps, with low heels, and large gold buckles on the side. Her dress sense was hideous, and even Grey himself, normally a most polite and politically correct gentleman, had been known to pass derogatory comments about Ms Jones's appalling dress sense. Though only when the woman herself was out of earshot.

She was sitting in front of a computer screen, scrolling through countless pages of information about their newly identified quarry. So engrossed was she, that it took Grey three attempts to attract her attention. Finally, she acknowledged him.

"Yes Major?"

"Immigration should have details of his entry into the country. Contact them and find out, when, where and how. I need to know everything about this bastards travel movements over the past couple of years. We need to ascertain if he's got what we might consider to be a home base. If he slips through our net we need to know what his next move is likely to be. Also, I want an alert posted at every airport. If this mongrel tries to leave the country I want him stopped. Once you've done that, would you please contact my driver? Ask him to be on standby, we may have to move at a moments notice. When you've done that, could you start looking into this chaps credit card or currency transactions. We need to find out about his movements over the last twenty-four hours. If we can place him anywhere near the scene of last nights murder, it will help immensely when we finally apprehend him."

Ms Jones confirmed she would be glad to assist and then went back to her computer screen.

Fifteen years I've been with Interpol, she reminded herself, fifteen years, ten of them as your personal assistant. And you still treat me like an imbecile, you arrogant, condescending bastard. One day the shoe will be on the other foot, Grey, and that's a promise.

Chapter 4

L ess than four hours later Major Grey gently placed the handset of his phone into its cradle and quietly cursed the day Ms Jones had been born. Years ago he might have gone into a rage. What was the term the young people used? 'Spat the dummy'. But not now. Now he took a more philosophical approach. It was better for his blood pressure and better for the Interpol image if he controlled his temper and refrained from choking the living shit out of the stupid, fucking bitch. It was hard though, so hard. He kept it undercover, bottled up inside where no one could see. On the outside he was cool, calm and unflappable. On the inside, absolutely fucking livid.

He remembered perfectly, telling the woman to inform the Australian department of immigration that Berswiski was not to be allowed to leave the country. It wasn't rocket science. You picked up the phone, dialled the correct number and explained to the bloke on the other end that a murdering psychopath might be trying to leave the country and would they be so kind as to stop the bastard at the airport. It was that simple. And yet that's exactly what she hadn't done.

Now Vladimir Mikhail Berswiski was on a plane heading for Athens. Yes, he would be stopping at Kuala Lumpur, Mumbai, and Dubai before reaching his final destination, but Grey knew that by the time he contacted the various embassies and organized an arrest warrant it would be to late, Berswiski would already be in Greece.

Shit.

He picked up the phone again and dialled Randall's extension. There was no point in calling that stupid bitch Jones, she obviously couldn't be trusted even with a simple task like booking a flight for the team to Athens. He gave instructions to Randall and then hung up and phoned his wife Marjorie. Perhaps here there was one tiny sliver of silver lining. At least she would be happy to know he would be a little bit closer to home soon. She had been a bit moody recently. She wasn't the type of woman to complain, she knew the importance of his work, but on the other hand, Edmond knew she wasn't exactly over the moon with the amount of time he had to spend away from England. Now that the kids had left home, she got lonely, and stiff upper lip stoicism could only be maintained for so long. Edmond knew the case needed to be finalized, and finalized quickly.

Peoples lives depended on it.

He forced himself to breathe deeply and regularly, making himself concentrate on the job at hand, rather than his anger at Ms Jones. There was no point in crying over spilt milk, what's done was done. The last thing he wanted to do was upset Marjorie, by discussing stupid office politics. The phone rang and rang, eventually switching over to the answering machine. Edmond left a message, telling Marjorie he would be in Greece by Friday at the latest and promising her he would arrange for them to have a short holiday together in Sibenic at the end of the month. Definitely, even if the case still hadn't been completed.

Edmond hung up the phone and picked up the green folder he'd left sitting on top of the mountain of evidence files the team had accumulated over the past three months. All that information had to be gone over again. Not because the Major was concerned they'd missed something crucial, but because he needed to ascertain what relevance, if any, the finger print found on the light switch, might have on all the other evidence.

The fingerprint had been the breakthrough the entire team had been praying for. According to the Interpol data base, it belonged to a Russian national known as Vladimir Mikhail Berswiski. Berswiski was a scientist, a nuclear physicist no less, and it was this, rather than any previous criminal activities which accounted for Berswiski's fingerprint being on the Interpol data base.

According to the suspect's file, he'd been somebody of great importance during the Soviet era. But the collapse of the soviet regime, the subsequent signing of the nuclear non-proliferation treaty and the gradual mothballing of most of Russia's nuclear arsenal, had meant that his standing with the Russian government had waned considerably. Eventually he dropped off the radar completely. He didn't reappear again until two years ago when his name suddenly started coming up on transcripts of covert surveillance audio recordings made by the CIA in North Korea.

It was also his rather unique qualifications which made Major Grey absolutely certain that Berswiski was the right man. There could only be one explanation why the fingerprint of a nuclear physicist had been found at the place where a young homeless woman had been tortured and killed, and that was that he was the killer.

Chapter 5

The bus swerved, its wheels locked and its tyres squealed in protest, as the driver hit the skids and took evasive action. A moronic Volvo driver with a psychopathic aversion to using indicators, slued across in front of the bus, shot across two lanes of oncoming traffic and disappeared up the driveway to the Indooroopilly Bowls Club. Iris was dozing and the lurching of the bus woke her with a start. She glanced around quickly to see what the fuss was about, then rolled her eyes skyward at the antics of the bloody Volvo driver.

Iris hated buses and the bus trip to Alex's place took over an hour. Alex was Iris's brother, twin no less and although they were of course, not identical, two siblings could not be more alike. They both had the same athletic physique, the same jet black hair and the same mischievous, piercing blue eyes. They also shared the same irreverent sense of humour and, at least until recently, the same adventurous spirit. Iris had to admit that Alex had changed.

Three years ago Alex met Pamela, a beautiful Toorak socialite with more contacts than a Telecom switchboard. Alex had fallen in love. Within just a few months he had resigned his commission with the Air Force, taken up a position with a corporate banking company in the city, bought a house in the upper class suburb of St. Lucia and settled down to wedded bliss. If Iris was ever asked to substantiate her theory that peoples lives were ruled by consumerism, then

14

Pamela would make a perfect "exhibit A" for the prosecution. She had to have everything that opened and shut, and it had to be the latest, best model, and with all of the most desirable features. Alex apparently earned what their Dad described as 'shitloads', but even that wasn't quite enough when it came to the financial requirements of the shopaholic Pamela.

Iris had to admit Pamela was gorgeous. Beautiful, there just wasn't any other way to describe her, and she definitely had a formidable business head. It was just that she was so much upkeep. As Peggy, Iris's best friend, had put it after the three of them had spent the day shopping together a few months ago. "It's surprising her credit card didn't spontaneously combust".

Ever since Iris had announced her intention to sail half way around the world with Alan Tew, Alex and Pamela had insisted she come over to dinner at their home each Friday. Because Iris had sold her car to raise some extra cash for the trip, she had been forced to endure the hour plus journey by bus. Today, as well as the near fatal collision with the Volvo driving lawn bowler, Iris had to endure the less than subtle attentions of a fat, spotty faced, grass stained schoolboy who had decided, despite a number of vacant bus seats being available, to position himself standing next to her so her could perv down her cleavage. "They're just tits mate", Iris said to the boy loudly as she stepped from the bus. "Just like yours, only not quite so big and saggy".

There was a five-minute walk from the bus stop to Alex's place and as usual his next door neighbour, Guido Spinozi, was in his front garden tending his roses when she walked past. It seemed to Iris that most retired people spent a great deal of time in their gardens, weeding, planting, watering and such. But Guido was just nosy, for him gardening was so he could keep his eyes on what was going on in the neighbourhood.

"G'day spunk rat" called Guido when he saw Iris, "How are things?"

"Both fine thanks Darling", snickered Iris, puffing out her chest "How are yours?"

" Oh! I'd have to show you babe," laughed Guido. "You'd think I was only bragging if I just told you".

"How's the garden going?" asked Iris, rolling her eyes in mock disdain.

"Oh I'm having lots of problems with nut grass Iris." replied the old Italian

"I suppose you could get a Brazilian," quipped Iris as she turned down the footpath to her brothers house.

Despite being nearly seventy, Guido was a terrible flirt, or perhaps terribly good flirt was a more apt description. Rumour had it he had seduced most of the women, both single and married, who lived at the old people's home up the road. The man's sexual escapades were legendary, though his prowess was no doubt due more to medical science than any natural aptitude. People said Guido took so much Viagra, he had to stand on his head to pee. Iris, forty-two years his junior, had frequently thanked her lucky stars that he was old enough to be her grandfather and respected Alex too much to ever try anything seriously. He could flirt though.

Guido was an enigma. He was proud of his Italian origins but was, first and foremost, a fiercely, almost fanatically patriotic Australian. Call him a Wog, Spick or Dago and he would simply laugh it off. Call him un-Australian, and he would go after you with a knife.

Back in 1957, Guido had been a merchant seaman. His first visit to Australia was on a ship delivering coal from Brisbane to Osaka. The first part of the trip was to central Queensland to load the ship with coal. Guido took one look at the city of Mackay and jumped ship. After a month in the area he hitched a ride south to Brisbane

The Captain of the ship was married to Guido's sister and at her insistence, didn't report Guido missing until the ship reached Perth. A manhunt ensued, but as the authorities were looking on the wrong side of the country, not a trace of Guido was found. It was not until 1973, when Guido and his now deceased wife Annette tried to get married, that immigration finally tracked him down.

Amazingly, so determined was he to make Australia his home, that from the moment Guido first set foot on the banks of the Brisbane River he had not spoken one word of Italian. Or so the story went.

The dinner at Alex and Pamela's house was a sumptuous affair. The food itself was the usual high standard, which meant Pamela had ordered a delivery from the local restaurant, and the company and conversation were both quite spirited. For the first time in months Alex seemed to be his old self again. He was articulate and animated and joked and laughed throughout the evening. Even Pamela, who was the most serious person Iris had ever met, joined in, making a few witty comments and giggling like a schoolgirl at Alex's antics. Pamela was not amused however when, after dessert, Alex belched loudly.

"Sorry everyone", he exclaimed, his voice full of contrition, "I meant to fart".

Around 11:00pm, while Iris, Alex and Pamela were sitting in the lounge enjoying an after dinner brandy, Alex's mobile phone beeped at him. He looked quite perturbed as he read the SMS message and shot Pamela a worried look before excusing himself to make a phone call from another room. When he returned a short time later he was ashen faced and extremely agitated. "Sorry honey, I have to go into work," he said to Pamela, "I'd better take Iris home".

Alex seemed miles away as he drove Iris back to her flat in Sunnybank. A number of times Iris asked what was wrong, but Alex would just smile and tell her there was nothing to worry about.

"Listen Iris," said Alex after a few minutes silence, "I'm afraid I won't be able to see you off at the airport on Sunday. I've been summoned to Canberra. The Minister for Finance needs me there first thing tomorrow morning. Sorry. Pam and I will fly out to meet you and Mr Tew in Portugal in a few weeks". Alex smiled his most charismatic and disarming smile and assured his sister once again there was nothing to worry about.

In just three days and fourteen hours, Iris would be boarding a plane for London. From there she would fly to Ankara. By the end of the week she would, for the first time in her life, be in a foreign country. She would be in a country where few people spoke English and she spoke no Turkish. She'd have no friends close by to call on in an emergency and only a limited amount of money. Her only contact would be a man she had never met before and had spoken to only once on the phone. A man she hoped to spend the next year with, sailing a small yacht, half-way around the world.

What the hell could there be to worry about.

Chapter 6

That Sunday Iris and her friend Peggy, sat at the airport waiting for Iris's plane to board. As they waited, they were entertained by watching the machinations of an obscenely overweight security guard as he demonstrated his expertise in megalomania. A frail, silver haired old lady with a walking frame, shuffled up to the obese security guard's desk and presented her handbag for inspection. With a snarl and a barely disguised look of contempt, Security Officer Lardarse snatched up the bag and thrust a massive paw inside. He bellowed triumphantly and with a flourish extracted a tiny metal object.

"You can't take that on the plane," snarled Lardarse. "It's a weapon."

"What?" queried the old lady, cupping a bony, porcelain skinned hand to her ear.

"I said", repeated Lardarse loudly, "you can't take that on the plane it is a weapon", and then he tossed the offending object into an enormous, overflowing rubbish skip labelled 'Nail files'.

An argument ensued. The old lady demanded that the security officer return her nail file immediately. Lardarse refused.

"It was a present from Queen Victoria" claimed the little old lady.

"Tell someone who cares", countered Lardarse, indicating a Salvation Army poster on the wall behind him. The altercation continued unabated until the security guard suddenly noticed that the queue behind the old duck had now reached the car park, and the other passengers were beginning to look decidedly pissed off.

"Look," said Lardarse retrieving the nail file from the rubbish skip, "I'm not supposed to do this, so just keep it in your bag until you get to your destination. Okay?"

The old lady nodded, took back the nail file and slowly, painfully, made her way towards the departure lounge.

Iris and Peggy agreed, the security situation since the September 11 attack on the world trade centre had reached absurd levels.

"I wish I was coming with you," declared Peggy. "What an adventure you're going to have. I'm so envious."

"So why don't you and Chris come and spend a few weeks in Portugal with me? I don't know if Mr Tew will have room on the boat for you, but if he doesn't, I imagine with all the financial shit that's going on in Europe at the moment, you should be able to pick up some ultra cheap accommodation. The Aussie dollar's never been better for overseas travel, so now's the time to take a holiday. Alex and Pam are meeting me in Lisbon around the middle of April, so Mr Tew has arranged for us to stop for about a month. Why don't you come too?"

"Oh, I'd love to, and you're right, now is definitely the time to go, but we can't afford it at the moment. Christopher is looking at buying an automotive repair business and we'll need every cent we can muster for that."

Iris looked at her friend as if she was mad.

"Chris is an unqualified labourer, what the hell does he know about fixing cars?"

"Nothing, but he reckons he can employ mechanics to do the actual repair work. He'll just be running the office."

Iris nearly choked. "Running the office? Peggy, you know I love you, but all your muscle-bound boyfriends brains are in his biceps.

He couldn't even count to twenty-one without taking his pants off. How in God's name is he supposed to run an office?"

Peggy didn't really have an answer to that. The simple truth was, Peggy loved Christopher. Love made her blind to the fact that, even though most of the time his heart was in the right place, Chris was as dumb as mud and should never be left alone in a room with sharp objects.

"Honey, listen, I know you love the guy," said Iris, "but when it comes to running a business, any business, he doesn't have a clue. Try to talk him out of it before he costs you both all your savings."

Peggy nodded and promised her friend she would set Christopher straight about his latest get-rich-quick scheme. Iris knew Peggy well and doubted the conversation would ever take place. She just hoped that when the inevitable shit hit the fan, her friend wouldn't get too badly burned.

A few minutes before eleven, flight Q734 was called and half an hour later Iris was on her way. If she had known then what the future had in store for her, she would have borrowed the old lady's nail file, hijacked the plane, and made them go straight back to Brisbane.

Chapter 7

Despite his name, Alan Tew didn't look Asian, and there was a very good reason. He was only one eighth Chinese.

Alan's Great Grandfather, Chu Sum Duc and his first wife, Chu Wai Fat left Kowloon in January 1872, travelled to Australia, by tramp steamer and headed for Melbourne via Darwin and Sydney. Their ultimate destination was the gold rush town of Ballarat in the state of Victoria, where Sum Duc and Wai Fat hoped to make their fortune.

Sadly for Alan's Great Grandfather, on the 15th of February, just two hundred nautical miles from Darwin, the steamer was struck by a category two cyclone. The ship was well-founded and weathered the storm admirably, but even so the conditions for the passengers and crew on board were treacherous. At the height of the storm the steamer was struck side-on by a huge wave and capsized. When it rolled back upright again, Wai Fat was nowhere to be seen. She had somehow been washed overboard.

With the storm raging outside, the Captain was hard-pressed just keeping the vessel afloat and headed into the wind. It was impossible to even consider a rescue attempt. Wai Fat perished at sea and was never seen again.

Despite his devastation at the loss of his wife, Sum Duc had continued on to Melbourne. There he had taken lodgings in a Williamstown boarding house and, over the following six weeks, assembled his supplies and equipment for the trip to the diggings at Ballarat.

By July 1875 Chu Sum Duc had come to the same conclusion that many others had, that prospecting for gold was pure folly. The mines had been pillaged since 1851, so after nearly a quarter of a century, the gold had all but run out. Supplying goods and equipment to those foolish enough to keep trying, however, was an opportunity too good to pass up. Sum Duc had started up a trading post. Initially, he operated from a simple bark and split timber hut, right in the centre of Poverty Point, the most heavily populated and lucrative part of the rapidly growing goldfields.

But within a year the store had tripled in size. A new building had to be constructed with sawn timber plank walls and a roof clad with sheets of corrugated iron which Sum Duc had shipped in especially from Melbourne. Soon the business became too large for a single operator and Sum Duc began to search for an assistant.

Sara Connelly, a twenty-three-year-old mother of two boys, Fergus and Shamus, twins of just eighteen months, threw her hat into the ring.

Like Sum Duc, Sara had been widowed by a terrible accident. Her husband Feargel had had his leg crushed in a rock fall whilst working down their tiny mine. Even though they were close to the city of Ballarat itself, there had been very little in the way of medical facilities available. Precious little could be done for him, and in an effort to stop the onset of gangrene, the local doctor, who in fact was only a glorified vet, had attempted to amputate Feargel's leg. The operation had gone horribly wrong. With no anaesthetic at hand the chances of Feargel surviving the operation were slim at best. In addition, without adequate surgical equipment to prevent the patient from bleeding to death, attempting such a difficult operation was little better than murder. Feargel died in agony on the table.

With no husband to provide for her and her children, Mrs. Connelly was forced to take drastic action. She sold the claim on her husbands mine, packed up her meagre belongings and walked the streets of Ballarat, knocking on every door she could find desperately looking for work. On the 18th of August she knocked on the door of Chu Sum Duc's hardware emporium and her life changed forever.

To Sum Duc the vision of a twenty-three-year old, one point three metre tall, pale skinned, painfully thin, red-headed Irish woman was a strange sight indeed. But he desperately needed someone to help in the shop, so after haggling for over an hour over what each thought was a reasonable stipend, Sara Connelly was given the job.

A few of the townspeople were not happy at the thought of a white woman working for a Chinaman and for the first few months they made their feelings on the matter quite apparent. In reply, for the first few months, both Sum Duc and Sara made it quite clear to anyone who came into the shop, that if they didn't approve of Mr. Chu's and Mrs. Connelly's, purely business relationship, they could fuck off and take their business elsewhere. An elsewhere that simply didn't exist. Not unless, of course, they were prepared to travel to the city itself. In typical mining town fashion, the townsfolk quickly came to realize there were more important thing to worry about. Sum Duc and Sara were left to lead their lives as they saw fit. So long as their relationship was solely on a business footing of course. No one was going to stand for a Chink shacking up with a white sheila.

For the next three years, Sum Duc and Sara continued to work side by side, six days a week, and in perfect harmony. Sum Duc admired the tiny Irish redhead for her attention to detail and her strong work ethic. Despite her size there was never anything that Sara Connelly wasn't prepared to do. Or at least prepared to give her best shot. Whether it was dragging out massive rolls of barbed wire from the store room out the back, cutting delicate lengths of lace ribbon for the school mistress's Sunday best dress, or painstakingly counting out dozens of tiny wood screws, Sara was ready, willing and able to put her best foot forward.

For her part, Sara grew to think of Sum Duc as her best friend. He was always willing to listen with a sympathetic ear to anyone who had fallen on hard times and would frequently put his hand in his own pocket to help someone truly in need. He was fair and reasonable in the prices he charged his customers and was always polite and courteous to her. He worked hard to adapt to his new homeland and spent many hours practising his rapidly, and constantly improving, English. Sometimes Sara wished that he would dress a little less Chinese, perhaps cut off that ridiculous pigtail or start wearing something that didn't look quite so much like a rich tarts evening gown. But it was not to be. Sum Duc was Chinese and although he loved his adopted home even more than his birthplace, he always would be.

Both of them were headstrong and Sara in particular, had a fiery temper. Occasionally they would argue, normally over some trivial matter which didn't really even rate a mention, and usually Sara would win. Sometimes because she was right, but more often than not, because Sum Duc let her.

With two such people, lonely and alone, thrust together by the cruelties of fate, it was little wonder that they eventually fell in love. Of course in nineteenth century, white Australia, the possibility of marriage between a Chinese man and a 'white woman' would have been unthinkable, so Sum Duc and Sara's love for one another had to be kept a secret. Sara and her two boys kept their rooms at the boarding house and Sum Duc continued to live in the tiny bedroom above the shop. For a further two years Sum Duc and Sara lived their lives apart but secretly together. They loved each other fervently and spent many an afternoon with the shop closed for 'stocktaking', a euphemism for shagging each others brains out in the back room. Not surprisingly, Sara eventually fell pregnant.

Before her condition became too apparent, she and her two boys left Ballarat and moved to Melbourne, where she found a place at a Christian Sisters convent. A place which was known to offer assistance to widows with orphaned children. The good sisters, totally unaware that Mrs. Connelly's husband had died over five years ago and was not the father of her unborn child, helped her through a difficult pregnancy and birth, and then found her work at a local bakery.

For his part, Sum Duc also kept busy. As soon as the opportunity presented itself, he sold the hardware shop. The purchaser was a Ballarat gold trader who could see that the heady, gold rush days of Ballarat were rapidly coming to an end, and was looking to hedge his bets by diversifying into other fields. He was hopeful that the hardware store would be his ticket to one last killing before the money dried up.

Sum Duc then moved on to Broome in the far north-west corner of Western Australia. Broome had a vibrant pearl fishing industry and a large Chinese and Japanese population. After six months he had started another hardware store, and within the year, Sara, Fergus, Shamus and baby Oscar joined him in Broome. Once again Sara became Sum Duc's employee, this time apparently a widow with three orphaned children. Sum Duc surmised that the inhabitants of such a town, remote and largely multicultural, would be more amenable to a mixed race marriage. Predictably he found that the reality was far from what they had hoped for. So once again Sum Duc and Sara were forced to keep their love for one another secret.

Oscar inherited his mothers red hair and pale skin, so even though his eyes were slightly hooded his half Asian heritage was not readily apparent. If the townspeople noticed any similarity between Oscar and his Chinese father they thankfully kept it to themselves.

Oscar Connelly, Alan's Great Grand father, was a happy child and quickly grew to be a happy man. He was a bright, though not exceptional student. While his elder brothers stayed at home and helped their parents in the shop, Oscar was considered 'worth the risk', and was sent off to boarding school in the state capital.

He hated boarding school with a vengeance. But he recognized that his parents were making a considerable sacrifice to give him a special start in life, so he studied hard, kept his nose clean and graduated somewhere near the middle of his class. He finished school in 1892. He was sixteen years old.

After leaving school he returned to Broome and started work at the newly opened branch of the Commonwealth bank. A job he kept for the next thirty-two years.

Sum Duc and Sara remained together for the rest of their lives. Sara died of heart failure in 1941 and her beloved Sum Duc died just four months later. They are buried together in Broome's city cemetery.

Oscar married late in life, meeting his future wife and the mother of his two children at a fund-raising event, in support of the troops overseas. Anzacs, battling the Hun, during the first world war in 1916. Oscars wife was a brash, loudmouthed, waspish woman called Bronwyn. A Welsh migrant, whose father had a weakness for drink and a passion for song. Bronwyn's Mother had died in childbirth and she had been raised entirely by her father. Mr and Miss Llewelyn had arrived in Sydney on a steamer out of Cardiff seven years previously and had been searching for a place to call home ever since.

Bronwyn gave Oscar two children, twins Cyril and Lionel, who were born in 1918. Bronwyn and Oscar were together for only sixteen years before Oscar died of a heart attack. The year was 1933. What became of Bronwyn after Oscar's death is unclear. Her father, homesick for the green and rolling hills of his homeland had returned to Wales a few years earlier and it is widely believed that after her husbands death Bronwyn followed him. Whatever her fate, Alan's Grandfather, Lionel Connelly, did not accompany her. The boy, then aged only fourteen, took lodgings at a boarding house and worked on a number of fishing trawlers to make ends meet. He had inherited his own Grandfathers wanderlust, and by the age of seventeen, had tired of life in the tiny city of Broome and left for the big city lights of Sydney. He was there for six years.

In 1941 Chu Sum Duc and Sara, Lionel's Grandfather and Grandmother died. Uncles Fergus and Shamus had both died during the great war leaving Lionel and his brother Cyril as sole benefactors to the substantial hardware empire which Sum Duc and Sara had built up over the past sixty six years. Suddenly the two brothers were both very rich.

They were also slightly confused. Although both brothers loved their Grandmothers Chinese employer and friend like their own grandfather, neither had had any inkling that Chu Sum Duc was in fact their actual Grandfather. Both boys had been told that Feargel Connelly, who had died in a mining accident in Ballarat in 1875 had been Oscar Connelly's Dad.

Lionel was amazed at the incredible lengths his Grandfather and Grandmother must have gone to keep their love for each other a secret. But he was also ashamed of his countrymen for making such a secret necessary. As a mark of his respect for his recently deceased Grandfather, Lionel changed his name to Tew, an Anglicized version of his real family name.

In 1941 Lionel moved to Brisbane, where he used the money from his inheritance to start up a munitions factory. The war in Europe was not going the way the allies had hoped and Lionel could see the writing on the wall. Sooner or later even Australia would be under threat and he was determined he was going to do whatever he could to make sure that when that happened, Australia would be prepared.

On the 7th of December of the that year, the Japanese Imperial Army decided to join the war in a most spectacular manner, attacking the American Navy base at Pearl Harbour, sinking 20 ships and killing nearly two thousand four hundred service men and women. Lionel correctly guessed that it would only a matter of time before the Japs made their way south towards Australia. Lionel's already substantial fortune, rapidly grew even larger

A year later Lionel met Lucia Randolph. Lucia was a first generation Anglo-Italian Aussie whose mother, Carolina, worked in the Tew munitions factory. Her father, who was purported to be a member of the British aristocracy, had been disowned by his family after eloping with Carolina, his younger cousin's Italian nanny. They ran away together away to Australia. Lucia was born just a few short weeks after their arrival. The day Lionel Tew first met the beautiful girl Lucia, William Randolph her father, was up north in New Guinea doing his bit to halt the seemingly unstoppable onslaught of the Japanese Imperial Army. Like many men of that era he had been forced to leave Carolina and Lucia at home to "muddle on as best they could," Fighting the Nips in the jungles of tropic New Guinea

Lucia was just sixteen years old when she came to work in the main office in Lionel's factory. She was a tall, elegant, raven haired beauty who turned the heads of both men and women alike. She had a sensuous, smouldering aura about her, and had already broken at least a dozen boys hearts. To Lionel she was the most exquisite creature he had ever laid eyes on.

As the owner of a very successful and very important business, it was easy for Lionel to find ways in which to impress his ravishing quarry. But Lucia, still a few months away from her seventeenth birthday, was not interested. Especially since Mr Tew was her boss and nine years her senior.

Still, Lionel persisted for almost ten years in his attempt to woo the beautiful Lucia and eventually, almost inevitably, she consented to go dancing. Three months later Lionel asked Lucia's father for his daughters hand in marriage and a year after their nuptials, on the eighth of August 1954, Patrick, Alan's father was born.

Chapter 8

In every family there's the occasional black sheep. For the Tew dynasty, it was Patrick. Generous people might have described him as wilful. The more honest would have called him an obnoxious little shit. Or worse.

Almost as soon as he could crawl, Patrick was a handful. Lucia only had to turn her back on the child for a second and he would be up to mischief. He would scurry off as fast as his tiny arms and legs could carry him, heading for somewhere he knew he was not allowed to be. His parents told him no. They scolded him, even occasionally smacked him, but nothing worked. If Patrick got something in his mind, nothing could prevent him from being naughty.

Lionel kept an office at home, somewhere where he could go, to finalize a tender to the Government, or correspond with friends, family and business associates. It was a small room at the back of the house, equipped with telephone, typewriter, a desk, bookcase, a standard lamp and a huge lockable filling cabinet in which he kept the documents he considered too important or personal to keep at the factory. The room also contained Lionel's most prized possession, On the corner of the desk, in a glass case which Lionel had had made specifically, sat Lionel's grandfathers abacus. The ancient Chinese device with which Sum Duc used to tally his days meagre takings all those years ago in Ballarat. For reasons which had never been made clear, most of Lionel's grandfather's possessions had

31

been sold or disposed of soon after Sum Duc's death. The abacus was the only precious item left to remind him of his secretive Grandfather. Patrick aged two and prone to clumsiness, sneaked into his father's office when his mother wasn't looking and somehow managed to knock over the standard lamp sitting next to the desk. It toppled over, smashed into the glass case and damaged the invaluable memento irreparably.

Of course Lionel should have understood that his son was just a toddler. A handful certainly, but just a toddler even so, and the breaking of the precious abacus was an accident, nothing more. But Lionel could never find it in his heart to forgive Patrick and the little boy knew it. Perhaps it was this event and Lionel's reaction which lead to the spectacular fashion in which Patrick Tew went off the rails.

In 1961, when Patrick was just seven years old, he had his first violent altercation with another boy. The boys name was Jonathan and he was eleven. He was much bigger and stronger than the small, slightly built Patrick. But size was irrelevant, at least when stacked up against the pure unfetted fury of the enraged Patrick.

Jonathan and Patrick had been playing hide-and-seek with a group of friends. When it came time for Jonathan to hide he chose a spot under the raised floor of the Principals office. Unfortunately for him his choice of hideout didn't prove very successful and he was discovered, just a couple of minutes later, by a little girl called Madeline Spring. Jonathan was embarrassed at being found so easily and by a five-year-old girl at that. He scurried out from under the building and stormed off. As he hurried past Madeline he pushed her over and she fell flat on her bottom, in the dirt and immediately began to cry.

Patrick was incensed by the bigger boys callousness and disregard for poor Maddie. Boys didn't hit or push girls, especially pretty little five year old girls. Everyone knew that. He began to yell obscenities at Jonathan, using words he had heard the men at the factory use. He didn't really understand their meaning, but he knew they were bad words, and that was all that mattered. Jonathan stopped mid stride, spun around and thundered back towards him, intending to give the little boy a thick ear for being so cheeky. It was something he would live to regret. Screaming like a banshee, Patrick launched himself at the elder boy and furiously pummelled him with his fists. In seconds he had Jonathan on the ground and began kicking him in the face. It took two teachers to drag him off.

That first instance of violence set the pattern for Patrick's entire childhood. He was an unruly child and would fly off into a rage at the slightest provocation. He had very few friends, preferring to be by himself, something which most of the other kids were quite happy with. Although he was only small for his age, everyone else quickly learnt of his explosive temper and steered well clear. Even so the inevitable bust ups were frequent and ferocious. Within his first year of high school he was expelled from three different schools for fighting, and eventually Lionel and Lucia were forced to keep the boy home and engage a tutor.

Patrick's sociopathic tendencies should have had Lionel seeking professional help for the boy, but in the late fifties such things were unheard-of. Unless they were unavoidable, most personality problems were swept under the carpet, simply ignored or passed off as lack of discipline. Patrick's problems went much deeper. His world began and ended with the people and things which directly effected him. Everything else was irrelevant. He had no empathy for any other person or creature and even the slightest deviation from what he expected should be the case, would send him into an almost psychotic rage.

In 1972, when Patrick was just sixteen years old, he left home. To everyone's horror and amazement, Maddie Spring still only fourteen years old went with him. While Patrick simply packed a bag and walked out, Maddie at least left her parents a note.

It read:

Dear Mummy and Daddy.

Patrick and I are in love and want to be together. He is leaving home to travel around Australia and I can't bare the thought of living without him so I'm going too. I love you Mummy and Daddy. I'm sure we'll come home again soon. Please don't worry about me. Patrick will look after me.

Love always

Maddie

Mr. And Mrs. Spring, never saw their little girl again.

Chapter 9

It was 1984 before Patrick Tew re-emerged. For the past twelve years he and Maddie had been travelling the world, now, suddenly and without warning, they were home. They brought with them their entire worldly possessions, all of which could have fitted quite comfortably inside a metre square cardboard box. All that is, except for the fifty-three-foot sailing schooner called Serenity they left anchored temporarily in the Brisbane river, plus a four-year-old son named Michael and his two year old brother Alan.

To their credit Lionel and Lucia accepted their prodigal son back into the folds of their family with very few recriminations. There were questions asked of course, (and an outstanding arrest warrant for Patrick for the abduction of a minor which had to be sorted out), but generally speaking they accepted the next generation of the Tew family wholeheartedly. Even though Patrick had been a nightmare as a child, he was still their son and as far as Lucia was concerned nothing would ever change that. Lionel too had missed his only son, and even though he was at first wary of once again opening his heart to him, he resolved to make the most of the situation, and to try to heal the rift that had opened up between them during the past twelve, long years.

But Patrick had changed. The anger and volatility of his youth was gone. Sadly it had been replaced by a debilitating, all-pervading sense of hopelessness. There was a good reason the pair had chosen that particular moment to return. Maddie was dying.

Five years previously Maddie's father had died of a heart attack and two years later her mother, Jean had followed. She'd contracted breast cancer. A particularly virulent form of the disease. She'd found a small, hard lump in her left breast which had grown at an alarming rate. The cancer spread to her lymph nodes and from there raced through her entire body. Less than six months after the initial diagnosis, Jean Spring was dead. As is frequently the case, it appeared poor Maddie had inherited her mothers weakness. She too had contracted breast cancer, and the prognosis was bleak. She had come home to Australia to die, and as she was an only child, and both her own parents were dead, Lionel and Lucia were the only family she had.

Lionel still owned the Brisbane munitions factory, but had retired from any active management role. On their retirement Lionel and Lucia had purchased a large, palatial house in the Brisbane suburb of Hamilton overlooking the river. They had more than enough room for their son and his family to stay for as long as they cared to. Patrick moved the Yacht further up the river to where he could keep an eye on it from Lionel's balcony, and the fourth and fifth generation of Tews moved in.

During the past few years Maddie had rarely spoken with her own family and the thought that Patrick might never see his parents again had filled her with an unbearable sorrow. She told Patrick, there was only one thing she wanted to do before she died, and that was to see him and his parents reconciled. For that reason, more that any other, Patrick had agreed to take Maddie and the boys back to Brisbane.

Patrick made it quite clear right from the start that he had no intention of sponging off his parents. He needed money, money for the general living expenses for his family, and money, lots of money, to cover the astronomical costs of the medical care Maddie required. In less than a week he'd scored himself a labouring job on a local building site. When he found that wasn't enough he took a second job, working behind a bar, Thursday to Saturday nights.

Maddie stayed at home with her two boys and her parents in law. It was from her that Lionel and Lucia eventually heard the story of what had happened to their son and his wife over the past twelve years.

The Tew family home in Hamilton, sat high on the hill with a magnificent view of the majestic Brisbane river and the city itself. It was only a small house by Hamilton standards, just four bedrooms, two bathrooms, a large lounge room, an equally large dinning-entertainment area. There was also a family room, kitchen, laundry, two car garage and, Lionel and Lucia's favourite place, a glass enclosed sun-room. It was spacious, airy, and comfortably appointed, with huge glass and aluminium windows looking out over the river. It was in this room that Maddie Tew would spend her last weeks. Patrick's parents new that the sun-room was a special place and would be perfect for Maddie's convalescence, so the day after their son returned home, Lionel set about setting up a folding bed for poor Maddie in the sun-room.

One Tuesday afternoon, while Patrick was still at work and Lionel, Lucia and Maddie were sitting in the sun-room enjoying, as best they could, the pleasant autumn weather, Maddie began to speak of the past dozen years. After leaving home, she told them, Patrick and she had travelled around Australia. They'd hitch-hiked north, heading for Townsville and then west to Mount Isa. Once there they both quickly found jobs, Patrick labouring in the huge nickel mine and Maddie doing house cleaning in response to an advert she saw on a notice board in the local supermarket. It took just a few weeks for them to save enough money to catch a bus to the city of Darwin in the Northern Territory, and from there to catch a plane to Broome, the city where one hundred and three years previously, Patrick's Great, great grandfather had first set up his new hardware store.

"It was a defining point in Patrick's life," Maddie told them, "Patrick told me he somehow felt a connection with the place. To stand on the exact same spot where a hundred years before Chu Sum Duc must have stood, suddenly made him feel very small and insignificant. He said it was as if all the responsibility that had been put upon him, the expectations of how he should act and what he should do with his life were lifted from his shoulders. For the first time in his life he felt at peace. He suddenly understood, his loyalties lay only with himself and me. Providing we were okay, everything else was unimportant. Does that make sense?"

Lionel thought it sounded like Patrick had been smoking something illegal, but Lucia seemed to understand.

"Where did you go from there?" she asked.

"We hitched a ride on a sailing yacht heading down the coast to Perth. We'd decided to have a look at the local yacht club and saw a notice on the board. There was a bloke who was heading for Perth and was looking for crew. We met him in the bar that night and moved onboard the following day. The skipper's name was Bruce. He was a really nice man and didn't worry that neither of us had any sailing experience. He taught us the ropes on the way down. We both loved sailing, right from the start".

"So where did you go from there?" asked Lucia.

"San Francisco. We saw another notice, this time in the Perth yacht club. This one advertising for crew going to the US. We applied, organized a couple of passports, and a month later we were off. It took eight weeks to make the crossing. Some days we would race across the ocean, the wind blowing freshly from astern, that's from behind, and we'd make good progress. Other days there wouldn't be a breath of wind and we'd just sit there, rocking back and forth, all the ropes and sails banging and crashing as we slopped about. I hated that sort of weather, but not Patrick. He loved every second of it, fair weather or foul. He just couldn't get enough." She began to cough and splutter from the exertion of speaking and had to rest for a while. Lucia went to the kitchen and poured her a glass of water. She held it to her daughter in laws lips until she'd drunk her fill and when Maddie had recovered enough she resumed her tale.

"We spent the next four years travelling around the US. Hitch-hiking, or sometimes we'd buy a car. Cars are so cheap over there, it's unbelievable. When I turned seventeen Patrick took me to Niagara Falls and we got married."

She smiled wistfully as she remembered that day and for a second the light in her eyes returned. Both Lionel and Lucia knew then, that even though they'd both been young, so very, very young when they'd eloped, Maddie had not regretted it for a second. She'd loved Patrick then and she still loved him now.

"So how did you get the yacht?" asked Lionel. pointing vaguely in the direction of Serenity, swinging lazily at anchor on the river below.

"Oh that happened in San Francisco," She waved her hand dismissively, as if the story was of no importance, but Lionel urged her to elaborate.

"We'd just come back from a cruise down to Costa Rica. Patrick met a guy in a bar who reckoned he could get us another trip back down that way again if we wanted it. A rich bloke he knew wanted someone to do a yacht delivery, through the Panama canal and around to New Orleans."

Lionel said he didn't understand. What did Maddie mean a Yacht delivery?

"Well sometimes the person who owns the yacht needs the boat moved from one place to another and can't or doesn't want to do it themselves. In this case the yacht's owner, a guy called Scanelli, wanted to go sailing around New Orleans but couldn't be bothered with all the hassle of taking the yacht through the Panama canal. So he paid Patrick and I to take it around for him.

"What a wonderful way to earn a living!" said Lucia.

"That's for sure. That was in early '79. I was pregnant with Mikey, but I hadn't really started to show yet so we said nothing and we got the job. It was the first time Patrick and I had skippered a boat by ourselves, but we had no problems at all. It was incredibly interesting taking her through the canal. Anyway, we got to New Orleans with a couple of days to spare. Patrick phoned Mr. Scanelli, who told us where to tie up the boat, He also arranged for us to be paid by the bloke who ran the marina. We figured that would be the last we'd ever see of him. But just a couple of days later he left a message for us at the yacht club and when we rang him back, he asked us if we'd take the boat back to 'Frisco because he'd had a change of plan and needed it back there."

Maddie started to cough again and had to rest for a while. The cancer had reached her lungs and liver now, and even the slightest exertion required a massive effort which left her totally drained. Lucia sat beside her on the bed, helped her sit up and drink a little more water. After resting for a while she felt much stronger and once again continued with her story.

Back in San Francisco she and Patrick again left the boat at the marina, only to be contacted just two weeks later and asked to do yet another trip, this time only as far as Panama city. And so it continued, running the boat up and down the coast, sometimes to Mexico, sometimes to Panama city, once even to Buena Ventura, a small coastal city in Columbia. In fact, during the next twelve months, the only time Mr. Scanelli didn't have them sailing the boat for him was a six-week break while Mikey was being born, a month whilst the boat was out of the water for maintenance, and the odd day here and there whilst Scanelli himself was aboard.

"Looking back now," explained Maddie, "we should have realized something wasn't quite right, but I guess we were a bit naïve. We were having the perfect life and didn't even want to consider that things were a bit strange. Then just after we'd got back from yet another trip down to Mexico, Scanelli sent a car for us. The driver said we were to come immediately, that Mr. Scanelli was in deep trouble, and so would we be if we didn't do exactly as he said."

She stopped for a moment to gather her thoughts and catch her breath. She was obviously finding all the talking hard going and both Lucia and Lionel suggested she rest for a while, but she was adamant she would continue. She needed to explain she told them. She and Patrick had done things, things neither of them were proud of, and she needed to get it off her chest, now, before it was too late.

"We got to Scanelli's and the place was crawling with people. Mean, tough looking people, some wearing shoulder holsters or with guns tucked into their belts. They were all rushing about, carrying boxes full of documents and other stuff out to a big truck around the back. I saw one guy with an armful of high-powered rifles, and another stuffing bundles of cash into a suitcase. Then Mr. Scanelli saw us and came over. He snapped his fingers at a man in a suit who'd been sorting through a pile of documents and he came over. Scanelli spoke to him in private for a few seconds and then the guy in the suit took us to one side and told us Mr. Scanelli was giving us 'Serenity.' Patrick asked him 'where does he want us to take her? The guy in the suit said, 'Wherever the hell you like. Don't you understand? He's giving you the boat. It's yours. Do whatever you damn well want with it. He spread a piece of paper out on the dining room table for us to sign It was a bill of sale for the yacht. The price was stated at $230,000 US. We didn't have that kind of money and we told the guy in the suit just that. He rolled his eyes and told us once again, Mr. Scanelli was giving us the boat, not selling, giving. The amount shown on the bill of sale was just for the IRS. 'Serenity' wasn't going to cost us a cent. Mr Scanelli had to leave the country for a while and rather than go to all the trouble of selling her, he'd decided to give her to us. He said he knew we would look after her."

"We both knew there was something wrong. Nobody, no matter how rich they are, gives away a $230,000 yacht. But what if it was legit? Mr. Scanelli had always been a bit eccentric. This could be the opportunity to own something worthwhile for once. To turn down what had to be the chance of a lifetime was stupid. So we sighed the document and grabbed a taxi back to the marina.

As soon as we got there Patrick got the yacht ready to go. In less than half an hour we were underway and heading for the open sea. We kept going until we were out of sight of land and then Patrick hove to, that means stopped, with the sails set so the yacht just sits there without moving forward or rocking around too much. Together we searched every square millimetre of the boat. Just before midnight we found it. The boat had a secret hold. Just a small space about a half metre square, between two bulkheads. That's like the internal walls on a house. It was packed full of cocaine, probably fifty or sixty kilos of the stuff."

"So that was the real reason for all those trips down to Panama and Columbia," guessed Lionel. "This Scanelli was smuggling drugs into the US? But why did he suddenly decide to give you and Patrick the boat?"

"Because of the drugs. We found out later that Scanelli had been indicted on a whole pile of organized crime charges. The cops somehow found out about the drug smuggling, plus a heap of other things. Someone had tipped Scanelli off and he was desperately trying to cover his tracks. He must have decided he couldn't take the risk of trying to move the drugs in case the yacht was being watched. So he set us up to take the blame. Patrick had noticed that the bill of sale for the Yacht had been backdated to December 78. A few months before we'd even met Scanelli. Our passports showed we'd been back and forth to South America nine times. If the DEA searched the boat and found a pile of drugs they'd understandably assume they were ours. As far as Scanelli was concerned he had nothing to do with them. He'd say sold us the boat over a year before."

Lucia was on the edge of her seat. Totally amazed at the nightmarish adventure she was hearing about from her daughter-in-law.

"Goodness Maddie, what on earth did you do?"

"We threw the lot overboard, scrubbed the secret hold out with detergent and gallons of water until we were sure not a trace of the cocaine was left and sailed north towards Canada. We stopped at Portland to clear customs. They must have been tipped off, because they went through the whole boat with a fine toothed comb. But they didn't find anything, and as we had that bill of sale, as far as they were concerned, as long as we complied with any and all customs requirements, the yacht was ours to take where ever we liked."

"Goodness, what happened then?" asked Lionel, "Didn't this Scanelli guy want his boat back? Not to mention his drugs?"

"That was three years ago. Scanelli was sent to prison shortly after we arrived in Canada. He's banged up for drug trafficking and a couple of dozen other offences. Patrick and I reckon he'll be inside for the next thirty years. If he comes looking for his boat when he gets out we'll worry about that then."

Both Lionel and Lucia knew Maddie and Patrick had more important things to worry about.

During October 1984 Maddie Tew took a turn for the worse. She, Patrick and the two boys had been living with Lionel and Lucia for almost seven months and Maddie's condition had progressively deteriorated. Some days were better than others, most were worse.

By then Patrick had quit his job and spent all his time caring for her. The two boys, aware that mummy was ill, spent their days playing quietly or went with their grandparents whenever one or both of them went out on an errand. Both Lionel and Lucia grew to love the boys, and even though they still found Patrick hard to get to know, they eventually warmed to him too.

Lionel regularly proclaimed, "He hasn't turned out such a bad person after all."

Perhaps they were swayed by her illness. Perhaps the pity they felt for their daughter-in-law tugged at their heart strings and affected how they felt, but Patrick's parents worshipped poor Maddie as if she were their own daughter. Maddie had always been a pretty girl and had grown into a beautiful woman, but there was no sign of that beauty now. Her tiny body had been emaciated by both the disease and the drugs the doctors had given her to slow the progress of her insidious illness. Her eyes were sunken, lifeless, and ringed with red. There were pale purple, greenish shadows across her cheeks, and her breath, shallow and rasping, smelt of death. Her skin, once lustrous and glowing, was pale and chalky and hung loosely on her pitiful frame. Once she'd had a glorious mane of curly red hair which had been the envy of every other girl she knew, now there was nothing left save for a few pathetic, limp wisps which had somehow managed to survive the onslaught of the merciless chemotherapy.

In many ways the drugs had been worse than the disease itself. Patrick felt sure that Maddie would have had a better chance of fighting the cancer if only she hadn't first had to battle with the effects of her medication. But that was not how it had been. Her oncologist insisted that if Maddie was to have any chance at all of a recovery or remission, then she needed to persevere with the drugs. So Patrick kept his opinion to himself and secretly prayed that, one way or another, his darling girls suffering would be over soon.

Some days were worse than others but none were pleasant either for Maddie herself or any of the others. The medication was doing little to slow the rapid onslaught of the disease. Eventually it was decided that the chemotherapy should be halted, but not before the toxic chemicals had done irreparable damage. All the doctors they'd consulted agreed, all that could be done now, was to make poor Maddie as comfortable as possible, load her up on morphine for the pain, and for her and Patrick to make any necessary arrangements for her passing

By November Maddie had little strength left and it became obvious that the time had come for her to be admitted to the palliative care unit at the Chermside hospital. They rang the hospital to let them know she was coming and then Lionel brought the car around as close to the house as possible. They packed a few necessities and Maddie's most treasured items into an overnight bag, and Patrick carried her tiny form out to the car and lay her gently on the back seat. With her head resting on Lucia's lap and with Patrick holding Maddie's hand, they drove to the hospital.

"Thank you, Mama," she whispered to Lucia, "thank you for your love and kindness." And then Maddie closed her eyes.

She died before they reached the hospital.

Chapter 10

Even the most charitable observer would have to admit that Dora Abernathy was past her prime. Worse still, somewhere in the deep, dark recesses of her mind, Dora was even starting to admit it to herself. It was not that she'd let herself go. It was simply that time waits for no man and it sure as hell wasn't waiting for Dora. She exercised religiously, ate healthily, didn't smoke, never drank to excess, and got plenty of rest. She was also happy, even proud, to admit that a well-known Beverly Hills plastic surgeon had done some fairly extensive renovations. She now had medically enhanced buttocks, a flat, trim tummy and a pair of breasts that were not only self-supporting but fitted quite nicely into the "Not many to the cubic meter" category. But despite all the effort on her part and the unquestionable skills of others, it had to be said, Dora was not only getting older, she was getting old.

Dora's late husband, Walter, had provided for her admirably in his will, but it was a sad fact that plastic surgery, especially when provided by a famous tummy tucker to the stars, does not come cheap. Regrettably Dora's bank account had shrunk directly in inverse proportion to the increase of her silicone augmented boobs. So with her last few thousand dollars, she purchased a round the world ticket on a cruise ship and set off with one purpose in mind. Dora was going to find herself a rich, new boyfriend.

The P&O round the world cruise for over 55's was secretly known by the entire ships company as 'The Gold Diggers Cruise'. Sadly for Dora it was, as always, filled to the gunwales with craggy faced old bags all hoping to find a rich, lonely old man who could keep them in the manner to which they would like to become accustomed. If that wasn't bad enough, the only rich, single men on board, were rich because they were astute and were single for exactly the same reason. As one silver haired oil tycoon from Houston was heard to remark.

"I have a bucket full of Viagra and a gold-plated American Express card! What the hell would I need a wife for?"

With such stiff competition on board and with such slim pickings to be had, Dora was forced to revert to plan "B". When the cruise ship berthed in Kea, Greece, she put on her hunting gear and headed for the City centre. She caught a taxi to one of Paris's daddy's hotels and headed for the lobby. If there was a rich, unattached, not too close to death, man to be found anywhere in Greece, then it was a good chance he would be staying at the Hilton.

She made her way through to the main bar and perched her medically reinforced buttocks on an available bar stool. There were a few dozen or so other people scattered around the room. They were mostly couples, but to Dora's delight there was also a smattering of possibly single, possibly suitable men strewn amongst them. Slim pickings at present, but then as the old saying went, the night was still young.

A few minutes before eight o'clock, Dora caught sight of the most suitable quarry so far. The best in fact, for the entire trip. He was a big man, almost one point nine metres tall and with the shoulders of a draught horse. He was impeccably dressed in what appeared to be a designer label suit, dark grey, with a muted, slightly darker, pin stripe. Dora checked for a wedding ring and found none, but what she did find was a pair of immaculately manicured hands, the right one adorned with a thick, yellow gold dress ring, set with more diamonds than a Swiss watch factory. Dora all but leapt from her seat.

"Hi!"

The 'arms dealer' glanced up from the ream of invoices he had been perusing, to find he was being addressed by a peroxide blonde. The old bat was at least seventy and appeared to be going to some kind of fancy dress party. Her hair, which had been teased to within an inch of its life, added a good 15cm to the old duck's height. Her make-up looked like it had been applied with a paint roller and her eye shadow and mascara made her eyes look like someone had just crept up behind her and screamed obscenities. She wore a minute tank top which barely contained what surely must have been the largest, most synthetic pair of tits he had ever laid eyes on, and to make matters worse, the silly bitch was wearing hot pants. He tried desperately to stop himself, but failed miserably. He burst out laughing.

"Do you come here often?" asked Dora, wondering exactly what it was the man found so amusing.

"No but I got a bit excited over there once", quipped the 'arms dealer' and once again he cracked up laughing.

$14,000 of rhinoplasty had arguably improved Dora's nose immeasurably, but when the meaning of what the large, obnoxious, lout had just said hit her, the work done did little to stop her from snorting half a glass of gin and tonic up it. She was immediately beset by a coughing fit, tears streamed from her eyes and her false teeth shot from her mouth and landed on top of the 'arms dealer's' paperwork.

He howled with laughter as he watched Dora snatch up her falsies and without so much as a wave goodbye, bolt for the entrance to the bar and out into the hotel's lobby.

Shit, he thought, as he watched the old cow rush off. Maybe I'd better go back to the gym and start watching my waistline. If that's the type of old bag I'm starting to attract, I must be looking really rough.

He placed his laptop computer on the table in front of himself, fired it up and logged on to the hotels Wi-Fi. Quickly he typed out a coded e-mail to his current customer and informed him of the progress so far. The meeting with Professor Vladimir Berswiski, although a little confronting, had gone well, he informed his buyer. Delivery of the merchandize to the agreed destination was on schedule.

The 'arms dealer' signed off and disconnected from the net. Even though he always changed location each and every time he logged on, and changed his e-mail address and ISP with every new transaction, he had learned many years ago that it was prudent to stay on line for only the barest amount of time necessary. There were people out there, dangerous people, dangerous not only to his business, but to his liberty, and maybe even his life, who would love to locate his whereabouts and glean information about his business. If he was to survive, he had to stay one step ahead of them. It was impossible to be too cautious.

Which was why he had found his meeting with Berswiski so confronting. The man was, how did the Americans put it? A loose cannon. The 'arms dealer' was no psychiatrist, but to his mind Berswiski was a bit of a psychopath. A megalomaniac with an ego the size of Texas, and if even half the rumours were true, with some very weird and violent sexual habits. The sooner he could finalize this current deal and be shot of the weirdo, the better he would like it.

Still! He had to admit, for two million dollars clear profit, he would willingly ignore a little weirdness from an eccentric Russian scientist.

Sometimes, unexpectedly, you might catch a glimpse of a stranger out of the corner of your eye. A reflection of a man or woman in the glass of a shop front window, or a mirror where you had not expected to find one. For a mere microsecond your brain fails to recognize that the reflection is your own, and for an instant, you see yourself as the rest of the world sees you. As you really are, before your mind alters your perception of yourself, with layer upon layer of ego.

Which is exactly what happened to Dora Abernathy as she stood in the Athens Hilton's, lobby powder room trying to regain her composure. She turned to leave, swivelled ninety degrees to her left, took a step towards the door, and for a split-second before it registered that she was looking in a mirror, she came face to face with an ageing, matronly, extremely odd looking old bat with a serious need to reconsider her dress sense. Before she could stop herself, her mind had registered her reflection as a joke. Mutton dressed as lamb as Dora's grandmother used to say. Silly old goat dressed as a kid was a more apt description.

No wonder the man in the bar had laughed at her she suddenly realized. She was a joke. What on earth had possessed her to spend her last few dollars on this ridiculous cruise. How in God's name had she fooled herself into thinking she might be able to find herself a 'Sugar Daddy' when she was so far past her prime herself. Sure there were a number of rich, powerful, intelligent, sexy, older men on board, but if Dora was honest with herself, they were not that much older than she was. Besides, those which fitted perfectly into the 'Sugar Daddy" category, had already lined themselves up with their opposing 'Sugar Baby'. Young, attractive women and girls, in their late teens or early twenties with smooth, youthful faces, flat tummies, pert, gravity defying tits and bums you could bounce bullets off. Dora hadn't looked that good even when she was still young. What chance did she have now.

Fighting back the tears of humiliation she rushed through the main entrance of the hotel and out onto the street. Tomorrow she would leave the ship, buy herself a cheap ticket on the next available plane and go home to California. Perhaps she would sell the old house Walter had left her and buy a little cottage in the country, or maybe a town-house in one of those gated communities she had heard so much about lately. If she could learn to live frugally and invest the little money she had left wisely, then she might enjoy a perfectly comfortable life.

In more ways than one, she told herself, it was about time she grew up and started taking control of her own life instead of relying on a man. Dora Abernathy was moving on, and hopefully moving up.

Then, just as she was about to cross to the other side of the street, a large black limousine pulled up to the kerb. The rear window rolled down and the occupant spoke to her. He said he'd noticed she looked distraught and asked if he might be of some assistance.

The man inside was an ugly little cretin. Almost rodent like in some ways, with sparse grey hair and yellowing bucked teeth. He spoke English with a heavy Russian accent. Still, at least he spoke English and despite his appearance, he seemed charming and was obviously very rich. Besides, after her recent epiphany regarding her own appearance, Dora felt it was time to lower her sights a little. After all, who was she to look down her nose at a someone just because they looked a little odd. And if the gentleman wanted to enquire after her well-being and offer her a limo ride back to the ship who was she to refuse.

The following morning, at five fifteen am, a forklift driver who worked at one of the dockside container terminals, found Dora Abernathy's body wedged between two massive shipping containers. She had been brutally tortured and left to die. By five thirty, the place was swarming with cops. By five thirty-two, a group of six, well-dressed men and women of various nationalities presented themselves to the Turkish Police's officer in charge of the investigation and, with the assistance of an interpreter, introduced themselves and requested that they be involved in the investigation.

It took a while but eventually the right ear was bent and word came down from the Turkish Chief of Police, that every courtesy was to be afforded to the six agents from Interpol. Though they were to act only in an advisory capacity, they were to be given access to all evidence collected, including the coroners report on cause of death. This proved to be asphyxiation. Dora Abernathy's mouth, oesophagus and lungs had been filled with silicon. Silicon which had been squeezed out of the breast implants her attacker had cut from her chest.

Chapter 11

The 'arms dealer' sat in the dingy hotel room and stared blankly at the television monitor. The thermostat on the ancient, gas, room heater had been wound up as high as it would go, but it did little to alleviate the freezing temperature. Outside the snow was beginning to thaw. Soon the trucks would be able to move.

Not a moment too soon, thought the 'arms dealer,' Novosibirsk was a shithole even in the summer. The whole world knew how dreadful Siberia was in winter. He had arrived, just before dawn that morning on a specially chartered aircraft, which had flown him, its sole passenger, from Athens. It had had cost him a small fortune, but he knew that the money spent would be recouped a thousand times over if he could pull the deal off.

On the TV the newsreader was expounding at great length about the latest success the government was having in the war against the Chechen rebels. The illustrious Government troops had uncovered and thwarted a plot to launch an attack on another school. Although it had happened six years ago, the siege at Beslan was still fresh in the minds of the newsreader's fellow Russians, and many people felt that President Putin's leadership was, when it came to fighting terrorism, weak and ineffectual. Most people still lived in fear of terrorist attacks. Many had removed their children from school and had not allowed them to return. This latest success was good news. It would give people hope for the future and it would give a massive boost to Putin's popularity.

Such a pity it was all bullshit. There was no Chechen plot. At least not one of the magnitude that the reporter was alluding too. If there had been, the Arms' dealer would have heard about it. They would've come to him with their truckloads of roubles or better still, suitcases filled with black market American dollars. They would have brought with them lists of the things they wanted. Guns, ammunition, grenades, automatic and semi-automatic weapons and bombs and he would have gone down the list, checking off the things he could supply and crossing out the things they could not afford.

He had been given such a list a few months ago. It was a comprehensive list that covered a broad spectrum of goods and the Arms' dealer had ticked each item, pricing them as he went. When he came to item nine he raised his head and stared at the buyer, trying to ascertain if the man was serious. The buyer looked back. He shrugged and looked embarrassed as if to say, "You couldn't really supply that, could you?" The Arms' dealer just ticked the item, drew a dollar sign, a number and added lots of zeros. The buyer smiled and nodded his head.

When the former Soviet regime had collapsed and the new, democratically elected Russian government joined the US in signing the nuclear non-proliferation treaty, the whole world breathed a collective sigh of relief. The threat of nuclear war appeared to be over. During the next few years, hundreds of nuclear weapons were disarmed, disassembled and mothballed, secured away in remote and secret locations all over the US and former eastern block countries, to be guarded by only the most loyal and trusted soldiers. The world turned its attentions to a new threat to world order, that of terrorism. For most of the world the threat of nuclear weapons was forgotten.

The collapse of the Soviet regime had brought not only the end of the cold war, but also an end to the careers of thousands of communist party officials. Hundreds of once powerful politicians and even more powerful KGB agents were put out to pasture. The Russian Mafia, which until that time had been just an ineffectual group of petty criminals, saw a way to utilize the knowledge and expertise of the ex-KGB agents and recruited many of them into their ranks. Over the next few years, billions of dollars worth of munitions were stolen from the government armoires and storage facilities, and sold to the highest bidder. Five years ago, when the Arms' dealer first did a little bit of business with the Russian Mafia, four nuclear warheads had disappeared from the Russian Governments bunkers. Now, although no one was going to admit it, there were seven missing. The latest one had been encased in a lead lined steel box which now formed a part of the chassis of one of the trucks waiting to leave Novosibirsk.

Chapter 12

At 182 cm or a bee's dick under 6 foot, Iris considered herself to be a tall woman. But when Alan got up from his chair in the yacht club to greet her, she felt like she must have been standing in a hole. The man was huge.

"G'day Iris", beamed Alan extending a large callused hand for her to shake, "Welcome to Turkey". Iris returned his warm greeting and for a few seconds they both stood there, not sure what was supposed to happen next. "Umm! take a seat Iris," offered Alan " I'll get us a drink. We'll have a chat and then I'll take you back to the boat and get you settled in. What would you like?"

"Brandy and soda please" she replied and then remembering that they would both be on a limited budget for the next few months, reached for her purse.

"Don't worry about that," said Alan with a conspirational wink "I get all my drinks for free here, I'm sleeping with the barmaid". Iris's mouth fell open, not at what Alan had said, but because she had seen the barmaid. She had everything a real man could ever want. Broad shoulders, big biceps, and a moustache. The thought that Alan, who she had immediately decided was exceedingly handsome, was involved with such a woman, if indeed it was a woman, was too horrifying to contemplate.

"Just joking!" chuckled Alan when he saw her reaction.

Alan returned from the bar and the pair chatted about this and that for an hour or so, before Alan suggested they return to the boat.

"Have you managed to arrange for anyone else to join us on the trip Alan?" asked Iris as they walked to the jetty where Alan had tied up his tender.

"Yes" replied Alan, "I had asked my brother, but I don't talk to him any more since he came out of the closet".

"He's gay?" asked Iris.

"No, just likes 'Hide and Seek' quipped Alan. "Sorry, I'm a bit nervous. I tend to kid about a bit when I first meet people. I guess it's my way of coping. cause I'm normally a bit shy. Anyway, I digress. A young Dutch guy called Stefan is going to join us. At least as far as Italy at this point. After that we'll see if we can pick up a backpacker or two. You'll have to share a cabin with him I'm afraid and you'd better watch out for him too. Apparently he's a bit of a lady-killer. At least I think that's what the cops said".

Iris smiled at Alan's joke. Tall, dark, handsome, obviously intelligent and with a sense of humour. Okay not a great sense of humour, in fact it was pretty lame, but at least he's trying. He just has to be gay, she thought.

As they walked to where the yacht's tender was tied up, Iris contemplated her first impressions of the man she would most likely be spending the next few months with. His physical appearance was very much to her liking. He was tall, well-built without looking like a body builder and had a devilishly handsome face. She liked the way he kept his hair trimmed short and although she normally disliked beards, Alan's suited him. It was a proper beard, not one of those silly scratchy things that looked like the wearer had forgotten to shave that morning. Iris wondered if it would tickle and suddenly found herself blushing at the thought of where it might tickle most.

It was far too early to make any informed judgement about his personality but he seemed nice.

Iris noticed Alan reach into his back pocket for his wallet. Just ahead, sitting on the edge of the dock was a little street urchin, maybe six years old, begging for alms from the passers-by. Alan handed the child a coin and patted him on the head. The child's face lit up and after bestowing his thanks on Alan for his generosity, he scurried away.

Iris waited for the "poor little tyke" comment or some other verbal crap that was designed to show her what a great bloke he was but Alan said nothing. He just looked a little sad, as if he was truly distressed to see the injustice of children still having to beg in the twenty-first century.

"So what does your family think of you travelling half-way around the world to go sailing with a complete stranger?" asked Alan.

"My folks weren't too keen on the idea initially, but I talked them round. I must admit I had a few concerns of my own at first. But the way I see it, I could die tomorrow, run down by a drunk driver or discover I have some horrible disease and only have six weeks to live. Then I would be berating myself for all the opportunities I've missed. Life's too short Alan, and too damn long if you're just going to sit around and watch it pass you by".

"I couldn't agree more Iris," he replied.

They walked out onto the jetty and then the big Aussie placed his hand gently in the small of Iris's back and guided her across until she was standing directly in front of him.

"That's 'Harvey' he stated, pointing over her shoulder at a beautiful white yacht bobbing happily a couple of hundred metres off shore. "Harvey and I are extremely happy you've come to join us".

'Harvey Wharf Banger' was a beautiful, Swarbick designed, 46ft (ca. 14 m) ketch. She was built back in 1999 in Fremantle and had been owned and maintained by Alan since the day she first came out of the boatyard. As a cabinetmaker Alan had expert skills perfect for looking after his pride and joy. The paintwork gleamed, the timber shone and the brass and stainless steel were polished to a mirror finish. Iris thought that 'Harvey Wharf Banger' was the most beautiful yacht she had ever seen. Down below deck there was a well-appointed galley and a comfortable, spacious saloon equipped with TV, DVD player, stereo sound system and a comprehensive library. There were also two cabins, one in the bow, which Iris would share with the other crew, and one in the stern underneath the cockpit, which was Alan's.

He still had a few days work to complete before he finished the cabinet making job he had undertaken to pay for the repairs to 'Harvey', and Stefan, the Dutch backpacker, was not due to arrive until the day before they left, so Iris spent the next few days sightseeing around Istanbul and familiarizing herself with the boat. She bought herself a small labelling machine and with Alan's permission went about identifying and labelling all the lines, halyards and winches so she could help with the sailing more efficiently.

Chapter 13

Just like his personal assistant, Avril Jones, Veronica Crystal was American. She was also female and white, and that more or less concluded any discernible similarities. If Edmund Grey was honest with himself though, he would also have to admit they were both of above average intelligence. As much as it pained him to say it, Ms. Jones was, in a lot of ways, as sharp as a tack. There wasn't much that got past her when it came to sifting through evidence, and she had an almost uncanny knack for finding the link between two or more facts that the others had simply overlooked. Though on paper at least, Veronica Crystal had vastly superior qualifications.

Mrs. Crystal, although fifty eight years old, and well past her prime, was also cuter. In Edmund Grey's eyes, infinitely cuter. Though of course he would never have admitted it to his wife Marjorie. Unlike Miss Jones, Veronica Crystal kept herself trim. She was tall and athletic, had dark hair, sultry, almond shaped, brown eyes, full lips and olive skin. Beautiful, olive skin in fact, encasing what Edmund considered to be a dynamite body. She had great legs, an undeniably magnificent bum and an irresistibly optically adhesive cleavage. She also had a PhD in forensic science, a doctorate in psychology and a high-powered job with the CIA.

Years ago, a few years after his discharge from the British Army and eight months into his first posting with Interpol, Edmund and Veronica Crystal had worked together briefly on an assignment in

Germany. Some time later, after she had retired from field work and taken on a more administrative role back in the states, he had attended a lecture she'd given on criminal profiling. That was the name given to the new fangled practice of using psychology to work out the personality type of the perpetrator of a particular type of crime. All psycho babble bullshit as far as Edmond Grey was concerned.

Even so, when he heard through the grapevine that Veronica was currently stationed in Athens, he felt he just had to see her again, and asking her to have a discussion with his team on the probable psychological make up of their quarry seemed like the perfect excuse. She'd readily agreed, and at the appointed time, arrived with a briefcase full of files and a laptop computer already loaded with her latest power point presentation. A document subtitled 'Criminal loonies and how to catch them.'

Interpol's headquarters in Greece was in the same building as the Hellenic Police headquarters. The two law enforcement agencies shared the large, two storey, building in the centre of Athens. With the global financial crisis hitting Greece and indeed the rest of Europe hard, there had been massive cutbacks, many of the rooms in the building had been mothballed, and as a result, the area allocated to Grey and his team had been drastically reduced. The obligatory guided tour Edmond gave Veronica took hardly any time at all, and as the session with the rest of Grey's group wasn't due to commence until ten thirty, Edmond invited Veronica to his office for coffee, a chat about the 'good old days' and mutual friends, and an informal briefing on the case so far.

"We've been tracking Berswiski, from London, since last October. He murdered a young woman at a disused warehouse near Hyde Park. Interpol got involved when he killed another two in France," he told Veronica. "We've been half-way around the world. A week ago we were in Australia, three weeks ago Thailand. Every time we think we're getting close he slips through our fingers. He always seems to be one step ahead of us."

He went on to present the evidence they'd amassed so far. He left nothing out in deference to her gender, spared no detail, no matter how gruesome. He knew he didn't have to, Veronica Crystal had seen the darker side of humanity before. In all probability, darker and more frequently than Grey himself had seen it. When he'd finished it was nearly ten thirty, so they made their way across the hall to the large, sparsely furnished, conference room which the team had set up as their operations base. He introduced her to the other five team members and then helped her set up her equipment before she began her informal lecture.

"The person you're seeking is, without doubt, criminally insane," she told the group. "From the evidence presented we're looking for a psychopath, rather than your more common paranoid schizophrenic."

"Is there a difference?" asked Randall, "They're both nut bags aren't they?"

"Well criminally insane is the more recognized classification," Mrs. Crystal replied, smiling, "but you're right, they're both nut bags. They're also two totally different creatures. I'll explain." She tapped the touch pad on her laptop and the huge plasma TV above her head burst into life. On one side the screen showed a list of the key markers, twenty in all, which psychiatrists used to identify patients suffering from Psychopathy, on the other a similar list showed the key markers for Schizophrenia.

The major couldn't help thinking that there were many items on the psychopath list which were repeated, or just put another way.

They were:

1 Glib and superficial charm: A tendency to be smooth engaging and charming without any shyness or self consciousness.

2 Grandiose self-worth: Arrogance and an over inflated ego.

3 Need for stimulation: Psychopaths get bored easily and require excessive, thrilling, and exciting stimulation.

4 Pathological lying: Will say anything to achieve their aims with no compunction.

5 Cunning and manipulative: Deceitful and deceptive.

6 lack of remorse or guilt: Lack of concern for others feelings or safety.

7 lack of emotion: cold-hearted and openly gregarious.

8 Callousness and lack of empathy: Inconsiderate and tactless.

9 Parasitic: Financially selfish and manipulative.

10 Poor behavioural control: Impatient, aggressive, abusive.

11 Promiscuous: Indiscriminate in their sexual behaviour.

12 Early behavioural problems: Lying, stealing, bullying prior to the age of thirteen.

13 Lack of long term goals: Compulsive, persistently failing in achievement.

14 Impulsive: Inability to resist temptation. Lacking in planning or deliberation.

15 Irresponsible: Repeated failure to honour obligations.

16 Denial of responsibility: Failure to accept responsibility for one's actions.

17 lack off long term relationships: Inability to make and keep friends, sexual partners,

18 history of juvenile delinquency: Behavioural problems exhibited from early teen years.

19 Low regard for recognized authority: Frequent revocation of probation and other similar institutions.

20 Criminal Versatility: Taking great pride in getting away with crimes.

"You can see here that there are a number of differences between the schizophrenic, which is a psychosis, a mental illness, and the psychopath who suffers from an inability to feel emotion or empathize with others. This is generally thought of as a behavioural abnormality."

"I'd have thought butchering six women would be considered more than just an behavioural abnormality!" interjected Jim Exeter, Dave Randall's partner.

"Yea, you're right. But what we're discussing here is the difference between two psychiatric conditions, not specific cases. Most peoples idea of madness is classic schizophrenia. Victims of this illness hear voices, experience visual hallucinations, that sort of thing. They have a delusional sense of reality. Most schizophrenics are totally harmless, some are only a danger to themselves. Occasionally however, we get one who decides to act on their delusions. We've all heard the defence, 'God made me do it.'"

She tapped the keyboard and another image filled the screen, this one a crime scene photo taken a few years ago. It showed the body of a murder victim. A young man who had been hacked to death with an axe in his own home. His killer had been found in the lounge room watching TV. He had gladly admitted to the crime, and explained that he'd done it because his victim was actually the devil and he was trying to protect Jesus.

"No need to ask if anyone remembers this guy. It was in all the papers for weeks. Lance Albert Horwich, thirty-nine, married, father of three. He'd first showed signs of schizophrenia when he was thirteen and had been in and out of hospital for years. The doctors finally found a drug which worked for him, and from the age of twenty-eight until his spectacular relapse last year, he'd been virtually symptom free. Which unfortunately led him to believe he didn't need his meds any more."

Veronica turned to face her audience and perched herself on the edge of the desk, unconsciously swinging her long legs back and forth under the desk like an overgrown school girl.

"Normally, no make that frequently, this type of perpetrator is easy to catch. More often than not, their attack, and it's rare that there's more than just the single offence before they're caught, is poorly planned or even spontaneous. Most of the time they don't even wish to avoid capture. In their delusional minds they often think they've done something good, not murdered an innocent person," she told them.

"This Berswiski bloke hasn't been easy to catch, and his attacks have been meticulously planned," interjected Exeter.

"Which is yet another good indication that the man we're looking for isn't schizophrenic. He isn't acting on orders coming from some imagined entity inside his sick mind. This man knows exactly what he's doing. And you can bet the farm he enjoys both the thrill of killing and the buzz he gets from getting away with it. Berswiski is a psychopath. Cold blooded, virtually emotionless, with no sense of guilt or remorse, totally unable to empathize with any other living creature. Berswiski doesn't kill for a reason, he kills for fun."

"I don't understand. You said he'd be emotionless. Isn't having fun, i.e. happiness an emotion?" asked Jones.

"Yea. Though I did say virtually emotionless. It's hard to say with any great certainty, but I suspect it's exactly that, which compels him to kill. For you and I, our feelings come easily. Someone tells us a joke, we feel happy, we watch a sad movie we feel sad." She turned and smiled cheekily at Edmond. "The boss gives us the shits, we get angry. It's all natural. Even small events trigger small emotions. Berswiski probably doesn't feel any emotion at all unless the trigger is extreme, and I suspect, they then come in a mighty big rush. Just like a narcotic. Also, the fact that his victims have all been women is also telling. It's not just violence that gets him off, there's also a large sexual component to consider."

Randall jumped to his feet excitedly. "So that's how we catch him then."

"What do you mean?" asked Grey.

Randall squinted, put his palms together as if in prayer and bowed deeply. Chinese style.

"We simply follow the psychopath of least resistance, Master."

The team groaned in unison. "Bloody mad Aussie," someone called. Someone else threw a notepad at him. But despite themselves everyone smiled.

James McTaggard, the young Scottish agent who'd been assigned to Grey's team as chief forensics officer, put his hand up like a schoolboy and then blushed deeply when he realized what he was doing. Veronica acknowledged him.

"According to his file, this Berswiski chap is ...", he checked his notes, "seventy-one years old. Is this psychopath thing....I mean, has this mad bastard always been like this? or has his condition developed more recently?"

"There are some records of people who have developed Psychopathy after trauma to the brain, but most Psychopaths are born that way."

"So how come this arsehole has suddenly started killing women?" asked Randall

Veronica slid down from her perch on the edge of her desk and clicked off her laptop. She had intended to show the group a pile of statistics, elaborate on the gruesome details of other murders committed by Psychopathic serial killers. But she'd realized there was no point. The men and women in this room had seen enough bloodshed and mayhem to last them a lifetime. They, more than most, didn't need reminding of the unspeakable evil human beings sometimes did to one another.

"There's no way of knowing for sure if it is a recent thing," she told them. "This Berswiski guy is obviously highly intelligent.

Smarter than anyone here I'll bet. He could have been killing women for years, but no one has ever caught him. You're right though, it does seem that, if nothing else, there's been an increase in his attacks. Also, the Major said his latest victim was in her seventies, so he's also getting less specific in his choice of target."

Randall sat back in his chair and let out a sigh.

"So how do we catch the bastard?"

"We wait for him to make a mistake. Trust me, no matter how intelligent he is, he will make a mistake. We just have to be vigilant and make sure we're there when he fuck's up. I'm sorry I can't be more help than that."

They talked about the case for about another hour and then she told them that, unless someone had more questions, that concluded the discussion. She began to put away her equipment. She stopped and once again addressed the room.

"Oh. Two things you might not like to know. According to some studies, up to one percent of the worlds population should be classified as psychopaths. The good news is, they're not all serial killers, or for that matter, even dangerous. Most hide their symptoms by imitating the emotions they see displayed by people around them. They tend to use their, shall we say character traits, to their advantage. Most are high achievers, corporate business owners, politicians, men and women with a huge influence on large groups of other people. A lot of their success is more than likely thanks to their inability to feel any compunction at the way they treat others. Or to put it another way they don't give a shit who they step on, on their way to the top."

"What's the second thing?" asked Jones.

"An agent who attended one of my lectures once expressed relief at the fact that he was sane. I told him something I want you all to remember. 'When it comes to our own sanity we should never consider ourselves a reliable judge.' In all probability, Vladimir

Michael Berswiski is quite convinced he's the only sane person, in a world full of very sick people. And that's where his weakness lies. As agent McTaggard alluded too, Berswiski is getting worse. This is substantiated by the change in his MO. His last victim, the woman in Istanbul, was an elderly woman, not his more usual, young, attractive female. The change may be due to opportunity. Dora Abernathy may simply have been in the wrong place at the wrong time. But maybe he's getting more desperate to get his kicks and correspondingly less cautious in his selection of victim. If that's the case, then he's going to start making mistakes sooner rather than later. We all need to be even more vigilant from now until this monster is caught."

Chapter 14

There was still two days to kill before Stefan the other crew member arrived and the tourist brochures for the Ayasofya Museum, Topkapi Palace and the Blue Mosque all looked very interesting, but what Iris really wanted to see was the ancient city of Troy. Crawling up a gigantic, wooden horse's arse and waiting for nightfall didn't seem like a feasible plan, so she took a bus 340 kilometres to Canakkale, booked herself into a hostel for the night and the following day joined a local tour company for an excursion to Troy.

The tour bus was a decrepit white, green and rust coloured Toyota Coaster that had seen better days and would probably not see many more. Its seats were ripped, the air conditioning didn't work, the tyres were bald and the glow plugs, an essential part of a modern diesel motor, which were needed to pre heat the motor prior to starting, had given up the ghost years ago. The result was, if the driver stopped the bus for too long and the engine cooled down too much, he was forced to employ the unusual and potentially hazardous practice of heating up the intake manifold with a small gas powered blowtorch. The tour group consisted of eleven other passengers of various nationalities, all of them backpackers and all of them a year or four younger than Iris.

The tour guide introduced himself as Nafti. He spoke excellent English but apart from that, his suitability as a tour guide was highly questionable. He had virtually no interpersonal skills. He was sloppy in both his dress and manner, and he had little knowledge or interest in his country's history. In fact the only interest he did have, was in a stunningly beautiful, nut achingly sexy 'Goddess' from Bologna called Rosa. Rosa spoke no Turkish and only a little English but she was fluent in body language and made it perfectly obvious to everyone, except the man himself, that Nafti didn't stand a snowballs chance in hell. Unperturbed, Nafti went after Rosa as if she was the last woman on earth.

Paul, a bleary-eyed, pasty-faced Brit, whose primary aim in life seemed to be to get legless as often as possible, noticed Nafti's dog like devotion to the delectable Rosa and renamed him Mustafa Root Asif. Unfortunately it didn't matter what you called him he was still a bloody awful tour guide.

During the drive to Troy, Nafti, who was clearly disinterested in what he was supposed to be doing, occasionally made a couple of vague, half-hearted, references to places of historical significance as they passed by, but was otherwise silent. Except that is when he wasn't trying to chat up Rosa. The poor girl had been deliberately delayed by Paul until all the other seats were taken and so she had to sit up the front next to Mustafa Root for the whole trip.

As soon as they arrived at Troy, Mustafa herded them off the bus and started his spiel.

"The city of Troy was built in 500 AD" began Mustafa.

"Fook off ya wanka" called Paul from the back of the group, "that's only fifteen fookin hundred years ago. I've got fookin underpants older'n that".

"I reckon you're wearing underpants older than that," said the girl next to him waving her hand in front of her nose.

"Actually " said a timid voice belonging to a podgy American with crew cut hair, titanium restrained teeth and coke bottle glasses, "Nafti is partially correct. The city of Troy, which was founded around 3000 BC has been invaded, destroyed and rebuilt nine times during its three thousand five hundred year history. The last time, as Nafti said was around 500 AD."

It transpired that Nigel, the podgy American, was a graduate in archaeology from the University of Salt Lake City. His final year thesis was entitled, "Archaeological Sites of Historical Significance in Asia Minor". A quick show of hands had the reluctant Nigel voted in as 'Official Unofficial Tour Guide' and Mustafa Root Asif was demoted to the lowly position of bus driver and handmaiden to the highly bonkable Miss Rosa. The rest of the tour was just wonderful. Slowly, Nigel overcame his initial shyness and entertained, informed and positively enthralled his audience with his lectures. He would scurry about the city ruins leaping from battlement to battlement, single-handedly re-enacting various battles and historical events and laughing at himself when he occasionally forgot some date that he should have mentioned. Of course, being from Salt Lake City, Nigel just had to be a fully-fledged member of the Mormon 'Tour de Suburbs Cycling Team' and whether from years of conditioning or just some inherent genetic predisposition, Nigel could not pass up an opportunity to spread the word of God. Thankfully he only tried it once.

"Our good Lord Jesus Christ once said..." began Nigel, just before an empty soft drink can, a half-eaten cheese sandwich and a torrent of abuse rained down upon him. Nigel took the hint and returned to the subject of Troy, so Iris never learnt what exactly it was that 'Our Good Lord Jesus Christ' had once said. Though to be honest, she didn't give a shit and had had enough of her cheese sandwich anyway.

The tour concluded back at the bus and as the group re-boarded a cry went up,

"Three cheers for Nigel the tour guide for a fookin' job well done". Everyone cheered, everyone clapped or shook his hand or slapped him on the back. Even Rosa, who despite her poor English had seemed to enjoy Nigel's efforts, went over and kissed him on both cheeks.

"Gratsi Proffesori" she gushed, and to Mustafa Roots Asif's annoyance, threw her arms around the American, kissed him enthusiastically on both cheeks, and squashed him to her ample bosom. Iris had never seen anyone blush quite so deeply.

The day before 'Harvey Wharf Banger' was due to set sail, Stefan came on board. He was a typical Dutchman. Tall, blond, blue-eyed, seriously self obsessed and speaking English with that same singsong, "nose full of snot" accent all Dutch people have. Iris was not a person that liked to put labels on people, but if she had been, Stefan's label would have read "Boring Pratt; shake well before use" There was no escaping the fact, the boy was as exciting as a rained out lawn bowls match. Iris tried everything to engage him in conversation, from discussing politics and religion to debating the existence of global warming, but nothing worked. His answers were direct, to the point and kept to a minimum. Nothing Iris tried extracted any sort of enthusiastic reaction. Damn thought Iris, now I'm going to have to spend most of my time talking to Alan. And then she smiled.

Alan just accepted Stefan as he was and immediately began to follow the tried and true Australian practice of taking the piss out of him at every opportunity.

Their first dinner together that night as the yacht sat comfortably at anchor was one Iris would never forget.

"So! Stefan" asked Alan with a look of intense sincerity on his face, "you come from the nether regions?"

"Yes Alan I am from the Nedderlunds" replied Stefan, nodding his head.

"Where in the nether regions do you come from?" asked Alan straight-faced.

"A little town called Hertogenborch," answered Stefan.

"Is that anywhere near Arsedend?" queried Alan

"No Alan" said Stefan "Ostende is in Belgium, not Holland ".

"They tell me that Holland doesn't have any mountains Stefan. Is that true?" asked Alan.

"Yes Alan," said Stefan and for the first time nodded with great enthusiasm.

"In fact 70% of the Nedderlunds is below the sea level".

"Goodness," cried Alan, as if this was the most amazing thing he had ever heard. "Iris, can you believe how flat Stefan's nether regions are?"

It wasn't that funny but the more Iris tried to stop herself laughing, the harder it became. She couldn't contain her giggling any longer and with tears streaming down her face and her hand covering her mouth to stop herself from laughing, she rushed from the galley and ran out on deck.

"I think she might be a liddle sea sick," said Stefan as she bolted outside.

Chapter 15

Had Berswiski read a transcript of the discussion between Veronica Crystal and Major Grey and his team, he would have, in all probability, concurred with most of what had been said. Though it was doubtful he would have agreed with the consensus that his mental condition was either an illness, or for that matter, a disadvantage.

For Vladimir Mikhail Berswiski, his inability to empathize with others was not a failing, it was a strength. Rather than a flaw in his biological makeup, Berswiski saw his Psychopathy as an inevitable side effect of his genius. He believed himself to be the next stage in evolution. An improvement over the primitive creatures who surrounded him and wished to inflict their asinine morals and standards upon him.

Those pathetic, ineffectual weaklings, like the ones who had been pursuing him ever since London, could never comprehend the things which drove him to kill. They did not understand the feeling of power, of omnipotence, that the suffering and eventual death of the women he murdered gave him. They were miserable, stupid creatures, every one of them. Like that ridiculous American woman Abernathy, how could anyone feel sympathetic towards such a shallow, self centred fool like her? Idiots like that had no reason or purpose in their lives, and were of no use to anyone except other idiots. The only thing of use the foolish woman had done during her whole life was when she'd died. At least then she'd given somebody a few minutes of happiness.

But another comment, one which Berswiski would have had to agree with Veronica Crystal on, was her assertion that the euphoria Berswiski felt after each attack would be short-lived. She was right there. Eventually Berswiski knew he would feel the compulsion to kill again.

He felt that urge now, which was why Vladimir had his head buried in a phone book looking for the same limo service he'd used a few days ago. He needed to go out into the night, seek out his next victim, find a pretty little thing, a beautiful yet stupid, young woman who might give him just a few moments of unbridled pleasure. He needed to feel the tug of flesh against his blade. He desperately wanted to hear the screams of the woman's agony and smell the sickly sweet metallic tang of freshly spilt blood. His need was palpable. He felt suffocated, almost unable to breathe, the craving for that rush of adrenaline, the amazing feeling of euphoria, was almost unbearable.

He finally found the number, picked up his mobile phone and dialled. The call went to message bank, and the female voice on the recording asked the caller, first in Greek and then in English, to leave a return number so that she might better service his requirements.

Berswiski left his number and a message requesting to speak to Tasos Meanopolis, the same chauffeur he'd engaged last time. Berswiski told the answering machine he would accept no other driver, it had to be Tasos. There was a good reason for his insistence. Not only would the man accept cash up front, which removed any chance of the police tracking him through his credit card transactions, Tasos could be trusted to keep his eyes peeled and his mouth shut. Or if not trusted exactly, then at least coerced. Vladimir knew he had enough evidence on Tasos's own peccadilloes to be sure the man would be too frightened to talk to anyone. He was a convicted criminal with enough previous form to ensure if he ever went to prison again, it would be for a very long time. What Berswiski had watched him to do to a young Italian woman early last year, before he himself took over, would be more than enough to have him arrested as an accomplice. Berswiski felt that that threat, plus the knowledge he would without hesitation, slice, dice and kill the fat fuck if Tasos overstepped the bounds of Customer/Chauffeur confidentiality, had him convinced he was safe in Tasos's podgy hands.

When the woman at the limousine hire service received Berswiski's message she rang him back. But not before she'd made a quick call to her local Police station. The cops had contacted all the taxi companies and limo hire establishments, urging them to call if someone called Berswiski contacted them. The Athens police then contacted Major Edmond Grey. Despite the late hour he immediately called Randall and had him track down Tasos Meanopolis's home address and set up around the clock surveillance. It was their second major lead and Grey was determined that this time Berswiski wasn't going to get away. They'd watch the chauffeur's home and when he went to pick up his passenger, Grey and his team would be right behind him.

Chapter 16

Alan inserted the winch handle into the halyard winch and began to wind. In less than a minute he had the big mains'l up and flapping lazily in the breeze.

"Okay Stefan", he called to the young man standing at the bow, "start bringing the anchor up please". Stefan leaned over the bow rail to watch as the anchor chain came up and stepped on the deck mounted switch. The anchor winch whirred, the chain clanked over the bow roller and then disappeared down the hawser into the chain locker below deck. 'Harvey' moved slowly forward, following the path of the chain lying on the seabed below, until she was directly above the anchor. The winch slowed, straining against the weight of the anchor, which had buried itself in the thick mud on the ocean floor, and then sped up again as the anchor broke free.

"Anchor loose", called Stefan and Alan pushed the big mains'l out into the breeze. The wind backed the sail pushing the boat slowly backwards.

"Helm hard to port please Iris", called Alan and Iris spun the big steering wheel to the left, causing 'Harvey' to back around until the wind was coming over her starboard side. Alan jumped down from the coach house roof and hauled the mains'l in, trimming it perfectly for a beam reach.

"Bring her around to a heading of two four zero degrees please Iris. Stefan, you and I will get the other sails up."

With Iris steering the slowly moving yacht, the two men quickly raised the genoa, mizzen and finally the stays'l. 'Harvey' dropped her shoulder into the oncoming sea and forged ahead. The voyage had started in earnest.

The one hundred and fifteen nautical mile voyage across the Sea of Marmara to Gelibolu, near the entrance to Canakkale Bogazi Dardanelles took one and a half days. Longer than expected due to light winds. No-one was concerned at the slow progress however. Alan had decided that because of the amount of shipping that passed through the Dardanelles, they should only navigate the narrow passage during daylight, which meant anchoring overnight off Gelibolu and making an early start through the passage in the morning.

Despite the light winds, Iris had enjoyed the sail immensely. The sea had been calm, the weather clear and the spring sun had been sufficiently warm for her to spend most of the daytime pottering around on deck in her bikini. Iris felt certain that as they were always a fair way off shore and the only people around to see were Alan and Stefan, the bikini was probably superfluous. Though this was her first major voyage, she'd spent a number of weekends sailing around Moreton Bay, and a couple of week long trips sailing up the Queensland coast. She knew from those longer experiences, that on a small boat with very little privacy available, it was inevitable that eventually everyone would see everyone else's jiggly bits. Iris had come to the conclusion, that if it was going to happen anyway there was little point in worrying about it now. However, as Alan was the skipper, she'd decided to let him decide if swimwear was required or not. As yet however, she'd been unable to think of a way of bringing up the subject without giving the others the wrong idea.

Just after 6:00 PM, whilst anchored off Gelibolu, Iris's phone rang. It was Peggy. The two friends did the "How are you? I'm fine.

How are you?" routine and then Peggy got around to the reason for her call.

"How would you and Alan like another crew member for a few weeks?" she asked.

"I'll have to ask Alan, but he said earlier another pair of hands wouldn't go astray," replied Iris "Who did you have in mind?"

"Me" said Peggy and then she started to cry. It was Chris or Christopher as Peggy insisted on calling him. The bastard had dumped her and was moving to Sydney with yet another lame brained scheme supposed to make him a fortune. A scheme that, as so many similar get-rich-quick plans had done before, would almost inevitably fail within the first three months. Iris wanted to say good riddance. She'd never liked Christopher, especially after he'd made a drunken lunge at her last Christmas. Also, as the break up had helped Peggy to make up her mind to come to Greece to join her, Iris was more than glad he was gone. Never the less Iris knew her friend was hurting and so decided the only thing she could do was offer her a Nokia assisted shoulder to cry on. By the end of the phone call, Alan had agreed to allow to Peggy join them. They arranged to meet her in Athens in a week's time.

If the sail from Istanbul to Gelibolu was slow, then the following day's sail through the Dardanelles made up for it. Overnight the wind picked up to about 25 knots and veered around to the north. Perfect for a roller coaster reach down the 35 nautical mile long channel. Alan sat on the side of the cockpit, lounging against a large cushion, steering the yacht with his foot. It was his second favourite sailing position. His most favourite involved a large sail bag stuffed with pillows; a young German girl named Dorotka and a can of whipped cream. But that was a different story and you had to be over eighteen to read it.

Alan looked around to make sure Stefan was still on watch in the stern. They were keeping well to starboard, so he had to admit, that even in a busy, narrow passage the chance of being run down by another vessel in the middle of the day was slight. But he had asked his two shipmates to keep watch anyway. A large container ship or oil tanker was not the most manoeuvrable vessel on the water. Fully loaded and at speed, such a ship would take three or four kilometres to stop. The only sensible course of action was to keep out of the way. Stefan gave a 'thumbs up' signal and smiled. Alan liked Stefan, though he wasn't sure he had figured him out yet. Iris said he was boring, but Alan was sure she was wrong. Despite very relaxed views on issues such as pornography and recreational drug use, the average Dutch person was a very conservative creature. In addition, although Stefan spoke English reasonably well, it was still his second language, and he still had to translate everything he heard in his head, consider his response, and then translate that into English before replying. Alan felt sure that this was a big problem. When he and Iris got into a lively discussion Stefan was simply left behind and could not join in. Iris misread this as disinterest.

The girl herself stood lookout in the bow. The cute little bikini of yesterday had been exchanged for a baggy, green tracksuit and a big fluffy blue jumper more suitable for the cold northerly wind. Pity, thought Alan. He liked that bikini. Four tiny triangles of Lycra that revealed as well as concealed. He liked the way it accentuated her cute bum, the delicate fabric stretching and contracting, caressing her buttocks as she moved around on deck. He liked the way it tried valiantly to contain her ample tits and the way it occasionally failed when she was engrossed in a physically difficult task, and a beautiful brown nipple slipped out. More than the bikini itself however, Alan liked the woman who wore it. As he watched her raise the binoculars to her eyes, Alan decided for the thousandth time since he'd met her that she was gorgeous. She was beautiful, sexy and alluring, but more importantly, she was intelligent and engaging. Alan liked that. He was sure that even if they did not become lovers, they must certainly become good friends. Dorotka had also been beautiful and sexy and alluring and they could hardly keep their hands off each other. But when the kissing and fondling and the sucking and fucking were over and their urgent lust for each other had been sated, Dorotka, who was so dense the Hamburg Scientific Society had her listed as a heavy metal, was painfully boring.

The ferry that runs between Canakkale and Eceabat crosses every hour on the hour. Whether it was 45 minutes late or 55 minutes early, Iris never knew but the delay meant that Alan had to reduce sail and slow "Harvey" down so that they passed to the ferry well to stern. Iris raised her binoculars to watch the ferry pass and there standing at the back of the boat was a bleary eyed, pasty-faced Brit with fifteen hundred year old underpants. Paul was on his way to the battlefields of Gallipoli. It was a small world, she thought. She had no idea just how small.

Chapter 17

The 'arms dealer' was pissed off. Not just angry or disappointed but totally, utterly and completely pissed off. Barrack fucking Obama's interference in the Middle East was severely affecting his business. He had to admit that it was a bit of a double-edged sword. On the one hand, over the past six months he had been approached by sixteen new groups. Radical, Anti-American groups with money to spend, who wanted nothing more in life than to get the Yanks out of Muslim territory and to kill as many of them as possible while doing it. For an illegal arms dealer, such hatred is good for business. On the downside, it was now almost impossible to ship goods to anywhere in the Middle East.

But the Palestinians had insisted that their requirements be delivered to Palestine. A reasonable request and normally easily fulfilled. The 'arms dealer' had long ago established a comprehensive network of Government Ministers, customs officials, border guards and military personnel who would, for an appropriate financial consideration, suddenly develop myopia on the night that his trucks passed through. Now, thanks to Obama's 'War on Terror', the Turkey-Syria-Jordan route was impossible. Turkey had welcomed the invading Americans with open arms and the Turkish borders had been closed. With just 6 weeks left before the delivery, the Arms' dealer had to find an alternative route. Such a pity one could not send nuclear warheads through the post.

Worse than having to find a new way of delivering the weapon, was the necessity of having to tell Berswiski about the change of plan. The 'arms dealer' hated Berswiski. He was frightened of him as well. But if a fully functional nuclear bomb was needed, Berswiski was the only man he knew who possessed the scientific know how to rearm one. The 'arms dealer' was left with a number of less than satisfactory options for transporting the bomb. Ultimately he decided he would join Berswiski in Greece and ship the warhead over the Mediterranean to Ghazzah.

The 1954 Leningrad University award for excellence was remarkable for two reasons. Firstly, at just fifteen years old, Vladimir Micael Berswiski was the youngest ever recipient of the prestigious award. The second reason was that the selection committee, comprising of some of the finest scientific minds in the Soviet Union, took a full three months to make the decision to present the award to him. The reason for the time lapse was not because the detestable little shit didn't deserve it; there was no doubt Berswiski's thesis on subatomic particle acceleration was a work of true genius. It was just that the entire selection committee would've preferred to give it to someone else. Anyone else.

Vladimir Berswiski's birth in 1939 caused a great deal of concern around the Berswiski household. His Russian mother and Polish father already had three children and another mouth to feed was the last thing they needed. He was a sickly baby, born far too small the doctors said, to have much chance of surviving more than a few days. Baby Berswiski however proved the doctors wrong. After three months in hospital, despite his frailty, Vladimir was taken home. His parents slowly came to realize that theirs was no ordinary baby. What Vladimir lacked physically, he more than made up for in intelligence. Before his first birthday, Vladimir was speaking. Not just Russian, but also Polish. Not only words but well-structured simple sentences. By eighteen months, he could read and write, and by the age of two, had mastered simple arithmetic. His first five years were spent in a wheelchair as his spindly legs were simply unable to support his weight for more than a few seconds. His eyesight was poor and his head so misshapen and pinched that most people thought he looked like some gigantic rodent.

Despite his success at school, or perhaps because of it, young Berswiski was not a popular child. His teachers would try to praise him for his achievements, but such praise would only bring forth a tirade of abuse from the boy. He simply could not believe that the fools thought he needed their approval. He was an unlikeable monster. Even his own parents despised him. In 1953, Berswiski's first year at university, the city of Leningrad was rocked by a brutal murder. The body of a young girl, barely more than a toddler was found in the basement of an old derelict building. She had been strangled and then the body had been hacked to pieces with an axe. The police never found the perpetrator.

After his graduation, the Soviet Government was advised of Berswiski's academic achievements and the Polit- Bureau concluded that such a man would be invaluable to their nuclear weapons program. Although the prestige of being the youngest person ever to work on such an important project should have been an honour, it did nothing to impress Berswiski. The money and perks he was offered however, were impossible to resist and so, in the spring of 1955, Berswiski moved to Moscow. Over the next 20 years he was moved all around the Soviet Union to work at various laboratories and research centres on the Soviet's nuclear weapons project. He left behind him a trail of death and destruction. Slowly but surely, the Russian police built up a strong case against him. A case so strong that even the Kremlin could not protect him. In 1975, instead of the plethora of murdered and mutilated prostitutes that normally surfaced whenever Berswiski was in the area, the body of a young and beautiful laboratory assistant had been found. Forensic scientists ascertained that she had been tortured for hours before she had died. Her hands and feet had been amputated, the nipples of both breasts had been chewed off and she had been repeatedly raped. Irrefutable evidence, in the form of photos of the unfortunate woman being tortured, were found in Berswiski's office and a warrant for his immediate arrest was issued. When the police stormed his home to arrest him, Berswiski was nowhere to be found. He had left just three minutes earlier. He resurfaced a few weeks later in Brazil.

Berswiski did not enjoy his years in South America. He found the country and it's people distasteful and the climate deplorable.

Berswiski had never enjoyed good health, or for that matter, anything even vaguely approaching good health, and the stifling heat and sweltering humidity of the summer wet season did nothing to improve it. His lungs would fill with mucus and his breathing would become laboured with the first onslaught of the monsoon. He would succumb to a racking cough that persisted for months. A cough which frequently left him bed ridden. He would find relief in the spring but even then, a debilitating attack of hay fever could be enough to send him back to his sick bed.

In the spring of '88 a recurring bout of pneumonia laid his frail body to waste, and he was convinced the time for him to go and meet his maker was imminent. He threw caution to the wind and wrote to his mother in Russia to say goodbye. Unfortunately the Russian Department of Science, interested in bringing Berswiski back to where he could be of some use to them, were informed of the letter when it was intercepted by a loyal party member in the local post office.

A large bearded man from the KGB presented himself at the door to Berswiski's mother's house, and forcibly enlisted the reluctant help of Vladimir's younger sister Svetlana, to bring the errant scientist back into the Soviet fold.

Two days later, Svetlana Berswiski arrived in Rio, and with the money given to her by the KGB, engaged the services of an expatriate German doctor who set about getting her elder brother well again.

Svetlana scrubbed and disinfected Vladimir's hovel from floor to ceiling. She threw out his soiled bedding, restocked the larder with fresh, wholesome foods and started Berswiski on an exercise and physiotherapy regime. The doctor too knew his stuff, in fact were it not for a particularly expensive penchant for cocaine, he would have almost certainly enjoyed a highly successful career back in Frankfurt. But he had fallen foul of the Deutschland medical authorities due to a number of irregularities in his class 1 drug record keeping and had been struck off. So now, having travelled to Peru and then Brazil in search of a cheap source of the white powder he craved so insanely, he was available at a fraction of the fee he would have commanded back in Germany. With the doctor's expertise and Svetlana's dedication, Vladimir gradually made a full recovery.

Each week, Svetlana would contact her benefactors back in Russia and inform them of her progress, promising each time that she would be bringing her brother back home as soon as he was well enough to travel.

After three months his health had greatly improved. Svetlana called the good doctor to the house. Vladimir slit his throat with a scalpel, dumped his body into the river. Then having disposed of the only person in South America who knew who or where he was, Berswiski and his sister disappeared without a trace.

In February '89, just months away from the collapse of the Russian socialist regime, Vladimir Berswiski turned up again, this time as scientific adviser at the nuclear enrichment plant at Kanggye in North Korea. President Kim IL Sung had decided that now was a good time to join the nuclear age, and having acquired a consignment of suitable spent nuclear fuel rods, wanted them reprocessed to produce weapons grade plutonium. Berswiski was in charge of this project.

With its more temperate climate, Vladimir found North Korea a much more suitable country in which to exile himself. Once a month the evil little rodent and any other scientists who had time off, were flown by charter plane the two-hundred odd kilometres from the facility in Kanggye to the capital for a bit of R & R. Now fully recovered from his ailments, Berswiski recommenced his depraved practice of mutilation and murder. He preyed mercilessly on the young female population of Pyongyang, sometimes killing more than once in a night. In mid 2003 Kim Jong IL, Kim IL Sung's son and successor, declared North Korea was withdrawing from the 'Nuclear non-proliferation Treaty' and announced it was developing a 'nuclear deterrent'.

But the fall of the Russian socialist regime meant that Berswiski could return home to mother Russia as soon as his contract with the North Koreans was completed. In May 2004 Vladimir Berswiski sent an e-mail to an Arms' dealer he had done some freelance work for over the years, and told him he was coming home. His timing was impeccable.

Chapter 18

The taverna on the Greek Island of Kea was known as "The Pegasus" or "The Olympus" or something, Iris wasn't quite sure. One thing she did know however, was after two hours of drinking Ouzo on an empty stomach, the taverna on the Greek Island of Kea was the best damned taverna in the entire Mediterranean. She wasn't pissed though, just mellow. Mellow as a parrot in fact. Poor Stefan, who had admitted to being 'not much of a drinker", was trying desperately to act sober and failing miserably.

"Kalimara" the taverna's only waiter greeted them.

"No thanks" joked Alan "I hate squid". Stefan burst out laughing and slapped Alan on the back.

"I like that joke Alan" he said and rolled his eyes in mock ridicule, "much better than your 'Nether Regions' gags". Alan and Iris looked at each other in disbelief, and then it was their turn to laugh.

The two hundred and twenty nautical mile voyage across the Aegean to the island of Kea took four days. Not because the sailing conditions were poor, in fact they were excellent, but because no one was in any hurry and there were so many interesting and spectacular places to see on the way. The Aegean Sea is littered with a myriad of ruggedly beautiful islands and each day they would sail for a few hours, then stop for the night somewhere spectacular. The weather was perfect too. The wind had dropped to a pleasant fifteen to eighteen knots from the east north east which not only drove the yacht along at a decent clip, but also took the edge off the hot spring sun. Iris discarded her baggy green tracksuit, and to Alan's delight, returned to wearing the cute little bikini. After four days, apart from four tiny, 'glow in the dark' triangles of flesh that nicely highlighted all the interesting bits, Iris's body had tanned to a glorious honey brown. Even Stefan, who could get sunburnt reading a post card and who had to use sunscreen on nights with a full moon, was starting to tan.

To Iris's astonishment and pleasure, Stefan was turning out to be an excellent shipmate. Until his first day on "Harvey Wharf Banger", Stefan's entire sailing experience was limited to reading the Dutch translation of "Mutiny on the Bounty". But he found that he loved sailing and now he wanted to know all there was to know about the craft. He would follow Alan around on deck asking questions "What is this called Alan?" he would ask, "Why did you need to do that Alan? Why does the compass go in the opposite direction when we turn the steering wheel Alan?" Alan would answer patiently and clearly, and Stefan would write it all down in the little notebook he always carried with him. Surprisingly Stefan's usefulness was not just limited to the sailing. The young man was a workaholic. Anything that needed to be done, and quite a lot that didn't, Stefan would be there to do. When Iris's first turn in the galley came around, Stefan offered to help.

"There is a cooking clup at my University in Amsterdam" he explained "I am the president of this clup. I am very good."

Indeed, he was. Stefan would cook up the most delectable, delicious meals from the most basic ingredients and when he once again offered to cook the following night, no one complained.

Iris was also happy with Alan. She loved his rugged charm and his kind and gentle manner. He never lost his temper, never complained and was always polite. His sense of humour was a bit lame, but as Stefan succinctly put it. "It's much better than if he was miserable."

He had one major flaw however, no matter how many times Iris flirted with him, no matter how many times she "accidentally" brushed up against him or complimented him on his talent as a sailor, Alan seemed impervious to her charms.

During the journey to Kea, the trio had discussed Peggy and formulated a plan for meeting her in Athens. Alan had been to Athens many times before, and although he said it was an interesting place and declared that monuments such as the Acropolis were not to be missed, he had no desire to go there again. It was decided that the best plan of attack was to sail to Kea. Alan would stay with the boat while Iris and Stefan would catch the ferry, which crossed the 20 kilometre strait to Lavrion on the mainland, and then take a bus to Athens. This would give them a day in Athens before Peggy arrived and another day after for sightseeing.

The evening at the taverna on Kea proved to be a huge success, and everyone had a great time. There was singing and dancing and the traditional Greek custom of breaking plates followed by the traditional Greek custom of sacking the waiter, and of course lots of drinking. There was delicious food. They drank copious amounts of alcoholic beverages, told tall and humorous tales and then drank some more. At Alan's suggestion Iris tried a dish containing braised octopus. Although she'd been out with a few in her time, Iris had never eaten octopus before. It was delicious.

Midnight saw the trio staggering back to the yacht. Iris had pitted herself against a bottle of Ouzo and had come out a dismal second best. She was only just managing to stop herself from falling over, throwing up, or passing out in front of the boys. Rowing the tender proved to be an amazing experience with the dinghy ending up facing the wrong way more than once. Poor Stefan, who was having trouble standing on dry land never mind in a rocking dinghy, ended up in the sea. When they finally reached 'Harvey', it was all Iris could do to climb up the ladder onto the deck. Iris said goodnight to the two men and turned in. Tomorrow she and Stefan would catch the ferry to the mainland.

The following morning, sunrise was at 5:16 am but Stefanrise was sixteen minutes earlier. Stefan staggered up on deck, relieved himself over the side and then sat on the coach house roof to watch the sun come up. He had woken dreaming of Jasmine, an English backpacker he had meet a few months earlier. They had enjoyed a brief, torrid and noisy love affair at the end of which, Jasmine had returned home to London for Christmas. In the dream they were once again at Frankfurt airport. Jasmine was heading home. In the real world they had embraced, kissed passionately and promised to write, which of course they never did. It was a ritual goodbye. Each one new that this had only been a holiday romance, perhaps not even a romance at all, rather just a sharing of lust and a few bodily fluids. It had been just a mutual enjoyment of each other's sexual being and neither Stefan nor Jasmine had any delusions it had been anything different.

In the dream however, things were different. This time at the airport Jasmine pulled away in disgust when he tried to embrace her.

"No Stefan", she snapped, "I never really loved you. I just wanted a shag. I'm not yours to paw and grope whenever the fancy takes you," and then she stormed off. Stefan had found the dream extremely upsetting.

Iris woke to the aroma of freshly ground coffee, the smell of bacon and eggs cooking in the galley, and the sound of Stefan whistling. The sound was so tuneless, so lacking in any form of tempo or rhythm that the pounding in her head sounded positively melodic by comparison.

"Stefan darling" sang Iris sweetly. "Would you be a dear and SHUT THE FUCK UP AND LET ME DIE IN PEACE".

There was a knock on the bulkhead next to her pillow. It was Alan. He was carrying a breakfast tray.

"Morning Snow White. Feeling Grumpy today are we?" he asked.

I'd rather be feeling you, thought Iris as she groaned and pulled her pillow over her head.

"The "Frying Dutchman" sends his apologies for waking you up, plus coffee, toast, bacon and eggs and a lumpy" announced Alan presenting the tray.

Iris sat up in bed. Her stomach didn't want to hear the words bacon and eggs ever again. "What's a lumpy?"

"It's like a smoothie but we don't have a blender", answered Alan. Iris picked up a glass containing a foamy yellow liquid.

"It's fizzy", she exclaimed.

"That would be the Berocca", said Alan. "Don't ask me what else is in it. It was made to Stefan's secret recipe "We haf a first day'd Clup at my University", said Alan imitating Stefan perfectly, "I am dur president oft dis clup. I am very good at making cure for han gofers", and he was.

Stefan's cure for 'han gofers' was miraculous and Iris made a solemn promise to herself never to tell 'Saint Stefan' to shut the fuck up ever again. By 6:30, an hour before the ferry was due to leave for the mainland, both she and Stefan were packed and ready to go. There was only one problem. Iris couldn't find her passport.

"I had it when we cleared customs" she wailed. "It must be on the boat somewhere."

After searching for nearly an hour, they had to leave without it.

As they had already cleared customs when they first entered Greek waters, the lack of passport was not immediately a critical problem. Not unless she needed to leave in a hurry due to some unforeseen emergency. Stuck in a foreign country without a valid passport wasn't a good idea, so she decided the best course of action was to go to the Australian Embassy as soon as they arrived in Athens, report the loss and try to arrange a new one.

The ferry to the mainland was packed full of tourists, holiday makers and commuters. Iris and Stefan found a spot at the back and settled down for the short trip.

"Stefan" yelled a male voice and a tall, blond, blue eyed clone pushed his way through the crowd. The two men shook hands, greeted one another warmly, then spoke to each other in Muppet for a few minutes before Stefan introduced his friend to Iris. His name was Roland. He and Stefan had met in Switzerland late last year and he too was now on his way to Athens.

Faced with the proposition of spending the rest of the day with Iris waiting for her to sort out the passport problem, or spending the day with Roland, the exciting world of bureaucracy came a distant second place. When they finally reached Athens, Iris and Stefan parted company, promising to meet again at the hostel later that evening.

According to Iris's 2014 edition of 'What Consulate is that,' the Greek city of Athens comes complete with it's very own, latest model, multi story, air conditioned Australian Embassy. It's conveniently located at Level 6, Thon Building, Cnr Kifisias and Alexandras Avenue, Ambelokipi. The taxi ride was speedy, life threatening and expensive, but at least the taxi driver somehow understood her clumsy attempt at the Greek language.

"I need to get to the Australian Embassy", she explained to the driver, using a combination of sign language and badly pronounced Greek, and then added that she'd lost her passport.

"Where did you loose it?" asked the taxi driver in broken English.

"I've looked everywhere" Iris answered, hoping the driver would understand.

"Ah! Australian" said the taxi driver as if that comment answered a multitude of questions and took her to the embassy.

Arranging for a replacement passport should have been a fairly straightforward operation. Simply supply one hundred and ninety-seven forms of identification, fill in the eighty-three-page questionnaire, pledge the soul of her, as yet unborn child to the devil, wait seven to ten working days, and with any luck she would have a brand new, 'expensive as hell' passport. There was, however one problem. After waiting in a cue leading to the window marked "Lost Passports" for over two hours, the snotty, 'my shit doesn't stink' bitch behind the counter refused to take Iris's documentation because:-

"The computers are down" and "You will have to come back tomorrow."

Iris was miserable. Spending four hours waiting in cues, filling in forms and being interrogated by the Consulate Gestapo was not what Iris considered a 'fun' afternoon. She was tired, hungry, severely dehydrated after last night's piss-up, and worst of all, Stefan's Nobel Prize winning han gofer cure was starting to wear off. That Mr. Microsoft, the arch nemesis of simple, fool proof office procedures should choose today of all days to decide he didn't want to play anymore, just wasn't fair.

According to her map, it was a good ten kilometres to the hostel where Iris and Stefan were to spend the night. Unfortunately the Athens public transport system was unfathomable, and as the cost of another taxi ride would probably necessitate the sale of one of her kidneys, Iris decided to walk. On the way she stopped and bought some post cards, found herself a passable looking café, and had a cup of the thick, liquid bitumen the Greek people call coffee.

With a population of 3.7 million, Athens has the largest Greek community in the world. The second largest Greek community, thanks to the very liberal immigration policies that existed during the 1950's and 60's, is in the city of Melbourne, Victoria, Australia.

On the wall of the café was a large, dog eared photo of the café owner, a woman Iris took to be his wife, and a couple of kids. They were standing in front of the Sydney Opera House. Iris pointed at the photo and then at herself.

"Australia" she said "my home. Did you like Australia?" The proprietor pointed at himself and shook his head, then pointed at the man in the photo.

"Brother", he announced. Iris raised her eyebrows in surprise. They were as alike as two peas in a pod. The proprietor recognized her confusion, cupped his arms in front of himself and rocked an imaginary baby.

"Me", he said and pointed to a date on the wall calendar, the sixth of November. "Brother" he said and again indicated the sixth of November. They were twins. Just like Iris and Alex. Iris smiled, nodded to let the man know that she understood, then indicated on the calendar that she and her brother were twins as well. Then, unexpectedly, Iris started to cry.

The loss of her passport was a minor thing. A nuisance admittedly, and an expense she could ill afford. But in the greater scheme of things it was hardly of earth shattering importance. What the loss of her passport had done however, was remind her that she was a foreigner in a foreign country. A stranger in a strange land. Apart from Alan and Stefan, everyone she loved, all the people she cared about, were on the other side of the world. Iris was homesick. She missed her friends back in Australia, her parents and even some of the people she used to work with, but most of all, Iris missed her brother Alex. It took only a few minutes for Iris to regain her composure but considerably longer to explain her despair to her distraught host. Eventually he came to understand and in a spontaneous display of solidarity at their mutual despair of absent brothers, dragged her into a tear drenched hug. He kissed her on both cheeks and then scurried back to the kitchen, returning seconds later with a couple of pieces of freshly baked pieta bread and a half full jar of Vegemite. Iris was in second heaven.

When she had finished her snack, her new friend refused point-blank to accept payment. He even went to the trouble of finding out where she was heading and then showed her which bus to catch, and where to catch it.

Such kindness from a perfect stranger far outweighed the annoyance Iris felt from the loss of her passport. The world was a beautiful place, and tomorrow Peggy would arrive. Now if a certain large, handsome, yacht skipper would just get his head out of his arse and notice that she had the hots for him, everything would be just perfect.

Between 6:00 and 7:00 PM that night, Iris received two phone calls. The first was from Stefan who rang to say that he and Roland had met a couple of other friends from Holland. He would not be coming back tonight and he would meet her and Peggy tomorrow at the airport. The second phone call was from Alan who rang to make sure she was okay.

Iris had a dream that night. A dream where she and Alan entered the world horizontal folk dancing championships. It was a great dream and of course they came away with the gold medal.

Chapter 19

The girl's name was Mars, like the planet. The red one, fifth celestial body out from the centre of the solar system. The planet some people thought might support intelligent life. Easier to substantiate was that Mars the girl didn't. Her name was an enigma. It seemed obvious she had never flown in a flying saucer, nor laid waste to the English countryside in a gigantic mechanical spider armed with laser cannons, so why her parents had chosen that particular name was a mystery. Also, as the ancient Greek God Mars was the God of war and not the Goddess of war, it really didn't really fit that way either.

Mars, the girl not the planet, had not come from outer-space or from ancient Greece, but she had once filled in an application form for a passport, made her way to the airport unassisted, and caught a plane flying from Melbourne to Athens stopping at Hong Kong and Beirut on the way. All clearly acts of a sentient being. So maybe Mars the girl not the planet did in fact support intelligent life. Or at least had done at some previous point in time.

The girl was nineteen years old. She was second generation Australian of Greek extraction and the purpose of her trip to Greece was to visit her ancestral home on Kea to find her roots. Alan felt that unless the girl discovered soap and water she wouldn't be finding any roots on Kea, at least not with him.

Mars had a serious personal hygiene problem. Her black, greasy dreadlocks were riddled with various life forms, her torn and grubby top, which had spent the first five years of its existence as someone's nightie, looked as if it had been used to mop up vomit, and her tie-dye flares were so stained it was impossible to discern what were the garments original colours. Worst of all, Mars stank, horribly. The type of repugnant odour that could make a skunk dry retch. As Alan later put it, if aromatherapy had any basis in reality, the girl's armpits could cure cancer.

The reason behind Mars's predicament became clear when she spoke. It was obvious from her slurring that Mars was stoned. Chemically not biblically, and had probably been that way for months. Apparently she only emerged from her marijuana induced stupor on days that began with a vowel.

"G'day" she drawled, teetering over to Alan's table and collapsing into the nearest chair. "Yur frum Oz ay? I saw duh flag on yur boat". Alan nodded and prayed to whatever deity listening that the feral woman would piss off.

"Not lookin' fur some crew are yuh mate?' asked Mars scratching her large unsupported tit through her nightie/top. "I'm lookin' tu earn some money so I can buy some tucker". Alan was constantly amazed at the way some people always accentuated their accents whenever they went overseas. Rarely did anyone of his generation or younger ever refer to food as tucker when back in Oz.

"Sorry mate", replied Alan, "I have plenty of crew at present. And to be honest, private yacht owners don't pay their crew anyway. It's more of a shared expenses basis. Crewing on a private yacht is more fun than work".

"Got any grass?" asked Mars varying her modus operandi by scratching her other tit.

"No" said Alan. However, his generous nature get the better of him, "but if you're hungry I can buy you something to eat". Mars, the girl not the planet, smiled and Alan discovered another flaw in the girls personal hygiene program, her teeth. The skunk ran for its life.

He ordered a large portion of pasta, which was not only nutritious, but cheap. The tavern keeper ladled a huge dollop of spaghetti into a plastic take-away container and waved his hand in the direction of the door. He had no wish to have vermin in his café, especially one too large for a rat trap. Against his better judgement, Alan accepted Mars's invitation to join her on the beach. The girl seemed lonely, in need of a friendly ear and with Iris and Stefan in Athens, Alan had nothing better to do.

"So what's yur name, mate?" asked the dread-locked feral. Alan replied with the obvious and inquired as to the moniker under which the girl travelled. "Name's Mars" replied Mars, "like the planet."

Just one of the many you're not on, thought Alan, but he was polite enough not to offend the woman by saying it out loud.

The pair chatted for the best part of the afternoon. Reminiscing about Oz and each discussing which part of Greece was their favourite. Mars explained her reason for her visit to the area, adding that it was also an excuse to get away from her mother who it appeared, was a bit of a tyrant. She was insistent that Mars was to marry 'a nice Greek' boy. One who would give her lots of beautiful grandchildren. Not only that, she should stop wasting her time at that silly university. All she needed to do was find a good Greek boy with a good job and he would take care of her.

"According to me Mum a man is supposed to take care of his wife. So women don't really need to go out to work. So yu got a girlfriend?" asked the feral, smiling and showing her teeth to their worst advantage.

"No," said Alan simply, but somehow the girl could tell there was more to this story than the big Aussie was letting on and pressed him for a more truthful answer.

"Well there is a girl, one of the people who's crewing for me at the moment. She's really nice. Well more than nice" and Alan went on to tell the girl, this perfect stranger, what he was almost unable to tell himself.

For the first time in a very long time Alan felt that with Iris aboard, he might enjoy something more than just sex or friendship from a female crew member. She was special. The way she smiled at him. The way she spoke. The way she tossed her hair and flirted with him. He knew it was stupid but all these little things made the world seem special with Iris Richards around. He felt he didn't have to just go through the motions anymore. With Iris on board, things felt right somehow. Alan felt that she belonged on board somehow. She wasn't just a temporary passenger. As a result, Alan's days seemed more worthwhile and important now. Quite inexplicably he felt more alive than he had done in years.

The night before she and Stephan had left for Athens, he had told her one of his corny jokes and she'd laughed, loudly and unashamedly. She'd punched him lightly on the arm, like a mate might do and then put her head on his shoulder and chuckled looking up at him with eyes that sparkled with sheer unbridled pleasure. He had felt a compulsion then to put his arm around her and pull her to him, to kiss her and never let her go. But he had not. Yes she was beautiful and sexy and intelligent and he wanted them to be more than just friends, but that was the whole problem. Her feelings for him mattered! If he was mistaken about her flirting, and it was all just meant to be a bit of fun and she rejected his advances, it would create a mountain of problems. They had to travel together for many long months and that would be impossible if they both felt uncomfortable about his declaration. If he made Iris feel ill at ease, she would leave and for many reasons, Alan found that prospect untenable.

Mars looked at Alan as if he were insane.

"So yu like this girl, yu think she like yu, but ya don't want to lose yur crew so yur gunna pretend yu just wanna be friends?" she asked. "Yur mad. Jump in head first mate. Yur gotta take life by the scruff of the neck and shake the shit out of it until summit falls out. If not, how the hell yur eva gunna see what's inside?"

The girl made a lot of sense. Even stoned out of her brain, dirty, smelly and with halitosis so bad it could stun an elephant at a hundred metres, she still made a lot of sense. Okay, it appeared Mars the girl not the planet did support intelligent life.

She finished her pasta and dropped the empty container into the nearby rubbish bin. She pulled out an expertly constructed joint, ignited the end with a disposable lighter and sucked in a lungful of smoke. Alan caught a whiff of a sickly sweet fragrance that was closer to incense than tobacco, and watched as the girl surrendered herself to its mind altering embrace. The ganja must have been top shelf produce because the effect was almost immediate.

"Yu hafta follow yur dreams Big Al" stated Mars, slurring her words even more than before "Don't let her get away, mate. Life ain't worth living without the one yu luv there beside yu". The feral's eyes glazed over and then closed, but in the split-second before they did, Alan saw a flicker of pain pass though them and a sadness that perhaps explained the real reason for the sorry state in which the young girl now found herself. Alan saw the loneliness in her eyes that the marijuana masked, and that vision helped him make a decision. Alone was not a place he wished to live in anymore.

Chapter 20

There was never a taxi when you needed one. Iris had completed her business at the Embassy and rushed outside with just one hour and forty-five minutes to spare before Peggy's plane was due to arrive. In his prime, Robert De Castella might have managed the run of fourteen kilometres to the airport, but Iris wasn't Robert De Castella and she was very, very lost. She scoured her map desperately and tried to make sense of the street signs, but nothing helped. She had no idea where the hell she was. In desperation she ran into a nearby shop and said "Airport" over and over again and ran around with her arms out making jet noises until someone got the idea and pointed in the right direction. A few minutes later she ran out onto the highway and there to her right was a sign. She had no idea what the words meant but there was a bloody big graphic of a plane on it and a huge white arrow. That was good enough.

She knew she shouldn't. She had lost count of the number of times her mother had told her not to hitch-hike.

"It's dangerous," she'd said. " And you'll end up dead in a ditch somewhere if you do."

But if people weren't supposed to hitch-hike, what the hell were thumbs for. It took three minutes before a big, black, chauffeur driven Mercedes limousine pulled up beside her. The passenger wound the window down and asked if he might give her a lift. He was a small, wiry man with thick glasses and protruding teeth. He looked for all the world like a large rodent and he spoke English with a heavy Russian accent.

"Thank you for giving me a lift" said Iris as she seated herself on the leather seat next to the little Russian. "I'm Iris by the way, Iris Richards" and held out her hand. The Russian took the proffered hand gently in his own and raised it to his lips.

"It is my pleasure Miss Richards. I am happy to make your acquaintance. So you are going to meet your friend from Australia?" asked Berswiski. Iris looked surprised. How did the weird little man know? Berswiski smiled, his teeth were yellow and jagged and Iris made a note to disinfect her hand as soon as possible.

"You go to the airport" he explained "yet you only have one small item of luggage". He pointed to the little rucksack Iris carried with her. "I assume, therefore, you are not the one who will be travelling. You are in a hurry; impatient to arrive at the airport, so I assume the one you meet is important to you. A friend, a lover, someone you wish to do business with, perhaps even a member of your family. But no, if it were a lover you would have dressed more prettily. You would have worn make-up and tidied your hair. If it were a business associate, you would dress more formally. Your family and you would have worn something more mature, something that would tell them you are an adult, that you are in control and do not wish them to worry or interfere. Therefore, I assume the person you meet is a good and valued friend. Finally, I recognize your Australian accent, so it is understandable that such a friend would also be Australian. These things are obvious to someone with an intellect such as mine".

Geezus thought Iris, who does this guy think he is? If he were anymore up himself, the retail association would have him listed as a tampon. But Iris still needed to get to the airport and was not about to bite the hand that fed her. She just smiled sweetly and nodded her head. They travelled a few kilometres further before the limo pulled to the side of the road and stopped outside a large but otherwise unremarkable red brick building.

"Regretfully Miss Richards I have a pressing engagement I must attend. So I will be leaving you now", said the Russian. "But Tasos, my chauffeur will take you to the airport so that you may keep your rendezvous. Goodbye my dear, I hope we will meet again soon." Berswiski opened the limousine door and without waiting for Iris to thank him, disappeared into the building.

Tasos was a big, fat, moustached Greek who had a prominent gold tooth and wore a chauffeur's uniform that was so tight it made body paint look baggy. To Iris's surprise he spoke very good English.

"Excuse me Miss Richards" he said into the rear view mirror, "I live just a couple of minutes away. Would it be alright if I stopped and picked up my airport parking permit?" He held up his hand so she could see and rubbed the thumb and forefingers together. "I might be able to make a little extra money if I can pick up some rich American tourists and show them around".

Given the circumstances, Iris didn't really think she should refuse, and as she now had almost an hour before Peggy's plane was due, gave her consent.

Tasos lived in a grotty apartment in an equally grotty apartment building somewhere in Spata near Athens airport. He had vanished inside twenty minutes ago and Iris was starting to worry. The limo was far too hot with the motor off and the air conditioning not working, so she had left the car and was waiting outside. Iris was beginning to wonder if she might have to start walking again, but realized that she had no idea in what direction. There was no alternative but to try to find the chauffeur. Her mother had told her a million times never to enter a strange man's house alone. But then Iris never listened to her mother.

"Hello, Tasos", called Iris as she reached the top of the stairs "are you there?"

"In here", replied the chauffeur. Tasos was standing near the doorway. He was big, he was fat and he was naked. He also had an erection. Iris hadn't had a root in nearly six weeks and was quite happy for it to continue that way. She bolted for the stairs. For a big, seemingly unfit man, Tasos was surprisingly quick on his feet. In a split-second he had her by the hair and had thrown her to the floor. He flopped on top of her, crushing the air from her lungs and stopping her from screaming. He ripped her t-shirt over her head and squeezed her breasts in his fat hands. Iris yelped at the pain and tried to push him off, but he was too heavy. Suddenly he sat up, shuffled forward and pinned her arms to the floor with his knees.

"Suck" he said forcing her mouth open with his fingers and trying to push his penis into her mouth. Iris bit down hard on the fingers and was rewarded with a blow to her face. She managed to turn her head at the last minute so he missed her nose, but she heard and felt the bones of her cheek shatter as his massive fist crashed into her face. Tasos raised himself up on his knees and raised his hand again for another blow. There was a loud wet slapping sound, a sound like someone hitting an overripe mango with a cricket bat. Tasos was flung sideways across the room as if hit by a truck.

Iris had never seen anyone who had been shot before, but it seemed obvious that this was exactly what had occurred. There was a small, slightly blackened hole about the size of a five cent coin just in front of his left ear. In contrast, the right side of his head, or at least what was left of it, was a mess. The side of his face had been blown off and splattered all over the wall. Tasos was deader than a Sunday night in Adelaide. Iris kicked the dead man off her and forced herself to breathe, slowly and evenly, forcing herself back from the brink of panic. Suddenly the phone on the bedside table rang. Iris nearly had a heart attack at the noise and had to calm herself once more. She picked up the phone

"Get out of the house," said a man's voice and the phone went dead.

Chapter 21

After nearly half an hour of sitting on the curb opposite the Spata Police Station, Iris finally summoned up enough courage to cross the road and report the chauffeurs murder. She didn't want too. She just wanted to run away, go back to the yacht, hopefully crawl into Alan's arms and have him tell her that everything was okay, that she was safe and that the bad man had gone away. But Iris had always considered herself to be a decent, honest, law-abiding citizen. And decent, honest, law-abiding citizens reported incidents like attempted rape and chauffeurs getting half their heads shot off to the police.

Especially, if that decent, honest, law-abiding citizen's fingerprints and DNA were all over the crime scene.

Iris looked at her watch. Peggy's plane would have landed by now. If she had been able to, Iris would have phoned Stefan and asked him to look after Peggy until she could join them, but her phone was missing. It must have fallen from her rucksack during her tussle with Tasos. She shrugged. Stefan was dependable and he would look after her friend without being asked.

She gently touched her cheek and winced. It throbbed mercilessly and her left eye had swollen so much she could barely see through it. Slowly she lifted herself out of the gutter and crossed the street to the Police Station.

The two Policemen currently on duty at the Spata Police station were not exactly what Iris had hoped for. The first was a scrawny, baby faced junior constable who probably still lived at home with his mum and borrowed his fathers' razor once a month when he needed a shave. His name was Dmitri. He was as eager as a sailor on shore leave and as thick as double whipped cream. His compatriot was his diametric opposite. Grey haired, pot-bellied, disenchanted and having equal contempt for criminals and victims alike. He had seen every crime imaginable during his thirty-five years of service, everything from assassination to parking offences, and with just four days till retirement, he didn't want to see any more. Unlike Dmitri, he didn't seem to have a name. Most people seemed to call him either Sarge or Bastard.

When Iris walked into the station with her face all swollen and bruised, Dmitri took one look and said, "Fuck". He knew another English word, one that rhymed with flat-bottomed rowing boat, but unfortunately those two words were the only English words he knew. After a few minutes of trying to understand the young woman, Dmitri turned to Bastard for help.

"Get Anastasia", he said in Greek without looking up from his newspaper. "She speaks English." Dmitri took Iris's hand and led her to a hard wooden bench at the front of the office.

"Stop", he said, remembering a third English word and scurried off to get the interpreter.

Anastasia -she pronounced it Anna sta seea- was nine, possibly ten years old. She wore a thick wool, tartan school uniform, a pair of equally thick wool stockings and the coolest pair of sunglasses Iris had ever seen. She spoke a reasonable amount of English, slowly, carefully and with an atrociously false American accent. Iris's report was slow and painful. She would say a sentence or two and then Anastasia would turn to Dmitri and translate, nervously glancing back at Iris every few seconds to see if she was getting it right. Dmitri asked a question.

"Can you take us to the crime place, please?" translated Anastasia. Iris replied she could. Dmitri looked to his superior for approval who waved them away with the back of his hand and went straight back to his crossword puzzle. Four days left, he said to himself, I'm not getting involved.

Dmitri herded his charges into the old Peugeot Police car and with blue lights flashing and sirens blaring, roared around the corner and raced the three hundred and fifty metres to the dead chauffeur's apartment. The black limousine was gone and so was Tasos. The place had been cleaned. The walls had been scrubbed, the carpet replaced and every trace of Tasos had been removed. That mad bitch on the "Spray and Wipe" commercials could not have done a better job. Iris ran over to the wall that had recently featured the remains of Tasos's head and rubbed her hand over the surface, the paint was still wet.

To Dmitri's credit he tried to find some evidence. He looked into cupboards and under beds, he put little bits of carpet fluff into little plastic, zip lock bags and even banged on a few neighbours doors and asked lots of questions, but in the end he just threw up his arms in defeat.

"Go away", said Anastasia after conferring with the junior constable, "nobody, no blood, no nothing and no case. Dmitri say you go away." So Iris did.

Chapter 22

With typical "Stefanesque" reliability, Iris's Dutch shipmate arrived at the airport a few minutes before Peggy's plane landed. The hostel where he, Roland and a couple of eager and very energetic girls from Switzerland had spent the night, had a minibus which was used to shuttled the hostel's guests to and from the airport. You were supposed to pay, but Stefan had charmed the big-breasted Greek girl who drove the bus and rode for free.

He didn't have a clue what Iris's friend Peggy looked like, nor had he any idea of her surname. All he knew was that Peggy's plane had landed and its passengers were already starting to trickle though customs. Iris still hadn't shown up and he was unable to reach her on her mobile. So he went to the bar, asked for an old cardboard carton, tore off a suitable sized piece of cardboard and wrote PEGGY, FRIEND OF IRIS in large black letters.

Where Iris was tall, dark and statuesque, her best friend Peggy was a cute little blonde munchkin. At 154 cm in stockinged feet -and 165 cm in high heels, suspenders and a push up bra- Peggy could almost be called diminutive. She had long blonde hair, green eyes, luscious cupid bow lips, pert, handful sized boobs, a trim waist, full round hips and a spankable bum.

"Hi! I'm Peggy," she said as she sashayed up to the sign-carrying blond boy. "You must be Stefan, where's Iris?" Stefan explained the situation as best he could and said that he was sure Iris had just been delayed and would be there shortly. They waited over an hour, before finally giving up and going back to the hostel. There was still no sign of her at midnight.

Stefan felt responsible for Iris's disappearance. If he hadn't gone partying with Roland, if he had stayed with her as initially planned, then she wouldn't have gone missing. Whatever had happened to his shipmate, he felt sure was his fault, and he was determined to do whatever he could to rectify the situation. He contacted Alan to find out if there had been any news and together they formulated a plan of attack. Alan would go to the Taverna and with the innkeeper acting as interpreter, phone all the Police Stations in the Athens area. Stefan would do the same for Hospitals, Casualty Centres and Ambulance Stations. They decided that they would use public phones, keeping their mobile phones free, just in case Iris tried to call. By the time Alan had contacted the Police Station at Spata, Dmitri had finished his shift and the Officer who had replaced him had never heard of Iris Richards.

Stefan left Peggy in their room and went down to find the hostel's assistant manager. The man had agreed to help if Iris hadn't returned by 10.00pm. It was after midnight before Stefan got back to the room. He'd phoned every one he could think of. In addition to hospitals, the assistant manager had suggested he phone the taxi companies and leave a message for their drivers. Stephan asked them to keep a lookout for a tall, Australian girl with long curly black hair and blue eyes, but no one had seen a thing.

Peggy was worried sick about her missing friend. She had not slept since leaving Brisbane 36 hours ago and was jet lagged out of her brain. Stefan found her sleeping fitfully on top of her bed when he returned to the room, and gently covered her with a blanket. As he sat watching the sleeping girl for a few minutes. he noticed a wayward hair that lay across her cheek. As he gently brushed it aside, his hand touched her face. Her skin was soft and supple, and he was almost overwhelmed by the desire to kiss her. He was certain that this petite, delicate young girl was the most beautiful woman he had ever seen.

Chapter 23

That was the trouble with mobile phones. They all had that electronic address book function. Someone gave you his or her phone number, you punched it into the keypad, stabbed "save" and then forgot about it, knowing you could retrieve it at any time. A simple, easy to use, brain cell saving feature that meant no one had to remember phone numbers anymore. That is until you lost your phone. During her walk from the Spata Police Station to wherever the hell she was now, Iris had passed a couple of public phones, all of them functional, all of them hungry for her euros. But as Iris could not remember either Alan's or Stefan's phone number, they were as useless as confetti at an arse wiping contest.

Iris was lost. She had been walking for nearly three hours and it was starting to get dark. She knew that the hostel where she was staying was close to the Acropolis, so she'd asked Anastasia to point her in that direction, but somehow she must have taken a wrong turn. Instead of sticking to the main road she'd taken a side street, mistakenly believing it would be a more direct route and would rejoin the highway as it curved back towards the city. But the side road itself had swung around to the west and now she was totally lost. If she strained her ears she could still hear the noise of highway traffic, somewhere over to her left and so she was still hopeful that the road would curve back again or that she would come to a cross street which went the right way. There seemed to be no other alternative other than to continue on the way she was going.

Suddenly she noticed a large red brick building that looked familiar. It was the building where Tasos had dropped off the weird little Russian. Iris wondered if he might still be inside. Perhaps he could explain what the hell was going on and who had shot the chauffeur. The limo had had a hire company's name in tiny gold letters embossed on the dashboard, so Iris was convinced that Tasos's attack would've had nothing to do with Mr. Berswiski. Surely he was just a client and wouldn't have had any idea that Tasos would try to rape her.

She felt a terrible sense of injustice. The Police hadn't believed her story and she needed to know more about what happened before she could put the whole, despicable event behind her. She didn't particularly like the strange little Russian, but he had been polite and helpful before, and Iris had no reason to suspect he would not be so again.

If she'd had any inkling of what she was about to do, Iris's mother would have screamed at her, smacked her backside and sent her to her room without supper for a year.

The building was a two story affair. Some kind of factory or warehouse. It had a series of small rectangular windows high up on each wall. They were glazed with frosted glass and secured with heavy steel bars. There were two large roll-a-doors at the front of the building, but both of these were closed and locked with heavy padlocks. Along the right-hand side of the building was a narrow driveway which lead to a smaller, heavy duty steel door. One which was just large enough for an averaged sized person to go through if he of she ducked their head a bit. There didn't appear to be a bell so Iris knocked as loudly as she could. After a few minutes there was still no answer and Iris was about to leave when she noticed a light shining at the back of the building. The window was high up on the wall and there was nothing around for Iris to climb on but she'd noticed another smaller window at ground level that seemed to lead into the basement. Iris went over to it and peered inside.

A second later someone or something hit her hard on the back of the head and for a brief moment stars danced in front of her eyes. Then everything went black.

When Iris came too, Berswiski was waving a small bottle of some revolting smelling liquid under her nose. Its pungent odour burnt the inside of her nose and brought her back to the land of the living with a jolt. Her arms had been tied behind her back and she was being supported by a thickset Greek man who smelt strongly of garlic and had more tattoos on his arms than bare skin. Iris's head ached painfully from the blow and she could feel warm, sticky liquid running down her back. Blood! There were four men in the room, the Russian rodent, two thugs, one of whom carried small, short barrel machine gun, and another, taller man who wore a suit and had an air of affluence you could take to the bank.

"Well, well, well if it isn't Miss Richards", sneered the little Russian, "how nice of you to drop in so unexpectedly". He lifted Iris's chin with his hand and inspected her face, admiring the chauffeur's handiwork. "That must have hurt", he said, and then stabbed his thumb viciously into her cheek to make sure. Iris yelped with pain and when Berswiski started to giggle, she knew she was in deep trouble. The chauffeur had been bad enough but he had only wanted his knob spit and polished. It looked like this bastard liked to hurt people.

The man in the suit spoke. Spat something out in rapid Russian. He seemed unhappy with Berswiski's actions Vladimir smiled and replied in English.

"Patience my friend," he pleaded. "We will conclude our business in just few moments. First I need to find out just who this young woman is and why she is following me."

Berswiski turned to the table behind him and picked up a small, black cylindrical object. It was about forty-five centimetres long and had two shiny metal points at one end.

"This is a modified stun gun Miss Richards, or whatever the fuck your real name is. A little present given to me by our debonair friend over there. You will now tell me who you are and what you are doing here or I will be forced to demonstrate how it works".

Iris was happy to oblige.

"I've already told you. My name is Iris Richards and I'm... "

Berswiski motioned to the thug that held Iris, to turn her around and lift up the back of her T-shirt.

"Very well" said Berswiski "if you want to play games then perhaps you will like this one." He pressed the points of the stun-gun to her back directly over her spine and pressed the trigger. Iris screamed in agony, her bladder emptied and her legs gave way under her. She had never imagined such pain was possible. It was as if her entire spinal column had suddenly been filled with white-hot molten metal. Iris went from frightened woman to a terrified animal in a split-second.

"Please, don't hurt me again" she sobbed "I don't know what you want. Please leave me alone."

"Answer the question truthfully and I will stop," yelled Berswiski. "Now, who are you?" Iris did not have an answer. Even in her terrified state she knew that the truth was not what the madman wanted to hear. Berswiski pressed the stun-gun to her spine once again. This time Iris's heart went into arrhythmia and for a few, brief, merciful seconds, Iris was rendered unconscious. She woke, face down in a pool of her own vomit and began to choke.

Suddenly there was a loud crash and a tinkling of broken glass. A soft-drink sized metal canister landed on the floor a metre or so from her head and started to belch thick, black, acrid smoke. There was more crashing, this time from the door at the end of a long hallway leading into the room. Someone was trying to break down the door. Iris's captors scarpered, racing for the narrow hallway on the opposite side of the room. A minute later the door jamb split and the door crashed open. Through the thickening smoke Iris could make out four, maybe five figures. They were all dressed in black military type clothing. Their heads were covered by balaclavas and they wore some sort of breathing apparatus. They charged into the room, firing machine guns at the retreating Russian and his cohorts, then raced off down the hallway after them. One of the soldiers stopped at Iris's side and lifted her up in his arms. He was tall and strong and had piercing blue eyes.

"It's alright now sweetheart," said the soldier, "We've got you. You're safe now." The nerve gas from the smoking canister finally took effect and Iris felt herself slipping into unconsciousness. She smiled. She knew she had nothing to fear anymore. She'd recognized the soldier's accent and knew she was in safe hands. Safe Australian hands.

Chapter 24

Veronica Crystal picked up her phone, pressed speed dial twenty-seven and then spun around, leaned back in her chair and lifted her feet up onto her desk. Someone on the other end answered.

"So. You lost him... Again?"

"Don't be a smart arse Veronica," demanded Grey. "I've been getting a bollocking from the men upstairs already. The last thing I need, is you rubbing salt into the wound."

"Bollocking? You English certainly have a way with words. I suppose that's like getting your ass kicked. Being dragged over the carpet?"

"Yes, that's correct," replied the Major. He didn't need to ask how Veronica had heard of his teams failure. She'd obviously taken an interest since her visit, and had asked her own people to keep an eye on any developments. "Anyway apart from your well documented penchant for shit stirring, to what do I owe the pleasure of this phone call?"

"I'll get to that in a minute if that's okay with you Eddie. But first, why don't you tell me what happened? How did the bastard get away this time?" asked Edmond. He swung the phone over to his other ear and like his comrade on the other side of the city, slouched back in his chair and put his feet up.

The warehouse where they had cornered Berswiski had once been a secure archive for some of the Greek governments more sensitive documents, Edmond told her. It had been closed down years ago but still retained the large vault where the most important bits and pieces were locked away. The vault was an impressive structure. Sixty centimetre thick, reinforced, concrete walls, no windows and a heavy, plate steel door with an eight pin locking mechanism set into the centre. Grey and his team had chased Berswiski and two others down a hallway which lead to the vault. They'd seen them clamber into the strong-room and close the door behind themselves just seconds before Grey and his team entered the room. By the time the Major had organized someone with oxt-acetylene equipment to come and cut open the vault door, Berswiski and his partners in crime had escaped. When they got the door open they found that Berswiski had cut a hole in the floor and escaped though the sewer pipe which went under the building.

"From the looks of the hole, it had been cut through a few days ago," explained Grey. "in fact it's quite likely that's how he got into the building in the first place."

"Jesus, Eddie. You're not having much luck with this asshole are you."

"You haven't heard the worst yet! You know how Berswiski used to work on the Soviets nuclear weapons program?"

"Yea!"

"Well one of the guys we saw escaping with Berswiski has been tentatively identified as a suspected illegal arms dealer. Nothing positive yet, we only caught a fleeting glimpse of the guy, but Jim Exeter reckons it's him. Oh! and there's another thing. The vault showed high traces of radioactivity."

"Oh Shit," sighed Veronica. "Well that settles it Eddie. I want in. I'll ring my supervisor and request a temporary transfer to your team.

Do you think Interpol would have any objections to a CIA operative helping out for a few weeks?"

"Let them try to stop you!" replied the Major.

Chapter 25

Iris's world slowly dimmed and swirled as she felt herself falling inexorably downwards, plummeting for what seemed like an eternity. Bile welled up in her throat and she fought back the nausea and the dread that refused to be quieted.

"Am I dying?" she thought. "Is this what it's like?" Gradually the fall slowed to a stop, but her suspicions that her time was up were lent further weight by the sudden appearance of a bright light. A light, like that seen from inside a very long tunnel, far off in the distance.

Everyone has heard tales of people who have had a near death experience. There was always the obligatory 'white light'. The one you were supposed to walk towards. Iris mentally shrugged her shoulders. If that's what one was supposed to do, then who was she to argue.

Like the fall into the abyss, the trek to the source of the light seemed to take forever. Iris's steps grew heavier, until she felt like she was trudging through treacle and she was overcome by a feeling of complete and utter exhaustion. She stopped for a few seconds and lay down on the ground that wasn't ground and found that she was floating, drifting dreamily towards the light.

Then, in an instant the darkness disappeared and the world became light again. A brilliant, incandescent light that filled everything with an intense, white glare. Iris looked down at her feet and was not surprised to find that she was standing on, well, nothing. Her feet dangling below her in midair and yet strangely, still supporting her body. She suddenly realized she was now clothed in a long flowing, white robe with a high neckline and sleeves that came down to her wrists. Her feet were bare and her dark hair had been tied in a long ponytail.

The angel was similarly attired, but with the addition of an enormous pair of wings which fanned the air slowly as he descended to where Iris stood.

"Hello Iris" sang the angel in a voice that filled Iris's heart with happiness to the point of bursting. "You're early. We were not expecting you for a while yet."

Iris tried to speak, to ask the angel what was happening, even though in her heart she already knew what the answer would be. To her surprise no sound came from her lips. The angel smiled at her and again Iris felt a joy that was beyond description.

"Ah!" he said knowingly "not quite ready yet hey? Well, I'd better send you back then."

Again Iris tried to speak, to yell out the questions she desperately needed answers to.

"When is it my turn to join you?" she asked silently, "How much time do I have left? Is there a heaven?" Again Iris's voice was mute, yet somehow the angel heard.

"There is a time to know and a time to wonder. This is your time to wonder", sang the Angel as he rose from beside her and flew powerfully away. "Go back Iris, fill your life with the things worth living for, fill your soul from the well of love, your friends have made for you. Now is not your time."

Far below a tiny black dot appeared, a pinprick of darkness, stark against the vivid white. It grew rapidly in size. Then the enveloping light started to swirl around her distorting and spinning, creating a vortex which spiralled down towards the void. Iris was amused to find that her own body was mimicking the light. It too was starting to spiral, wringing itself into a grotesque corkscrew. Suddenly she was thrown outwards, out to the very edge of the whirlpool of light. The current caught her and dragged her around in circles, spinning, tumbling and turning, faster and faster, until she was plummeting downwards at breakneck speed towards the abyss. Iris screamed as she reached the edge of the black hole. The darkness tore at her body and she watched in horror as first her feet and then her legs were sucked into the blackness and began to dissolve like a sugar cube in boiling water. She clawed vainly at the air, trying to stop herself from being dragged into the black hole, but there was nothing to hold onto. The blackness itself engulfed her, her mind quietened, the panic subsided and finally Iris fell into a deep, but troubled sleep.

In life there were times when Iris dreamt and later remembered every detail, and there were times when she dreamt and everything disappeared from her mind as soon as she woke. Mercifully that was how it was this time.

Chapter 26

The morning after the day Iris disappeared, at exactly 7:00am, Stefan's phone rang. A man speaking Dutch told Stefan that Iris had been found, that she had been in an accident and had sustained some minor injuries. The caller stressed the injuries were not serious, but Iris would be kept in for observation for a few days. He said Stefan, Alan and Peggy could expect to see Iris back at the yacht in about three days. Before Stefan could ask the caller who he was or what hospital Iris was in, the line went dead.

Stefan immediately called Alan, only to find that his skipper had received a similar phone call only moments before. Everyone was ecstatic at the good news, but Peggy was still a little concerned because they still didn't know Iris's whereabouts. She and Stefan decided to stay in Athens for another two days just in case the caller, or Iris herself, called again. It would give them some time to do some sightseeing and they would be close by, should Iris need them.

Peggy was feeling so guilty. Poor Iris was lying injured in hospital somewhere, while she was having the most wonderful time imaginable. Peggy loved Athens and was positively enthralled with the historical sites they visited. On the first day they saw the Acropolis, The Horologion of Andronicos, Hadrian's library and a couple of the Byzantine Churches. She had bought herself a new camera and took so many photos that by the end of the day the memory was full and she had to buy a second card. On the second day, they visited the archaeological site at Kerameikos and the museum nearby. In the afternoon, as a complete change of pace, Stefan took Peggy to a fairground, something she hadn't done since she was a child. The fair was great fun, with roller coaster rides, side-shows, the inevitable pathetic ghost train, as well as lots of very unhealthy junk food. But as far as Peggy was concerned, the best thing of all was Stefan. He was attentive, patient, generous and simply fun to be with. When he offered Peggy his hand as she stepped down from the boarding platform for the Big Dipper, Peggy took it and didn't let go. Later that night as they lay in their room at the hostel they kissed for the first time.

Peggy was an old-fashioned girl at heart, so on their first night together they only fucked in the missionary position.

Chapter 27

Someone had taken up residence inside Iris's head and the bastard had brought his drum kit. He wasn't a terribly good drummer, in fact he only knew one beat. THUMP- THUMP- THUMP- THUMP, but what he lacked in variation and talent, he more than made up for in persistence and pure unadulterated volume. Iris opened her eyes and a thousand painfully brilliant flashbulbs went off inside her skull. She groaned and fought to stop herself from vomiting as wave after wave of nausea washed over her. It was a loosing battle. She rolled over onto her side and lunged for the plastic bucket by the side of the bed, spewing half a litre or so of viscous, brown-green bile into it. She flopped back onto her pillow and received a painful reminder of the gash on the back of her head. Someone had cleaned the wound, stitched it up and dressed it. Over the past twelve hours or so, Iris had acquired a bruised and broken cheek, a puffy, constantly weeping black eye, four small stun gun supplied electrical burns to the base of her spine and now, a small unexplained incision just in front of her left ear. She would have to remember to ask about that. Runner up in the "Things that hurt I wish I didn't have", stakes was the pounding headache, piped at the post by the dreadful, "surely I'm going to die", nausea.

Iris struggled to sit up, then assessed her situation. Someone, perhaps the someone who had attended to her wounds, had stripped her, scrubbed and disinfected her and dressed her in one of those delightfully chic, totally impractical hospital gowns. The type that tied at the back and showed the whole world your bum every time you stood up.

The room in which she found herself had been decorated in 'Early Stark'. The walls and ceilings were plain white and the floor was covered in that cheap, grey patterned vinyl, which from a distance of five or six metres, looks a bit like ceramic tiles. Unless you were small enough to fit through the tiny air conditioner vent above the bed, the only way in or out of the room was through a solid looking, locked door opposite Iris's bed. In the centre of the room was a cheap, imitation wood, kitchen table, surrounded by three similarly cheap vinyl covered kitchen chairs. Except for a stainless steel toilet bowl and the bed, these were the only pieces of furniture in the room.

Another wave of nausea washed over, she lunged for the bucket once more and then lay down again and closed her eyes. She was asleep again in seconds.

Almost three hours passed before Iris woke for the second time. Her headache had gone- sort of- the nausea had subsided and the pounding had moved from inside her head to outside the door of her room/cell. Iris sat up and swung her legs over the side of the bed just as the door opened a crack.

"Are you decent?" asked a terribly British, male voice.

I am when you get to know me, thought Iris before answering that she was. The door swung open and a man who introduced himself as Grey, and a woman who didn't, filed in. The woman carried a briefcase and a large plastic shopping bag. Grey carried a breakfast tray. To Iris he looked incredibly elegant. He was in his late sixties, had silver hair and wore small rectangular, wire-framed glasses. He was dressed in an immaculately laundered, crisp white shirt and blue tie with some sort of logo, worn under a stylish, expertly tailored, grey pinstripe suit. His female cohort was called

Ms Jones, an American from her accent, probably somewhere in the north-west. She was also in her late sixties, had grey hair and wore spectacles, but there the similarity ended.

Jones was a hatchet faced, hook-nosed, old hag who had all the style of an airline sick-bag. She wore a pink frilly, low cut, puffy sleeved blouse that showed off her gnarled and wrinkled cleavage, and a beige, tight-fitting skirt that was far too short for someone whose legs wouldn't look out of place in a butcher shop window. The skirt and blouse clashed horribly and Iris felt that the material the skirt was made from would make a very flattering top for someone who was flat chested. It sure made Jones' arse look big.

Grey placed the tray on the kitchen table and motioned for Iris to take a seat.

"I have brought you something to eat Miss Richards," said Grey "nothing too elaborate I'm afraid. Your tummy won't be able to take anything even remotely rich until the CT18 wears off completely."

Iris decided she liked Grey. His use of the word tummy made Iris feel like a little girl and his kind smile and quiet, yet authoritative voice somehow instilled a sense of confidence. He was in control, and as long as he was, Iris felt safe.

"What's CT18?" asked Iris. The Major handed Iris a plate of honey covered toast, then poured three dainty cups of tea.

"CT18 is the nerve gas you inhaled at the warehouse" he replied " I'm most dreadfully sorry about that Miss Richards. It was rather unavoidable I'm afraid. However, I can assure you that there will be no long-term side effects. You will be right as rain again in a few days."

Iris smiled. "Major Grey if you had anything to do with getting me away from that mad Russian, then you could lock me in a decompression chamber with a flatulent elephant and you'd still end up at the top of my Christmas card list. I can't thank you enough for saving my life."

It was Grey's turn to smile.

"You're most welcome Miss Richards", he said. "Now finish your breakfast and then we can have a nice little chat about what happened."

The nice little chat consisted of Iris talking a lot, crying a lot, and answering a lot of questions. Most of which she didn't know the answers to. She told them the whole story, from the time she decided to join Alan to the moment she inhaled a face full of CT18 and passed out. The Major listened attentively and patted her hand or offered her his handkerchief whenever the memory became too painful and Iris's emotions overwhelmed her. Jones sat there stony faced and took notes on a small note pad. Occasionally she would roll her eyes impatiently, She was a cold heartless bitch and Iris couldn't help wondering if she'd been spayed yet.

When she'd finished, Jones took some photos from her brief case and asked Iris if she recognized anyone. There were three. The Russian rodent, Tasos, the would be rapist and the man she had seen at the rodent's warehouse, the one that looked like an affluent businessman. All the others were unknown. That more or less concluded the interview.

"By the way Miss Richards", said Grey, "we found your phone at the chauffeur's apartment. We retrieved your friends' phone numbers and took the liberty of contacting them to let them know you were all right. We also bought you some new clothes to replace those damaged during your ordeal."

The Major placed Jones's shopping bag on the table and emptied its contents. Apart from Iris's phone there was a new, 'brand name' sundress that had probably cost more than Iris earned in a month, a pair of similarly expensive sandals and some very, very expensive lingerie.

"I hope that's alright Miss Richards," said Smith "I have a daughter-in-law about your size. It was she who chose the clothing, ordered the items on line in England from a boutique with a branch here in Athens. I'm afraid I had no idea what your style might be so I just had to rely on Janet's taste."

Iris thought Grey's daughter-in-law had more than enough of an idea for both of them.

"Okay," said Iris, "I've told you my story, now tell me yours."

"Well...We have been wanting to question the Russian man who attacked you in relation to a number of other attacks on women", answered the Major. "We were trying to apprehend him when...."

"Yes, but who are 'We'?" interrupted Iris.

"The police of course."

"No disrespect but that's bullshit" said Iris "You're English not Greek, Jones or whatever her name is, sounds American, and the soldier who rescued me from this Berswiski guy was Australian. Why would foreigners be working for the police in Athens? Also, attempted rapists don't get shot by unknown snipers who then clean up after themselves, and psychopathic murderers don't hang around in groups carrying sub-machine guns. I'm sorry Mr. Grey but your story has more holes than a nudist's negligee."

"You're right Miss Richards," admitted Grey, "my comrades and I belong to Interpol. I'm sure you've heard of us. But I'm afraid I am not at liberty to tell you much more than that. It's become a matter of international security. I will tell you this much however, we are the good guys and it is most important that you return to your friends, continue your holiday and try to forget that any of this ever happened.

Iris reneged. "Okay, I believe you when you tell me you're the good guys, and I guess I should do as you say, but just answer me one question. Where the hell am I and how do I get back on the ferry to Kea."

"Ah! That part is easy. We will provide transport for you back to the ferry tomorrow or maybe the next day." he held up his hand to stop her when Iris started to object. "Of course you are not obliged to stay, you can leave right now if you want, but the doctor who treated your wounds told me he would rather you stayed close by for twenty-four hours, just in case you have an adverse reaction to the CT18. Also, I'd like you to talk to Mrs Crystal. She's a profiler with the CIA and wants to ask you a few questions about Berswiski's actions. If you're up to it of course?"

Iris didn't feel up to anything other than crawling under a bush and hiding, but she knew it was necessary to help Major Grey and the others as much as possible. Slowly she nodded her head in agreement.

Chapter 28

David Randall was in his late twenties but looked and acted a good ten years younger. Depending on his mood, and on how well Randall performed his job, Major Grey would describe him as being either full of youthful enthusiasm or infuriatingly childish.

Apart from his striking blue eyes he could never be called handsome. A mop of unruly, ginger hair, pale skin, a weaselly nose, and ears which were perhaps just a little too big for his head, put paid to that. But what he lacked in good looks, he more than made up for with bucket loads of charisma.

He was always red cordial energetic, and eternally cheerful and optimistic. It was as if he had seen all the misery and despair in the world he could cope with and had decided it was up to him to single handedly swing the pendulum back the other way. To put it another way he was a good-natured larikin, and even those who didn't know what the word larikin meant, seemed to warm to him instantly.

As Berswiski had once again evaded capture, and with no other new leads to go on, Dave was faced with the certainty of yet another eternity of rehashing the mountain of evidence they'd already collected. Fruitless hours sifting through stuff, all in the futile hope of uncovering something they had missed the first six times, held no appeal for him whatsoever, so he presented himself to the Major and offered to baby-sit Iris until her ferry left for Kea the following day.

"I'm the closest to someone her own age," he told Grey, "and we're both Aussies, so I'm the best person to look after her. She's had a terrible time of it, Sir, we can't keep her locked up downstairs and I don't think she should be left on her own if we release her."

The Major nodded and gave his approval. Iris Richards was the least of his concerns right now and he was happy to have her taken off his hands.

"She's going to need a place to stay tonight," said the Major, "Book her a room near yours at the hotel you're staying at and charge it to us. Oh, and Randall, it hasn't escaped my notice that the young lady is quite attractive. I'll remind you that she has been through a very trying and extremely harrowing experience. I'm relying on you to behave accordingly."

Dave Randall sprang to attention and saluted his superior.

"Yes Sir," he replied. "You can rely on me sir. To be honest sir, I'd never even noticed she was a such a babe until you pointed it out just now sir.'

"Yea. Right." Edmond mumbled under his breath.

"So you're a spy?" Iris asked Randall after the elder Interpol man had left the restaurant.

"I'm an undercover operative with Interpol."

"Sounds like a spy to me."

Randall shrugged his shoulders. "I suppose I am. No, not really. I'm just a detective, but with a bigger beat than your regular cop. Whatever you call it, it's a lot more interesting than being stuck in an office."

Originally Major Grey had had no intention of telling Iris who her saviour was and why they had been tailing Tasos the chauffeur for the past few days, but her revelation that she knew the operative to be Australian, plus his request to look after her for the next twenty-four hours, put an entirely different complexion on the matter. Dave Randall had told the Major even before she'd regained consciousness, he was sure Iris had recognized his accent and he'd been correct. Major Grey could see her curiosity had been aroused, and that worried him slightly. The prospect of the young woman ferreting around, asking questions and trying to find out what the hell was going on could prove dangerous to the whole operation, so Grey was forced to revert to plan "B". Tell the truth. Well, get Randall to tell the truth. Or some of the truth. There was still a little matter of international security. He hoped that would assuage the young woman's curiosity somewhat and stop her snooping around where she wasn't wanted.

Earlier the Major had asked Iris to get dressed and to wait for Mrs Crystal. The American woman turned up a few minutes later and once again Iris was questioned mercilessly on the events of the last twenty-four hours. Mrs Crystal stated that she was a criminal profiler, a psychiatrist trained in working out the way a criminals mind works. She then used that information to work out, amongst other things, where the perpetrator might strike next. Iris tried her best to helpful, but her knowledge of Berswiski was scant at best and Iris was sure nothing she could say would be much use.

The Major returned an hour later and took Iris to a small café in the centre of Athens. Randall was there waiting. Where Ms Jones had gone Iris wasn't sure but she suspected she'd gone off somewhere to hump someone's leg.

"So how the hell did you land a job as a spy with Interpol Dave?", asked Iris.

"Well, I was in the RAAF back home. I ended up with Airforce Intelligence, which as you can imagine, turned out to be a bit of an oxymoron. But the RAAF didn't really suit me, I felt I was just wasting my time, playing war games and spending my days collating, analysing and re-analysing old, out of date information just in case Australia ended up at war with someone. Then I spent a few months in Iraq and that was the final straw. It seemed to me, Iris, the Iraqi war was nothing more than a personal vendetta against Saddam Hussein, and it was a pretty transparent attempt to get control of the oil in the area. September 11 was a terrible day in the world's history and we should all do everything we can to assure such a horrific event never occurs again. But if we are to be successful in our fight against terrorism, then we have to make sure we choose the right target. That is why I quit the RAAF and started up with this crowd."

"Don't tell me, there was an advert in the paper", exclaimed Iris.

"Of course not", replied Dave. "Uh! It was on the Internet".

Grey, who had better things to do than sit around all day while Randall and Miss Richards got acquainted, interrupted.

"Miss Richards. Randall, that is David, and I have decided it would be best if we were to tell you a bit more about what is going on. I must warn you it is imperative that you keep what I am about to tell you to yourself. You must not tell anyone, not even your closest friends or relatives. To do so might put the whole operation, not to mention your own life, at risk. Do you understand?"

Iris said she did and Grey proceeded to explain.

Her head was spinning by the time he had finished. Being told she had inadvertently stumbled onto an illegal arms deal where the item for sale was a nuclear bomb, and that she had narrowly escaped from an insane Russian nuclear scientist who was probably responsible for the death of a dozen or more young women, was not something that happened every day.

"So what's the story with the chauffeur?" asked Iris "Who was he and who shot him?"

"Tasos Meanopolis was nobody," explained Grey. "He was just a thug who did some driving and ran a few errands for Vladimir Berswiski. He had numerous convictions and had been in and out of prison more times than some of the warders. We'd been following him for about three days. We hoped he would eventually lead us to his boss. Unfortunately he had to be eliminated before he could do so. It was one of Interpol's snipers who dispatched him"

"You, Dave?" asked Iris

"Not me. I couldn't hit the side of a barn" answered Randall smiling. He knew what the young woman's next question would be and continued before she could ask.

"We're sorry we didn't come and get you after that bastard tried to rape you Iris but we figured you were just some local girl who had got herself in a bit of bother and would just go home to her family". He reached into his jacket pocket and pulled out a small cylindrical object. It was connected by a long, thin wire to what looked like a digital camera. Dave clipped the object to the peak of his cap and handed the display unit to Iris. She looked back at herself from the tiny screen and was horrified to see her black eye. It looked nearly as bad as it felt. Dave turned his head and looked around the room. Everything he saw the miniature camera relayed to the screen.

"All operatives use one of these whenever they are on assignment," explained the young agent. "The sniper, the one who shot Meanopolis, recorded him arriving at his apartment and the attack on an unidentified young woman. He believed the young woman's life was in imminent danger and was forced to take Meanopolis out. It wasn't until a couple of hours later, after we'd brought you back from the factory, that we saw the recording and realized that Berswiski's victim and Meanopolis's victim were the same person."

"Well I suppose at least you rang that arsehole's phone to tell me to get out," she told him, once again fitting back tears. "But you and your mates left me all alone. You knew I was in trouble, I was lost and confused and frightened half to death. All someone had to do was take me to hospital. Instead, you just left me to my own devices."

"You're right Iris. We should have done more" replied the Major. But even as he said it, Iris knew that it was not true. It was a bad, bad world out there. A bad world with a madman running around, quite possibly with a great big nuclear bomb. Compared to that, a young woman with a black eye looking for some sympathy and someone to take her to hospital, was of no importance at all.

Grey looked at his watch and asked to be excused, telling Iris he had a rather important meeting to attend. He told Randall to look after her and to answer any other questions she might have, keeping in mind of course, that she did not have clearance for much of the information concerning the case. He reminded Iris that her friend's back on Kea would be expecting her the following day. Then he said goodbye.

After Grey left, to lighten the mood a little, Dave picked up the miniature camera and clipped it to his shoe. The waitress who was serving at the next table had a short skirt and obviously bought her knickers at the same place as Grey's daughter-in-law. Iris was shocked but couldn't help laughing.

"Dave Randall Interpol spy", she commented, placing her head on the table and sighing theatrically, "what chance has the world got".

'It's okay," he told her. She doesn't mind me being a bit naughty. She's my girlfriend, though for god's sake don't tell Grey. He tapped the waitress on the shoulder and said something in Greek. Showing her the footage of her bum he had just taken. She smiled widely, slapped him playfully on the shoulder and then, making sure her boss was looking in another direction, wrapped her arms around him and kissed him ferociously.

"The Major doesn't approve," he told Iris. "fraternizing with the locals I mean. So we keep things low key when we're in public."

After lunch, Dave took Iris back to his hotel. He had already arranged the room opposite to his to be available for the next two days if she needed it.

"The furnishings are a bit Spartan," he told her with a mischievous twinkle in his eye.

Iris groaned, "Oh shit Randall, if you keep that up I'm going to be sick again."

To be honest the room was a bit of a dive, but it was clean, had its own bathroom and a huge double bed. There was a full length wardrobe along one wall and a large window, which looked out over the road below beside it. It had two bedside tables, a small fridge, tea and coffee making facilities and a medium-sized flat screen TV, which was bolted to the wall opposite the bed. In other words a typical, middle of the road hotel room. Comfortable but nothing out of the ordinary.

She sat on the edge of the bed and found its softness adequate. The doctor had commanded she rest for the remainder of the day, but her mind would not keep quiet and she knew she would find it impossible to sleep. Suddenly she felt lost, unsure about what to do next. Luckily Dave Randall once again ducked into his fictitious phone booth, whipped on his cape, tights and bright red underwear and sprang to the rescue.

"Listen, you can stay here if you want too, you know, get some rest or whatever. I'm just across the hall if you need anything. Or if you'd prefer some company, we can trudge over to my place. I've got tea and coffee and stuff. Plus there's a half a bottle of rough red plonk waiting to be polished off. Oh! and I've got a packet of what I've come to regard as a very reasonable Greek, facsimile of our beloved Tim Tams in the fridge." He paused, shrugged and looked at her expectantly.

Iris didn't mind the occasional glass of rotgut red, and when it came to chocolate biscuits, like most women she could either take it or take it. So they trekked the two and a half paces across the hall to Dave's room and settled in for the afternoon.

"Dave," she asked, a few Tim Tams or so later in the day. "What happens if you don't stop Berswiski? Do you know where the bomb is headed?"

"I'm not supposed to tell you.....but we believe that the buyers are a radical Palestinian splinter group. We don't know where their target is for sure, but I wouldn't be buying real estate in Tal-Aviv any time soon if I were you".

"Jesus" said Iris, "what the hell is wrong with people? Why is there so much more hatred in the world in recent times?"

"I don't believe there is so much more hatred", he replied. "It's just that the media reports more of what goes on today than they did a few years ago. Also, because of the Internet, any loony who thinks he has an axe to grind, knows how to mix a bit of oil with a bag of fertilizer, blow himself up and take a few dozen people with him. That's the terrible thing about terrorism Iris, it's a game anyone can play."

Dave was right. Just the other day President Obama had received a feminine hygiene product through the mail. Osama Bin Laden was furious and berated the minion responsible mercilessly. "I said Anthrax you idiot", he screamed, "not Tampax."

Just after six, Jim Exeter, Randall's partner and fellow occupant of the hotel, arrived home from work bearing gifts of Pizza, Pasta, salads and, as he and Dave were on standby and were prohibited from drinking until Berswiski was safely under lock and key, some non-alcoholic beverages.

Like Grey, Jim was English. Hailing from somewhere call Sarf Lundun, he was in his mid thirties and of mixed Scottish and West Indian descent. He was short and stocky and built like a wrestler. Olympic not Sumo, and wore his hair pulled back in a long, thick, black plait which hung halfway down his back. He had a tiny goatee beard and moustache and a prominent gold tooth which flashed whenever he smiled. He also wore a full length leather coat which made him look a little like someone out of 'The Matrix.' Jim was, Randall explained, the teams weapons expert. If you needed something mechanical which was designed to kill or injure someone,

Jim was the man to see. In addition to his technical expertise, he was a third dan Aikido, whatever that was, and Iris thought he looked like could quite probably knock out a street lamp with one punch. Despite this, he turned out to be the quietest and shyest man of the bunch.

"So Iris, has carrot top here done his Spartan existence joke yet?" Jim asked as he served a large dollop of piping hot marinara onto a plate and handed it to her.

Iris nodded and rolled her eyes. "Yep. Variations on the theme anyway."

Exeter turned to his comrade and shook his head. "You gotta stop doing those shitty jokes buddy. There is such a thing as justifiable homicide you know."

Randall just grinned, and everyone knew it would take much more than a death threat to quell his use of not so humorous quips.

"If you're the weapons expert, then I guess you must be the person who shot Tasos." Iris asked.

"Who?"

"Tasos Meanopolis! The man who tried to rape me! Berswiski's chauffeur."

"Sorry Iris," said Exeter, "I've never heard of the bloke. What about you Dave?"

Randall looked thoughtfully at the ceiling. "Nuh, sorry name doesn't ring a bell with me either. But I'm sure whoever he is he hasn't been shot. He's probably just disappeared, Iris. I mean if he was dead, and one of us had done it, there would have to be an inquiry. Poor Old Tran would get suspended or maybe even charged on suspicion of unlawful killing. Of course eventually it would be found that this Tasos's death was unavoidable, your life was at risk after all. But in the meantime Tran would have to be locked up in jail, or at the very least spend weeks cooling his heals, without pay I might add, back in France. Eventually internal affairs would get it through their thick skulls that the shooting was justified, but in the meantime we'd all be faced with a shit load of extra paperwork and, with one team member down, Berswiski might even get away. I'm sure Meanopolis isn't dead, the fat ugly arsehole is just holed up somewhere waiting for the nasty men from Interpol to go away. Don't you think?"

At first Iris wondered if she might be going mad, but as Dave spoke she began to understand what had happened. This wasn't James Bond, there was no licence to kill. The men from Interpol didn't have a Carte Blanche directive to kill whoever they thought necessary. The fact that Tasos had been shot had to be covered up. If not, all sorts of shit might hit the fan. The official version was that Tasos had taken off to places unknown, presumably because he had realized Interpol was after him.

"Who's Tran?" she asked.

Exeter answered. "Tran's one of the other operatives on our team. Vietnamese French guy. You didn't meet him or his partner Helmut back at the office. They're on stakeout until midnight. Which reminds me, I gotta hit the sack. Veronica Crystal and I are due to relieve the boys when their shift ends."

He got up, took his empty plate into the bathroom and washed up. Seconds later he headed for the door. "Nice to meet you Iris," he said smiling. "Sorry about the circumstances. Maybe next time it'll be a bit more pleasant."

Then, once again Iris and Dave were on their own.

A little while later, around nine thirty, they had another visitor, or rather resident. Iris had noticed that Randall's room, though ostensibly the same as hers, had a bit more of a homey feel to it. A female, homey feel to it. There were flowers in vases, clean tea towels hanging on the rail in the bathroom and framed photos of Randall and the waitress from the café where they'd stopped earlier in the day. Plus there were a number of other little indications, like a sexy white bra drying on the shower curtain rail in the bathroom. All of which led Iris to suspect that Dave's hotel room wasn't strictly a bachelor domain.

The girl's name was Marika and she spoke virtually no English. Luckily Randall must have warned his girlfriend about Iris, so there were no awkward moments while Marika tried to find out just who the fuck this bruised and battered woman sitting in her supposedly faithful boyfriend's bedroom was. She simply breezed into the room, said,

"My name Marika," kissed Iris, very gently, on both cheeks and then threw herself into Dave's arms and kissed him until they both nearly collapsed from asphyxiation. After, she helped herself to some Pizza and wolfed it down whilst Randall and Iris chatted away about their homeland.

Dave came from Melbourne and had been to Brisbane, Iris's home city only once. Just a couple of months ago in fact, when he and the rest of the team had investigated the murder of an aboriginal woman. It transpired that his dad had been a cop and so it was inevitable that he would, eventually at least, follow in his fathers footsteps. He had always been good with languages and took an active interest in learning as many as he could. So far he had mastered French, Italian and of course Greek. Like Jim he had been trained in martial arts and knew which end of a gun you were supposed to point at the bad guys. He'd been with Interpol for just a couple of years and found the work both frustrating and rewarding in equal portions.

He'd met Marika the day the team arrived in Athens. He asked her out two days later and she moved in, more or less, a week after that. Whether their relationship was supposed to be serious or just a brief fling that both knew would end when Randall moved on to his next assignment, was not discussed, but from the way the couple looked at each other, with complete, unabashed adoration, Iris could tell they were very much in love. Considering Dave's transient life style, Iris couldn't help wondering how either of them would cope when the time came for Dave to move on.

With Randall translating, Iris was able to tell Marika about herself and explain the reason behind her rather obvious and gruesome injuries.

The trio chatted happily until a little before eleven, at which time Dave politely suggested that, as Marika had an early start in the morning, they should call it a night. Iris thanked her hosts for a pleasant evening and made her way back to her own room.

She hurried across the hallway, unlocked her door, reached around the jam, fumbled for a few seconds for the light switch, and then dashed inside and locked the door behind her. Suddenly she felt very alone and frightened. The mad Russian had escaped and he was out there somewhere. Inexplicably she began to worry that he had followed her back to the hotel and was waiting for the right opportunity to break in and kill her? She knew she was being illogical. Berswiski was probably kilometres away by now, running for his life. But still she was unable to shake off the feeling that she was being watched.

She worked her way around the tiny room, checking inside the wardrobe, behind the bathroom door, even under the bed. She knew she was being foolish, but she just had to be sure.

"I need to calm down," she said to herself. "I'm falling apart here."

She once again checked to see that the door was locked and the security chain latched, and then went into the bathroom to draw herself a bath. A few minutes later she was soaking in the tub, luxurious, piping hot water lapping at her chin, and all the knots and aches and pains gradually ebbing out of her bruised and battered body. When the water began to chill off, she reached out with her big toe and turned on the hot tap, refilling the bath until the water was almost too hot to bear.

After nearly half an hour of soaking she clambered out and towelled herself dry. She was just combing the knots out of her long dark hair when there was a knock on the door. She wrapped a towel around herself and crept quietly towards the entrance. There was another knock.

"Who is it?"

"Irisi, is Marika."

Iris slipped the security chain off the latch and opened the door a crack. Marika was standing in the hallway dressed in a pair of bright yellow, floral, flannelette pyjamas. She was carrying another pair, these in blue. "You put on, yes?"

Iris hadn't thought about sleepwear. Somehow wearing the clothes she'd worn all day didn't hold much appeal, and after the attack, she suddenly realized being naked, even in the privacy of her own room, would leave her feeling terribly vulnerable. Marika was obviously a very thoughtful person. She opened the door wider and waved the Greek girl inside.

"You put on," repeated Marika and gently pushed Iris towards the bathroom. When she came out again, Marika had turned off all the lights except the two bedside lamps and was sitting up in bed with the covers pulled up around her chin. She patted the vacant side of the bed and waved Iris over.

"It's okay Marika," said Iris, "I'll be fine. You go home to Dave."

"DAVEED" called Marika and the door slowly opened and Dave Randall shuffled in carrying a sleeping bag, a pillow and dragging a single bed mattress. He was wearing a pair of shiny, light blue boxer shorts and a black, 'I'm with stupid' T-shirt. Iris smiled when she saw the arrow was pointing at his crotch.

"Sorry about this Iris. Marika insists we keep you company tonight. She reckons she'd be cowering under the bed if she had to be left alone after what you've been through. Don't worry, neither of us snore."

With that he threw the mattress down on the floor, right in front of the door, unrolled his sleeping bag and climbed inside. He rolled over and wished them both a good night and then said something to Marika in Greek.

The Greek woman groaned, reached over the side of the bed and hurled a slipper at him.

"What did you say?" asked Iris.

"I told her I was unhappy. I'd always wanted to sleep with two women at the same time, but this wasn't how I'd imagined it."

Iris groaned too.

Chapter 29

Alan had just settled down to eat breakfast, his latest, favourite book propped up in front of him, when the phone rang. It was Iris.

"I'm so happy to hear from you Iris. I...I, mean we, have all been worried to death about you", declared Alan. "What the hell happened?" Iris said she would tell him and the others as soon as she got back to the boat. She would be arriving on the 4:00pm ferry. Iris had already contacted Stefan and Peggy and when she learnt they were still in Athens, had arranged for them all to travel back to Kea together. Iris explained to Alan that she had to go as the battery in her phone was running low, and then added that she was looking forward to seeing him tomorrow.

Dave Randall didn't really like shopping, but he'd had more than the odd girlfriend in his lifetime and knew from personal experience that for most women, psychotherapy or even trauma counselling, were mere Band-Aids, compared to the miraculously recuperative powers of three or four hours of shopping. At 8:00am, Dave dragged Iris out of bed, sat her in front of a bowl of cereal and arranged for a taxi to pick them up at 8:45.

Iris had come to realize her new friend had many admirable qualities. One such quality was his generosity. As they entered the first of many dress shops, Dave pulled out a sizeable wad of euros and stuffed them into Iris's hand.

"Don't worry," he said with a conspirational wink, "Interpol can afford this. I'll just tell Grey I had to pay off an informer". Iris smiled and took the money, but only after she'd made it clear that the money was only to be a loan. She would repay the money as soon as she got back to the boat and arranged for some more funds to be transferred into her bank account. She suspected that Randall had no intention of making the bogus claim, the money would come directly out of his own pocket.

Iris's first purchase was a new pair of shorts and a T-shirt. She loved her new sundress, but wanted to keep it for a special occasion. Probably when her injuries had healed and her face no longer looked like Quasimodo's scrotum.

Dave had chosen a part of town that was close to the major hotels, correctly assuming the shopkeepers in the area would be more used to dealing with tourists, and so have a better command of English. As the day progressed, Iris began to understand why Randall, who was not the most handsome creature ever to draw breath and Marika, who was gorgeous, were together. The man's charisma was astounding. It was a good thing Marika was beautiful. Only a woman possessing extreme confidence would be able to cope with the amount of female attention Dave drew everywhere he went. Maybe it was his red hair, unusual in a country where hair normally came only in either black or grey. But whatever it was, young schoolgirls gazed adoringly, ancient grandmothers hugged him and pinched his cheek and female shopkeepers and assistants flirted outrageously, making it perfectly obvious they thought he had an interesting face and wouldn't mind sitting on it. Even Iris herself started to feel a little bit jealous of all the attention he was getting. All the men they saw showed no interest at all. Which was something Iris hadn't experienced since before she'd grown tits. Still, she thought, if I didn't have an eye that looked like a ruptured haemorrhoid I'd give him a run for his money.

She bought a little something for everyone on the yacht. Stefan got a new snorkelling mask, Peggy a t-shirt with the words 'You've been a naughty boy, go to my room' on it and Alan would receive one of those black fisherman's caps that all Greek fishermen seemed to wear.

The morning ended much too soon and after a sumptuous lunch at a nearby café, Dave took her to the dock and her ferry.

"Sorry Iris", he said, "but I can't wait with you until the ferry leaves. I have a meeting back at headquarters in about half an hour, so I'll have to leave now if I'm to make it".

He hugged her and kissed her on the good cheek. Promising they would meet again soon. He jumped into the waiting taxi and was gone. It was twenty minutes before the ferry was due to leave and Stefan and Peggy were nowhere to be seen. It was the first time since her ordeal that Iris had been alone and out in the open. Berswiski was out there somewhere and although she knew that the mad Russian must surely have left the area by now, she just couldn't shake off the dreadful feeling he was watching her and waiting for the opportunity to attack. She began to panic and started to shake and hyperventilate. She had to find somewhere to sit down. Fifteen minutes later, Stefan found her cowering, hiding near a large shipping container. She was almost paralysed with fear.

Chapter 30

Vladimir Berswiski had to admit, the arms dealer had been as good as his word. Berswiski hated loose ends, and as far as he was concerned, Iris Richards escape was a major loose end.

At first the 'arms dealer' had refused to become involved.

"Just forget about her," he'd said. "There are plenty more fish in the sea."

But that was not an acceptable course of action as far as Berswiski was concerned. Captain Ahab had not relinquished his pursuit of the white whale simply because there were other whales to be slaughtered. Moby Dick had cost him a leg and escaped the captains harpoon, a situation which Ahab needed to correct. In the same way, Berswiski felt compelled to rectify the fact that Miss Richards had failed to adequately experience the fatal caress of his blade.

The 'arms dealer' had contacts in the Greek department of Customs and Immigration and could trace Iris Richards whereabouts quite easily. Knowing this Berswiski had attempted to explain a simple fact to him. That he needed, desperately needed, to find the woman and conclude what he had already started.

But his words fell on deaf ears. The 'arms dealer' would not be swayed. Then the Russian explained that if the arms dealer wouldn't help, then he would have to search for Miss Richards himself, and if he failed in that task, there was a good chance he might also fail in his endeavour to re-arm the decommissioned war head. That in turn, might lead the Palestinians to suspect that the 'arms dealer' had tried to sell them a sub-standard product. They would definitely want their money back. They might even try to extract some form of retribution against him as compensation for their wasted time and effort.

So the 'arms dealer' made a few phone calls and three days later he received the information he'd requested. An Australian woman named Iris Richards had cleared customs into Greece on the fourteenth of that month. She was travelling as a crew member on a private yacht called 'Harvey Wharf Banger.' The yacht was due to leave Greece, headed for Alexandria, Egypt, in about a week. There was also additional information revealing that Miss Richards had somehow lost her passport and a replacement had been issued. There was a further notation that the replacement had been expedited at the request of Major Edmond Grey of Interpol.

Ah! Thought Berswiski, it is always nice to have friends in high places. So now he knew the name of his nemesis, Major Edmond Grey of Interpol. He also knew something else. It appeared Berswiski had been wrong about Iris Richards. He'd been convinced that her sudden, and unexpected, arrival at the warehouse was not merely an accident. He been sure she'd been following him. Until now he'd been certain she was an agent of Interpol, and that was how the cops had found his hideout. Now it looked like, she was exactly who she said she was. Her appearance, hitch-hiking to the airport and then again at the warehouse, was nothing more than a happy coincidence. Well happy for Vladimir.

To go after the girl now, so soon after her escape, would be foolhardy. He needed to wait, let the woman's confidence return. Let her think that she was once again safe. Then, when she least expected it, he would strike, and this time the Australian bitch would not escape.

Once more he asked the arms dealer for his help. This time he demanded the arms dealer supply him with some way of keeping tabs on the woman. he needed a way of tracking her until he had finished recommissioning the warhead and was ready to proceed with her recapture.

The arms dealer was wary and sought assurance from the Russian that he would wait until their business was completed before chasing after the Australian woman. Eventually Berswiski convinced him of his loyalty, and the arms dealer gave him a small electronic homing device. Once attached to Iris's luggage or perhaps the boat she was travelling on, Berswiski could follow her to the ends of the earth.

The Russian learned something extremely interesting that day. The GPS unit which the arms dealer had given him, looked suspiciously familiar. It was identical to the tiny piece of equipment he'd found, under one of the warheads inspection covers, the first time he inspected the bomb.

That evening, thanks to a local fisherman he employed specifically for the job, Berswiski had the second little tracking device securely attached to the hull of Alan Tew's yacht. Now, no matter where Iris fucking Richards went he would be able to follow. All they way back to Australia if necessary.

For his part, the arms dealer was profoundly unhappy with how Berswiski, had nearly landed them all in very hot water. His penchant for hurting young women was not to his liking, not one bit, especially when it interfered with business. He wished to God he could just put a bullet in the bastard's brain. But there was no one else who could re-arm a disabled nuclear warhead. Unlike some of his previous customers, the Palestinians knew a dud when they saw one, and his life wouldn't be worth two Euros if he tried to sell them a bomb that didn't go bang with the appropriate intensity when they wanted it to. Now there was no other alternative. But now his customers would have to wait. There was no way known to man he was going to try to move the bomb while the cops were skulking around. He'd have to delay his departure until things died down a bit. Then again, he thought, Uranium 234 has a half-life of about a thousand years, which meant that Tal-Aviv would be uninhabitable till about 2350 ad. So what the hell difference would two or three weeks make anyway?

Chapter 31

Alan was very pleased to see Iris, but horrified to see the damage to her face. He was not a violent man, in fact he abhorred violence of any kind. But he had seen enough bar room brawls in his time to know Iris's story about being involved in a car accident was untrue. Stefan's report of finding Iris cowering in fear at the ferry terminal only confirmed Alan's suspicions. Though she seemed happy and relaxed now she was back amongst her friends aboard 'Harvey', it was clear all was not as they had been told. Alan decided he would find out what was really going on at the earliest opportunity.

The rest of the day was spent welcoming Peggy and hearing the latest news from Australia. Once again Stefan insisted on cooking dinner and once again, he produced a spectacular meal.

"That was simply delicious darling", enthused Peggy when they had finished.

"Darling?" said both Iris and Alan at once.

"You know me Iris", shrugged Peggy, "a real sucker for a handsome face. I hope you don't mind, but I think he's just gorgeous". Iris didn't mind one single bit. The original plan was for Iris and Peggy to share the for'ard cabin and for Stefan to sleep in the salon, but now Iris was the one to move out.

Much later that night, after everyone had retired and Iris found she couldn't sleep, she went up on deck to enjoy the cool night air.

Alan was already there, watching the lights on the shore and the stars in the night sky. He patted the cushion he had placed on the deck next to him, inviting Iris to share the view. Below them they could hear the sounds of Peggy and Stefan embarking on a night of unbridled passion, followed by bridled passion, and finally some whips, spurs and leather straps' passion.

Once she was seated, Alan gently took Iris's hand and placed it in his own. It was a gesture designed to be non-confronting but at the same time offered support.

"Do you want me to kill him?", asked Alan in a matter of fact voice.

"Who?"

"The man who did this to you" replied Alan indicating her injured face.

"You're too late," said Iris, "he's already dead." Then in an uncontrollable torrent, Iris spilled out the whole story.

"Okay", said a stunned Alan when Iris had finished. "Let me see if I have this straight. You met a group of guys who work for Interpol".

"Yes."

"And they're in Athens because this Berswiski character has sold a nuclear bomb to the Palestinians who are trying to blow up Athens?"

"No, Berswiski is a nuclear scientist. He's needed to reassemble the bomb which was taken apart by the Russian government after the cold war. Without him, the bomb is useless. Major Grey thinks the bomb is headed for Tal-Aviv. It's only in Athens, if indeed it is in Athens, because they can't take it to Palestine through Syria. There are too many US soldiers around at the moment", explained Iris.

"Okay. So how come this Grey character is in Athens? I mean aren't there enough Interpol spies in Greece without flying in others from half-way around the world?"

"I suppose so", replied Iris, "but Berswiski was in Australia a few months back and Grey and his team were involved with the case then. In fact I think they were even before that there were other murders elsewhere which they were investigating. When the little Russian turd surfaced here, Grey and the others were brought over to liaise with the Greek cops".

Alan nodded his head.

"I'm sorry I didn't tell you the truth before Alan, but Grey made it clear that it was all hush, hush and top secret. I'm glad I've told you now though".

"You have one more problem Iris", said Alan pointing in the direction of the cabin underneath them, "Tomorrow, when 'Mr. and Mrs. Shagalot' have finished trying to knock the barnacles off the bottom of the boat from the inside, you're going to have to tell them the truth as well. Neither of them seemed convinced with your original tale about the car accident."

Alan was right of course, so the following day, Iris repeated her story for the benefit of the other two. Peggy was horrified that her dear friend had been so close to being raped and murdered. She spent the rest of the morning comforting her, and never strayed more than a few metres from her side. Easy to do on a fourteen-metre yacht.

Later in the morning Alan decided to move the yacht to a quieter, more peaceful location. Last autumn, when he passed through the area on his way to Istanbul, Alan had discovered a beautiful, secluded little cove on the South West side of the Island. It was only about an hour's sail away, and as the winds were light and the boat's batteries could do with being recharged, Alan decided to start the yacht's diesel and motor to the new anchorage.

Stefan, Peggy and Iris tidied the boat and got ready to move, then Alan gathered them around and showed them how to start the big diesel motor.

"Firstly, we have to ensure that the boat is out of gear and the throttle is set in the starting position", explained Alan, moving the two levers to the appropriate position. "Next we have to warm up the glow plugs. Glow plugs are like an element on an electric stove. Turn on the power and they heat up the intake manifold making it easier to start. If you don't do this, the motor won't go."

Alan turned on the ignition key and a small yellow light lit up.

"The glow plugs are connected to a timer. When this light goes out, you press the starter button and...."

Alan pressed the button and the motor throbbed into life. A few minutes later they raised anchor and steamed to the other side of the Island.

"So, what's the story with Alan?" asked Peggy a few hours later when they were snuggled down safely in the new anchorage. The man in question was out of earshot, fishing off the back of the boat, propped up on a huge cushion with his feet up on the pushpit. "He's cute and from the way he keeps checking you out, I'm pretty sure he'd like to get into your pants. Pity about his sense of humour though. it's a bit lame."

"That's for sure," laughed Iris "but I'm afraid as far as I can tell, what you see is what you get, I really like him and I've dropped enough hints, he seems interested, but doesn't follow through. To be honest, it's starting to give me the shits. I'm hornier than a Viking trumpet player and if I don't get a root soon, I'm going to have to cut my finger nails".

"I know what you mean," said Peggy. "When Christopher and I split up sex, was the thing I missed most, and like Bill Gates said 'digitally remastering your software is a poor substitute for a nice big hard drive".

"I think he was talking about computers!", said Iris.

Peggy, whose greatest technological achievement to date was to put rechargeable batteries in her vibrator, thought this was unlikely.

"He's got very big feet", said Peggy. "Is it true what they say about men with big feet?"

"What?"

"That they work in a circus," answered Peggy rolling her eyes. "You know! Men with big feet are supposed to have big ......"

"How the hell would I know?" interrupted Iris with a look of exasperation on her face. "Am I supposed to grab a tape measure and go up to him and say 'excuse me Alan can I measure your cock?'"

Peggy didn't answer but simply got up and called to the skipper.

"Alan is it safe to swim here?" she asked. Alan replied he thought it would be. "My bikini is still packed away in my suitcase" continued Peggy, "You're not going to be offended if I swim naked are you?" Before Alan could answer Peggy had stripped off her T-shirt, shorts and knickers and was standing on the deck naked as the day she was born, but with bigger tits and considerably more pubic hair. "Come on you lot, get your gear off", she called as she dove over the side, "the water looks delicious."

Stefan followed his girlfriend's lead and dove over the side, his lily-white bum shinning in the sun. Iris looked at Alan and shrugged before peeling off her sexy green bikini.

"Come on Alan", she said. "I know what Peggy's like, if you act all modest now, she'll just do something like wait until you're in the shower and hide all your clothes." Alan laughed and he too stripped naked. From the distinct lack of any tan lines, Iris could tell it wasn't for the first time. And yes, he did have big feet. Very big feet.

After lunch, the wind picked up, gradually rising until it peaked at about twenty knots. Luckily, it continued to blow from the north-east so although the sea got quite rough outside the anchorage, inside it remained millpond calm. Even though there was no reason to suspect that the world was about to end, Stefan and Peggy were not about to take any chances. So off they went to their cabin to fuck each other's brains out just in case they didn't get another chance.

"Are you afraid of heights?" asked Alan as he and Iris finished drying the lunch dishes.

"No."

"Great", said Alan. "Go and put on some good walking shoes and some sturdy clothing and meet me up on deck as soon as you can. I'll take you over to the island and we can climb to the top of the hill".

The 'hill' was only about a hundred and fifty metres high, but it was covered in a moraine like rubble that occasionally slipped away from under their feet as they climbed. Alan was carrying an enormous backpack, but he was still able to outpace Iris easily, stopping now and then for her to catch up.

"You've done this before haven't you?" panted Iris, "climbing mountains I mean".

"This isn't a mountain" answered Alan. "This is just a little hill. But yes, I have done a bit of climbing over the years" and listed a number of very impressive 'real' mountains he had either climbed or attempted to climb.

When they reached the summit of the hill, Alan unpacked the backpack. It contained two nylon-webbing harnesses and a huge black mound of some sort of lightweight sailcloth. The same sort of stuff that was used to make yacht spinnakers.

He helped Iris into one of the harnesses, put on his own, spread the black sailcloth out in front of them and attached a couple of fasteners to his own harness. Finally, he stood behind her and clipped Iris's harness to his own.

"Okay", he said "start walking backwards into the wind." As she did so, a dozen or so thin ropes snaked out from underneath the pile of sailcloth. When they were fully extended, Alan asked if Iris was ready.

"Ready for what?" she asked in a confused voice.

"This," answered Alan and gave a short sharp tug to the control lines, opening the throat of the para-glider to the wind. The huge wing filled with air and carved a majestic curve upwards until it was directly above them. Iris screamed as she and Alan shot up into the air a hundred meters or so and then spun around like a top, 180 degrees, to face into the wind. Alan cackled with delight and hauled on the left line banking the para-glider around to the left like a speeding motorbike on a hairpin bend.

"Y-Y-Y-You lunatic" yelled Iris. "Put me down!"

"In a minute," yelled Alan over the howling wind. "Just enjoy the ride. It's perfectly safe. I've done this hundreds of times before."

Iris gasped and dug her nails into the palms of her hands. The huge para-glider hit a thermal and rocketed upwards another hundred metres. There they hung in midair, the big wing describing lazy circles across the bright sky.

Alan tugged on the control lines again and the para-glider slipped to the right, corkscrewing downward, the centrifugal force throwing its two passengers outwards like an enormous fairground ride. Iris squealed again, but this time with delight. The abject terror of a few moments ago had been replaced by a heady rush of euphoria.

"Look," yelled Alan, "down there about forty-five degrees to your left."

One hundred and fifty metres below them, a tiny toy sail boat sat on a mottled turquoise sea.

"It's 'Harvey'," Iris called, "can we get closer?" Alan eased the control lines and soared around to the other side of the boat. With the wind behind them the para-glider began to drop.

"There's not enough wind here Iris, we have to go back" and Alan skimmed back towards the island where he knew he would find the updraught they needed to regain height.

The two spent nearly an hour souring above the island. Alan showed Iris how to control the big kite and where to look for the all-important thermal currents. By the time they'd landed, Iris was a firm convert to the wonderful world of unpowered flight.

Chapter 32

No one who new agent Dave Randall would ever consider him a wimp. Sometimes he could be a bit quiet, though not often, and he wasn't the most imposing person physically. But only people who didn't know him, ever considered these traits to be a sign of weakness. And they only did it once. The truth was, Dave was as tough as a porn star's clitoris and everyone at Interpol knew it.

The problem was, when you're shaking like an epileptic sex toy and you're bent over spewing your guts up, it's hard to exude an air of toughness. Major Grey placed a paternal hand on Dave's shoulder and gave it a squeeze. He understood what Randall was going through. The sight of the poor creature inside the old farmhouse had almost had the same effect on Grey himself. What Berswiski had left of the as yet unidentified Greek girl, was barely recognizable as human. The remains hadn't even reached the coroners office yet, but Grey already knew what the answer would be to his question about the cause of death.

"Take your pick!"

Chief Superintendent Vladmiros Hatzidakis had phoned Grey as soon as the gruesome discovery was reported. The old farmhouse belonged to a wealthy businessman. A weekender vacant except for when the businessman and his secretary went there to 'conference' each other's brains out while the businessman's wife stayed at home and did the same thing with the gardener. The secretary arrived first, poured herself a drink, oozed into something a little more comfortable, and then went upstairs to wait for her lover. Seconds later she fled screaming from the house and ran to the next door neighbour for help, quite oblivious to the fact that she was wearing nothing but a peephole bra, suspenders, stockings and a pair of crotchless knickers.

"There is a dead girl upstairs in our bedroom," the secretary told the neighbour, "Can you call the Police?"

The Major was astounded that Berswiski had struck again so soon after his near capture. He had been sure the Russian would flee the area, or at least lie low for a few weeks. Edmond expected him to keep his head down until the heat died down a bit. But something was amiss. Berswiski was normally extremely careful, making sure there were no clues left behind to tie him to the crime scene. This time, however, Berswiski's fingerprints, semen and a host of other clues were all over the farmhouse. It was almost as if the Russian wanted to be caught. Or maybe Randall was right. Maybe this time Berswiski had transcended his normal state of insanity and had reached totally fucking mad.

Chief Superintendent Hatzidakis came out of the building and approached the two Interpol agents.

"Have you and agent Randall seen enough?" asked Hatzidakis in Greek. "I would like to send my forensic team in as soon as possible."

With Randall translating, the Major replied he wanted one last look around. Then he and Randall returned to the farmhouse.

Berswiski had chosen the site for his latest butchery well. It was at least fifteen kilometres from the nearest town, and the only neighbour was a teacher who worked at a boarding school in Athens and only came home on weekends. Berswiski's victim was a young girl, barely out of her teens. The team later discovered from a friend of the victims- a girl named Ioanna Voulgaris, who had been with the victim at the time of her abduction- that Berswiski had met them both at a railway station. She and her friend, Haro Karistani were new to the city. In fact they'd only arrived from the country that morning and had nowhere to stay. Berswiski had offered them both a meal and a bed for the night, which they'd foolishly accepted. On the way, a few kilometres from the farmhouse, Ioanna had asked if they could stop at a petrol station as she needed to pee. When she came out of the restroom Berswiski and Haro had gone.

The big double bed upstairs in the vacant farmhouse, was the last bed Haro Karistani would ever lie on. Berswiski had tied her down and systematically tortured her to death. He had amputated each of her fingers and toes with a pair of bolt cutters, sliced strips of skin from her breasts and peeled them back like the petals of a flower. Then he'd dripped molten lead onto her stomach and pubic area. Finally, he strapped the girl's legs to some sort of winch and slowly pulled her legs apart until the flesh tore and her hips snapped.

"How could anyone do such things to another human being?" Randall asked Grey.

"I don't know my friend," replied the Major, "but I promise you when we get the fucking bastard, and we will, he will not be given the chance to explain. Three seconds after he's in custody, I'll make sure he'll never do something like this ever again."

Chapter 33

During the time the four shipmates spent at the secluded anchorage Stefan and Peggy's love for each other continued to grow unabated, as did their progression through the Karma Sutra. The other two fared much worse. Alan continued to delay letting Iris know he cared for her, while she doggedly stuck to her belief that it was the man's place to make the first move. She simply refused to take Peggy's advice of pretending to mistake Alan's wedding tackle for her snorkel the next time they went skinny-dipping.

The noise from the erotic symphony conducted in Stefan and Peggy's cabin each night. The fact no one ever wore swimwear anymore, plus Peggy's continual reference to Alan as 'Tripod' was not helping Iris's plight one bit. Eventually she was forced to cut her fingernails and began to contemplate which of the kitchen appliances in the galley was her favourite.

One evening, when it was Iris's turn to do the dinner dishes and she was in the galley while the other three shipmates were up on deck enjoying the cool night breeze, Stefan, who the girls were beginning to realize was a lot more perceptive than they had originally given him credit, broached the subject.

"Alan," he asked, "if you like Iris, why don't you tell her?"

Alan, who like most people in love had no idea he was being so obvious, started to deny everything, but before he could utter a word Peggy joined the fray.

"Stefan's right Alan," she said. "Subtle as a cheese grater, but right. You two can hardly take your eyes off each other. Blind Freddy's deaf, dumb, and thick as shit cousin Eugene, could see you two are in love. To be quite honest Alan, if you don't do something about it soon, you're in real danger of losing the best thing that ever happened to you. Iris is old-fashioned. She'll never make the first move."

Alan threw his hands up in despair.

"Of course I like her. In fact I'm absolutely mad about her, but that's the problem. I've never felt this way about anyone before, and I'm terrified that she might reject me. She's been attacked and tortured just recently, I need to give her time to recover from her ordeal before I go barging in trying to jump on her bones...."

"They sound like excuses to me," interrupted Peggy. "Why don't you just jump in and see what happens? What the hell have you got to lose?"

"Just a very good friend!"

"That'll never happen." It was Iris. She had finished the dishes and come up the companionway behind them. "Now that I know for certain how you feel about me, I'm sure it would be easier for you if I told you I feel the same way about you"

She walked over to him, sat on his lap and threw her arms around his neck. Then she turned to Stefan and Peggy.

"Piss off you two" she commanded. "Tripod and I have some serious catching up to do."

To be honest, Iris had not been the only one to suffer from the ravages of celibacy. Alan too had found the going rough and for the past two nights had been so horny, when he needed to take a leak, he had been forced to either stand on his head or piss out the window. As a result, their first night together was not the romantic, loving, dreamy night that Iris had hoped for. But then earth-shattering, nerve jangling, multiple orgasms are much better anyway.

The following morning, Iris rose late. She had slept deeply, her mind at peace, all her desires sated and any anguish laid to rest by the knowledge that Alan loved her just as much as she loved him.

The man himself was up on deck, sitting at the rail, his trusty fishing rod dangling over the side. Iris stood behind him, leant down and wrapped her arms around his muscular body, twirling her fingers through the dark, curly hair on his chest.

"Hi," breathed Iris into her new lover's ear.

"No, just happy," replied the big Aussie. "Did you sleep well?"

"Yea! When you finally let me sleep. I'm glad the boats made of fibreglass. I'm sure we would have sprung a couple of planks last night if this had been a timber yacht". Iris rubbed her cheek against Alan's beard and then searched for his lips with her own. They kissed again and Alan felt a pleasant tingling sensation in his groin. Iris couldn't help but notice the effect she was having on her man and giggled like a schoolgirl.

"C'mon Alan," Iris called as she dove over the side. "I'll race you to the beach. First one there gets to go on top". Alan had been able to swim like a fish since the age of six, but that looked stupid, so he chose freestyle and shot past Iris as if she were treading water. She didn't stand a chance, but then she didn't really want to go on top anyway.

The little beach on which they found themselves was the perfect place for a romantic interlude and the couple spent most of the morning cuddling and just lazing in the sun. Alan spoke of his childhood for the first time, describing to Iris the many facets and events in his life that brought him to be the person he was today. Slowly Iris began to understand that her new man was far deeper and more intense than his carefree manner had led her to believe. Of course his happy-go-lucky nature was much more than just a facade. Alan was not only a genuinely optimistic and cheerful person, he was also caring, generous and quietly unassuming. He was a private man though, cautious in his dealings with other people and sometimes wary of getting too close quickly. He was definitely not the type of man to wear his heart on his sleeve.

"So how did you get into sailing Alan?" asked Iris, as they lay on the sand, the salt water on their skin rapidly drying in the warm sun.

"I've loved boats and sailing since I was a kid. In fact I was born on a boat."

Iris was impressed. "You're kidding."

"Nuh! On my parents yacht 'Serenity'. My place of birth is at 28.3 degrees north, 142.5 degrees west. Just about half-way between San Francisco and Honolulu. They'd left America nearly seven weeks earlier on the first leg of their voyage back to Oz, but we got stuck, slopping about with no wind in the middle of the Pacific Ocean, for the best part of a month. Add to that the fact that my folks got it wrong about when I was due and Instead of Hawaii and a modern, well-equipped hospital, I got fifty-three feet of teak and Huron pine. Not that I remember much of that time. My first memories, vague ones, were of the time we spent in the Philippines. Then we spent almost a year in Honiara. I was two years old by the time we got back to Australia."

"Wow" said Iris. Then came the question Alan had been dreading. "So where are your parents now?"

Alan sat up and crossed his legs, leaned forward, gently resting his elbows on his knees.

"My parents are both dead. My brother Michael and I were brought up by our paternal grandparents." He replied.

"Shit. I'm sorry Alan. How did your parents die?"

For the next hour, Iris and Alan sat together on the sandy beach as Alan told the story of his mothers battle with breast cancer and his father's subsequent slide into depression and eventual suicide.

Patrick Tew had not coped well with the death of his beloved Maddie. She had been his soul mate and he simply didn't know how to live without her. Lionel and Lucia had watched helplessly as their only son became more and more morose and despondent. Six months after her death, Lionel finally convinced Patrick to seek professional help. He went to a counsellor, one who specialized in helping people cope with the grief of losing a loved one. After nearly a year of therapy, he eventually seemed to be making some progress.

He got himself a job, driving a forklift three days a week at the Rocklea fruit markets. At first he travelled from Hamilton by public transport, changing buses three times each way to cover the thirty or so kilometres. Then, when he had saved sufficient money, he bought himself a cheap car, a 1979 Holden Commodore. It was white, or at least it had been when it was new. The tyres needed replacing, it used heaps of oil and there was an alarming whine which came from the gearbox in third gear. But the motor was sound and it was reliable enough to get him to and from work.

Sadly it was also reliable enough for Patrick to start it, put a hose into the exhaust pipe, lead it through the back window into the cars interior and sit quietly and alone until the toxic fumes killed him.

"Jesus Honey! I'm so sorry." said Iris.

"It's okay Iris, I was only three and a half years old. I don't remember my parents much anyway. And Lionel and Lucia, they're my grandparents, did a wonderful job of bringing up Michael and I. They heaped love on us both, taught us the difference between right and wrong and made sure we got a decent education. All the things a parent should provide for their kids. Plus they were quite rich. Mick and I wanted for nothing."

Even so Alan's tale left Iris feeling quite down. She pulled Alan back down beside her and kissed him. The big Australian rolled over onto his back and stretched out his arm so that Iris could snuggle in against his chest. Three hours later, Stefan found them still in each others arms, fast asleep.

Chapter 34

Dave Randall flicked on the computer and downloaded the forensic report on Berswiski's latest massacre. Since the discovery of the young girl's body at the old farmhouse four days ago, Berswiski had struck three more times. Four bodies in four days. The last murder had occurred yesterday, at an abandoned warehouse in the dock area, just a stone's throw away from Interpol headquarters. He was goading them.

Randall could not bear to be reminded of the gruesome details of the insane Russian scientist's latest obscenity, so he scrolled through the information quickly until he found the section he was looking for. The evidence list and the preliminary summation prepared by Veronica Crystal about what it all meant.

Once again Berswiski seemed to have taken absolutely no precautions to prevent himself from being linked to the crime. The evidence that Interpol and the Greek constabulary had against him was now totally overwhelming. There was not a court in the world that would not find him guilty. Not that he would ever see the inside of a courtroom if Dave Randall had anything to do with it. Grey had unofficially issued a 'shoot on sight' order for Berswiski. They were not going to let this one get away. To many times in the past some smart-arse lawyer had been able to find a clever loophole and as a result, the criminal the team had been pursuing got away. But not this time. Berswiski was a dead man. He just didn't know it yet.

As well as Mrs Crystal's report, there were two other pieces of evidence that were of interest. Firstly they had found traces of residual radioactivity at the vacant warehouse. Nothing that could be considered dangerous but enough to indicate that the missing nuclear warhead may have been there recently. It appeared the bomb was still in Athens. Secondly, Grey and his team now knew Berswiski had an accomplice.

At the farmhouse and again at the warehouse, the forensic team had found traces of another person, a female other than the victim. In the first instance they'd found three long grey hairs and there was a high heel shoe print in a pool of blood at the foot of the bed. At the warehouse, they'd found lipstick marks on the body of the murdered woman, or rather on what was left of her. The forensic team had isolated DNA from the hair and tried to match it to all of Berswiski's known associates, but to no avail.

Veronica Crystal felt extremely uneasy. The Russian should not be acting in this way. It was almost as if he was daring his pursuers to catch him. A more frightening theory was that Berswiski had lost it entirely and had decided he had nothing to lose. If that were the case there was no telling what he might do next.

Dave returned to the evidence list and perused the information pertaining to the mystery woman. Forensic had ascertained from the grey hair, that the woman would be aged at least in her late fifties or early sixties. From the footprint they found at the farmhouse, she would be of medium height and heavy build, but apart from that, there was precious little to go on. Veronica felt the mystery woman was the key in the whole case. If they could find her, she could lead them to Berswiski and the bomb. It was that simple.

They had to find the woman. But who was she.

Veronica Crystal came up with a theory, a possible answer to Dave's question, which she decided to discuss with the Major that evening over dinner.

Despite the financial woes the world was currently experiencing, a CIA operatives expense budget left that of the Interpol employees looking like pocket money. So Veronica's digs were at the Crowne Plaza Hotel, a far cry from the hovels Grey and his compatriots had to endure.

Mrs. Crystal wanted to put her hypothesis to the Major in private, away from the others. If her guess was right then the fewer people who knew about it the better. So that evening she invited Edmond to join her at her hotel for dinner.

She'd booked a table for 7:30, giving herself ample time to prepare her report. She had a quick shower, and then dressed for the evening. She chose one of her favourite outfits, a long, full length evening gown in a silvery blue fabric which hugged her body like a glove. It had a high neckline, which she felt was more appropriate for a woman of her age than the low cut gowns she might have worn the last time she and Edmond had worked together, and a slit at the side which occasionally revealed her still shapely legs.

The Major arrived a few minutes after 7:30, apologizing profusely for being late and nearly bowling over the Matre'd in his hurry to get to their table. Veronica thought he looked extremely elegant. Not handsome, but as the English so eloquently put it, definitely dapper. Once again he was dressed in an immaculate grey, pinstripe suit, but this time it was accessorized with a pale lemon shirt and a blue and silver tie.

Veronica felt that in all probability, as a baby Edmond Grey had worn grey pinstripe diapers, and a Secret Seven tie in his crib

The waiter came over and presented them with menus, poured water into their drinking glasses and then left for a few moments while they made their selections. Both Veronica and Edmond had had enough of the rich, over spiced, over flavoured Greek fare served at the restaurants they had frequented over the past four weeks, and so chose a simple repast of a dozen oysters followed by a medium rare fillet steak for Veronica and prawn cocktail and roast beef for the Major. The food was simple but delicious.

Half way through their entrée Veronica put down her fork.

"Do you remember the last time we dined together Eddie?" she asked smiling. "We were in Berlin, following that dangerous terrorist. The one operating out of the Argentinian embassy."

The Major laughed. It was good to see him enjoying himself for once, thought Veronica. He'd become far too serious over the past fourteen years.

"Yes, I remember it well, back in... uh 97? One of your guys intercepted a 'suspicious' phone call. Someone trying to arrange for the assassination of the German foreign affairs minister. We spent weeks listening in on hundreds of calls, following suspects from one end of Europe to the other, trying to gather proof, only to find that the Argentinian bloke was a good friend of the ministers and was only trying to arrange a surprise birthday party."

"Thank you, Edmond."

"For what?"

"Not reminding me that the 'guy' who intercepted the call was me. I felt such a fool."

Edmond reached over the table and gently touched the back of veronica's hand.

"I seem to remember telling you at the time V, there was nothing foolish about your actions, nothing at all. Just imagine if you'd decided not to act on your suspicions and someone had died. You'd never have forgiven yourself. Far better to be safe than sorry. Don't you think?"

Veronica nodded. She didn't entirely agree with the Major. She had made a fool of herself and of the CIA, not to mention cost the agency heaps. But she knew it was a point that she and Eddie would probably always disagree on. He was ultra conservative and over cautious. Whilst she was infinitely more compulsive. Neither side could ever say with any conviction that their way was the correct one. Besides, what had happened had happened and as always, what ifs simply didn't come into consideration

They chatted about the good old days all through dinner, dessert and later in the bar until nearly midnight. It was good to reminisce about all the fun and excitement they'd had together all those years ago. Though Edmond would never have admitted it as both of them were after all happily married, he liked Veronica almost more than was good for him. She was beautiful, sexy, interesting, intelligent and despite all that, one of the most down to earth women Edmond had ever met. There were no airs and graces with Mrs Veronica Crystal. There had been a dozen times at least during their time together when Edmond had come close to telling her how he felt, but he had always pulled back just at the last minute.

They finished their drinks at the bar and moved to a quiet table in the corner. Then Veronica reached for her briefcase. She opened it and pulled out the five-page report she had written on her theory regarding Berswiski, who the mystery woman might be, and where their investigation might go next. She handed Edmond the document and directed him to pay particular attention to her comments on page four.

"So, you're sure about this?" asked Grey after he had finished reading.

"Positive. I'm American and my family's got money Eddie, I've been skiing in Colorado almost every winter since I could walk. Trust me, there is no Regal Hotel in Aspen."

Major Grey didn't swear often. In fact Veronica had only ever heard him cuss once before. He looked again at her report.

"Shit."

He paused for a second and gathered his thoughts. What Veronica was alluding to had huge ramifications. It also explained a hell of a lot. Like how Berswiski always seemed to be one step ahead of them. In the past three months there'd only been one occasion when they'd come even close to catching the bastard.

"There could be another, simpler, explanation though. Most of us have some sort of skeleton in our closet. Something we'd rather remain secret. You've considered that, haven't you? he asked.

"Yes and you're right, there could be another reason," she agreed. "But everything fits. Psychopathy frequently appears in siblings. Svetlana Berswiski could be just as much a psychopath as her brother. All the signs are there. I've checked and double-checked. It's a text book case. As I said at my lecture, most of them exist in society totally undetected. They learn to imitate the emotions and reactions of others by watching and copying. I'm sure I'm right Eddie. Trust me on this."

"Okay. So what do we do next? How do we prove your hypothesis?"

Veronica pulled another sheet of paper from her briefcase, leaned over and placed it in front of him.

"You collected semen samples from the Australian woman you found murdered in Brisbane, plus we've samples collected here, so I assume you've got Berswiski's DNA profile handy?"

Edmond Grey nodded.

"Great. So check it against this one and I'll bet you a thousand bucks you'll get a positive result."

Chapter 35

Alan stretched sleepily and turned onto his side, carefully lifting his hips, rolling over on his shoulder and lowering himself gently back down onto the mattress. He was trying not to disturb the sleeping woman beside him, as he silently slipped out of bed and crept to the galley.

Not that anything short of an earthquake could have disturbed her. She was a good sleeper this Iris Richards. A gold medal Olympiad sleeper. Sure she was energetic when they first went to bed, and gentle and loving as they kissed and cuddled afterwards, and they often talked until the early hours of the morning. They chatted about many subjects, from politics or religion, to their dreams and aspirations for the future. But when it came time to go to sleep, she'd close her eyes, her breathing would become regular and deeper and she would sleep the sleep of the dead until the sun winked through the tiny portholes of their cabin and a swallow on the island farted and heralded in a new day.

Alan too normally slept like a baby, though without the need for a two a.m. breast feed and a nappy change in the morning. But sometimes he didn't, and he would lie awake, watching Iris sleep, marvelling at her presence, unable to believe he could be so lucky.

It was a bit Mills and Boon, but Alan had to admit, he was in love and although he revelled in this new sensation, it also terrified him.

What if one day he woke to find her gone? Or worse, that her love for him died. Or what if...?

He chided himself for being so melodramatic and then excused himself with the explanation that he had never felt love for a woman in quite this way before. Iris Richards was his soul mate, of that he was one hundred percent sure, and the thought that he might lose her was unbearable. So sometimes he lay there in their bunk, wide-eyed and listless, listening to the creaking of the hull and the clanking and twanging of rigging, as 'Harvey' rolled gently with the swell, straining and tugging at her anchor, until exhaustion finally overcame him and he dropped off.

He had lost loved ones before, his parents and grandparents. His mother and father had died when he was barely more than a toddler and even though he had long ago forgotten even what they looked like, the confusion and grief he'd felt at the time had burned into his heart and left a scar that even today, nearly thirty years later, still felt raw. Lionel and Lucia had died too. The old man lived until he was seventy two, active and lively right up until the end. The headaches and nausea he had suffered with during the last few months of his life, proved to be undiagnosed high blood pressure. One day it became too much for the old man's heart to cope with, and it burst like an overripe watermelon.

Lucia, who was younger by some years than her husband, lived on for another decade. But she too eventually succumbed to the ravages of time and died in her sleep on the eighteenth of June just four years ago. The doctor who performed the post-mortem declared an brain aneurysm to be the cause of death

The death of Alan and Mick's guardians meant the two brothers became the sole benefactors of the once mighty Tew estate. The arms factory in Brisbane had been sold a short time before the death of the boy's parents and the cataclysmic collapse of the stock market in the mid eighties meant that most of the Tew fortune had been whittled away.

Even so the stipend the two brothers received after all the taxes and duties and expenses had been paid, was a sizeable sum. Alan bought his treasured yacht and invested what was left of his share in government bonds. Mick frittered his away in less than six months and had nothing in the end to show for it. Many people said; the two men were alike in many ways physically, but in all other ways, two brothers could not be more dissimilar.

'Harvey' languished in the tiny, secluded anchorage on the island of Kea for three more days. They were wonderful days. Days filled with sunshine and happiness. Balmy days, in which Alan's love for Iris and hers for him, grew.

They spent hours curled up together in bed or up on deck chatting about their past lives and making plans for the future. One morning they awoke to someone banging up on deck.

"Geezus," remarked Alan, "don't those two ever take a break?"

He crawled out of bed and wandered outside, picked up his snorkelling gear and speargun and dropped quietly over the side. He cleaned the face mask in the water, spat a huge gob of spit onto the glass and rubbed it in. While he did so, he breathed deeply, priming his lungs with air for the first dive of the day.

Free diving was one of the things Alan liked best. Sure there wasn't the heady rush of adrenaline that accompanied paragliding, nor was there the sense of surging power he felt when 'Harvey' heeled over in a stiff breeze, but diving gave Alan a sense of calm and inner peace. Something he could not find anywhere else. It was a more relaxed pastime. The feeling of weightlessness lulled away any tension in his soul and the closeness to nature reminded him of the beauty and goodness that still existed in the world. Alan took a deep breath, bent forward at the waist and then lifted his legs out of the water using their weight to push himself down towards the ocean floor. There were rocks down there, and a myriad of small fish scuttling to and fro, searching the bottom for sustenance.

Alan yawned, thrusting his jaw forward, and his ears squeaked as the pressure inside his eardrums equalized. He hung there motionless for almost a minute, and then headed to the surface for a fresh lungful of air. He repeated the procedure for nearly ten minutes before the creature he was looking for got used to his presence, and crawled out from its hiding place. A huge crayfish almost forty centimetres from the end of its tail to the tip of its two gigantic claws, ambled out from under a rock. It walked slowly across the bottom, fanning its claws towards its mouth, scooping up tiny bits of food from the ocean floor. The bolt from the speargun hissed through the water and pierced the creature's body just behind the neck and Alan once again felt the familiar, inexplicable double-edged emotion of euphoria at his success and dismay at the death of another of nature's beautiful creations. The sadness was palpable and always lasted much longer than the fleeting joy of a successful hunt. Alan had wrestled long and hard with his conscience about the dilemma of killing another life form versus the need to put food in his stomach, and he had eventually reached the conclusion that all he could do was ensure he always did whatever he could to make sure the fish he caught and the animals he hunted died as quickly and as painlessly as possible. And he only ever caught enough for his immediate needs.

Lunch that day was delectable, with Stefan once again winning first prize in the Harvey Wharf Banger version of 'My Galley Rules'. While the young Dutchman cooked, the two girls entertained the group with an extremely spirited rendition of 'Zorba's dance' to the Greek music playing on the radio.

"Tell me about the others who have crewed for you Alan," commanded Iris as they all tucked in to the 'Crayfish a la Stefan'. The big Aussie was only too happy to oblige.

"Well" he began, "there was Janelle. She was an English girl who had crossed eyes. They were so bad that when she cried, the tears streamed down her back. Then there was Helga from Germany. She was so uptight the pharmacy guild had her listed as a suppository. Mary who was so dense world heritage listed her as a rainforest. Wendy who was as useless as a g-string in a dysentery ward. Linda was a pommy bird who talked so much even Helen Keller asked her to shut up..."

"Oh very funny, NOT. But hang on," interjected Peggy, "are you telling us that all your previous crew have been women? What about the blokes?"

"Apart from Stef' here, I've only had two other men on board for any length of time," replied Alan. "Neil, a kiwi bloke and my brother Mick".

Alan got up from the table and wandered off to his cabin, returning a few moments latter with a dog-eared photo album. All three crew members noticed the distinct lack of masculinity within the album's pages, but only Peggy mentioned it.

"See" she announced "nothing but girls. I reckon you're a bit of a dark horse Al! Trying to see how many women you could shag in as many countries as possible hey?" To Iris's amazement, Alan looked extremely embarrassed.

"It just seemed to happen that way," he protested, sounding like a school kid who had just been caught perving down Auntie Mabel's cleavage. "For some reason, nearly every time I advertise for crew, only women apply. I think it must be because women have a more romantic perception of sailing. They think it will be all balmy nights, sun drenched days, long, deserted, sandy beaches and endless glasses of chilled champagne while relaxing on deck. But blokes don't want that. They just want to get to wherever they're going as soon as possible. Somewhere where they can get drunk and get laid. I'm sure you've noticed, when it comes to getting anywhere on a yacht, 'as soon as possible,' has an entirely different connotation."

It took a while for Iris to realize that Alan's embarrassment was because of her. Of course he had had girlfriends before her. He was thirty-two, handsome, sort of witty, well-built and had that certain, quiet confidence women always find attractive. But it seemed he felt uncomfortable talking about his previous women in front of her. She smiled to herself guessing she knew the reason why. Alan considered her special, the others had meant nothing to him and he didn't want her to think she was just another notch in his bedpost. She slipped her arm through his and squeezed, laying her head on his shoulder as he continued to leaf through the pages. Rather than feel jealous or threatened, Iris felt a sense of triumph. Every girl in the album was past history. Alan was hers now. What went before was of no consequence.

Then Alan turned the page and there was Dorotka.

The picture was not in the least bit erotic or sexily posed. In fact both Iris and Peggy had themselves stood behind the wheel of the yacht and enjoyed the feel of a cool breeze on their naked skin. It was just that this woman did it so well. She simply oozed sexuality. She was about twenty-two years old, tall, blond and voluptuous. The type of women Iris believed all men lusted after.

The next photo was more of the same. Once again the long limbed honey known as Dorotka was naked, but this time she languished seductively on one of Alan's big boat cushions. Her luxurious, long, blond mane was no longer stuffed inside a hat, but hung loosely, draping itself around her shoulders and cascading gently across her ample, pert nippled breasts. The sun had burnished every inch of Dorotka's beautiful body to a deep, rich tan, which contrasted noticeably with the tiny, curly blond triangle of pubic hair nestled between her legs.

Stefan said wow. Quietly, but not quietly enough to prevent him from getting a sharp jab in the ribs from his girlfriend's elbow. But there was simply no arguing with Stefan's sentiment, the German woman was hot, and from the photo, it was obvious that at the time, all of that heat was directed towards Alan. In the picture, Dorotka's huge hazel eyes twinkled mischievously and her luscious lips and perfect, white teeth conspired together to form a smile whose meaning was clear. When Alan put down the camera he was going to be fucked. Not like a blender fucks a jellyfish, but with just as much certainty.

"She's very beautiful", said Iris. Thankfully Alan had more sense than to try to deny the obvious.

"Yea, she was. That's Dorotka", explained Alan. "We spent a few torrid months together last year sailing up the East Coast of Africa". Alan went on to tell of how they met in Capetown and travelled together as far as Dakar in Senegal.

Dorotka, explained Alan, was not the brightest of God's creatures and frequently did silly things that got her into a great deal of trouble. She'd arrived in Capetown from Germany a few days prior to meeting Alan with nothing but a backpack, a hundred dollars or so in traveller's cheques and a phone number of a South African man who had promised to 'look after her' when she got to town. The phone number belonged to an elderly woman who knew nothing of Dorotka or of Dorotka's friend, who, it transpired, was not really a friend but a complete stranger the silly girl had lent some money to a few weeks earlier. Alan took pity on the girl and invited her to come on board until they got to Senegal where she was to meet up with a another friend, a real one this time, from Frankfurt.

For the next half-hour or so Alan entertained the group with tales of Dorotka's exploits. Like the time she dropped her mobile phone into the toilet and the time she forgot to tie the dinghy to the back of the yacht and Alan had to swim nearly a kilometre to retrieve it. The water had been rough and the shoreline rocky. Also, the swim was made even more harrowing, by the knowledge that if the water he was swimming in wasn't shark infested, it was only because the crocodiles had frightened them all away.

As Alan told his tale, Iris became aware of two things. Firstly, apart from a healthy interest in ugly bumping, Alan and Dorotka had precious little in common. Secondly, despite the numerous times the German girl put her foot in it, you couldn't really think of her as stupid. She totally transcended stupid. In a competition to see who had the most common sense, Dorotka would probably come a distant second place to a hairball.

As Alan succinctly put it, "She had the face of an angel, the body of a goddess, and the head of a lettuce."

She may have been sex on a stick, but that was all she was, and knowing this made Iris much more confident about her relationship with Alan.

The Dorotka photos finished and after a couple of 'short term crew' photos, Alan arrived at a section featuring his brother Mick.

Mick and Alan had not seen each other for nearly ten years when, just a few weeks after Dorotka left 'Harvey' in Dakar, Alan received an urgent telegram from his long-lost, elder brother.

They hadn't seen each other in years, in fact Alan didn't even know for sure if his brother was alive or dead. But back in Australia, Mick had by chance met a friend of Alan's who had remarked that Mick was the spitting image of someone he knew. In typical 'small world' fashion, the similarity proved to be genetic rather than just coincidental and the brothers were subsequently reunited.

Mick had not fared as well for himself as his younger brother, but he was still able to scrounge, scrimp, save, beg borrow and steal the money for the airfare to join Alan in the Canary Islands. From there, they would sail together to England.

Mick had squandered his inheritance years ago and had been forced to get a job. Like his younger brother, Mick had decided to earn a crust by using his hands. While Alan chose a career in cabinet making, Mick decided to become a glazier. A job that not only earned him a meagre but liveable income, but as his windows never fell out, also provided him with irrefutable evidence that he did in fact, know the difference between shit and putty.

The Canary Islands are some of the most spectacular islands in the world, but unfortunately, Mick who spent almost the entire time they were in the archipelago in one of the many bars, did little to disprove Alan's theory about male crewmembers and their narrow outlook on travelling. It wasn't quite true to say Mick had a drinking problem. Admittedly he got pissed with monotonous regularity, and he had a habit of becoming persistently annoying and annoyingly persistent whenever there was a member of the opposite sex around, but as far as Mick was concerned, this wasn't a problem. Of course Alan thought differently. Luckily the younger Tew found that his older brother wasn't an aggressive drunk. In fact Mick inevitably became over-friendly. It was also true that Mick had a terrific sense of humour. It was just that when you are trying to have a romantic, candle lit dinner with your fiancée or you are trying to explain to your soon to be ex-husband just how much of a dud root he really is, you don't want some pisshead coming over, turning the insides of his pockets out and asking you if you would like to see his world-famous impression of a white eared elephant.

On one typical occasion, Mick decided that a particularly attractive black girl, who was enjoying a quiet drink with some friends, was worthy of his attention.

"Howyagoin?" slurred Mick, directing his question to the woman's chest.

"Je ne comprends pas" answered the woman.

Mick quickly and loudly explained to the woman he was Australian and didn't speak more than a few words of French. Had the woman had her wits about her, she may have used this fact to her advantage and played dumb. Unfortunately, she let slip that she spoke English quite well. Mick latched on to her for the next three hours and the poor woman did everything she could think of to get rid of him.

A little after midnight, the French woman tried to leave. Mick followed her back to her hotel, walking beside her with his arm around her waist, pulling her towards him. Finally, she'd had enough and told him in no uncertain terms that his advances were unwelcome and that he should piss off, but Mick ignored her protests. A few hundred metres from her hotel, Mick made his move, swinging around in front of the woman and kissing her squarely and passionately on the lips. She responded by lifting her right knee forcefully and with perfect accuracy, catching him in such a way that he was rendered helpless with pain and for the rest of his life had to dress to the left.

Although Alan was back on 'Harvey' at the time and did not actually witness the impact of the woman's knee as it crushed poor Mick's nuts, he claimed to have heard the thump. He came up on deck just in time to see Mick hobble down the jetty, bent over double, bow-legged like a Hindu mahout who had just been rogered by his elephant.

Many years ago, Alan had decided there was little to be gained in trying to make his older brother see the error of his ways. They were, after all their years apart, virtual strangers. Besides, Mick wasn't a child. But after the "noix ecraser" episode, Alan rethought his previous decision and took Mick to task about his drinking. To his surprise, Mick took it all rather well and promised to amend his drinking habits to a more suitable, non life threatening level.

All went well for a few days, but soon Mick found an excuse to celebrate and proceeded to leap, rather than simply fall off, the wagon. Alan took the matter in hand and announced they would be moving to a quieter, more remote area, one that did not feature the plethora of bars to be found in places like Las Palmas or Santa Cruz.. Unfortunately, half-way through the passage to the Island of Lanzarote, Alan discovered that his younger brother had taken it upon himself to sample a few of the bottles of wine he had stored away. Mick, who was supposed to be at the helm, was passed out cold, snoring away loudly, curled up on one of the huge cushions Alan kept in the cockpit. Luckily he had set the auto pilot before he'd succumbed, but even so, they were both extremely lucky they hadn't been run down by one of the numerous cruise ships which regularly traversed the area.

The big Aussie had had enough. He raided the storeroom and galley and poured every drop of alcohol he could find over the side. Mick was not impressed and the two brothers came close to physical violence. Eventually Mick calmed down and the two discussed what should be done. The older brother slowly came to accept that he had a problem and promised to let Alan help him.

As sometimes happens, fate stepped in to lend a hand. After leaving Lanzarote, the pair returned to Las Palmas to clear customs and then headed for the Portuguese Island of Madeira, a mere five hundred kilometres to the north. The trip should have taken about four or five days, but after only fifty or so kilometres, the weather changed for the worse. The wind died.

There are few thing sailors hate more than no wind. Strong winds can be frightening and damaging to the sails and rigging, but most experienced sailors will simply reduce sail or if necessary, hove to and wait until the blow has eased. However, the situation where there is no wind, is maddening in the extreme. The boat rocks and rolls incessantly making it extremely uncomfortable and hard on the sails and equipment. By midday, with hardly any wind at all, 'Harvey' had all but stopped. Alan rigged the MPS, a huge, lightweight sail designed to make the most of even the lightest breath of wind and once again, the boat began to creep slowly forward By 16:00 the wind died completely and the yacht stopped completely, or to be more precise, all forward motion stopped completely. The south-westerlies which had blown continuously for the last few weeks had set up a sizeable swell which set the boat rocking violently from side to side. The sails would empty as 'Harvey' rolled one way and then fill again with a loud bang as she rolled back. The main and mizzen booms flicked back and forth, swinging across before being brought up short by the line Alan had rigged to stop the sails accidentally gybing, that is, crashing from one side of the yacht to the other. To prevent them being damaged by the constant flogging, Alan and Mick dropped all sails except for the MPS, which was polled out on the whisker pole ready to catch the next zephyr.

For the next four days 'Harvey' drifted aimlessly, never moving more that a few hundred metres from where she had started. Mick could not believe such boredom and frustration could exist.

"So, how about we start the motor Alan?" he regularly suggested. But his request was denied.

"We have plenty of food and water", replied the younger brother "and although we have ample fuel to get us to Madeira, it's probably best we don't use it all up now. We might need every drop later on in an emergency".

Mick felt rolling from side to side incessantly and making no visible headway was an emergency, and said so in no uncertain terms. But as Alan was a far more experienced sailor and it was, after all, his yacht, he had no option but to sit it out and wait until the wind returned.

On the fifth day, Mick complained of feeling unwell. He began to feel nauseous and started to sweat. By mid-afternoon, he was shaking uncontrollably and had a very unpleasant, hollow feeling in his chest. He felt like he was dying, though Alan believed 'dying for a drink' was a more likely scenario. To his credit, Mick recognized the symptoms as those of alcohol withdrawal and admitted to Alan that he now realized he had a major problem.

The next few days were the most distressing and unpleasant that both Mick and Alan had had to endure for many years. Mick went through a series of highs and lows, his normally placid, happy-go-lucky nature, was destroyed by the cravings for booze. He ranted and raved at the sea, the yacht, his brother, but mostly, he raved at the cursed wind. The sea turned to glass and took on an almost oily appearance. The surface stained with swirls of greasy brown plankton which had died and floated to the surface. It filled the air with a pungent, dead fish smell that permeated throughout the entire yacht.

For two more days the wind was virtually non-existent, and then it returned with a vengeance. Shortly before dawn on the eighth day, while Alan was asleep in his bunk, he awoke with a feeling that something had changed. They had reset the mains'l, sheeting it in tight and flat to try to slow the lazy rolling of the yacht. The MPS too was still rigged, drooping loosely from the peak of the mainmast, waiting for the next breath of wind.

Suddenly a ripple raced across the face of the huge sail, and it filled with a loud pop, backing against the wind and wrapping itself around the forestay. At the same time the mains'l began to pump, the leach, or leading edge of the sail, flogged rapidly for the few seconds it took for the MPS to push the bow around. When the gale hit the mains'l side-on, 'Harvey' heeled over, nearly pushing her gunnel under. Mick who was on watch at the time, slid off the bench he was laying on and landed with a crash on the cockpit floor. It took many long minutes before the two brothers were able to bring the yacht back under control, setting a reefed mizzen and a small stays'l which had 'Harvey' hove-to comfortably.

As if to make up for the pathetic efforts of the previous eight days the wind began to howl, regularly gusting to sixty knots. The gale set up a banshee like wail through the rigging, screaming so loudly that even when below deck, the two brothers were forced to yell just to be heard. At 13:30 that afternoon the clew on the stays'l, the stainless steel eyelet through which the sheets or control ropes were tied, let go, tearing itself free from the corner of the tiny sail. Within seconds the sail had flogged itself to ribbons. Alan was forced to brave the elements and go up onto the foredeck to change the sail for an even heavier fabric storm-sail.

With no heads'l to hold the yacht steady, 'Harvey' kept trying to steer herself until she was facing directly into the wind. Had this been allowed to occur, the mizzen too would have shredded itself in minutes. So while Alan changed the stays'l, Mick dropped the mizzen, lashed the helm and scurried for'ard to help, leaving the yacht to her own devices. Laying a-hull in this fashion is not an uncommon heavy weather practice on a more modern, fin-keeled, boat, but it is rare in an ocean going ketch with a full-length keel. Never the less, Harvey took it all in her stride.

Even so, she was much more comfortable when the boys had her hove-to with a bit of sail up once again, to hold her steady, with her bow pointing just a few degrees off the wind. In this way the waves would simply lift her up, pass under her and lower her gently down the other side, repeating the exercise over and over again until the wind eased.

Or something broke.

"Get your safety harness on and stay at the helm." screamed Alan over the shrieking gale. "You're much more use back there". Alan sat at the base of the forestay struggling with what was left of the torn sail. A huge wave broke over the deck and washed him sideways but his harness was securely hooked onto the lifelines and stopped him from being swept over the side. Both the genoa and stays'l were fitted to furlers which rotated around their respective stays, rolling up the sails a bit whenever the wind increased, or totally when 'Harvey' was at anchor. But to lower what was left of the destroyed stays'l Alan had to unfurl the whole sail, pull it out of the luff groove, feed the new sail into the groove and winch it up. The task, which would normally take only a few minutes in good conditions, took Alan over an hour.

For the next thirty-two hours, the gale continued unabated. The two men stayed below deck as much as possible, venturing outside for only as long as it took to scan the horizon to make sure they were not in any danger from shipping. They were a long way offshore and the wind was blowing them even further away, so there was no chance of them being driven ashore. But other vessels would be travelling to Madeira and with visibility at less than a few hundred metres, a regular lookout was needed.

At around 01:30 a loud rumbling noise could be heard over the howling wind. Alan heard it first and recognized it for what it was.

Even large ocean swells seldom display the ferocity exhibited by a smaller, yet far more turbulent, coastal breaker. The watery giants roll in, one after another, some as tall as a multi story building and yet they are of little concern to a well found yacht in the hands of a competent sailor. The wave may be high, but the crest of the one following, may be fifty to one hundred metres behind it so the face of the wave presents a gentler incline than the near vertical wall of water of a large coastal breaker. Occasionally, however, one wave will decide it no longer wishes to play the game. For some inexplicable reason, it will slow and its following sibling will catch up, climb up onto its back, and join with it to create a monster rogue wave. They can be huge and worse, may begin to break, like a surfer's worst nightmare. It was a wave such as this that caught 'Harvey' napping.

Alan heard the wave coming and knew from first-hand experience that the shit was about to hit the fan. The two brothers felt 'Harvey' lift her nose out of the water, rising at the bow until she was standing almost vertically against the face of the oncoming wave. For what seemed like an eternity the yacht hung there in midair, stalled in her climb and then Alan felt her falter and start to slide backwards down the wave, turning side on to the wave as she did so.

"Hang on", yelled Alan as the yacht started to broach. "She's going to roll over". As she swung around, 'Harvey's' keel dug in and the enormous wave rolled her over 180 degrees. She hung there, upside down, for what seemed like an eternity. Both Alan and Mick fell down onto what had once been the roof of the main cabin. The overhead cupboards flew open and they were bombarded with books, coffee cups, tins of food, anything and everything that had not been properly secured. The large timber cover, which normally concealed the diesel motor, hurled itself through the air and smashed itself into a dozen pieces just millimetres from Mick's head.

"Geezus fucking Christ," cursed Mick, "we're upside down."

"She'll come back up," Alan assured his brother, "provided we don't sink first." As if to add credence to Alan's comments the sea started to pour in past the weather seal on the main hatch. 'Harvey' began to shudder and shake and once again the brothers whole world, slowly at first but with increasing speed, started to roll back upright. When the yacht had regained her correct orientation the floor was awash with almost half a metre of water sloshing and swirling around the two men's feet. Alan bolted for the hatch, eager to asses any damage done by the capsize. If one of the masts had come down, it would still be attached by the stainless steel wire stays, and there was a very real danger it could flail about in the rough seas and pierce the hull.

Remarkably, both masts were still standing, though the genoa furler was bent beyond repair and numerous items had been washed overboard. Once again, the stays'l was just a tattered mass of rags and this time the mizzen had also been shredded. There was nothing left to do but pull down what was left of the shredded sails and leave the yacht to her own devices. The next few hours were the most uncomfortable Alan had ever experienced on a yacht. Without some sail to keep the boat headed into the wind, she was like a cork in a washing machine. She was tossed from side to side, with nothing to slow down the violent motion of the tempest outside.

At daybreak Alan noticed a change in the weather. The storm was beginning to abate, the wind was easing and the waves were no longer quite so fearsome. The two brothers were able to assess the damage fully. In addition to the bent furler, there was a large gouge in the deck where the spare anchor, normally securely lashed in its cradle, had broken free and bounced up and down on the deck during the capsize. Thankfully, it was still attached to the anchor chain and had not been lost overboard.

The whole day was spent pumping out water that had found its way into the cabin, repairing those things that could be fixed, and re-packing all the items that had been catapulted around the boat the previous day. Around dusk Alan decided that conditions had improved sufficiently to raise what sail they could, and once again 'Harvey' swung around to the north and headed for Madeira.

Much later Mick was to comment that the storm had been a pivotal occurrence in his life. At the height of the gale, when the yacht was lying upside down and Mick thought he was going to die, he suddenly had an almost unbelievable craving for a drink. The absurdity of that craving was not lost on him and it was then that he made a promise to himself. If he got out of there alive he would go back to Australia and at the first opportunity, sign on with the local chapter of 'Alcoholics Anonymous' and never touch a drop of booze ever again. And, Alan told his three shipmates, that's exactly what his brother did.

Chapter 36

The major hadn't actually seen the inside of Veronica Crystal's suite at the Crowne Royal, but he surmised you wouldn't have to be a crack investigator to work out that her accommodation was far more salubrious than his digs at the 'Something unpronounceable in Greek' Hotel on the other side of the city. In turn, as befitting a person of his seniority and ranking with Interpol, his room was better than the ones enjoyed by Randall and the rest of the team, but not by much.

His new room was small and rectangular, and was furnished with just a double bed, two vaguely comfortable chairs, an eighty centimetre, flat screen TV, two bedside tables complete with lamps, a digital alarm clock, and the obligatory bible. There was a tiny bar fridge wedged under the full length, bolted to the wall, work bench/ table-top, a tiny combined bathroom and toilet. And that was it.

At night the view from the rooms solitary window was quite pleasant, the city lights making quite an impressive backdrop, but during the day, the grey, dirty, tired metropolis stretched out as far as the eye could see, a perfect depiction of urban squalor. The proprietor of the hotel claimed than from the balcony one could, if you stretched out a bit, see the Acropolis. Edmond tried, and even though he was taller than the rotund manager by a good twenty centimetres, failed to catch even a glimpse.

Edmond had let himself in, thrown his briefcase on the bed and unclipped his mobile phone from his belt. He'd pressed 1 and the device dialled his home in London. The phone rang and rang. There were a few seconds of electronic, echoing, silence and then Edmond heard himself tell him that he and Marjorie were not at home at the moment, and if he would like to leave himself a message, he would get back to himself as soon as he was able. The Edmonds both hung up and then he tried Marjorie's mobile, with ostensibly the same result.

It was late, but not too late. He considered the time difference between Athens and London and judged it to be around nine thirty in the evening GMT. Marjorie should have been at home, watching TV, with Grombletic the moggy curled up on her lap. If not watching TV she should be snuggled up in bed with a book, and the phone right there next to her on the night stand.

Of course should have and was, were two different things. There was a good chance she had simply gone to the cinema, or to visit friends. Or maybe one of the boys had felt like a night out with their wife and had asked Granny to baby-sit the grand kids. In fact there was any number of simple, innocent, explanations why Marjorie hadn't answered the phone. Sadly Edmond had to admit to himself that the most plausible of these was that she was at home and had ignored the phone's incessant ringing because she was giving him the cold shoulder.

He had let her down once again. She had been ever so excited about the prospect of the two of them spending a weekend together in Sibenic. Over the moon. She'd told the boys all about it and before anyone knew it, the weekend for two had morphed into ten days for the entire extended family. The boys and their wives had taken time off work, Charles, Emily and Rachael had permission to be absent from school. The villa had been booked for ten days, airline tickets to Dubrovnik had been bought and paid for, and the hire car arranged.

Ten whole days. Two weekends for Edmond, Marjorie and the gang with five days in the middle for Marjorie and the kids and grand kids to explore the area, and finally, a day at the end to pack up ready for the trip home. Perfect.

But Edmond couldn't make it.

"Every man and his dog is looking for this Berswiski character now," she argued when he broke the news. "Surely the mighty Major Grey can have a couple of days off. You can't save the whole world Edmond. Not on your own at least."

She was right of course. Every Intelligence Agency, every Police Force, and all Defence Force personnel from Ireland to the Bering strait and South to Kenya were desperately seeking out the insane Russian scientist. In reality, the Major's authority in the matter had been usurped many times over, by the fact that the situation had escalated to one of international security. It wasn't just a simple case of chasing a serial killer half-way around the world anymore. The Russians were still refusing to admit that one of their nuclear weapons was missing, so there hadn't been actual confirmation that the bomb even existed. But if it did... Well, that simply didn't bear thinking about. Millions of lives might be at risk, not just from the bomb itself but from the repercussions which might arise after the fact. Marjorie was right. Edmond couldn't save the whole world. But Berswiski was still out there, and his entire team all agreed, it was only a matter of time before he resurfaced and attacked another helpless young woman. Edmond Grey was going to be waiting when he did. There were seven billion people in the world. Saving even one of them seemed like a good day's work.

He tried both phones again with the same result. Unable to decide what to do next, he sat on the edge of his bed and stared unseeingly at the bare, insipid lemon walls of his hotel room. What if something had happened? What if Marjorie had been in an accident? He dialled Damian, his eldest son's mobile. Thankfully this time his call was answered, but Damian had no idea where his mother could be. He'd spoken to her earlier the previous day and she'd seemed fine, he told his father. He promised to make some calls and get back to him as soon as possible.

Edmond called a few mutual friends back in England, but to no avail. Then, realizing it was getting late and not wishing to disturb people unnecessarily, decided there was no more to be done until the morning. If, as he feared, she was ignoring him on purpose, eventually she would calm down and start answering her phone. If not, Damian would find her much sooner and easier than he could from Greece. There was little else he could do tonight except wait to hear from her or their son. In a daze he wandered into his tiny bathroom and prepared for bed. He was worried, but as he stood under the shower, piping hot water cascading over his aching, tired body, he realized Marjorie's disappearance wasn't the only thing worrying him. Veronica's assertion regarding Berswiski's sister was very concerning indeed. It certainly answered a lot of questions, questions which had been plaguing the whole team since the very beginning.

But more importantly, it also gave the them the lead they had been so desperately searching for. If Veronica was right, then they knew where Svetlana Berswiski was, and if she didn't suspect the team knew her secret then she could quite possibly lead them to her brother.

The Major had already phoned Randall from the restaurant, explained the situation and instructed him what to do next. By now, everything should be in place.

But there was something else which in a way, was even more worrying, something which had happened later, when he'd seen Veronica to her room and wished her good night. She had kissed him.

"Goodnight V," he'd said and then leaned forward, as he had done so many times before, to give her a peck on the cheek. His head turned right, her head turned left and their lips touched. It was chaste and fleeting and probably meant nothing, but then she'd reached up and stroked his face, gently, tenderly. Was it just one of those little mishaps? Something not even worth thinking about? Or had it been deliberate? The more he thought about it, the more it seemed that she had turned her head intentionally at the last second, so that the kiss was unavoidable. It was all very disconcerting. Of course Edmond liked the woman, liked her more than he cared to admit. He'd also been away from home too long. He was lonely and missed Marjorie more than he'd thought possible. Veronica was nearby and the thought she might have feelings for him left him in a place he simply didn't want to be. It was easier to put his attraction for her to one side if he felt he didn't have a snowballs chance in hell anyway. Now he was faced a question he'd rather not know the answer to. It was all so very distressing.

He drew back the shower screen and stepped out into the bathroom. He reached out with a hand towel, wiped the condensation off the steamed up mirror and stood looking critically at his reflection. It was true he was past his prime, and had that dreadful, badly washed ashtray complexion, but he had to admit, for sixty-two he didn't cut such a bad figure. He worked out every day in the gym for at least an hour. He ate well. Didn't drink too much. Didn't smoke or do drugs, and more importantly, at least when it came to attracting a more mature woman, one who was likely to want a companion with more than just good looks, he had charm, wit and..... And what?

Suddenly he felt very foolish. Who was he trying to kid. Even if he hadn't been married, she was out of his league. She was stunningly beautiful, sexy and if that wasn't enough, she was also rich, rich even by American standards. Veronica Crystal wasn't the type of woman to look twice at someone like Edmond Grey romantically. She was a friend. A good friend yes, but even so just a friend. The kiss had been accidental. Of course it had. What an idiot he was being. Or was he?

He towelled himself off, went back into the bedroom and put on his pyjamas. Then he sat on the bed, opened his briefcase and pulled out the report Veronica had given him, plus the DNA profile on Vladimir Berswiski he had collected from the office on the way back to the hotel. He didn't for even a second profess to understand the intricacies of the printouts in front of him. That was for the geeks and boffins in the lab to know and understand. But he knew enough to realize that when the peaks and troughs of the two graphs virtually mirrored each other, as these two did, then it meant that the two DNA samples must come from close family members. Probably siblings. Damn, Veronica Crystal had been right.

He knew she would still be awake and he was just about to call her and tell her the news when there was a knock on the door. Another mystery was about to be solved, when he opened the door, Marjorie Grey stood there, suitcase in hand and a big grin on her face.

Chapter 37

If Alan Tew was to be asked about his religious persuasion, he would almost certainly answer that he was agnostic, laced with a large dose of disinterest. He didn't have a lot of time for religion. It wasn't that he had anything against religious people, nothing he could use anyway. But it was a fact that religion, all forms of religion, had the unhappy knack of sometimes producing the odd radical. Such a person was not content to be smug in their beliefs, sit quietly at home waiting to die and be taken up to heaven, they had to go and try to show the non-believers the error of their ways and try to convert them. Such a man was Cyrus Wimple.

Cyrus and his equally intrusive wife Sofia, was a fully-fledged, card-carrying operative with the Jehovah's Witness Relocation plan and as such, felt it was his right, if not his duty, to convert as many sinners to the way of the Lord as he could.

Cyrus was American, fat, balding, well past his use by date and fortunately for him, rich. Cyrus's yacht, 'The Light', was an enormous motor launch that cost more to run for a single week, than most middle class, two car families would spend on fuel in a year. When Alan went up on deck early in the morning, he found 'The Light' had moved into the anchorage and Cyrus's tender was bearing down on them at a great rate of knots.

"Hi!" drawled Cyrus in a broad Texan accent. "May we come aboard?" Alan replied that they were welcome and lowered the boarding ladder. Cyrus introduced himself and his partner and launched into the reason for his early morning visit. "We wanted to talk to you about Jesus", he announced.

"Sorry", replied Alan "I can't help you I'm afraid, I'm allergic to dairy products." Cyrus and Sofia looked as confused as a bisexual's address book.

"What's that got to do with Our Lord Jesus Christ?"

"Oh, sorry Cyrus", said Alan, "I thought you said cheeses. I've just been in the shower and I've got a bit of water in my ears."

At that moment Iris decided to come up on deck. She was still wearing her normal night attire, that is, a pair of blue, floral pyjama shorts and a pair of earrings. She was naked from the waist up and was busily scrubbing away at her teeth with her toothbrush, her golden tipped breasts jiggling rapidly as she did so.

"Morbing Darbing", she mumbled to Alan around a mouthful of foaming white toothpaste. She saw they had company and so walked to the side of the boat to get rid of the toothpaste. She spat over the side, rinsed her mouth from the glass she carried, spat again and then turned to the two strangers and introduced herself.

"Don't you think you should put some clothes on dear", whined Sofia, her voice turbo charged with three thousand volts of moral indignation. Iris contemplated the question, formulated an answer but then decided that 'Get Fucked' was probably a little too strong. In an instant she had recognized the two Americans for what they were, interfering old busy bodies.

"No", she replied, "no one can see."

"We can", whined Sofia.

"That's easily fixed," said Iris and stripping off her pyjama shorts, dove naked over the side.

As Iris's beautiful body hit the water, Stefan came up on deck. He too was dressed in his night attire. The Wimple's quickly decided that as the wearer was a male member of the human species, a pair of shiny satin shorts was quite an acceptable form of dress. So they were not too concerned. But to Cyrus and Sofia's dismay, Stefan also dropped his pants and after grunting his good morning, dove over the side to join Iris.

It should be mentioned at this point that as loveable and adorable as Peggy was, she was not a morning person, and 7:42 am was definitely not her favourite time of the day. Not even close. She came up on deck, and snarled a greeting to Alan and the two Americans. She had been listening to Cyrus's initial comments about the 'Good Lard Cheeses' from her bed below deck and had it not been for the imminent explosion of her bladder, would have remained cowering below until the God botherer's had gone back to their own boat. Peggy's night wear was different from that of the other female sailor, consisting of a very short, highly transparent 'Baby doll' nightie, under which she wore what at first looked like a pair of tiny fur covered knickers, but of course, it wasn't.

"Good Lord", snapped Cyrus and Sofia in unison, "doesn't anyone on this boat have any decency?"

"Oh! Fuck off, you sanctimonious bastards" roared Peggy. "Nudity has nothing to do with decency. Decency is about how you treat people. What you wear is called fashion. Decent people treat others with respect and honesty. For example, decent people don't go around annoying other people at ungodly hours in the morning..."

Cyrus and Sofia Wimple did not hear the rest of Peggy's outburst. They ran to the side of the boat, scurried over the side and roared off back to 'The Light' as fast as their overpowered tender could take them. To their credit they did not let the sinful little Australian woman's antics drive them away totally and remained in the anchorage until around midday. Peggy calmed down eventually, and although later that morning she decided to do her yoga exercises, naked, and up on deck and in full view, it was not she assured everyone, to annoy the Wimples. Yea Right.

Chapter 38

Marjorie Grey was shocked at how sickly her poor husband looked when he opened the door and found her standing there grinning like a mischievous schoolgirl. Twelve hours ago she'd been angry with him, livid, because he'd once again put his family second after his beloved job. But she'd calmed down and forgiven him, berated herself in fact, for being selfish when what she should have been doing was supporting him when he obviously needed her most.

Then she'd received a phone call from the American woman, Veronica Crystal. Marjorie had a vague recollection of meeting her, twenty years ago or more. Edmond and she had worked together in Germany shortly after he joined Interpol. If Marjorie's memory was accurate she was with the CIA and had been seconded to Edmond's team at her own request. She'd introduced herself with the words,

"I don't know if you remember me but..."

Then she'd gone on to explain the reason for her call. She was worried about the Major. He was working himself to the bone she'd said and Veronica believed he was letting himself get emotionally involved with the victims. He wasn't eating properly or even regularly, and Veronica was sure he was getting precious little sleep in the evenings. The stress was taking a terrible price on his health.

Marjorie interjected. Told the American woman about their plan to spend some time together over the next two weekends and how Edmond had cancelled at the last minute.

"I've told him he doesn't have to worry so much now that your lot and all the others are taking an interest. But you know what Edmond's like. Always feels like he has to save the world," she'd said.

"Yea you're right," replied Veronica, "that's the reason I decided to stick my nose in where it might not belong. Now would be the perfect time for Edmond to take a few days off. We've all suggested it to him but he ignores us. I hope he'll listen to you."

"So what do you think I should do?"

"Jump on the next plane to Athens and get him out of the place. If not for the weekend then at least for a few hours. Eddie needs a shoulder to lean on at the moment and because of his position, and with his stiff upper lip, British stoicism, he won't accept it from me or one of the others in the team."

Perhaps she was right, perhaps Eddie needed her support. Or perhaps the American woman was just being a busy body. Or maybe there was an ulterior motive behind her phone call. Perhaps she wanted Edmond off the scene so she could run things her own way. Whatever the reason, Marjorie Grey wasn't going to give anyone the opportunity to claim she'd been warned and had ignored good advice. So she asked the two boys to go around to the house to feed Grombletic the cat and water the plants for the next few days, and then booked herself a flight to Athens.

Airfares were incredibly cheap at the moment, what with the global financial crisis and things. And as she'd already informed the girls at her bridge club she'd be away for two weeks, there was precious little reason to stay at home vegetating, when she could just as easily hop on a plane and visit Edmond in Greece. Not to mention, keep an eye on the interfering Veronica Crystal.

But as soon as Edmond opened the door Marjorie knew that Veronica's intentions were honourable and her concerns warranted. He looked dreadful. Dead on his feet. His eyes were red rimmed and bloodshot, and even though he was obviously glad to see her, Edmonds greeting lacked any real enthusiasm.

"Marjorie! What are you doing here?"

"Well Eddie, if Mohamed won't come to the mountain..."

They embraced and pecked each other on the lips old fart style, Edmond invited her in and then ducked out into the hallway to recover her luggage.

"I've been trying to get you one the phone for the past hour," he told her, "I've been worried sick."

"Yes, I know. Damien phoned me. He and the others are all in on my little plot to surprise you. When I got off the plane there were messages from you and one from Damien telling me you were worried. Sorry about that, but you can't surprise people if you let them know in advance now, can you?"

The major agreed and for the first time since her arrival smiled broadly.

"Well," he said, "I think this calls for a celebration. I think a bottle of Moet and a dozen oysters are in order." He picked up the phone and dialled the front desk. It wasn't really the type of establishment which offered room service, but because of his busy schedule, the Major had already had the occasion to ask the desk clerk to run across the road to the twenty-four-hour market for midnight supplies. He was a big tipper and the desk clerk had a large extended family to support. The young man was more than happy to oblige.

Marjorie had Edmond heave her suitcase up onto the bench and began to unpack. While she did so she chatted away at a mile a minute telling Edmond all the news from home and setting out the itinerary for the next three days. She realized the Major had work to do and that it was work of the utmost importance, but that didn't mean Edmond had to work himself into an early grave. He'd be no use to anyone, least of all Marjorie and the kids, if he died of a heart attack due to stress and overwork.

"So," she proclaimed as she draped a final blouse over a coat-hanger and hung it in the wardrobe. "I suggest we have mornings off. You can go into work after lunch at one and work until..say...seven at night."

Edmond smiled. Whenever Marjorie decided to take control of the situation, it reminded him of that old saying 'Behind every great man is a nagging bitch who can't be ignored or dissuaded.'

"I'm afraid it isn't quite as simple as that dear. I can't just take time off whenever it pleases me. I have people who rely on me."

"It's all arranged Edmond. I spoke to your young Mr. Randall. He's reworked the roster with the others to cover for you for the next three mornings."

Despite the realization he would be wasting his time, Edmond was prepared to argue the point, but just at that moment supper arrived. In typical Greek fashion the oysters had morphed into some sort of smoked mussel dish and the Moet had been replaced by a bottle of cheap sparkling crap from Italy.

They consumed it all anyway and found it surprisingly palatable. Despite his misgivings, the next three mornings of R&R proved to be just what the doctor ordered.

Chapter 39

Marjorie Grey spent the next nine days in Athens, and even though the Major managed to wrangle only two afternoons off to spend with her during that extra time, her visit proved to be very cathartic. She was there waiting for him in their tiny hotel room each evening when he finally finished work, and she sent him off each morning with a kiss and a wish for a pleasant and hopefully successful day. For Edmond, each and every moment they spent together was like a breath of fresh air. Every waking second the Major and his team had spent during last few months had been taken up by the murdering bastard Berswiski or his bomb. Marjorie brought back a little normalcy to Edmonds life. At dinner each evening the topics they discussed were simple, even mundane. Things like the grand kids, how they were doing at school or kindergarten. How the garden at home was desperately crying out for a little masculine TLC. Or how Marjorie's friend Clara was taking the world of acting by storm. At least she was as far as their tiny local theatre group was concerned. This type of stuff brought Edmond back to earth with a thump. It gave him a sense of reality and at the same time gave him something else to think about besides Berswiski.

Initially, Marjorie hadn't intended to tell Edmond of Veronica Crystals phone call, but it had somehow slipped out. So on the fourth night of Marjorie's visit, the Grey's invited Mrs Crystal to dinner to thank her for her kindness and sensitivity. Once again they patronized the wonderful restaurant at Veronica's hotel and as with the first evening both the food and the company were excellent. The two women hit it off and were soon chatting together like old friends.

Of course Edmond would never mention to anyone, least of all either his wife or Veronica about his concern about 'that kiss'. Looking back at the incident, he now realized he'd been very foolish. Veronica was a caring, thoughtful and insightful woman and the kiss meant nothing. But he began to believe Veronica's call to Marjorie was not entirely charitable. He suspected she had noticed his attraction to her and had called his wife to nip things in the bud before they got out of hand. Veronica Crystal was very astute, as her discovery of Svetlana Berswiski's involvement had proven.

Chapter 40

When he'd said that Avril Jones was a genius, and that she could find ground breaking information that everyone else missed, the Major should have stood and taken a bow for being astute. He was right on the money. Though if he was honest with himself, he'd have to admit that this time it was due to a huge dollop of luck.

Once it was revealed that this was more than just a serial murder case, that there was a good probability there was a fully operational nuclear weapon lying somewhere in Greece, it understandably became a matter of international importance. The CIA got involved, the MI5 and every Police force and Secret Service agency in Europe. All Governments and Ministries of Defence, of every country from France to Russia and south to North Africa, also got involved. And everyone wanted to be kept informed of any development, as soon as it happened.

Each and every day Edmond Grey and his team received requests from a multitude of desperately interested groups wanting to know what the hell was going on and what progress had been made in the search for Vladimir Berswiski, and more importantly, the nuclear weapon he was reputed to have in his possession.

The Major decided the best way to cope with the enormous workload these requests generated, was to issue a daily update, by e-mail, to any authorized person who requested one. The list grew inexorably by the hour.

Three and a half weeks into the investigation in Athens, the Major received a request from NATO that another name be added to their list. The name was Karl Sigmund Schnauzer.

The request was passed on to Avril Jones who promptly entered it into her data base. But for some reason the name rang a bell in Avril's mind. Of course with a name like Schnauzer he could have just been someone she'd dated, but the thought that she'd seen the name before, and just recently, kept niggling at her. She clicked open her file on Berswiski's known associates and trolled down through the list. There it was, Karl Sigmund Schnauzer.

Schnauzer was German. A few years ago, before the wall came down and Germany was reunited into one great uber Deutzland he would have been classified as East German. A communist. In fact he was a member of the dreaded Stazi. He had spent time working as what today would be called a systems analyst, and it was in this capacity he had come in contact with their quarry.

What if this man was the same, Karl Sigmund Schnauzer?

Avril made a few inquirys, called in a couple of favours and formulated a plan. It was brilliant in its simplicity and Avril Jones couldn't think of a single reason why it wouldn't work perfectly. She'd show that asshole Grey and the rest of them who was the real brains behind the team. Later that day, at the end of her shift, she packed up her laptop, stuffed it inside her briefcase and called a taxi.

The following day, for the first time in nearly five years, Avril Jones didn't show up for work.

Chapter 41

Dave Randall gazed down at his beautiful wife Marika, and smiled. He was the happiest man alive. The door to the private hospital room swung open and a nurse carrying something small wrapped in a tiny blue blanket entered and presented Mr. and Mrs. Randall with their new baby boy.

"Congratulations to you both", beamed the nurse, "you have a beautiful son."

The nurse's face changed into a look of disgust and she held out the bundle at arm's length,

"It's a pity he's such a naughty little boy". Dave Randall took his son in his arms and looked down at him. He had a pinched look to his face, a nose that seemed much to big for his small head and a pair of bucked teeth that looked for all the world like incisors.

"Hello Daddy", said the child and with a start Dave realized that the child was speaking Russian. "I'm hungry", screamed the baby and launched itself out of Dave's arms and onto Marika's lap.

"Feed me", he commanded. Marika smiled and opened the front of her robe and offered a swollen breast to her new son.

"No", bellowed Dave as Baby Berswiski bit down onto his wife's nipple. She screamed and gallons of blood poured down her stomach soaking the bed.

"Excuse me Mr. Randall", interrupted the nurse, "but your phone is ringing".

And it was.

Dave Randall sat up in bed with a start. The dream had him covered in sweat and his heart was racing. The phone on the bedside table jangled noisily until he picked it up. Grey was on the other end.

"There will be a car outside your hotel in about three minutes", announced the Major. "A security guard at the airport has reported seeing a man fitting Berswiski's description. He followed the suspect to a small hotel in Athens. He has a young girl in the room with him, so we must move quickly. Full assault gear please Mr. Randall."

The line went dead. Dave was pleased that something was finally happening. He had spent the last few days pouring over every scrap of evidence and hearsay they had on the mad Russian, and he had begun to suspect Berswiski had once again slipped through their fingers.

As promised, the car was waiting when Randall burst through the door of his hotel. He sprinted the few metres to the passenger side and jumped in. The driver was a local Athens man who had been assisting Grey's team since their arrival in the city.

"Hi Spiros" greeted Dave, as he buckled himself in for the breakneck race to Berswiski's hotel. "Good to see some action at last, hey? Any further information come to light since Grey's call to arms?"

Spiros replied in heavily accented English.

"Still no confirmation that the target is Berswiski, but from the description it has to be him. The girl is thought to be a prostitute. The Major he thinks she's safe for the time being, there would be too many witnesses and too much noise for Berswiski to try anything while their both still at the hotel. He'll have to take her to a quieter location before he makes his move."

"What's the plan of attack?" asked Dave.

"The target is on the third floor, room 307, nine others on the floor. Access is by stairs and elevator to a common hallway and by a fire escape. Two operatives will secure the downstairs foyer and the rest of the team will pair off and move in. Grey will let us know the details when we get there".

For the rest of the drive, which took less than four minutes, the two Interpol agents travelled in silence. Randall rechecked his equipment automatically as his mind raced through every conceivable scenario that might occur during the next half hour or so. He was glad of one thing. Even though Grey was confident the girl in Berswiski's room was safe for the time being, the assault would commence as soon as humanly possible. The risk was just too great to do otherwise. Besides, after weeks of following one dead end lead after another, Dave's nerves were not up to sitting around for hours waiting for something to happen.

The car screeched to a halt outside a dingy, run down hotel that backed onto a vacant block. It was the perfect place for someone on the run to hide out. Grey and the rest of the team had massed in an alleyway across the road and as soon as Dave and Spiros arrived, he set out the plan of attack.

"Dave and Jim will take the fire escape. Berswiski is on the third floor, fourth window along. Tran and Santos will take the lift, sorry elevator, and Spiros and I will take the stairs. The foyer has already been secured by Veronica and a few members of the local constabulary. There are more blockading the streets as we speak. We go in on my command not before. Understood? Any questions?"

No one raised their hand, so the Major issued the order to take up their positions. Randall clipped on his video camera as he ran for the fire escape and adjusted the tiny microphone of his communication unit so it was directly in front of his mouth. He and Jim Exeter reached the bottom of the fire escape and cautiously started up. The fire escape was old and rickety, and despite their best efforts at being quiet, it rattled alarmingly. Someone on the second floor had the radio blaring and Dave mentally crossed his fingers, hoping that the noise of Judith Durham and Ozy Osborne's latest musical collaboration, 'The Carnival Is Over So Fuck Off', would cover their noisy ascent. When they'd reached the third floor and made their way to the fourth window along, Dave tapped rapidly four times on his microphone and listened. A few moments later two taps sounded in his earpiece. Team two was also in position. Soon all four teams were in place, and after a few moments Dave heard a high-pitched beep indicating that the ten-second countdown had started. Exeter raised a grenade like object above his head and pressed the button on top.

"Three, two, one, go, go, go" yelled Grey's voice in Dave's earpiece and he swung the butt of his machine pistol through the glass window. Jim lobbed in the grenade and covered his eyes. Rather than an explosion, there was a pop and a brilliant flash of light which left the room's occupants blinded for a few seconds, long enough for the six Interpol agents to storm the room and capture the man and woman inside. The plan went like clockwork and the male occupant was easily apprehended. There was however one minor problem. The man inside was not Vladimir Berswiski.

When six heavily armed gun men smashed their way into his room, threw him to the floor and held a machine gun to the back of his bald head, Fabrice Delaine had nearly soiled his pants. No small feat considering his pants were on the back of a chair on the opposite side of the room. He was in Athens on business and like many other French men, when he was away from home, he frequently liked to sample the offerings of the local women of the night. The security guards mistake was understandable. Delaine was bald, short, scrawny and had a prominent nose but there the similarity between him and Berswiski ended. Nevertheless, Grey had him taken in for questioning, just in case he had seen something since arriving at Athens airport an hour and twenty-seven minutes ago.

The prostitute was also a surprise. Rather than a Greek woman, the girl was an Irish backpacker. She'd run out of money and had foolishly decided that the quickest and easiest way to supplement her travelling kitty was to do a bit of freelance work as a sperm donor recipient.

It was Interpol protocol that all females taken in for questioning be interviewed with a female agent present. Mrs Crystal was only on loan from the CIA and had already gone beyond the call of duty many times already, so Grey didn't want to stretch the friendship too much, but he really didn't have any choice. There was still no sign of Ms Jones and she hadn't answered the numerous calls he'd made to her mobile. He'd considered sending a car to fetch her from her temporary home in Koropi, but he wasn't even sure she was there. Pity, she'd have liked to be picked up and driven to work, there was little Jones liked better than a ride in the back seat of a speeding car, with her head thrust out the window, her tongue hanging out and her ears flapping in the breeze.

When Veronica arrived, Grey took the young girl to the interview room and put on his 'Concerned Gentleman' alter ego. The young Irish woman went on the defensive immediately, professing her innocence and then when that didn't work, she became abusive and demanded to see a lawyer. Grey smiled charmingly.

"My dear young lady", he said in his best upper class twit accent, "we pose absolutely no legal threat to you. You have not been arrested and we have no intention of doing so. We merely wish to make sure you're alright. There have been a number of attacks on young prostitutes in this area over the last few days and we felt you might be in danger".

The Irish girl thawed slightly. Delaine had been her first trick and if she was honest with herself, she was happy they had been interrupted. She explained as much to the Major, admitting to him that she had been a fool, and promising she would never bob for apples in a strangers lap for money ever again. Smith was not convinced and although it was not his concern, he decided that the silly girl needed a little extra persuasion.

"That's excellent news my dear", he continued pleasantly, "perhaps you might look at these photos and tell me if you recognize anyone. They are pictures of the other prostitutes I mentioned, the ones that have been murdered. You may have seen them around."

The girl glanced down at the first photo and gasped. It was a colour photo of Berswiski's latest victim. The poor woman had been brutally mutilated, her eyes had been burnt out with a blowtorch and she still had the large electric drill Berswiski had used protruding from between her legs.

"Sweet Jesus, Mary and Joseph", cried the Irish lass, "what sort of monster would do that to another human being?"

Grey decided it was time to get tough.

"Well", he snapped angrily, "it might have been the man you were with tonight or perhaps the next man you decide to show a good time to."

He threw the next photo onto the table in front of them. It was of the girl from the old farm house.

"Oh fucking hell", said the Irish girl, choking back tears and trying desperately to stop herself from throwing up.

"You see you stupid bitch," snarled Grey. "This is what you risk every time you sell yourself to a stranger. These girls died in agony to satisfy the perverted desires of a madman and if you continue on the path you have chosen, you might well be next".

The girl sobbed and once again promised that she would never again turn to prostitution, this time with more conviction. Grey put his hand in his pocket, pulled out his wallet and extracted a large wad of notes. He handed the money to the girl.

"Now go home or if you must, continue your holiday in Greece, but keep your nose clean and don't ever go anywhere, night or day by yourself. Is that clear?"

After the girl had been escorted from the building, Grey spent a few minutes writing up his notes on the night's events.

"You didn't have to do that" commented Veronica Crystal.

"It's only money" answered The major. "My own money, I might add, not the agency's."

"I know, but I was actually talking about the lecture, scaring the girl like that. It's not our job."

Grey was angry.

"It has nothing to do with the job V. That girl is somebody's daughter. Somebody has to make her see sense. Point out to her that she is on a very dangerous path. Whether it was Berswiski, some other bloody loony or just someone with a horrible disease, if she continues to work as a prostitute, she will end up dead. I do what I have to do and I refuse to apologize for it."

Chapter 42

Over the past few centuries. the Mediterranean Sea had been fished to the point where some forms of sea life are now almost non-existent. Nevertheless, both Alan and Stefan regularly wet a line or jumped over the side with a spear gun. Somehow they always seemed to manage to catch something edible for dinner. Alan had taught himself to fish during his many years of sailing while Stefan was, predictably, the president of his university's fishing club. One day, Peggy decided she would like to try her hand with a fishing rod and enlisted her boyfriend's help.

"It's quite easy", said Stefan, as he stood beside Peggy, fishing rod in hand. "You just take the rod in your right hand like this, hold the line in your left hand, pull back this lever which lets the reel spin freely, swing the rod out and let go of the line".

Stefan demonstrated, swinging the tip of the rod in a lazy arc over the side of the yacht. The baited hook and heavy lead sinker whistled through the air and plopped into the water about ten meters away.

"Now you try," said Stefan after he had reeled in the line. Peggy held the rod as instructed, flicked back the aforementioned lever and with a mighty heave scythed an arc through the air right next to Stefan's ear. The fish-hook and sinker clattered onto the deck at Peggy's feet. Iris, who had been watching from what she considered to be a safe distance, moved another couple of metres further away.

"No honey, not like that, do it gently. It's all about inertia, not brute force", explained Stefan. Peggy tried again, this time the tip of the rod flew through the air with a hiss. The line went tight, the rod's motion stopped with a jerk. Stefan yelped, Iris gasped, and Peggy screamed. The big fish-hook had buried itself into the back of Stefan's leg. It was not a pretty sight. The hook was well and truly stuck.

Luckily, both Alan and Stefan knew what had to be done. As the fish-hook was barbed, there was no chance of just pulling it out. To try to do so would either tear a chunk out of Stefan's leg or worse, the hook would snap leaving the barb behind. Alan raced below deck and returned a few seconds later with a pair of pliers and some small bolt cutters.

"What the hell are you going to do with those things?" asked Iris who had run off to get the first aid kit.

"I have to push the hook through the skin and then cut off the barb so I can pull it back out" explained Alan. "Pass me the bottle of antiseptic please Iris, and then go down below and get the wooden chopping board from the galley".

When she returned, Alan had swabbed Stefan's leg with the antiseptic liquid and cut the fishing line. A large purple bruise had already appeared on Stefan's leg and Iris could see the fish-hook lying deep below the surface of his skin. Peggy had wrapped herself tightly around Stefan's neck. She was weeping great pools of tears and continually apologizing for the hurt she had caused.

"Iris!" called Alan "come here please and hold the chopping board like this". He demonstrated what he wanted, holding the corner of the board directly over the point of the fishing hook. "Sorry Stef, but this is going to hurt a bit I'm afraid."

The young Dutchman looked pale, but he nodded indicating that he understood.

Alan picked up the pliers and grasped the shank of the fish-hook. He pushed down firmly on to the chopping board so that the point of the hook had something to press against. If he didn't the hook would try to tear through the skin rather than piercing it cleanly.

"Ready?" he asked and when Stefan nodded his head, Alan pulled strongly on the pliers and the barb erupted through the skin. Stefan yelled something in Dutch that didn't need translating and went even more deathly pale.

"Okay", said Alan with a smile, "that's the worst part over. Now we just snip off the barb and pull the bugger back out". Alan picked up the bolt cutters. They looked like the tree pruners Iris had seen her father use around the garden at home. Alan placed the jaws of the cutter over the barb and squeezed the handles together. There was a metallic click and the barb shot off into the air. Seconds later the fish-hook had been pulled out.

The following day Peggy decided to try her hand at spear fishing. But quite inexplicably, the spear gun had gone missing.

Chapter 43

Like Alan Tew, Vladimir Berswiski did not believe in God, though perhaps Berswiski's theological determination was closer to absolute atheism than Alan's more open minded agnostic tendencies. The Russian was a scientist, and in his mind religious belief was ridiculous. It made no more sense to believe in Santa Clause, than in any of the multitude of fairy tales people of faith subscribed to. There was, as far as he was concerned, not one, single, solitary shred of evidence indicating in any way, that there might be an omnipotent force or being who had created the universe, and until there was Berswiski would remain a disbeliever. He had no time for religious people, with the exception of those who followed Judaism. For the Jews, he had all the time in the world. In fact the longer he could take killing one, the more he liked it.

Veronica Crystal would argue that as a psychopath, Berswiski was incapable of love, but in a way, she was wrong. Berswiski considered himself to be someone special, very special indeed. He believed himself to be the next stage in evolution, one unencumbered by the emotions or empathy of the worthless creatures who preceded him. He had an unshakeable ego, and an ego such as his could quite rightfully be considered as love. Self love. So, in a way, Berswiski was indeed capable of love. He was also capable of hate.

Just a few weeks before his twentieth birthday, Berswiski met a stunningly beautiful, raven haired Jewess. The girl's father was a major with the KGB and Berswiski figured such a man would be worth knowing. It seemed obvious to him that the best way to get to the father was to first ingratiate himself with the daughter.

He felt no love for the young woman. In fact, apart from a distaste for her simpering ways and her seemingly indefatigable obsession with her appearance, he felt nothing at all. But he was determined to win her over. He had observed how other men of his age wooed the objects of their desire and proceeded to emulate their actions. He lavished gifts upon the girl, all of which she returned unopened. He wrote her reams of poetry, which she threw unread into the fireplace, and he sent her flowers, which she buried in the compost heap at the bottom of her garden. Eventually, unable to bear the thought that he might fail in his attempts to win her heart, Berswiski went to her home, got down on one scrawny and deformed knee and asked for her hand in marriage. Predictably the beautiful Jewess rejected him. She informed him that she would not marry him, even if he were the last man on earth. She told him he was ugly, deformed, depraved and ate the flesh of swine. The girl finished by saying that she would rather be dead than marry him, and predictably Berswiski was only too happy to oblige. From that moment on, Berswiski hated all Jews.

It was this hatred that had convinced the 'arms dealer' that Berswiski would be the best man for the job. There was little chance, he felt, that the evil little rodent would have an attack of conscience and pull out, or worse still, inform someone of the Palestinians plans. But now the little shit had disappeared. And he'd taken the nuclear warhead with him.

The 'arms dealer' had been keeping an eye on things, remotely at least, while they waited for the heat to die down. He had made regular checks of the disused warehouse where they were storing the warhead, making sure it was safe until they were ready to load it onto the Iran bound freighter he arranged for the following day. Plus he had rigged an alarm to be sent to his computer should the GPS device attached to the bomb be moved anymore than a few centimetres. The tracking device was still sitting in the warehouse. The bomb itself was gone. All of which left the 'arms dealer' frightened, very, very frightened. The Palestinian group that had engaged him would not be happy with the unexpected turn of events. The fact that their deposit of two million dollars would be returned to them, really wouldn't compensate for the loss of their prized acquisition. All the efforts they had put into planning the destruction of Tal-Aviv would now have to be discarded. And that would be unacceptable.

Two days later, in response to the 'arms dealers' urgent phone call explaining what had happened, he received a visit.

"You have two choices", growled the angry Palestinian spokesman as he sat opposite the 'arms dealer.' "You will find this Russian scientist and retrieve our property or you will supply us with another nuclear weapon. You have one month to achieve one of these options. If you fail, we will find you and when we do, we will kill you. Very slowly".

As the 'arms dealer' was tied to a chair, had three broken ribs and had his mouth covered with tape, he was unable to answer. But the Palestinian didn't need an answer. He leaned forward and pulled out a huge, evil looking knife, reached up, grasped the arms dealers ear and sliced it off.

"I will return this to you when you have returned our property", the Palestinian said, as he calmly slipped the severed ear into the pocket of his robe. He rose and left, leaving the 'arms dealer' writhing in agony.

It took a little time to figure out a way of extracting himself from his bindings and a little more time to figure out what he was going to do next. The Palestinian had no way of knowing it would not be what he was expecting, and that he had, in fact, just signed his own death warrant.

If a person wished to purchase some serious weaponry, there were a number of avenues one could take. However, if the purchaser wanted the best weapons available, then he or she had no better recourse than to contact the 'arms dealer.' But to do so required a little bit of effort. Firstly one had to log onto the Internet and visit a number of web sites, each of which contained a coded message that translated to a single number. When the purchaser had decoded all of the messages, he or she then had a phone number which when dialled, led to a recording which simply said you had called a wrong number and you should check the number before dialling again.

However, things did not end there. A few minutes after making the call, the purchaser would be called back, and a man with an English accent would ask for details of the purchaser and the goods required. If he was satisfied that the inquiry was genuine, he would then arrange a meeting with the 'arms dealer'

The Englishman's name was Roland Crookwell, a nondescript little man who worked for a nondescript office supplies company somewhere in Kent. He was the only man in the world who knew how to contact the 'arms dealer' directly. This kept him, as much as humanly possible, out of reach of the law and earned Roland Crookwell a cool one thousand pounds, paid into a numbered Swiss bank account each and every week. After acting as a go-between for over seven years, Roland was a rich man and although he didn't know it, he was far more valuable than the mere grand the arms dealer paid him.

Two days after the Palestinian had visited him, the arms dealer flew into London's Heathrow airport. He hired a car and headed for Kent, then made his way to Rockwell's company and asked the receptionist if he might see him.

The receptionist was in her early thirty's and had died blonde hair, long tanned legs and large breasts, all of which indicated that it was highly unlikely the woman had been hired for her office skills. Unless of course you considered fucking the general managers brains out in the photocopier room, office skills.

"Mr. Crookwell?" the dizzy blonde receptionist said into the intercom, "there is a man here that wishes to speak to you. Shall I send him through?"

"Who is he?" asked an obviously frustrated Crookwell. The bloody stupid bitch wouldn't make a receptionist's arsehole. If she wasn't shagging the boss, she wouldn't have a job at all. How many times did he have to tell her? She must ask any callers for their name?

"He won't say, but he said you know him", she answered and then whispered "he has a German accent and his head is covered with bandages". Crookwell put two and two together and decided this was a visitor he could not refuse to see.

The 'arms dealer' carried a walking cane. It was a beautifully crafted piece, a sturdy oak stick topped by a skilfully carved sterling silver handle that had been fashioned in the shape of a wolf's head. It also contained a highly charged cartridge of compressed air and when the cane was pressed against the chest of the dizzy blonde receptionist and the hidden trigger pressed, it blew a hole right through her heart. The arms dealer made his way to the office of Roland Crookwell, opened the door, pushed the walking stick against the chest of his former employee and pressed the trigger. An hour later he was on a plane headed for Africa. He would have to create another system by which his customers could reach him, but for now his main concern was to prevent the Palestinians from finding him. He had to disappear for a short time. At least until he could devise a plan to extract his revenge for the loss of his ear. He also wanted to be as far away as possible from that mad bastard Berswiski, and the missing nuclear weapon.

Chapter 44

Milos Constantine, not his real name, lifted the large plastic tub full of dirty dishes, rested it on his portly stomach and staggered towards the kitchen. He pushed the 'in' door open with his shoulder and sidled past the throng of waiters, waitresses, chiefs and kitchen hands who were scurrying around the kitchen with all the frantic energy of puppies let loose in a kindergarten. Milos dumped the tub next to the sink, extracted a plate, scraped the uneaten food into the bin, rinsed the plate under the tap and placed it in the dishwasher rack. He extracted the next plate and repeated the procedure. When the rack was full, Milos pushed it into the automatic dishwasher, closed the lid and pressed the button. Whoosh went the dishwasher, and clouds of steam billowed from the machine saturating the air. Milos sighed. At fifty-one years of age he was beginning to realize his plan for a meteoric rise through the ranks of the hospitality industry, culminating in the managership of his very own five star resort was not proceeding as well as he had hoped.

Milos was born and lived the early part of his life on a desolate, unnamed, wind swept island in the middle of the Aegean Sea. The eldest son of a poor, simple fisherman and his wife, Milos spent his formative years helping his father with the nets, going to the islands tiny, one room school, and assisting his mother in caring for his younger siblings. There was precious little for his parents to do on the island in the evenings, so his siblings were numerous. In fact so often did his mother give birth that Milo's dad developed grave concerns about her ability to sit on a barstool. At fifteen, he got his first job as a dishwasher at the island's one and only taverna. The place was a dingy, flea bitten hovel which catered for a meagre handful of tourists who visited the island each year. Now, thirty-six years later, his career had progressed exactly nowhere. Sure the beautiful island of Sifnos was certainly not the desolate place his home had been, and the resort where he now worked was a far cry from the dump where he had started. But which ever way he looked at it Milos was still a mere dishwasher.

The huge infestation of tourists, and the correspondingly obscene amount of money they brought with them, was rapidly reaching plague proportions these days, but it made no difference to Milos. Very little of the money made its way into Milo's back pocket. At the end of each shift the dishwasher was so exhausted it was all he could do to walk the few hundred metres to the staff quarters, let himself into his tiny one room accommodation and collapse on the bed.

Milos sighed. It wasn't fair. He was a good employee and he worked hard. He was never late and over the past thirty-six years, he'd had exactly four point six days off due to illness.

He had also taken steps to make himself more attractive to each prospective and consecutive employer. He had learnt three languages, English, French and German and had taken every hospitality-based correspondence course he could find, passing every one with flying colours.

There was one consistent flaw in Milo's plan. Every time he got close to being promoted, someone would phone his manager and make an outrageous accusation.

"So", the caller would say "you have Milos Constantine working for you? You know that he fucks goats, don't you?"

Milos would be called to the office to answer the terrible accusation. He would vehemently deny everything, but even if the manager believed him and didn't fire him on the spot, it would only be a temporary reprieve. Soon the rumours would start to circulate and his friends would desert him. Inevitably his co-workers would begin to call him names or bleat at him whenever he passed by. At a resort he worked at two years ago, one apprentice chief even went so far as to ask him if he had ever done it with an Angora goat, and if so, was she a sweater or a jumper? Eventually Milos would be forced to leave his job and go somewhere else and to try to start again. The accusation was of course, ludicrous. How could anyone confuse a sheep with a goat? There was simply no comparison.

Milos turned once again to the enormous pile of dirty dishes and started to fill the next dishwasher rack. Scrape, rinse, stack: scrape, rinse, stack, working mechanically, without pause. Tonight it was well after midnight before he'd finished, and as he was getting ready to leave, one of the waitresses, a pretty little thing from a tiny village near Thessaloniki, told him that the manager had asked to see him before he went home. Milos took off his apron, collected his meagre belongings and left. He did not bother to see the manager. The man was a bastard, the type of person who it was rumoured, had once broken into a blind woman's home and moved all her furniture as a practical joke. He was an arsehole of colossal magnitude, someone who would be happy to have some new ammunition to make Milo's life even more miserable. There was no point in confronting his boss, Milos already knew what the outcome would be.

As he walked slowly back to his lodgings down near the waterfront, he thought once again about the events that had dogged his every step for the last thirty-five years. He had been a fool, a disgusting, despicable, deplorable fool and even now he had no idea what had possessed him. Sure he was young, insanely horny and his hormones had been jumping around like a spring lamb. But how many young men went through times like that? The answer was all of them, and they didn't feel the need to stick their willies into sheep. The truth was, he told himself, he was a deviate, a low life, a sheep fucking scumbag who wasn't worth the steam off a decent fart.

What had made him do it? She wasn't even an attractive sheep. She was old, mutton dressed as lamb in fact. But she had looked at him with those big brown eyes and in a microsecond she had turned from hotpot to sexpot. He had a terrible crush on her, those Acme sheep crushes were always terrible, and he had been unable to stop himself from walking around the back and giving lamb chop some pork chop.

Milos shuddered at the memory. God how he regretted his actions. He regretted he had been unable to control his urges. He regretted he had taken advantage of a defenceless animal, but most of all, he regretted that the sheepdog trials were on and the TV cameras were still rolling.

Around 1:00 am Milos found himself down by the harbour. He walked out along the old stone jetty stretching out into the bay and stood looking down into the lazily, swirling inky blackness of the water below him. The water looked deep and strangely inviting and Milos suddenly felt an inescapable desire to end it all. The water would envelop him and shut out all the pain and suffering he had caused himself with his despicable actions. He kicked off his shoes, and without a seconds hesitation, dove in.

"Shit", said Alan as he rowed the dinghy back towards 'Harvey Wharf Banger' "Some bloke's just jumped off the end of the jetty. He must have hit his head or something 'cause he hasn't come up again".

Alan turned the dinghy and pulled with all his might back towards the end of the jetty.

"There he is", cried Stefan, pointing at a dark shape floating face down in the water just a few metres away. Alan changed course and headed in the direction Stefan had indicated, ploughing through the water until they were less than a metre from the inert form floating face down in the water. He dug the oars in, stopping the row boat dead right next to the man. Alan was over the side in a split-second. He had been born in a time and place where the first thing a boy learnt to do was swim, and the second was how to stop your mates from drowning. Treading water, he rolled the unconscious man over onto his back, tilted his head back, pinched his nose closed and blew three quick lungfuls of air into him.

Alan slipped his arm under the shoulder of the unconscious Milos, and supporting his head with his left hand, swam around to the back of the dinghy. They needed to get him out of the water, but although he was short, he was very overweight and there was no way they could lift him over the side without capsizing the dinghy.

Alan held onto the stern of the row boat and told Stefan to head for shore. Iris and Stefan grabbed an oar each and rowed as if they were possessed. It took only minutes for them to reach the beach, but it seemed like an eternity. Stefan clambered out of the boat as it grounded on the pebbly beach and helped Alan drag the unconscious man out of the water. The two men then lifted him by his belt so that he hung upside down. Water poured out of his mouth and nose. They laid him down on his back and Stefan placed his fingers to his neck feeling for a pulse.

"No pulse", he said and pounded his fist into the man's sternum. Placing the heels of his hands he began to pump. "One- two- three-four- five", he counted out loud until he reached thirty. He stopped and Alan recommenced the mouth-to-mouth resuscitation, three breaths and then Stefan once again took his turn pumping the man's heart. Each time they changed, Stefan would check for a pulse. Suddenly, Stefan put his ear to Milo's chest and held up his hand for silence.

"I've got a pulse", he announced and a micro second later, Milos gasped a huge lungful of air and started coughing. "Turn him on his side", commanded Stefan.

Milos Constantine, not his real name, lived to fuck another sheep.

Chapter 45

Veronica Crystal was wrong in one other way about Berswiski. Psychopath or not, the man knew how to hate. For example, he absolutely loathed and detested the ocean. The constant, unbearable, nauseating motion made him feel ill. Very ill. Add to that the stench of the diesel, the stifling heat and noise in his cabin and Vladimir Berswiski would have rather dug out one of his eyes with a spoon than spend another second on the ancient timber freighter he had chartered to take him and his deadly cargo across the Mediterranean sea.

The only two things that gave him any comfort at all from his debilitating Mal-du-mer, was the certainty he would soon be digging someone else's eye out with a spoon, and, of course, the knowledge he had well and truly fucked up that arrogant 'arms dealers' plans.

For nearly three weeks he'd sat and watched the screen of his lap top computer for any sign that Iris Richards and her friends were about to make a move. But until four days ago they had stayed put. Now they were on their way, and according to the 'arms dealer's' wonderful little tracking device, they were headed for the island of Crete. From there, according to his contact in the Greek Customs and Immigration department, they were to sail onto Egypt.

Right from the very beginning the Russian had had no intention of fulfilling the 'arms dealers' wishes. There was, he admitted, a certain amount of appeal to detonating a nuclear device in the middle of Israel. But that plan was childish and moronic compared to the use Berswiski had in mind. The Palestinians were not thinking it through. Sure lots of Jews would die and as far as Berswiski was concerned that was a good thing. But once again the Jews would be seen as the victims and no one would blame them when the Israelis inevitably struck back, undoubtedly with far greater firepower.

So the Russian scientist had decided to steal the weapon for his own uses. He found himself a ship, or maybe it was a boat, he wasn't quite sure on that point. When exactly did a boat become a ship? One thing he did know was that it was timber. It had to be. Timber boats, or ships, were harder to detect with radar, and for obvious reasons that was imperative. It was also seventeen meters long and powered by a huge diesel motor. The ship was, according to the ship's Captain, capable of twenty-two knots. This was apparently quite rapid. Berswiski knew little about such things and cared even less. As long as the thing could get him and the Palestinians warhead across the Mediterranean to Egypt, he would be satisfied.

He had arranged the charter of the vessel in the age-old manner of parking his arse at a bar frequented by sailor types down at the docks, and making a few surreptitious inquiries. Within a matter of hours, he had ferreted out the Captain of a Panamanian registered vessel, who was willing to take Berswiski and his unspecified cargo to Egypt. For a further monetary consideration, the voyage could be done under the cover of darkness and without the knowledge of either Greek or Egyptian Customs and Immigration.

Berswiski's original plan had been to shadow Iris Richards across the Mediterranean to Alexandria. But the Captain had pointed out that this, while possible, was a really bad idea. Sailing yachts of the type sailed by Alan Tew had an average speed of about six knots. Or to put it another way, you could run faster. Not only that, but it wasn't as if you could hide behind traffic and watch from a distance. They would easily recognize they were being followed and would quite likely report it to the Greek Water Police. So it was decided that they would head straight for Alexandria and Berswiski would wait there for his new playmate to arrive.

However, things were not going according to plan. Just sixty nautical miles out from Kea the heap of shit motor broke down. It was something to do with the diesel injectors according to the ship's captain. The mechanic, who was also the navigator and the ship's cook, was trying to rectify the problem as quickly as possible.

For the next three days the ship, or boat, sat becalmed one hundred and thirty-two nautical miles from the nearest land, or as the captain joyfully told him, about two hundred metres from the nearest land, if you included the bit directly below them. Berswiski did not. The mechanic stripped the injectors, cleaned them of carbon build up and reassembled them. The motor refused to start and the Captain flattened the batteries trying.

"Is not problem," said the Captain in heavily accented English. "We have generator to recharge batteries."

The generator was an old Cummins diesel beast which refused to start.

"Is not problem," said the Captain. "We clean injectors. Good as new"

It took another day to get the generator going and a few hours to charge the batteries and nearly another day to clean and bleed the air out of the fuel lines on the main motor. Eventually the engine roared into life and the Captain pointed the old tub south.

During the whole time Berswiski remained in his tiny, claustrophobic cabin, only leaving his bunk when he needed to urinate, defecate or throw up. Even so he spent the time constructively. He came up with a whole knew gamut of ways he was going to make that Australian bitch Richards pay for escaping the first time.

Chapter 46

When Milos hit the water, he swam down, as fast and as deep as he could, blowing out every vestige of air as he went. He didn't want to have time to change his mind, but just as he reached the point of no return, change it he did. He was a fool, he didn't need to do this. With the advent of the EU, travel around Europe was now quite simple. He could move to another country, assume another identity and get himself another job, a job out of the industry that knew and despised him so much. Milos turned for the surface, but it was too late. He was starting to black out and as he did, his reflexes took over and he opened his mouth and filled his lungs with seawater. As Milos died his whole life flashed before his eyes. Unfortunately it was so boring he fell asleep half-way through. When he woke again there was a large Australian man trying to kiss him. There was also another man standing by and two young women. All looked extremely relieved to see that Milo's attempt at suicide had been unsuccessful.

Iris tried to ask him if he was alright, but her Greek wasn't really up to the task. Peggy started to giggle. "What?" asked Iris.

"I think you just asked him 'What's it like?" answered Peggy.

"Shit, does anyone know what's Greek for 'Are you alright?'" No one knew the answer except Milos, but he was still trying to get his breath.

"It's okay (cough, splutter)", said Milos "I know (hack, wheeze) how to speak (gurgle) English. Thank you for saving my life. (Cough, cough, cough) I will be alright in a minute."

The four shipmates conferred and came to the conclusion that he most certainly wouldn't be. The man had nearly drowned. He had stopped breathing and his heart had stopped. You didn't just shrug something like that off. Milos needed medical attention and as soon as possible.

No one was sure whether there was a hospital on Sifnos. And even if there was a doctor, he or she would almost certainly be based at Apollonia, in the centre of the island. So it was decided that the best course of action was to take Milos back to 'Harvey'. The most important thing now was to get him dry and warm and to get some antibiotics into him. Lung infection was a very real risk.

Laying in the bottom of the dinghy on the way back to the yacht, Milos had time to reflect, and to think up a story that explained his situation. One without alluding to his unique interpretation of animal husbandry.

"My name is Milos Constantine," said Milos Constantine, (not his real name), when they were all settled back on the yacht. "Once again let me thank you for saving my life. I am afraid I have been very foolish. My dear, sweet mother died just recently and I didn't have any money to pay for her funeral." The audience made the appropriate 'sympathy' noises and Milos continued. "I borrowed the money from my employer without asking him and he found out before I could repay him. I lost my job and felt that no one on the island would employ me if they thought I was a thief. I was so distraught, I tried to take my own life. But I now realize, that where there is life there is hope. I will just have to move to another place and start again"

Milos looked forlorn. No one on board had had clothes that would fit the plump little Greek. So after removing his sodden clothing, Alan had given him an old sleeping bag to wrap around himself. As he sat shivering in the salon. He reminded Iris of a news item she had seen on television a few years back during the 1998 Sydney to Hobart yacht race. There had been a terrible storm and many yachts had foundered, six men lost their lives and many more had to be rescued by Air Sea Rescue. Iris had seen an interview with one of the rescued men. He was wrapped in a blanket, shivering uncontrollably, distraught at the loss of his friend but trying, as Milos was, to find some hope for the future.

"I will go now", said Milos, "if you would be kind enough to row me back to shore, please" The others would not hear of it. Milos would have to stay on board overnight so Stefan could keep an eye on him. Stefan felt he might be suffering from hypothermia and the risk of pneumonia was very real. Peggy suggested she and Stefan give up their bed for the night so that Milos could get a good night's sleep. They would decide what was to be done in the morning.

Milos did not get a good night's sleep. In fact he could not sleep at all. He tried counting sheep, but that just made him horny. Providence had provided him with an opportunity to change his life and his excitement was palpable. This was an opportunity he was determined to grasp with both hands.

In the morning Stefan pronounced Milos to be greatly improved, adding that medically speaking, as he had been clinically dead just a few hours ago 'greatly improved' was entirely subjective.

"I have pounded on his back to help him cough up any sea water still in his lungs and injected another 5cc's of antibiotics into his substantial buttocks", explained Stefan "Now we wait and see. If his condition deteriorates, then we will have to get him to a doctor as soon as possible."

By the end of the first day of Milo's recuperation he was sitting up in bed, chatting amiably with his benefactors, seemingly no worse for wear.

"So where are you headed after you leave Sifnos?" asked Milos.

"Crete" answered Alan.

"Might I ask you a favour, please Alan?" ventured the tubby man, "Could you take me with you?" Milos went on to explain that the hospitality industry in the Aegean Islands was a very tight-knit community. The news of his sacking and the reason for it would, by now have travelled via the grapevine to every resort, hotel, and taverna in the area. He had little or no chance of ever working in the industry ever again.

"I hope to make a new start in a different field somewhere. Crete would be an excellent place to try", explained the fat little Greek. "I could catch the ferry, but I am afraid I gave every Euro I had to my ex boss. I admit that it was not all that I owed him, but I intend to pay him back in full as soon as I can. I know that stealing is wrong and I am deeply ashamed of what I have done. If you could help me, not only would I be able to make amends, I would also be eternally grateful."

One of the things that Alan had told Iris when she had joined him on "Harvey" was, if there was to be any addition or deletion to the crews company, then all existing crew would have a vote on the subject. If anyone already signed up did not want the new person to join them, then the applicant could take a hike. However, in practice it wasn't as simple as that may sound.

Alan, Peggy and Stefan were all enthusiastic about helping Milos and so Iris felt she had little choice but to cast her vote in Milo's favour as well and make it unanimous. The truth was, Iris was not at all happy about having the fat little Greek join them. She was, however, magnanimous enough to recognize that she was being selfish. She was deliriously happy with the tiny world she had made for herself and Alan. Peggy and Stefan were happy too and she didn't want anyone upsetting the status quo.

Her love for Alan had grown stronger each day and she knew beyond any shadow of doubt that Alan loved her in return. He showed it in so many ways. He would pick her wild flowers at each of the islands they visited. He carved their names inside a heart on a tree on Kithnos near the hot springs and he had invented cute pet names for her like 'Princess', 'Angel' and once, when she'd had PMS, 'Irrational'.

The sex too was great, both in quality and quantity, though Iris had to admit that unless Peggy slipped and broke her pelvis, the chance of her and Alan usurping the younger couple in the quantity stakes was very slim indeed. They were just too prolific, and knowing Peggy, Iris was pretty certain Peggy would have to break her jaw too. And both her arms.

Iris was extremely happy with Peggy and Stefan, both as friends and as shipmates. Stefan in particular was proving to be extremely handy to have around. Poor Stefan, Iris had severely misjudged the young Dutchman. He was not in the least boring, just a bit introverted. Apart from rapidly becoming an excellent sailor and a magnificent cook, Stefan was also invaluable as the ship's medical officer.

The day before they'd left Kea, Stefan inspected Iris's injuries and announced it was time to remove the stitches in the small incision the Interpol doctor had made just in front of Iris's left ear.

"I'm a bit perplexed about that Stef'" said Iris. "It looks to me to be a deliberate cut rather than an injury."

"Your cheekbone has been broken" explained Stefan, "the doctor made this small incision and then pushed a piece of wire, like a coat hanger wire but stainless steel, into the hole in your skull your ear canal goes through. It is hollow behind your cheek, so a doctor can push the pieces of broken bone back into place with the wire".

Iris felt sick at the thought of someone rummaging around inside her head with a bit of coat hanger. That was when Iris realized Stefan seemed to know a hell of a lot more about medical procedures than someone whose knowledge was supposedly derived from a university first aid club. Too much even, for someone who was the president of the club. Iris put two and two together and got four.

"So when do we have to start calling you doctor? officially I mean?" she asked.

"I have one more year at medical school and then I have to do my internship", answered Stefan and to Iris's surprise, the young Dutchman blushed. Iris felt ashamed. Until that moment, she hadn't even bothered to ask Stefan what he was studying.

So if Iris had been wrong about Stefan, maybe she was also wrong about Milos. Perhaps she was concerned because she felt threatened? It was, after all, only a little over three weeks since she had been attacked by Tasos and his insane boss Berswiski. No matter how much the little fat man seemed to need their help, it was an inescapable fact that Milos was a stranger. Luckily for Iris, she was blissfully unaware just how much stranger.

'Harvey' sailed out of the Port of Kamares two days later, with Milos officially welcomed aboard as fifth crewmember. The harbour was crowded, but Alan had decided it would be good practice for the crew to sail out rather than fire up the diesel.

"What would we do if the motor suddenly stopped and we were in the middle of the harbour with boats everywhere?" he asked. "We need to know how to manoeuvre the boat under sail, just in case we have to".

The mains'l was raised and then Stefan brought up the anchor. As soon as the anchor was clear of the bottom, Alan unfurled the big genoa backing it against the wind. 'Harvey' spun round slowly, taking little more room than her own length to do so.

"Okay Stefan", called Alan, "raise the mizzen please. We will have to get pretty close to windward, to get around that red fishing boat and we'll need the mizzen for balance. Peggy, you take the helm please. Iris, haul in the main and then tighten the Genoa for windward. Peggy, bring her round till she's aimed at that speed boat...."

Alan continued to call out his instructions until they were past the first line of vessels and then announced he was going below to check the navigation charts.

"Try not to hit that rock wall please Peggy", he said, before disappearing through the hatch.

"Jezusfucincrist" yelped Peggy at anyone who would listen. "What the hell is he playing at? Go and get him Iris. He has to tell us what to do".

"I've just fallen overboard or had a heart attack and died", called the skipper from somewhere in the bowels of the yacht, "so you have two choices. One, you lot can sail the boat out of this harbour like I know you can, or two, you give up and throw out the anchor. Option two means the three of you have to buy me dinner at the restaurant of my choice when we reach Crete."

Iris could almost feel Alan rubbing his hands together in anticipation. The gauntlet had been thrown down and the four crewmembers were not going to let Alan win, at least not without putting up a fight.

"Okay let's do it", yelled Iris to the others. "Stefan unfurl the stays'l and pull it in tight. We need to increase our speed before we can tack. Peggy steer a little closer to the wind... that's good, hold her there. We'll stay on this tack until we are close to that speedboat and then come about as quickly as we can". No one questioned Iris's authority. They were all aware that she had considerably more sailing experience than they had, and were happy to have someone else take charge.

"Okay Peg', hard to starboard please", Iris commanded as they drew close to the speedboat. "Stef', loosen the Genoa a bit more, please". 'Harvey' turned into the breeze rapidly slowing as she passed through the eye of the wind. Suddenly, as the wind caught the back of the big heads'l, she swung around onto the other tack.

"Pull the genoa in tight Stefan" called Iris, and he did, winding the big sheet winch a fast as he could 'Harvey' picked up her heels and surged forward. Iris was pleased to see that Milos had scurried forward to help Stefan. He had already told everyone that he had absolutely no idea about sailing, but was very willing to take orders. The genoa was a huge sail and even in the light wind that blew into the harbour and with Milo's considerable weight helping with the winch, it was hard work to haul it in quickly.

The turn put them close-hauled on a port tack, that is with the wind blowing across the left side of the yacht at about forty-five degrees to their heading. A sailing boat cannot sail directly into the wind, and while a modern racing boat can get as close to the wind as thirty degrees, a ketch rigged cruising yacht like 'Harvey' can only manage about forty-five. 'Harvey' would have to tack or zigzag out of the harbour, hopefully missing all the other boats, buoys and bits of land on the way.

Six times Iris had the crew tack the yacht before she was certain they had gone far enough out to miss the headland that stood between them and the open sea. Six times Stefan and Milos hauled in the big genoa until it was as tight as a drum and pulling like a train. An hour later they cleared the headland, turned the yacht southward and trimmed the sails for a beam reach. Once she had checked the heading and made sure the two men were not about to expire from exhaustion, Iris went below to announce the obvious fact they had made it and to gloat. To her chagrin, Alan was lying on the bed fast asleep.

When Alan woke a half-hour later it was to the clattering and clanking of kitchen utensils and to the delectable aroma of gently sizzling aubergine. Milos had volunteered to prepare lunch, a repast of delicious, traditional Greek dishes. Moussaka followed by an octopus dish he claimed was peculiar to his home village, served with freshly baked focaccia bread. The food was just heavenly.

Unfortunately while the food was scrumptious, the wine Milos had purchased was not. It was a mottled red colour like sangria, had the viscosity of paint stripper and tasted vaguely of brake fluid. It was also so wildly alcoholic that the uninitiated could be rendered unconscious just reading the label.

Milos apologized profusely, explaining that the wine had gone off, then he re-corked the bottle and hid it away until a toxic waste facility could be found.

While at sea, away from the dirt, grim and pollution of the land, 'Harvey' stayed remarkably clean. But when she had been at anchor for a while, the dust settled on her decks and wet feet left tell-tale footprints all over her top-sides. After lunch, Iris and Peggy were directed by the skipper to scrub the decks, while he and Stefan checked the navigation.

One of the many things Iris loved about her best friend Peggy was her happy disposition. While many people were bemoaning the state of the economy or the weather or the size of their genitals, Peggy danced through life, singing and laughing, seemingly oblivious to the fact that the world wasn't always the picture postcard perfect place we would like it to be. People who didn't know her thought her naïve, but they were wrong. Peggy had the happy knack of being able to separate the confusing peripheral garbage associated with a problem and getting right to the crux of the matter. For example, when scrubbing down the deck, a person tied some rope to a bucket, hurled it over the side, pulled the bucket back up and then sloshed the water all over the place before scrubbing with a soft broom. Problem: your clothes got all wet. Peggy's solution: 'don't wear clothes'. So while Iris went off to hunt for the famous green bikini, Peggy got her gear off and started to scrub the deck. Of course in times gone past, when 'Harvey' was in a Milos free state, Iris too would have stripped for action. But the little fat Greek man made her feel uncomfortable and even though she'd chanted Peggy's often repeated mantra of 'decency is about how you treat people, what you wear is called fashion,' Iris just couldn't bring herself to be naked in front of Milos. For his part Milos thought Peggy looked gorgeous, though he would have preferred her in a sheepskin jacket.

Dinner at sea while underway, usually followed one of two procedures. If the voyage was through a busy area, then the evening meal was taken in shifts, so that a constant lookout could be posted and the chance of collision minimized. On evenings such as tonight however, where the way was clear, the moon bright enough to see a reasonable distance, the weather fine and mild and the possibility of chancing upon another vessel slight, the autopilot was turned on and everyone enjoyed the communality of sharing their evening meal together. But such events were always held up on deck, so that the essential practice of making regular checks for the unexpected vessel or dangerous flotsam could still be rigorously adhered to.

Stefan had once again volunteered to cook and prepared a feast fit for royalty. As the meal progressed the conversation meandered its way from topic to topic, eventually settling on Iris's recent attack. Milos was amazed. He had read in the newspaper about all the poor young women who had been murdered in Athens over the past few weeks.

"You mean you were actually attacked by the madman who has been killing all those women?" he asked, "I just cannot understand how anyone could do such evil things".

Iris once again described her ordeal with Berswiski in detail, only leaving out the names of the Interpol Officers to protect their anonymity.

"So did they find the bomb?" asked Milos.

"No, unfortunately", replied Iris. "I just can't understand these terrorists. Why can't the Palestinians learn to live in peace with the Israelis?"

Milos looked intensely at his new shipmates, trying to gauge what their reactions might be before he made his next comment.

"They don't think of themselves as terrorists Iris, they see themselves as freedom fighters. They're trying to drive out the invaders," said Milos.

"That's a crock of shit!" declared Peggy. "The Jews have a right to be there. Judea is where the Jews first came into being".

"You are right" agreed Milos. "I too support their right for a Jewish homeland, but you are also forgetting what most people forget. Judaism is a religion, not a nationality. I agree with their right to live there, or for that matter anywhere else they choose. The problem is with the formation of the Israeli State. Imagine if someone annexed a part of Germany, drove out all the people who lived there and said only Lutherans can live here. It's exactly the same thing. Israelis come from all over the world, Europe, America, Africa even Australia. Their commonality is their religion, not their nationality."

Milos had obviously researched the topic at great length and launched into a lecture on the history of Israel and the conflict with Palestine.

During the First World War, the Middle East or Ottoman Empire as it was then called, had allied itself with Germany and lost. So, at the end of the war it was carved up and put under the protection and governance of either England or France. The area now known as Palestine and Israel was under British rule. Back in England the Zionist movement was gaining momentum and its members lobbied the British government to allow the formation of a Jewish homeland. In 1917 the British issued the 'Balfour Declaration' which basically supported their request. Soon after the

United States issued a proclamation that they too supported the supposition and the League of Nations was forced to allow migration of a number of Jewish people to Palestine.

The Arabs, led by Grand Mufti Haj Amin El-Husseini, were not happy about Britain giving away their land without any authority. They rioted repeatedly, which finally led to Britain halting Jewish immigration into Palestine.

After the Second World War and the Holocaust in which six million Jews were slaughtered by the Nazis, there was renewed pressure for Britain and the rest of the world to allow further immigration to Palestine. In 1947 the United Nations partitioned the area into Arab and Jewish states. Understandably, the Palestinians refused to accept the partition and war broke out. The Jews, who had received millions of dollars in aid from the US and could equip themselves with far more sophisticated and effective weaponry than the Palestinians, won a decisive victory and expanded their territory displacing several hundred thousand Arabs in the process. Further wars broke out in 1956, 1967, 1973 and 1982 and skirmishes go on even now. In the 1967 six day war, Israel once again expanded its area, this time occupying the West Bank and the Gaza strip. It is this area that is now the biggest bone of contention. In 1988 the Palestinian Liberation Organization agreed to accept a two state solution provided Israel withdrew from the West Bank and Gaza Strip. The Israelis refused. It is estimated there are about four million Palestinian refugees who have been driven from their land and now live in exile in Jordan, Syria, Lebanon and Iraq as well as hundreds of thousands who live in squalid camps scattered around Gaza and the West Bank.

"Please do not think that my comments are anti-Semitic," concluded Milos, "and don't think for a minute that I condone the use of violence by either side. I assure you my comments are not pro one side or the other, rather they are pro-peace. The only hope for the Middle East is for everyone to learn to live together. Perhaps that means getting rid of the concept of an individual 'homeland' for either group."

The group was quiet for a while and Iris took the opportunity to wander for'ard to the bow rail and scan the horizon for other vessels. The wind blew cold off the sea and Iris shivered violently as it chilled her to the bone. Standing there on deck she pondered the state of things in the world today and Milo's interpretation of the Israeli situation. She tried to tell herself she understood his point of view, but it still came out sounding a little bit racist. Or maybe that should have been religionist. Then she looked down at the heaving deck and wondered. There she stood, her entire world just under her feet. A world only forty-six feet long, a world she happily shared with four other people. Why can't other people be happy with so little, she thought but then she remembered 'Harvey' wasn't her home but only somewhere she currently lived. Home was on the other side of the world and she found herself hoping desperately that no one would ever try to take it away.

Chapter 47

In these modern, electronics riddled times, the ancient and mystical art of celestial navigation is rarely practised. With the advent of the inexpensive, reliable and pinpoint accurate satellite navigation system called the Global Positioning System, previously treasured equipment like sextants, chronometers and nautical almanacs have been relegated to realms of antiquity. Everyone uses GPS these days, including Alan Tew.

On odd occasions however, Alan would take his old sextant out of its polished timber carry case, take some sun shots and work out where the hell they were the old-fashioned way. Whether he did this to keep in practice just in case the GPS shit itself mid Atlantic or because of some nostalgic yearning was unclear. But what was clear, was that Stefan saw him using the sextant and being an inquisitive, nosy little bugger asked Alan to show him how it worked.

So, while Iris took the helm and watched out for errant cruise liners, Peggy lay on deck working on her tan and Milos languished under an awning dreaming of greener, sheep filled pastures, Alan sat Stefan at the saloon table and revealed to him the dark secrets of celestial navigation.

"It's really quite simple", explained Alan. "The earth revolves on its axis once every twenty-four hours. This gives us the impression that...."

It was not really quite simple. In fact it was really quite bloody complicated, but Stefan was one of the sharper chisels in the toolbox and after an hour or two of tuition, he felt ready to have a go.

"You simply take the sextant in your left hand", explained Alan as they stood on the deck, "flip down these filters so the sun doesn't microwave your retina when you look at it, set this indicator...."

Just like the theoretical instruction, it was not simple at all, but after a few attempts Stefan was able to get a decent sun sight. The two men then retired to the saloon to do the necessary trigonometry.

It took Stefan nearly half an hour to calculate what the sextant reading of forty-nine degrees taken at 1200 hours 6minutes and 37seconds, meant in latitude and longitude, and to confidently declare they were at 52.2 degrees North, 21.1degrees East.

"Poland?" asked Alan

"Shit", answered Stefan and picked up his pencil and tried again. The next answer was closer, but the centre of Saudi Arabia was not quite as wet as the middle of the Mediterranean, so Alan felt another attempt was needed.

"I'm just going up to get a breath of fresh air", announced the young Dutchman as he headed for the companionway steps. He looked sheepish, very sheepish, so much so, it not only aroused Alan's suspicion but aroused Milos too. The little bugger was going to look at the GPS.

"I turned it off Stef," called the skipper and waited for his shamefaced pupil to return. "Tell you what mate," continued Alan, "I'll show you where you're going wrong and you can try again. Oh! and as an added incentive, if you don't get it right this time, I'm going to buy Peggy her own fishing rod."

Stefan put his hand over the still tender scar on the back of his leg and went pale. But this time he got it right.

'Harvey' sailed into the port of Chania just before lunch the following day. It was a beautiful, picturesque harbour and the five travellers felt confident the port would be an excellent place to make their temporary base while they played tourist on the island of Crete. It was close to the famous Sammarian Gorge and other places of interest, yet far enough from the hustle and bustle of Iraklion, Crete's capital, to ensure a continuation of the low key pace they preferred.

Milos had decided to leave the ship here. He felt that in the smaller town he would have a better chance of going unrecognised. He had enjoyed the trip with the four youngsters tremendously and wished he could go further with them, but it was now time to find a job, save some money and set the wheels in motion for the next phase of his new plan. Milos had decided to emigrate to Australia. The three Australians, and one Dutch man, had shown him such kindness and understanding during the last few days that Milos could not help wondering if all Aussies were this way. During his recuperation and again as they sailed to Crete, the three Aussies had waxed lyrically about the beauty and wonder of their country. Alan in particular, despite the fact he spent a lot of his time travelling outside Australia, seemed the most proud of his homeland and entertained all those on board with tales of his exploits in the land down under. Australia seemed like 'a top place' as Iris put it. A place where a man could make a new life for himself. A place where he could escape the cruel taunts and looks of disgust of his countrymen. And, to Milo's delight, it was a place where they reputedly had over thirty million sheep.

Before he left their company for the last time, Milos thanked each of 'Harvey's' four crewmembers by taking them to a nearby taverna for lunch. This time, both the food and the wine were excellent. Except for Iris's choice of fruit salad, which came out of a tin and was described as being as tasteless as tan Lycra bike pants.

Outside the taverna after lunch, Iris hugged Milos goodbye and kissed the man's plump cheek.

"Goodbye Milos", she said with a smile. "I hope we will meet again soon". It was then Stefan's turn to make the appropriate noises, followed by Peggy. Alan stepped up, grasped the fat Greeks podgy hand and pumped it vigorously.

"I'm afraid I'm not very good at good-byes," said Alan. "So fuck off."

And Milos did.

The Samarian Gorge is an eighteen kilometre long chasm that ends at the village of Agia Roumeli. It was also the first place the four shipmates wished to explore. The following morning they packed a picnic lunch into Iris's little rucksack and jumped on the bus to the village of Omalos. During the short bus ride, Alan struck up a conversation with a Belgium backpacker who had been travelling around Crete for the last three days. He was a student geologist and was visiting all the areas of geological interest. There was another gorge, he told Alan, on the eastern peninsular. This Gorge was known as the valley of the dead because it contained many ancient Minoan tombs and was an incredible archaeological site. Unfortunately, the area had been closed to tourists recently because of the danger of wild animals. There had been bears seen in the woods nearby and they had been searching for toilet paper.

The trek through the Samarian Gorge was an arduous slog, worsened by the fact that not a fly fart of breeze penetrated the ravine to cool the place down. As the day progressed and the group trudged further along the stony path, the temperature soared. The sun beat down, baking the ground at their feet. The heat was reflected back at them from the valley floor, and from the near vertical cliffs on both sides of the ravine, until the air felt as if it came from an open blast furnace.

Crete had enjoyed a very mild winter that year, and the seasonal rains that normally came with the colder weather had not eventuated. Now with the hot summer well and truly in attendance, the river had shrunk considerably. Thankfully there was still enough water bubbling and gurgling its way along the valley floor for the group to occasionally jump in, fully clothed to try to get cool.

"Whoever had the brilliant idea of coming to this godforsaken place deserves to have their arse kicked", declared Peggy, bending over. "I've never felt so hot in my entire life".

Around midday they came to the deserted village of Samaria and a stand of very popular poplars which offered some shade from the merciless sun. Amongst the ruins nearby, a number of Kri-kri, the wild goats of Crete, scavenged around the old deserted village looking for food or for titbits from any tourists that passed by.

Despite the blast furnace heat, Iris had to admit that the gorge was without doubt the most beautiful and spectacular place she had ever visited. From Mt Giglios and Xiloskalo through to the 'Iron Gates' where the ravine narrows to just 3 meters wide and beyond to the village of Agia Roumeli, every single footstep brought another stunning, breathtaking vista or amazingly interesting sight.

For the next three days, the four shipmates spent every waking moment visiting the many places of interest that Crete had to offer. They hired a car and drove to the Toplou Monastery, a Byzantine building housing the famous icon of Theotokos the immaculate.

Next they went to Iraklion and the spectacular ancient city of Knossos. There they joined a tour group and listened enthralled as their guide explained how the Phoenicians had founded the island of Crete and built the town of Knossos as its capital. The island had fertile land which was highly suitable for growing grapes and olives, so Crete developed into a land of wine and honey, or rather olive oil, and grew to be wealthy and culturally significant. The citizens of Knossos, who were known as the Minoans, enjoyed opulent lifestyles and Crete itself became a commercial centre, unsurpassed anywhere in the then known world.

Mythology also played a large part in Crete's history. Apparently, Rhea the earth mother who was shacked up with some guy named Cronis had a son named Zeus who was a god. Whether he was really a god or that was just something his mother cried out during his conception, is not clear. What is clear is that Zeus had a son called Minos who became the king of Knossos, Crete, and all of the Aegean. King Minos built the palace at Knossos and eventually sired a son of his own called Androgeus. According to the legend, Androgeus was a hunk and ended up humping half the women in Crete and then went on to do the same thing on the mainland. The king of Athens got jealous and murdered him. This enraged King Minos who declared war on Athens. A war which the Cretans won.

As spoils of war, King Minos demanded that every nine years, Athens send seven young men and seven young virgin women to Crete to be sacrificed to the Minotaur, the fierce half-man, half-bull creature we now call a politician. The nine-year gap between sacrifices was initially thought to be of some astrological or historical significance, but archaeologists now realize it was simply because it took nine years to find six virgins.

One year when the sacrifices were due, Theseus, the son of the king of Athens, volunteered to go as one of the seven young men. He would try to slay the Minotaur.

"If I succeed and the Minotaur doesn't kill me," he told his father, "I will change the sails of my ship from black to white. That way you will know to get the beer cold before I return."

Theseus, with the help of Ariadne the town bike and daughter of Minos the king of Crete, managed to kill the Minotaur. Then Theseus set out for home.

"Now, did I tell Dad it was white sails if I won or black sails?" he asked his crew on the way home. Sadly no one could remember and Theseus took a punt and guessed black. When the king of Athens saw the black sails, he assumed that his son had failed and had been killed by the Minotaur. Grief stricken, he threw himself into the sea and drowned.

The tour guide also pointed out interesting frescos on the walls of the various buildings depicting life in Knossos between 7000 BC when the city was first built, to1250 BC when it was captured by invading hordes of Mycenaens. The Mycenaens then inhabited the city right up until Roman times. In addition to the many frescos illustrating birds, dolphins and people wearing the unique fashions of the period, including the bare breasted court attire women used to wear, there was some marvellously preserved architecture. The Royal Villa, with its polytheistic altars, stone pillars and double staircase, and the Temple tomb's crypt, were two of Iris's favourites.

Anyone who has even the slightest knowledge of ancient history knows that the world owes a huge debt of gratitude to the ancient Greeks. The world would have been an entirely different place if not for Greek scholars such as Plato who first conceptualized democracy, Archimedes who gave us the lever or Pythagoras who invented pastry.

What most people don't realize was that the Minoans, the forbears of ancient Crete, also left a considerable legacy for future generations. They not only gave us the world's first flush toilet, but topless restaurants and bull fighting as well. The Minoan bullfight was radically different to the Spanish/Mexican massacre we see today. The young men would test their courage in the arena with feats of both daring and agility. The bull would be made to charge the men, who would grab it by the horns, somersault over the beasts back and land safely behind the charging animal.

Why they did this is unknown, but popular consensus is that they were nuts. Thankfully today, after considerable lobbying by groups such as the RSPCA, bullfighting has been outlawed in all but a handful of countries. Today, most young men now have to limit their demonstrations of bravado, to getting really pissed and yelling,

"Look mate I can stop the blades of this food processor with my dick".

The Island of Crete was a truly awe-inspiring place with literally hundreds of things to see and do. In fact the group had intended to stay at least two weeks on the island, but the best laid plans of Mycenaean men seldom come to fruition. So it was with the crew of 'Harvey Wharf Banger'. In the evening of the fourth day, Stefan's phone rang. His matriarchal Mother was calling to take Stefan to task over his recent action, or rather inaction, concerning his studies.

No one besides Stefan himself could speak more than a few words of Dutch but it was obvious to the others from the heated tone of the conversation, the relationship between Stefan and his Mother was not the sweet smelling rose garden he may have liked it to be. Stefan explained to the others later that his Mother was flying to Cairo on business in a few days time and had demanded that Stefan meet her there to discuss his future. Stefan had explained to his Mother that it was impossible for 'Harvey' to sail to Cairo in such a short time. Further discussions ensued and eventually it was decided that, provided Alan and the others agreed, Stefan's Mother would travel by car from Cairo to Alexandria and Stefan would meet her there in four days.

The news was as welcome as a fart in an oxygen tent, especially for poor Peggy. The thought of losing the man she loved had frequently been in the back of her mind over the last few weeks. She knew he intended to leave the boat once they reached Portugal and she also knew eventually he would have to return to his studies. But now, with that possibility imminent, she was unable to cope and ran from the cabin in tears.

Alan was his usual philosophical self. He had said goodbye to many crew over the years and although he liked Stefan and would miss his quiet, unassuming ways, he knew that life would go on.

"Okay", said the skipper when Peggy had regained her composure and returned, "let's have a vote on it. All those in favour of rescheduling our departure date for Egypt and taking Stefan to see his Mum say aye!" All of the group, including Peggy, put up their collective hands.

"All those in favour of learning how to say get fucked in Dutch and phoning Stef's Mum back say aye!" proposed Peggy. Again every hand went up, but this time the vote was declared null and void.

The following day 'Harvey' motored out of the harbour and headed for Egypt. The wind was light and almost directly from the stern so Alan asked for 'The Twins', two enormous headsails, poled out, one on either side of the yacht, to be raised. In this manner 'Harvey' rolled along nicely, as if led by the nose and no one had to touch the helm for hours. Around midday the wind began to die and the yacht slowed almost to a stop. Alan went to the bow and surveyed the horizon. In the distance, huge, black, hammerhead clouds had formed and were beginning to roll towards the east, directly into 'Harvey's' path. Below the clouds was a grey green sheen of rain. Rain that hit the water at a steep angle rather, than straight down.

"Better get everything down Iris", said Alan calmly "and get everyone into their wet weather gear, including life harnesses. We have a blow coming and it looks like a big one."

Half an hour later Iris was beginning to wonder if her boyfriend was any good at weather predictions. The wind had died completely and the sea was millpond calm.

However just a few hundred meters away the clouds were scuttling towards them, the rain was teaming down and the ocean churning and boiling as it hit the water. Suddenly 'Harvey' started to quiver, her rigging pumping and vibrating as if some huge sea monster had grasped the top of her main mast and had given it a good shake. Iris heard the wind before she felt it. A howling, screeching wind that tore through the rigging as if the hounds of hell themselves had been unleashed. Despite her lack of sails to offer resistance to the wind, 'Harvey' tipped slowly onto her side until her gunnel were under water. The knock down lasted only seconds before the yacht righted herself and began to move through the water, sailing under bare poles.

"Stefan can you raise the mizzen please?" asked Alan. Stefan did as he was instructed and 'Harvey turned her bows slowly up into the wind. Alan then unfurled a small amount of the stays'l, backed against the gale to balance the yacht and 'Harvey' settled with her nose slightly off the wind. Hove-to in this fashion the yacht sat comfortably, drifting slightly downwind with the rapidly growing waves passing harmlessly under her. Most people who sailed more modern yachts chose the practice of running down wind in a gale, but with an old-fashioned ketch, with a large, full length keel and a more adaptable sail plan it was safer and more comfortable to hove-to. Iris was impressed. Although heeled well over, the yacht remained stable, slowly rising and falling with the waves as if on a giant roller coaster.

Then the rain started, huge dollops of water landed on the deck with a roar, a sound like waves breaking in the distance. The surrounding sea turned white as the downpour hit the water, splashed back up into the air and was turned to spume by the screeching wind. The sea was getting wilder. 'Harvey' would rise up on the crest of a wave, hang there momentarily and then plummet down into the trough before repeating the whole thing again. Suddenly a larger than normal wave crashed over the side and for a few seconds the decks were awash, the icy sea swirling around the crew's legs. No one saw Peggy go over the side, but they heard her scream.

Alan was the first to reach the lifelines where Peggy had gone over. The stainless steel clip that was part of the safety harness everyone wore in a storm was still attached to the lifeline but the stitching on the webbing strap had parted. Peggy still had her harness on, but it was no longer attached to the yacht.

Every yachtsman knows that the most dangerous aspect of sailing is not the risk of sinking or capsizing but of falling overboard. To do so on a swiftly moving yacht in poor visibility or rough weather, means almost certain death from drowning. By the time the vessel has turned around, many minutes may have passed and more often than not the person in the water will have been lost from view. To find that person again, when all that can be seen above water is his or her head, and even that is frequently hidden in the trough of a wave, is nearly impossible. As 'Harvey' was hove-to, she was moving only slowly, but still it seemed an eternity before Peggy was spotted.

"There she is", yelled Iris trying to be heard above the wind and pointed to a spot about fifty metres off the port side. Everyone strained to see through the blinding rain.

"Where?" pleaded Stefan. Then the next wave lifted 'Harvey' high into the air and at the same time another lifted Peggy and they all saw her.

"Watch her", yelled Alan, " I won't be able to see her when I'm in the water. I will look back at you for directions. Everyone point at Peggy."

As he spoke he was stripping off his heavy wet weather gear. He pulled on a pair of swim fins, slipped a life jacket over his head and went over the side.

Alan swam like a man possessed. Each time he reached the crest of a wave he would look back at the crew for guidance and then strike out again. After what seemed like hours but what was in fact only a few minutes, Alan saw that Iris had left the rail and was busy at the wheel trying to keep the yacht on course. With a terrible sinking feeling in his stomach, Alan realized the wind was changing and 'Harvey was starting to drift away from him.

"Over here", yelled Peggy and at the next wave they saw each other. Peggy had done the right thing and remained calm, knowing that panicking would only expend her energy faster. She could see 'Harvey's' twin masts and realized that she was drifting away from her. She flipped over onto her back and floated, using her legs to push herself towards the yacht. When she saw Alan coming towards her she could have cried.

"Shit harness skipper!" she said as Alan reached her. "I'm going to be really pissed off if you don't get me a new one when we get to Alexandria".

It's good to hear Peggy's keeping it together thought Alan.

"That's right blame someone else for your clumsiness", he replied, panting from the exertion of swimming through the maelstrom. "If your bloody legs were a bit longer that wave would have hit you in the back of the legs instead of in the arse and you wouldn't have been knocked over. Put your arms around my neck and I'll take us back to the boat." He lifted his foot out of the water to show Peggy he was wearing fins. The big Aussie turned around and started towards the yacht but stopped after only a few strokes. The wind had changed and Iris had been unable to keep 'Harvey' stable. The yacht had swung around and was now sailing away from them. Peggy saw it too and shuddered. If Iris couldn't turn the yacht around, they didn't stand a chance.

Stefan stood at the rail and watched as his whole world crumpled before him. His friend Alan and girlfriend Peggy, the woman he loved more than life itself, were slowly being dragged further and further away from the boat.

"For Christ's sake Iris, do something" he pleaded sinking to his knees.

"I am" yelled Iris from the cockpit. "You just keep your eyes on them. Don't loose sight of them for an instant. If you do they've had it. I'll get them back if it's the last thing I do".

Iris turned on the GPS and wrote down the latitude and longitude and then busied herself with getting the yacht around. On a cruising ketch like 'Harvey', the mizzen and stays'l which were the only sails set at present are self tacking, so Iris was able to sail the boat by herself. It was hard however, to get the old girl to turn around with such small sails and in such rough weather. She ran the yacht down wind until it started to surf down the face of a wave and had picked up enough speed to make the turn. She threw the helm over as hard as she could and the yacht slued sideways. 'Harvey' hit the bottom of the trough side on and then as the wave lifted her stern, the wind caught the mizzen and pushed her around. Iris left the helm for the few seconds it took to sheet in the two sails and then headed back for Alan and Peggy.

"They're going to miss us," cried Peggy. "They're too far to the left. Sure enough the yacht surged past them and then turned back. "Shit is the woman blind?" growled Peggy, spitting out a mouthful of seawater. "Now she's too far the other way".

"No she's not" replied Alan, "She's a frigg'n genius. Look, behind the yacht, there in the water!". Trailing in the water behind 'Harvey' was a rope nearly 30 meters long. Periodically along its length they had tied plastic bottles, boat fenders, empty fuel drums anything that would float and keep the rope on the surface. Iris had deliberately sailed in a wide arc around the two in the water trailing the rope. Now it formed a loop, which was rapidly closing around them. "Grab on to the rope" yelled Alan. Peggy didn't need telling twice.

Stefan had been, as Iris put it, as frantic as a blind lesbian in a fish shop. Now, with his girlfriend back on board safe and sound, he took stock of the situation he found himself in and made a life changing decision. He had to return to Holland to finish his studies. That was something he wanted but he would return when he was ready, not when his domineering mother demanded it. He also decided that when he went home, he would take Peggy with him.

"Peggy, would you come with me to meet my mother when we reach Alexandria?" he asked later that night as they sat on deck watching the stars. The storm had passed and the sea had calmed markedly. Peggy suddenly felt very nervous. Stefan seldom spoke about his mother, but when he did, it was not in glowing terms. She was sure that he loved his mum, but the old bat certainly sounded like a major force to be reckoned with.

"S-sure" answered Peggy, "that would be nice."

"Bullshit it will", countered Stefan, "but it will have to happen sooner or later. Can I ask you another question?"

"Yea" said Peggy and he did.

Chapter 48

Rabbi Shai Simon was in a dilemma and not just because the butcher on the corner had pork chops at half price. The young Arab boy, Mousa, the one who liked to play football with Shai's youngest son, had been telling tales again. The imp told more lies than anyone Rabbi Simon had ever met and Shai normally considered him as reliable as a fat woman's g-string, but this time, the young boy's fibs made the Rabbi uncomfortable. There was an uneasy ring of truth to them. For instance, how could the mind of an eight-year old, poorly educated child from the Gaza slums dream up such a complicated fabrication? The child claimed that his uncle belonged to a group, and the group had bought a bomb, a nuclear bomb and they were going to take it to Tal-Aviv and detonate it. The bomb had been acquired from a German arms dealer the child said, and soon the blood of many millions of Jews would be spilled and the people of Palestine would reclaim their homeland once and for all.

Somehow the whole story smacked of the truth. It seemed that the boy had been listening to his uncle talking and was repeating what he had heard. There was little possibility he was simply making it up.

Rabbi Shai Simon decided that the only course of action was to inform the authorities. They could take the boy's uncle in for questioning, interrogate him and discover if there was any truth to the child's wild stories.

The local police were extremely doubtful about the accuracy of Shai's tale and simply fobbed him off, telling him to report the matter to the Israeli Secret Service. This was easier said than done as the Israeli Secret Service took the secret nature of their organization very seriously and finding them proved as difficult as finding a squid's clitoris.

Eventually however, Shai was successful and the Mossad forces duly arrived at the door of Moura's uncle. The house was empty.

"He has gone to Greece", said one of the neighbours.

The officer in charge returned to headquarters and filed his report. The document joined the millions of other reports circulating through the plethora of 'In' and 'Out' trays strategically placed on the myriad of desks in the busy headquarters. After a few days of circumnavigating the office, it disappeared into a waste-paper bin and was never seen again.

Chapter 49

'Harvey entered the port of Alexandria just twenty-six hours later. Alan had radioed customs an hour before and they directed him to anchor in the eastern section of the harbour near another recently arrived yacht. 'MV The Light', Cyrus and Sofia Wimple's floating Jehovah's Witness temple. Peggy groaned.

"Shit, not those two bible bashers again".

It took two hours before the Egyptian customs had inspected the group's documents, searched the yacht for contraband and completed the necessary paperwork allowing then access to their country. Money exchanged hands rapidly and their visas were stamped.

"Welcome to Egypt, the land of the Pharaoh's" said the customs official in practised English.

At the mouth of the Nile River sits the city of Alexandria. A city, that in the past had been one of the busiest sea ports in the known world. For centuries Egyptian barges plied the waters of the Great River, carrying slaves, grain and riches beyond imagination to the palaces of the Pharaoh. From the East and the Ottoman Empire came Arab Dhows laden with rare spices and silks. From the North, Roman galleys came carrying ingots of bronze, livestock and that powdery cheese that smells like sick.

Today Alexandria is a mere shadow of its former glory, but the port is still busy, or so Iris found when she climbed out of the dinghy onto a rusty, deformed ladder and made her way up onto the dock. The jetty simply seethed with hundreds of Arab faces, all jostling for the best position from which to sell their trinkets. A large ocean liner had entered the harbour filled to the brim with rich American tourists who had come to see the Pyramids. Every merchant, self-proclaimed tour guide and con man was on hand to take advantage.

As Iris joined Alan and the others on the dock, a squeaky childlike voice rang out from somewhere within the crowd.

"Alan", it called and a few seconds later a little Egyptian boy of eight or nine years old erupted through a gap in the crowd and hurtled himself at the big Australian's legs.

"Naim", cried Alan, lifting the boy into his arms and hugging him to his chest. "What are you doing here?"

"I have a friend who works for the..." The boy searched for the right word for a moment. "They meet the boats and take money from visitors", he explained.

"Customs Office" offered Alan

"Yes, Customs Office. My friend look to see 'Harvey Wharf Banger'. When you come, he telephone mother. Say 'Alan he's back.'"

The boy threw his arms around Alan's neck and hugged him with all his might.

"Naim", said Alan remembering there were others waiting on the dock. "This is my girlfriend, Iris and this is Stefan and his girlfriend, Peggy.

"Hello" said the little Egyptian, bowing and touching his forehead in the approved manner. "I am Naim Abdulla Saihd Tew, Alan's son."

Chapter 50

The arms dealer smiled smugly to himself as his taxi wound its way through the suburbs of Athens and headed out to the airport. In his pocket was a deposit receipt from the bank for nine million US dollars, the amount he had transferred to a numbered account in Zurich just an hour before. It comprised of the two million deposit he had returned to the Palestinian two weeks ago and the balance of the money meant as final payment for the bomb.

If there was one character trait the arms dealer was most proud of, it was his ability to keep a cool head when things went pear shaped. When the tall Palestinian with a penchant for removing body parts had first threatened his life, he had assumed the German arms dealer would do one of three things. One, find the nuclear weapon and deliver it as originally arranged; two, run away and hide somewhere or three, come after the Palestinian with a machine gun and try to take him out. When the arms dealer disappeared off the face of the earth eight days ago and no one could find him, the Palestinian assumed that option number two had been chosen.

For the arms dealer all three options were unacceptable. Firstly, he had no idea where Berswiski or the bomb was. Secondly, he wished to continue in his line of work and running away and hiding was not good for business. Thirdly, even though the thought of blowing a great number of holes in the man who had cut off his ear was very appealing, killing the Palestinian would not be the end of it.

He was, after all only the mediator, the spokesman for the real people who wished to acquire the nuclear warhead. Killing the Palestinian would serve no purpose other than to set the others on his heels. So option four was the only acceptable solution to the problem left open to him.

Nine million dollars is not the king's ransom it used to be thirty years ago, but it still has to be considered a large sum of money. Such sums cannot be brought into a country as hand luggage, but provided the money is 'clean', it can be transferred between banks quite simply. However such a sum would attract unwelcome interest. Particularly if it suddenly turned up in a small suburban branch. Knowing this, the arms dealer felt sure the money would have been transferred, in many small stages, to one of the large banks in the city centre. This meant the Palestinian would be staying somewhere close by so that he could get to the money quickly if needed.

After three hours sitting in his hotel room with a lap top computer hacking into the registers of the major accommodation establishments, the arms dealer ascertained that his quarry was staying at the Dionysos Hotel Athens, room 602.

On the same floor were three other Arabs, probably his security detail, who were on hand to look after the money.

The arms dealer phoned the Palestinian at 2:30pm on Friday.

"I have the item you asked for", he said when his call was answered. "Meet me tomorrow morning at 7:00am, usual place, bring the money" and hung up.

This gave the Palestinian just two hours to go to the bank and get the nine million dollars. The 'arms dealer' felt sure the three thugs would go with him. The arms dealer waited across the road until he saw them leave, then went to the reception desk and asked to see the man from room 602. When he was told that the gentleman was out, he left a gift-wrapped bottle of wine and a note written in

Arabic. Although the receptionist did not know it, the note simply said "Compliments of the Management".

Of course the Palestinian was a devout Moslem and should not touch alcohol. But he had eaten the bacon he'd ordered with his breakfast each morning and he had soiled his purity by shagging all those infidel prostitutes that came to his room each night and so the arms dealer was quite sure he would also drink the wine when he returned to the hotel. What he wouldn't do was drink it in front of his comrades. For that reason he could be confident the Palestinian would be alone in his room when he returned from collecting the transfer details for the money later that afternoon.

Just before midnight, the arms dealer crossed the road to the hotel and re-entered the lobby. He waved goodnight to the concierge as if he was a guest of the hotel returning home after a night out, went to the house phone and dialled room 602. When he received no answer, he walked to the elevator and went up to the sixth floor.

After knocking on the door to room 602 and again getting no answer, he picked the lock, cut the security chain with the bolt cutters he had brought with him, and slipped inside. The wine, or more precisely the strychnine he'd laced it with, had done its job. The Palestinian lay dead on the bed, chained to his wrist was a briefcase containing the account details, including the security personal identification number for the nine million dollars. Without these details transferring the money was impossible. It would never leave the bank it was now in. It had been a gamble, but the arms dealer had been sure that the numbers would be written down somewhere in the Palestinians room. The Arab would have needed them to conclude his purchase in the morning, and there was no way his superiors would have allowed such information to be committed to memory by only one person. If something happened to him, then the deal couldn't be finalized. one of the others still needed to be able to access the money.

Phase two of the plan then came into action. The arms dealer cut the chain attached to the briefcase with the bolt cutters, stuffed the dead Arab into a dirty laundry bag and shoved him down the laundry chute, in the hallway, outside his room. Under the bed, where the three Arab heavies would find it, the arms dealer placed a passport sized photo of his victim, replaced the security chain with the new one he had brought with him, picked up the empty wine bottle and the briefcase, and left. Five minutes later he had collected the dead Palestinian from the bottom of the laundry chute and was driving towards the outskirts of Athens.

In the morning, the Palestinians comrades found room 602 empty and contacted their superiors to report his disappearance, mentioning at the same time the passport photo. After some deliberation, it was suggested that the three men search the area for other clues, and over the next few hours they found other passport photos, glue, scissors and a scalpel in the hotels rubbish bins. They also found pages of writing that appeared to be someone practising their signature. The name on the pages was Salem Mohamed.

At 7:00am one of the three Arabs showed up at the appointed rendezvous to find the arms dealer ready and waiting to hand over the location of the bomb and receive his final payment. Or so the Arabs believed. The 'arms dealer' was there waiting for them, seemingly oblivious to the fact that something had gone wrong Their boss had gone missing, as had all the money. All the evidence pointed to one inescapable conclusion. Their leader had double-crossed them. The passport paraphernalia made it appear the Palestinian had given himself a new identity and stolen the money. Hadn't he insisted that he be left alone in his room during the previous night, the thugs would say. Further investigations at the airport had revealed that according to the ticketing records a man by the name of Salem Mohamed had flown out at 1:30 am for Morocco. According to the bank the money had been transferred out of the country, to a numbered account in Switzerland. An account they concluded, which belonged to their former comrade. No one ever saw the Palestinian again, only the arms dealer knew where he was, and unless he was accidentally dug up during an excavation of a building site on the outskirts of the city, that was the way it would stay.

Chapter 51

The bus trip to St. Raphael's orphanage took just over an hour, long enough for Alan to explain his sudden and unexpected plunge into fatherhood.

"So he's adopted?" asked Iris indicating the small Egyptian child sitting on the bench seat next to them and clinging to his 'father's' hand as if his life depended on it.

"More like sponsored", answered Alan and went on to explain that eight years ago a policeman had arrived at the gate of the orphanage they were en-route to and deposited yet another new-born baby. The child had been found abandoned at a nearby building site under a pile of timber trusses. No one had any idea who the baby's mother was but she was probably one of the local prostitutes. The good sisters of the orphanage called the baby boy Naim and over the next six years, loved him and cared for him and taught him to speak English. Sort of. Then, when he was old enough, they sent him with the other orphans of St. Raphael's off to the nearby government run primary school.

It was here that young Naim first encountered the cruelty of his fellow human beings. The school was attended by a variety of children from the local village. Except for Naim and his fellow inmates from the orphanage, all of the students had at least one parent to care for them. The orphans were teased mercilessly and as poor Naim was believed to be the offspring of a whore, he was singled out for particularly harsh treatment. He fought back as often and as well as he could, but there was no escaping the fact that he was a sickly child and fought about as well as a drag queen with a broken finger nail.

One day about two years ago, a ruggedly handsome Australian yachtsman called Alan arrived at the orphanage and quickly made friends with the children. That evening as he sat talking to the Mother Superior, Naim climbed up onto the Aussie's lap and asked if Alan would be his Daddy. Sadly adoption was impossible. Alan was single, had no fixed address and no permanent form of employment. After consultation with the Mother Superior however, Alan agreed that he would send money each month to assist with the cost of educating and caring for the little boy. After a lot of legwork on Alan's part, visiting numerous bureaucrats and self impressed government officials, the surname Tew was officially added to Nail's. It wasn't official adoption but as far as the young boy was concerned he now had a father.

A few days later Alan went to the school to collect Naim and to take him into town. Supposedly on the pretext of buying him some new clothes, but in reality to introduce the child to the heavenly pleasures of ice cream. The sudden appearance of Nail's. new father must have caused quite a stir at the school, for Nail's. lowly status of 'Son of a whore' was rapidly elevated to the Egyptian equivalent of 'Cool Dude with the Aussie father' and no one ever picked on the little boy again.

Maybe it was the commonality of being an orphan himself that convinced Alan to help Naim or maybe Alan just recognised that the little boy needed someone to love him. Whatever the reason, he had opened his heart to the child and would never regret it.

For the next three days Iris and Alan spent their time working their arses off at 'St Raphael's Orphanage'. Luckily they both grew back. Alan introduced Iris to the sisters who ran the place, as well as the children he recognized from his last visit. Sadly there were many more who had arrived since that time. The Mother Superior greeted Alan like a long-lost son and insisted they stay and enjoy the meagre hospitality of St Ralph's. Alan could not refuse. In fact, as Stefan and Peggy were staying in the city with Stefan's mother for the next couple of days, the invitation was quite opportune. Unfortunately, Catholic nuns are not the most open-minded of people when it comes to the cohabitation of unmarried Australians, so Iris was given a bed in the girl's dormitory while Alan slept in the boy's. Not that he actually got any sleep. As Alan explained to Iris the following morning, "There is a big difference between light and hard," he told her, "for example you can sleep with a light on".

With a cheeky grin and a wave he headed off towards a run down building that looked like a barn. "See you in a couple of hours. I just have to check in on her Royal Highness."

"Who's her Royal Highness?" Iris called after him but all the big Australian did was turn and wink and then disappear into a large corrugated iron shed.

Alan connected the recharged battery, turned on the fuel tap and pressed the little brass button on the side of the carburettor until neat petrol pissed out of the breather hole. He flicked on the ignition switch and with a tremendous heave, stabbed downward on the kick-starter with his foot. At the third attempt the ancient and decrepit motorcycle coughed. At the fourth it fired, spluttered and then clattered into life, belching a thick, black, acrid pall of exhaust fumes into the air. Alan blipped the throttle a couple of times and then let the old girl warm up properly before making some final adjustments to the 'carby'.

The bike was an old, nineteen seventy-something, 350cc Royal Enfield 'Bullet' or at least it pretended to be. In reality it was a clone. She and a hundred thousand or so of her siblings had been manufactured, under licence, in India and it was a sad fact, but true that she was not the quality motorcycle her cousins from Blighty had been. Still she had turned out to be a reliable old bike and had served her dozen or so owners admirably.

Alan had worked on the bike four times. The last time in the autumn of last year when he passed through on his way to Istanbul. Each time he had repaired the bike, it was the same three problems. Lack of maintenance, incorrect use, and the one thing he could do nothing about, old age.

years ago the motorcycle's previous owner had been an Egyptian man, a carpenter by trade, handyman by default. A man who had worked tirelessly for the orphanage for many years for no other payment than a bed for the night and three meagre meals each day. He had fitted the bike with an enormous sidecar, an addition which proved invaluable for carting the weekly shopping from the village. When he died, the sisters at the orphanage got to keep the bike.

Sister Regina, a young novice hailing from British Colombia took it upon herself to learn how to ride and maintain the motorcycle and for the next three years, dressed as a man and wearing a false beard to stop wagging tongues and the disapproving looks from the locals -a group who frowned upon women even driving cars let alone a motorcycle,- piloted the big black beast to and from the shops every week.

In those days the orphanage was about ten kilometres from the nearest shop and post office, and even though the good sisters at the orphanage grew most of their own food, there was still the mail to be collected and the odd thing to be purchased. A book perhaps, some clothing for one of the children or perhaps a kilo or so of hashish so that Sister Agnes could continue her research into the effects of long term narcotics addiction. Then one day, Sister Regina accidentally discovered her clitoris, renounced both her faith and her calling and returned to Canada to start an Internet porn site.

It then fell to Sister Mary-Magdalene to do the shopping run, more often than not in the company of the perpetually stoned Sister Agnes. Once again with both nuns dressed as men to avert the wagging tongues of the locals. Each Thursday after vespers, Sister Mary-Magdalene would push the ancient motorcycle out of the shed and jump up and down on the kick-starter until the bike fired. Then with Sister Agnes perched on the pillion, they would roar out of the orphanage gates and hurtle up the road, rattling, clanking and farting huge clouds of fumes all the way to Alexandria. When the rattling, clanking and farting became too ominous for comfort, Sister Mary Magdalene would leave Sister Agnes at home with a bowl of prunes and a newspaper and make the trip by herself.

Over the ensuing years, the suburbs swelled inexorably towards the old orphanage, eventually engulfing it in the maws of its urban sprawl. Someone built a shopping centre nearby, a bus ran regularly past the orphanages' front door and a rich benefactor donated a brand new Toyota Corolla to the orphanage. But as any Nun will tell you, old habits die hard and although they now had their groceries delivered, Sister Mary-Magdalene continued the weekly run to the city to collect the mail.

A few years ago the wheel bearing on the sidecar gave up the ghost, and with ingenuity born of necessity, the good sisters at the orphanage attacked the sidecar with axes, hacksaws and shifting spanners and converted the old Enfield back to its original two wheeled form. When Sister Mary-Magdalene made the painful discovery that two wheeled motorcycles fall over when you stop at a stop sign and forget to put your feet down, Sister Margaret took on the post woman's role. She rode side-saddle, which made it a bit obvious to anyone who saw her that the rider wasn't the masculine devil he appeared to be. But Sister Margaret knew perfectly well where her clitoris was and whether it was living or just mechanical, she was not letting any big, black, throbbing thing anywhere near it.

One day in the middle of Alexandria, the Royal Enfield broke down and a large ruggedly handsome yachtsman from Australia used fencing wire and a tin can to get the bike running well enough for Sister Margaret to make it home. Two days later Alan turned up at the gate of the orphanage, his trusty tool kit in one hand and a huge bag of toys for the kiddies in the other. Christmas came early that year at the orphanage thanks to Alan. The kids loved him, the Nuns loved him, Naim found a new 'father' and after two days of tinkering, the soon to be sweetly running Royal Highness, Princess Enfield of India, loved him too.

Chapter 52

Katja Van Kesling squeezed herself into the driver's seat of the tiny hire car, inserted the ignition key and gave it a twist. With typical Japanese reliability the little motor fired immediately and screamed loudly to what sounded like eight million RPM. Stefan's mother hurriedly took her foot off the accelerator and the engine slowed to a burbling idle. It sounded tinny, hollow, the engine noise echoing from somewhere under the bonnet like someone gargling in a toilet bowl. Twenty minutes earlier, Katja had entered the office of 'Pyramid Car Hire' and asked if she might arrange a vehicle for the next three days, something nice, perhaps a Mercedes? The booking clerk giggled and shook his head. A BMW? more giggling and shaking of heads, perhaps a Volvo? Eventually a deal was struck. Forms were completed and signed, credit cards were swiped and the keys to what transpired to be the only car left available, were handed to Mrs. Van Kesling. The keys belonged to the minute, electric blue, Nissan Micra in which Katja now sat.

Stefan's mother groaned and reached to adjust the rear view mirror. As she did so, she caught sight of herself scowling and mentally slapped herself across the face. Don't be such an arrogant bitch she chided herself. It's just a bloody hire car. You haven't been condemned to drive the thing for all eternity. It has four wheels and an engine and that's all you need to get from Cairo to Alexandria and back.

The hire car did indeed have four wheels and an engine. It also had a CD player, air bags, tinted windows and most importantly air conditioning. As today's temperature was expected to eclipse 45 degrees C, this last feature was more of a life saving necessity than an optional extra.

Unfortunately the car also had a clutch.

Of course Katja had driven a manual car before, a '72 Triumph Stag no less. The classic British sports car Stefan's father had bought himself while in the throws of yet another midlife crisis. The Triumph had had a clutch, though if Katja was honest with herself, reversing three metres down the driveway so she could get her Range Rover out of the garage really didn't constitute driving. Still she felt she knew the basics, so she threw in the clutch, mashed the loudly whining gearbox into 1 and bunny-hopped out of the car park. Three hours and numerous unintentional detours later, the little blue Micra hurtled into the underground car park of the Alexandria Hilton and screeched to a halt.

For the remainder of the day and for a considerable amount of the evening, Katja Van Kesling stayed in her hotel room, pounding away at her laptop and attending a number of Tele-conferences associated with her business. Stefan had never mentioned it to Peggy, but Katja Van Kesling was the founder, director and principal shareholder of Europe's third largest pharmaceuticals company. Katja was rather proud of her business achievements. She had built the company from the ground up, and to her credit, she had done it without trampling over anyone else. She had done it through hard work, determination, good business sense and most importantly, through an almost uncanny ability to see any problems long before they actually eventuated. She was also an excellent judge of character.

The following morning Katja took an early breakfast in her room, made a few phone calls and then readied herself to do battle with her errant son. At 9:45 am as Katja sat in her underwear in front of the mirror, expertly applying her make up, her room phone rang and the desk clerk announced that Mrs. Van Kesling's son had arrived and was waiting in the lobby. He was fifteen minutes early. Surprisingly, Stefan's early arrival unnerved Katja. He had never been on time in his whole life, never mind early. The little bugger had had her in labour for eighteen hours for Christ's sake. How the hell could he be early? Katja was also very annoyed. She could not be angry with Stefan if he was early and she really wanted to be angry with him. Hurriedly she threw on a dress, slipped on a pair of Gucci shoes, locked her room on the way out and caught the lift to the lobby.

Stefan looked like a million dollars. His hair had been cut stylishly short. He was clean-shaven and wore a crisp white open necked shirt which showed off his tan magnificently. His slacks were clean and pressed and his feet were enclosed in polished leather shoes. Real shoes, not those dreadful bloody sandals he usually wore. Over one arm he had draped a dark blue sports jacket and on the other a cute little blond in a pretty little sundress.

"Hello mother", greeted Stefan warmly, "it's lovely to see you again. You look wonderful." He embraced his mother, hugging her affectionately. "This is my girlfriend Peggy" he continued switching to English.

"Hello Mrs. Van Kesling," gushed Peggy. "It's so nice to meet you at last. Stefan has told me so much about you" The cute little Australian proffered her hand for the elder woman to shake and then offered her a seat. Over the next few hours the three chatted pleasantly about this and that. "You must be so proud of Stefan", Peggy said clinging to her boyfriend's arm. "He will make a wonderful doctor", she declared. "Did you know he saved a drowning man's life on Sifnos?" she asked.

Katja smiled. She had had enough dealings with marketing executives and public relations people to recognize a sales pitch when she saw one and the young Australian woman's 'Stefan and Peggy' proposition was a good one. It was obvious to Katja that it was Peggy who had ensured that she and Stefan arrived dressed to kill and it was she who had orchestrated that they arrive early and meet in the lobby on neutral ground. Later, when the three had retired to the restaurant for a bite of lunch, Katja was not in the least surprised to find that Peggy had already booked a table for three in her own name. Predictably, the young couple sat close together with their backs to the wall, presenting a united, numerically superior front against the enemy, Stefan's mother.

"Take a seat please Katja," offered Peggy "I'll have the waiter bring us something to drink." During the luncheon Peggy once again took control, skilfully steering the conversation in directions that suited her agenda. She spoke about her future with Stefan, about the things he would do when he received his doctorate. Delicately and gently sewing the seed in Katrina's mind that her proposition was the only one worth considering.

Katja was not surprised by the young woman's actions. What did surprise her was that she was letting her do it. The truth was Katja liked the cute little Australian woman. She had an energy, a strength of character and determination that Katja felt would be the perfect foil for Stefan's more impulsive nature. Peggy was perfect. She was pretty almost beautiful, obviously intelligent and confident without being arrogant. She was nothing like the rich bitch, conceited, shallow as mud flats, narcissists Stefan had dated in the past. There was something else too. Something that had made Stefan's mother throw up her arms in defeat almost as soon as she recognized it. Stefan loved this woman. This was no lust-induced infatuation. Her son had found his soul mate and Katja could not fight against those odds, even if she wanted too. She would, however, make damn sure his feelings were reciprocated before she would lie down completely.

When they had finished their lunch and Peggy was, predictably, attending to the account, Katja asked Stefan if he would wait for them in the lobby.

"I have a few things I would like to discuss with your girlfriend in private," she explained.

Peggy returned to the table and sat down, ready for a fight. Katja leaned forward and crossed her arms comfortably in front of her on the table.

"You're good young lady, very good" said Katja. "If you ever decide to live in Amsterdam and want a job in marketing there's one waiting for you with my company." Peggy smiled at the compliment, understanding the elder woman's meaning instantly.

"Thank you, Mrs. Van Kesling", she replied. "I have every intention of eventually living in Holland, but I already have a job. A job I intend to dedicate the rest of my life to". Katja raised an eyebrow quizzically. "I'm going to make your son the happiest man in the world"

Katja Van Kesling reached across the table and gave her future daughter-in-law's hand a gentle squeeze.

"In that case we had better be friends."

Chapter 53

St. Ralph's was not one of those strange orders that expected the sisters to take a vow of silence. Just as well because Sister Elizabeth's head would have exploded. Sister Elizabeth was a chatterbox. A jovial, plump, moon faced woman of fifty-three who constantly spouted such inane drivel that she made the speaking clock seem eloquent and interesting. Unfortunately for Alan and Iris, the excitement of having two new and interesting people all the way from Australia to talk to was an opportunity Sister Elizabeth simply could not resist. She followed them everywhere, filling the air with inane, boring chatter until the two Australians were ready to scream.

"She's driving me nuts!" exclaimed Alan when they finally managed to sneak away for a few minutes by themselves.

"Oh? Where to?" asked Iris, seductively nibbling at her boyfriend's earlobe and playfully walking her fingers up his thigh towards his groin. "I hope she brings them back".

"Very funny", said Alan taking up the challenge without missing a beat. "Can you believe how much the woman can talk? I heard that she was expelled from a scuba diving school for talking in class."

"Yea", countered Iris, "and I heard that sparks from her fillings once started a bush fire."

"That's nothing. I heard that she learnt sign language and killed three deaf people in unarmed combat". Iris started to giggle a sure sign for Alan to continue. "I just hope she puts on some more weight", said Alan

"What?" asked Iris with a confused look on her face.

"Well think about it honey", explained Alan, "If she gets fat enough there's a good chance someone will wire up her jaw."

Iris chuckled at Alan's weird sense of humour. He sat on the ground and pulled his girlfriend down on top of himself. He put his arm around her, drew her close and kissed her deeply and passionately.

"I suppose we shouldn't be so critical, She's not a bad old stick really," he admitted.

"They're all really nice people," Iris agreed, "But I find it hard to understand how a group of obviously intelligent women can dedicate their whole life to the worship of a God that in all probability doesn't exist."

"Perhaps they have no choice", replied Alan. He hugged her closer, settled himself comfortably, leaned back against the wall and told her about Thomas Ngaddi.

A dozen or more years ago, just after he had completed his indenture as a cabinet makers apprentice, Alan decided to go and see the world. He bought himself a backpack, signed on as crew on a huge private motor sailer and headed for Africa. The yacht was a rich man's toy and came complete with a paid skipper, two crew and two young beautiful and voluptuous hostesses. The girl's responsibility was to ensure that the champagne was correctly chilled, the Colombian party powder flowed freely and that the boss never forgot his dick could be used for other purposes besides urinating.

On the surface, the motor sailer was immaculate. Everything gleamed and in top shape, even the engine room was spotless. But inside the diesel itself, things were not quite so shipshape. The owner of the yacht had no time for sailing in its true sense. The diesel was run continuously in an endeavour to reach Capetown as quickly as possible. A few days out of Fremantle, the skipper noticed that the temperature gauge was reading higher than normal and sent Alan below to investigate. Alan found a number of fairly dire problems. Firstly, according to the maintenance records, the oil had not been changed in almost five thousand hours. The oil was as thick as treacle and felt gritty when Alan rubbed it between his fingers. Secondly, the sacrificial anodes on the raw water side of the heat exchanger had not been replaced when necessary. This meant that the cooling system was full of corrosion. It was so bad, very little coolant was getting through to the cylinder head. Alan reported his findings to the skipper who after informing the owner, ordered Alan to fix the problems as soon as possible. Alan was not a mechanic, but he had gleaned a basic knowledge from his grandfather who, after his retirement, had developed a passion for most things mechanical. He changed the oil and fuel and oil filters plus flushed out the heat exchanger with some acidic tile cleaner he found in the galley. But before he started, Alan informed the skipper that the engines cooling system had to be flushed out, or it would continue to overheat. He warned him that as the system was badly corroded, the acidic tile cleaner would probably eat through in some places causing leaks. Sure enough, when they restarted the diesel, water pissed from its side, filling the engine room with steamy hot seawater. It took Alan almost three days working with bits of copper plate, rivet guns and exhaust putty to get the system working effectively, though even then, the motor still leaked slightly and continued to overheat, if operated above three-quarter throttle. When the yacht finally reached Capetown the motor needed new rings. As did the two hostesses.

For the next few months Alan travelled around the African Continent, caught a weird bladder infection and then travelled around incontinent. Eventually he reached Angola. It was not a pretty place. After decades of civil war, the country was on its knees.

Now, when Angola could least cope with it, the country was in the grips of the worst drought in living memory. Thousands of people left their homes and headed for Namibia, sometimes walking hundreds of kilometres in search of food and water. Predictably, when they reached the border, Namibian soldiers were there to prevent them from going any further. With nowhere to go and no strength left to go there, hundreds of thousands of men, women and children simply lay down and waited to die. Some of the more affluent economies in the western world threw the people of Angola a few crumbs in return for political or strategic considerations, but generally it was left to non government charitable organizations to try to prevent the genocide of an entire nation.

The Red Cross was in the process of building a field hospital near one of the larger refugee camps and Alan asked if they might be able to use a cabinet maker or carpenter during its construction. It was here that Alan first met Thomas Ngaddi.

Thomas was a tall, lanky, hook-nosed Ethiopian who worked as an aid worker at the refugee camp. Every morning before sunrise, Thomas would fill his truck with supplies and head out into the camp. He would dole out meagre handfuls of rice or bread, dispense basic medicines and perform simple first aid for those who needed it. Then, at the end of the day, he would load his truck with the bodies of those poor unfortunates who had not made it and take them to some nearby wasteland to bury, in one of the many mass graves. Thomas worked tirelessly all day and for a good part of the night, only stopping to rest when the need became too great. He would not return to the Spartan barracks the Red Cross provided for its workers until late in the night. Then he would kneel down at the side of his bed and pray.

Alan was young and less tolerant in those days. He asked how Thomas, in the light of the enormity of the suffering and injustice that was occurring not more than a stone's throw away, could believe that a benevolent God existed.

Thomas rose to his feet and smiled knowingly.

"There has to be a God Alan", he answered, spreading his arms as if to encompass the multitude of sick and dying people outside. "There are so many people who need our help. Surely we cannot be expected to help them all by ourselves".

Alan did not believe in God and never would, but Thomas's words helped him understand those that did. They believed not because God's existence was irrefutable, but simply because to do otherwise was just too horrible to contemplate. Alan believed it was the same with the sisters of St Raphael's. They cared for the orphans because the orphans needed someone to care for them. But the sisters couldn't do it without their faith. Their belief in God kept them going when things seemed hopeless.

Iris looked up at the man she loved and smiled. She was slowly beginning to realize, that Alan's philosophy of helping those in need, was for no other reason than the need itself. It was probably the thing she loved most about him she decided. Thomas Ngaddi was right. We shouldn't be expected to do so much by ourselves. Alan was glad that with Iris by his side, he no longer needed to.

For the next two days Iris and Alan worked side by side, slaving away at every 'fixit' and maintenance job the sisters of St. Ralph's threw at them. They repaired broken furniture, fixed leaking pipes, painted the girl's dormitory, serviced the generator and the old motorbike, and of course, made Sister Agnes a new bong.

In the afternoon after school young Naim would join them, shooing Sister Elizabeth away with a torrent of Arabic obscenities that thankfully the chatterbox nun did not wholly understand. Naim would follow the two Australians around like a puppy, holding his 'Father's' hand and gazing up into his eyes adoringly. In the evening, the three would retire to the sisters' common room. It was a small private room where the nun's went to get away from the children for a short while and to chat. Here they could contemplate the day just past, and watch porno movies. As a treat, sometimes Naim would be allowed to join them until his bed time. Alan would sit with the little boy perched on his knee, and with Iris sitting opposite, they'd talk. Sometimes about the past, but more and more frequently about the future.

"Mother!" said Naim, prodding Iris in the arm to try to get her attention. "Do you think that one day you and Father might take me to Australia?" Iris's jaw dropped to the floor. She was not quite sure if she was comfortable with the thought of an eight-year Egyptian old boy she'd known only two days calling her 'Mother'.

"I think that's really up to Alan", replied Iris, burying her head in the book she was reading and hoping it would all go away. She had fallen in love with Alan knowing that there was bound to be some things she wouldn't be entirely happy about. He was handsome, charming and certainly knew his way around a bedroom, so Iris was prepared for there to be the odd ex-girlfriend in his past, but she'd never expected to be lumbered with a complete family. Alan on the other hand was delighted with the situation and teased Iris for the rest of the evening by calling her Mother at every opportunity.

The following evening they were to return to 'Harvey' and rejoin Stefan and Peggy. From there they would sail up the Nile to Cairo. In the morning however, Alan must have had a brain seizure or lapsed into temporary insanity or something, because he decided to borrow the old motorbike and offered to take Iris shopping for an hour or so. Of course had he been lucid when he'd made the offer, he would've remembered that in a woman's mind, the critically important task of shopping and the phrase 'for an hour or so' have no business being in the same sentence.

Finishing the painting of the girl's dormitory took most of the morning, but after lunch Alan wheeled the old Royal Enfield motorbike out of the shed, started her up and took Iris to a local shopping area. Iris had never been on the back of a bike before and initially she was quite nervous, but as her confidence in Alan's riding skills grew, she relaxed and found herself enjoying the euphoric thrill of the ride. The bike was normally ridden sedately, rarely getting up to more than a brisk canter. In Alan's skilful hands however, the bike became a different beast entirely. It hurtled up the road with a throaty bellow, barking loudly when Alan down shifted for the first corner and banked steeply round the bend like some deranged fighter jet. Iris squealed with delight each time the old bike rocketed out of a corner and roared up the road.

Alan had chosen to visit an older part of Alexandria where he hoped he would find a more realistic side of Egypt than the modern, tourist infested city centre. He was sadly misguided. Even in the back streets, the call of the mighty tourist dollar was deafening, and the shelves of the shops and roadside stores were littered with tawdry, cheap, made in china souvenirs like stuffed toy camels and Great Pyramid snow domes.

The two Australians moved on to an even older part of town, closer to the waterfront. Here they found a more promising collection of goods on sale, and for the next few hours scoured the shops for 'something interesting'. Late in the day they came upon a dingy hovel selling second hand goods, Alan looked through the door and immediately spied an old 'Stanley' wood plane, a tool used by carpenters and cabinetmakers for shaping and smoothing timber.

"I'm just going in here for a bit, honey", explained Alan. "I'll be back in a couple of minutes". Iris nodded and said he should join her in the shop across the road when he was finished. The plane was a beauty. Sure there was a bit of surface rust and the blade was as dull as a television cooking show, but it was complete and would be as good as new with a little maintenance. Alan took it to the counter and following tradition, started to haggle.

Iris's shop was also interesting, filled with traditional women's clothing and some exquisite silver jewellery. Her eyes fell upon an intricately crafted silver anklet festooned with tiny bells. As she picked up the anklet to inspect it, she became aware of a strange smell, it was like rubbing alcohol only more pungent. Suddenly something or someone struck Iris hard across the back of the legs and she stumbled to her knees. Before she could turn around, a choking arm wrapped around her throat and a rag soaked in chloroform was held tightly over her nose and mouth. Iris tried to drag her attackers' hand from her face, but he was too strong and she soon felt herself slowly slipping into unconsciousness. As she slumped to the floor, Iris looked up. Peering down at her was the most evil face she had ever seen. The face of Vladimir Micael Berswiski.

Perhaps Thomas Ngaddi was right, perhaps there was a god, a 'supreme being' who watched over us and leant a hand in our hour of need. Maybe it was divine intervention that made Alan leave the second hand shop just in time to see a scrawny little man with bucked teeth and a big nose and an overweight, grey haired old woman bundling Iris into the back of a white Mercedes 140D van. But then maybe it was just luck. Alan yelled and ran towards the van, but they were too far away and Berswiski had the van started and was driving off before Alan could reach them. He had the old Stanley plane in his hand and threw it with all his strength at the receding vehicle. It shattered the back windscreen but did nothing to slow down Berswiski's escape. Alan raced back to the old motorbike, threw his leg over the saddle and stabbed at the kick-starter. The bike fired instantly. Alan whipped in the clutch, stamped on the gear lever and fishtailed up the road after the van, twisting the throttle as far as it would go. Alan saw the van turn right at the next intersection, about three hundred metres ahead. Suddenly an ancient Peugeot 304, filled to the brim with a family of shoppers, shot out of a side street directly into Alan's path. He hauled on the anchors and then swerved up onto the footpath, scattering pedestrians and street merchants as he went. The Enfield jumped the curb again back onto the road, swerving around between the back of the old Peugeot and a hand cart filled to the brim with pumpkins. He down shifted, set himself up for the corner and leaned into it. The back wheel started to drift so he opened up the throttle, controlling the slide like a speedway rider, coming out of the corner sideways. The van was up ahead about one hundred meters away driving rapidly, but it was no match for the far superior acceleration of a motorcycle and Alan was gaining quickly. The van turned again, to the left, heading for the wharf. Alan dropped the bike into the bend, sliding his weight backwards and lying flat on the tank to try to stop the back wheel breaking free. This time she stuck to the road like glue, banking over until Alan's knee was merely millimetres above the asphalt. He opened the throttle again and accelerated hard till he was just a couple of metres behind the Mercedes. Berswiski hit the brakes hard and at the last instant spun the wheel and rocketed down a side street. Alan went after him but this time providence was not on his side. The front wheel slid out from under the bike, the hardest slide of all to control on a motorbike. He went over the handlebars and hit the road with a sickening thump. Alan picked himself up and stared helplessly after the van as it turned sharply down the turn-off towards the wharf and vanished into the distance.

His right calf and knee were badly grazed, and his ankle was badly sprained and was already starting to swell. He hobbled back to the bike and lifted it back up onto its wheels. Pain shot up his right arm from his hand. His little finger was twisted out at right angles to his wrist, obviously broken. Eventually Alan got the bike running again and despite the pain in his hand whenever he twisted the throttle or squeezed the front brake too hard, rode off to try to find Iris.

The old abandoned furniture factory with the name Ishmael and Sons written in both Arabic and English on the sign had a three-metre-high wall all around its perimeter. Luckily for Alan its front gate was made of chain link mesh and galvanized pipe, or he would have missed the white Mercedes van, the one with a broken back windscreen, parked in the car park.

He killed the bike's motor, kicked down the side stand and limped painfully over to the gate to peer in. What he saw was not to his liking. The factory was guarded by four heavily armed Arabs, one stationed at each of the buildings four corners. The windows were secured with steel bars and there were only two doors, a large roller door directly facing the gate and another small personnel doorway next to it. There were skylights positioned all along the roof but even if he had been able to get past the guards, the sides of the building were corrugated iron and would be impossible to climb.

Despite these obstacles, Alan began to formulate a plan. Calling the police was not an option. He did not speak more that a few words of Arabic. Explaining what had happened and more importantly, getting them to believe him would take too long. Iris would be dead by the time he got them to respond. Assistance was needed now. Major Grey had to be contacted, but Alan was unsure how to reach him. He thought Iris had his number stored in her phone but that was attached to her belt and was now inside the warehouse with its owner. He used his own phone to call the orphanage, asked the Mother Superior to put Naim in a taxi to the Harbour as quickly as possible. If Grey could not be reached, then he would send have to send Peggy to the police with Naim acting as both guide and interpreter. Finally, Alan phoned Stefan, explained what had happened and asked that they all meet back at the yacht as soon as possible. As he ran back to the bike, Alan went over the plan in his mind. It all hinged on one thing. Iris had appeared to be unconscious when Berswiski was stuffing her into the back of the

Mercedes. If that was the case, Alan felt there was a good chance that Berswiski would wait until she was awake before he started having his fun. If that didn't happen, then Alan would not have the time to execute his plan and his girlfriend was as good as dead.

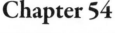

Chapter 54

Iris's cloud drifted lazily across the azure sky, eventually coming to rest atop a majestic, snow capped mountain. She picked up the mooring line and heaved it towards the 'shore'. A tall crocodile dressed in a long, white, flowing robe and turban caught the rope, tied a bowline and dropped the loop over a bollard.

"Nice cloud", said the crocodile as Iris stepped down. "Have you had it long?"

"I don't think so, I can't remember", answered the girl. "Who are you?"

"Oh sorry! My name is Nile. Welcome to Olympus. I'll be your guide for the day. You must be Iris. They told me to expect you. You've come to see the Gods I suppose", replied the crocodile.

"Is there more than one?" asked Iris.

"Sure, shit loads, young ones, old ones, male and female. To be honest, the place is infested with the buggers. They breed like rabbits you know", declared Nile. "So who told you there was only one?"

"I read it in the bible, I think".

Nile rolled his eyes back in his head in an expression of exasperation.

"Shit girl, don't believe everything you read. Next thing you know, you'll be telling me you believed there were weapons of mass destruction in Iraq."

"Don't be silly", replied Iris. "No one believes that".

Nile the crocodile indicated they should start walking along a path which led through the snow to the top of the mountain. As they walked, he asked Iris lots of questions about her journey so far. Where had she been? What was Australia like? When did she first realize she was in love with Alan.

"Also, can you explain to me why you are naked?" he asked

Iris looked down at herself and found that she was indeed nude.

"Well this is a dream, isn't it. I'm always naked in my dreams. It used to embarrass me when I was younger but now I don't think twice about it. Is it a problem?"

"Oh yes" replied Nile. "You can't visit the gods with nothing on. Don't you have a radio or TV or CD player or something?"

Iris chuckled to herself. This certainly was a weird dream.

"I have earrings on", said Iris, suddenly realizing she was wearing the pearls Alan had given her on Sifnos, "so the problem is solved."

Nile agreed. The pair walked on for what seemed like an eternity, never getting any closer to their goal. The crocodile reached into the folds of his robe and pulled out a paper bag filled with something that looked like lumps of solidified, clear slime.

"Dried Jellyfish" he explained, popping one into his mouth, "they're delicious. Would you like to try some?"

Iris declined, knowing that even in a dream they were bound to taste awful.

Suddenly they reached the crest of Olympus and looked down into the valley below them. There they saw the Gods, playing in the sunshine. Barking, chasing balls, chewing bones, lying on their backs with their legs spread wide or licking their genitals. They were dogs not Gods

"You have dyslexia don't you Nile", exclaimed Iris.

"Do I?" asked the crocodile with a look of horror on his face and Iris laughed out loud. This was such a silly dream.

She suddenly felt very tired and lay down on the snow to sleep. Surprisingly it was warm and soft. Iris grabbed hold of a handful and pulled a fold of it over herself. She snuggled down and closed her eyes. Without warning a wave of nausea washed over her and she groaned, holding her stomach.

"Don't wake up Iris" pleaded Nile kneeling at her side with a look of desperation on his face. "Whatever you do don't wake up".

But it was too late, Iris was already racing towards consciousness and Berswiski was waiting for her.

Chapter 55

It only took a few minutes for Alan to ride the short distance to the wharf but by then the sun was already setting. Stefan and Peggy along with Katja, who had driven them there in the Micra, were waiting for him on the dock. Hot on his heals came Naim and Sister Elizabeth. Mother Superior had decided that sending an eight-year-old child in a taxi was not the safest thing to do and as it was an emergency, asked Sister Elizabeth if she would take Naim to his 'Father' in the orphanage's Corolla. This was great news and Alan was able to change his plans accordingly. After he had explained the situation to the group, he asked Sister Elizabeth if she would take Naim to the police station and report Iris's abduction.

"Give them this address" he told the nun, handing her the piece of paper on which he had scribbled the factory name and street details. "Tell them the man is known to Interpol and is considered extremely dangerous".

"I'll go with them", offered Katja, throwing the keys to the little hire car to her son. "It will add weight to the report if I'm there too and I can phone my companies contact with the Egyptian government on the way. He's only a trade delegate I'm afraid, but he may carry some clout".

As soon as the Corolla drove off, Alan and the others headed back to the yacht to collect the equipment needed for Alan's assault on Berswiski's stronghold.

"I'm pretty sure it's not broken", said Stefan as he inspected Alan's little finger when they were back on 'Harvey', "just dislocated. Peggy, can you hold Alan's wrist please? As tight as you can with both hands if you would".

Peggy did as she was asked and braced herself against the side of the saloon table.

"Sorry, this is going to hurt I'm afraid," explained Stefan.

"JESUSFUGGINCRIST" bellowed Alan, as Stefan gave the dislocated digit a firm tug and popped the knuckle back into place. "Next time I take a bloody doctor on board, I'm going to make sure the bugger's heard of anaesthetic".

"I've heard of it," replied Stefan, "but that doesn't help if we don't have any."

As Stefan taped the damaged finger to the one next to it and immobilized the pair with a splint, Alan had Peggy get a screwdriver from the tool kit. In the centre of the saloon, directly under the main mast was a large, solid, compression post. A round wooden pillar designed to take the huge loads generated by the mast and transfer them to the heavy keel. On the front of the post was a polished brass plaque which read:

"Harvey Wharf Banger"
Fremantle Boat Builders
Launched
20th May 1982

Alan got Peggy to unscrew the plaque. Behind it was an opening in the hollow compression post. Inside was a double barrel, sawn off shotgun and six boxes of ammunition.

Alan laid out his plan of attack to his two shipmates as he gathered up the equipment he required.

"What I need from you Stefan", he concluded, "is a diversion. Any ideas?" Stefan thought for a moment and then smiled

"Leave it to us Skipper", he replied "I have just the thing."

Chapter 56

I ris rolled over on the cold, hard, concrete floor and threw up. The world was spinning. Her head was splitting and someone had tied her hands together behind her back. The dream had ended, but surprisingly she was still naked. So was Berswiski and so was Avril Jones. Iris turned onto her back again and sat up quickly. Her head spun and heaved as she glanced around the room. She appeared to be inside some kind of factory. There was machinery, large, heavy wooden workbenches strewn with bits of timber and woodworking tools and various pieces of unfinished furniture. Everything was covered with a fine coating of sawdust and cobwebs. There were no windows and the only way in or out, seemed to be a single doorway that opened into a large vacant warehouse. She knew why she was there, Berswiski had kidnapped her. But what the hell was Ms Jones from Interpol doing there? And why, now that the dream had ended, was everyone naked?

"Ah, Miss Richards you are awake at last. I was beginning to fear that you were going to miss the festivities completely," said Berswiski, as if he was referring to a pleasant garden party. "I can't tell you how pleased I am that we were able to meet up again so unexpectedly. I was so happy to find that we will be able to continue our unfinished business. Svetlana, could you fetch a chair for our guest please. We can't leave the poor girl sitting on the floor."

Ms Jones dragged a simple, wooden, straight-backed chair over to where Iris was sitting, grabbed her by the hair and lifted her bodily to her feet, pulling her backwards so that she stumbled and fell heavily onto the seat.

"Ms. Jones, what's going on? Why are you helping this madman?" asked Iris

"Svetlana has been kind enough to help me with a perfectly ingenious plan for my nuclear warhead," answered Berswiski.

"Svetlana?" Iris had a vague recollection of Dave Randall mentioning a Svetlana Berswiski, "She's your sister?"

Berswiski smiled crookedly. His mouth a cavern of misshapen and crooked teeth.

"Congratulations Miss Richards. Well done. You are correct. Ms Avril Jones is in reality my dearly loved younger sister, Svetlana. She has been working, how would you say? Undercover? For Interpol. Keeping her eyes and ears open for me. Letting me know whenever the bastards were getting too close."

So that was how he had been able to evade capture for so long, he had his sister warning him of Interpol's every move.

Iris realized her only hope of survival was to delay Berswiski until someone came to her rescue. She had to try to keep him talking.

"And where is the bomb? What do you intend to do with it?"

It was an obvious ploy and the evil little Russian saw right through it.

"Oh all right", sighed Berswiski. "I'll play your pathetic little game. No one is going to find you here anyway."

The Russian bowed and with a sweeping gesture indicated a large, shiny, steel conical object sitting in the middle of the factory floor. It was about one and a half metres tall and a metre wide at its base. On its side was the classic hammer and sickle insignia of the former Soviet Republic. There was a numbered keypad and a red LED display visible though an open hatch in the side of the warhead.

Iris assumed that the display would show important information such as the countdown to detonation. The display was flashing.

"That's right Miss Richards", continued Berswiski, "the bomb is all primed and ready to go. In a short time everything within a five-kilometre radius of this point will be vaporized. Every man, woman and child in Alexandria will be dead, either from the blast itself or from radiation poisoning within a week."

Iris could not believe her ears.

"Why? I though the Palestinians were going to destroy Tal-Aviv."

"The Palestinians have nothing to do with our wonderful plan Miss Richards," replied Berswiski. He preened and pranced around the room as if he were in some amazing theatre production and he was the star.

"Those Palestinians are fools. I am doing them a favour by detonating the bomb here. The Jews are the most powerful people on earth today. Do you know why?"

When Iris shook her head, Berswiski replied, "Because of Adolph Hitler."

"You're insane" snapped Iris. "Hitler slaughtered millions of Jews. How did that make them the most powerful people on earth?"

"Of course I'm insane, you dumb bitch", hissed the mad Russian, "but I'm not stupid. Hitler didn't just kill six million Jews. He created six million martyrs. For the past seventy years every time someone said the Jews shouldn't do something, they pounded their chests and pulled out their hair and cried anti-Semitism and reminded the world of how Adolph Hitler murdered six million of their poor comrades. No one is game to criticize the Jews anymore and so they get their own way every time. If the Palestinians had set off the bomb in Tal-Aviv, they would have created many more martyrs, and the whole world would have united with the Jews in a war against the 'Evil Palestinians'. A war in which the Arabs would have been wiped off the face of the earth. But my sister has come up with the most delightful plan. The repercussions of what we are about to do tonight will be so far-reaching, so devastating, the holocaust will seem like a pleasant little picnic."

Berswiski continued his tirade for a few more minutes. Expounding further on his theory of the inexorable growth in the political and financial strength of the Jewish people. He paced around the factory floor, gesticulating wildly, becoming more agitated and angry with each passing second. He suddenly stopped in mid sentence and a look of utter terror passed over his face. He screamed and flailed his arms in the air, trying desperately to ward of the demons in his mind, clawing at his head, trying desperately to rip the pain out of his skull. Berswiski dropped to the floor and curled himself up into a ball, covering his face with his hands. Svetlana Berswiski came to him then and cradled his scrawny misshapen body in her arms, hugging him tightly to her naked bosoms.

"It's alright Vladimir", she cooed stroking his bald head and wiping the tears from his eyes, "you don't need to be afraid anymore my darling. Soon it will be all over and we will be safe forever."

Berswiski shook violently and then slowly, the seizure passed. After a while he dragged himself painfully to his feet and continued his ranting.

"In a short while," said Berswiski, panting heavily, "the computers at the NATO missile detection facility in Dresden will register the launch of a ballistic missile from Israel. Not a real launch of course but merely a computer generation, a virus designed by a colleague of mine, to make it appear a missile has been launched from inside Israel. When our bomb detonates, the whole world will believe that the Jews were responsible."

"Bravo my love", cried Svetlana and she threw her arms around him and kissed him passionately. "You are a genius!"

"Oh my God," exclaimed Iris. "If the rest of the world thinks that Israel has launched an unprovoked attack against a Moslem country, the Islamic nations will slaughter every Jew they can find. Not just in Israel but all over the world. Not only that, but Egypt is also an ally of the US. America would be hard-pressed to continue supporting Israel if it thought the Jews had launched a nuclear weapon against a friendly country."

"Well done Miss Richards" congratulated Svetlana Berswiski. "No one else I have told of our plan has picked up on that before. Both Major Grey and Dave Randall said you were intuitive."

"Enough of this idle banter", interrupted Vladimir Berswiski and grabbing Iris by the hair, dragged her over to a heavy wooden workbench. She struggled with all her might to get free, but the combined strength of her two captors was too much and they easily overpowered her. The mad Russian had tired of Iris's efforts to delay his enjoyment and now he wanted to have some fun. To her horror, Iris noticed that Berswiski, the brother, was getting an erection. He picked up a knife, sliced through the rope that bound Iris's wrists, dragged her to her feet and then pushed her, face down onto the bench.

"Hold down her left hand," he commanded his sister. The woman did as she was told, holding Iris down with a fat arm across the back of her neck. Berswiski picked up a hammer and held the point a large, barbed nail to the back of her hand. Iris screamed as the nail pierced her flesh and was driven into the wooden bench.

Chapter 57

Cyrus Wimple thought that the big Australian man must surely be mad. At first he had refused outright to help.

"If this Russian man is as dangerous as you claim, then you should go to the police", he'd advised. But Alan had explained that there was not enough time. Iris would die if Cyrus didn't help. Again Cyrus Wimple refused. It was too dangerous. Alan would only get himself killed.

"You don't understand Mr. Wimple", pleaded Alan, staring at Cyrus with the eyes of a man who had almost lost all hope. "I love her. I don't know how I'll ever live without her. You have to help. Please."

A few moments later Cyrus Wimple stood at the wheel of 'The Light's' powerful ships' launch, speeding up and down the harbour. He was towing a crazy Australian, who floated thirty metres above him, attached to rope and hanging from a Paraglider. Cyrus had been told to wait for Stephan, the Dutchman and his rude little girlfriend, who would soon send some sort of signal. The American Evangelist began to wonder if maybe it was he himself who was mad.

High above, Alan searched the darkened city below him, trying to make out which building held his lover prisoner. There, near the main highway, was the mosque whose position he had noted earlier in the day. The factory would be a kilometre or so to the north, but he could not tell exactly where. He swung the Paraglider back over the land and the slight up-draft from the warmer land lifted him higher.

Alan's wristwatch alarm sounded, indicating that if all was going to plan, Stefan's diversion should happen any second.

"Come on mate, now would be a good time", said Alan to himself and as if on cue, there was an enormous explosion in front of the gates of the 'Ishmael and Sons' factory. Flames shot twenty metres into the air, a plume of smoke erupted and the heavy steel gate was torn from its hinges and thrown into the air, landing, Alan noted with some satisfaction, on the roof of Berswiski's Mercedes van.

"Well done Stef', that's what I call a diversion", he said.

With the fire at the gate of the factory acting as a beacon, Alan had no difficulty identifying his target. He released the tow-rope and hauled on the control lines, steering the Paraglider towards the roof of the factory. Moments later he landed, unhooked the chute, stuffed it into his rucksack and made his way to the nearest skylight. Within seconds he had it open and had slid down a rope into the warehouse.

Stefan and Peggy looked at each other and hooted with glee. The home made bomb had not only worked, it had performed better than their wildest expectations. When he, Katja and Peggy had been waiting for Alan on the dock a little over half an hour ago, Stefan had noticed the unmistakable stench of fertilizer. There was a broken pallet of the stuff, ruptured bags of it, strewn all over the jetty. At the time Stefan wondered what fool had left such a dangerous substance lying around. When Alan asked the young Dutchman for help, Stefan 'borrowed' a bag of the ammonium nitrate, filled a steel, ten gallon jerrycan with it and added some old sump oil. He then took one of the glow plugs out of 'Harvey's' diesel motor, wired it up to a length of electric cable and stuffed it into the top of the jerrycan. The 'detonator' was activated by connecting the other end of the electric cable to the twelve-volt battery in the little blue hire car. Stefan had no idea what the proportion of oil to ammonium nitrate should be, but from the size of the explosion he must have got it just right.

"Wait here", said Stefan and started to run across the road to the factory. Peggy grabbed him by the collar and pulled him back.

"What the hell are you doing?" she asked. "Alan told us to stay here and wait for the police to arrive."

"He also said there were four guards. He is just one man, injured and with only a shotgun to protect himself. Alan and Iris need my help", replied the young Dutchman.

Peggy thought for a moment.

"No Stefan, they need 'our' help". There was no time to argue, so Stefan ran to the Micra and retrieved the spear gun and fishing knife he had hidden there. Keeping to the shadows as much as possible, the young couple scurried across the road and through the factory gates.

Thomas Ngaddi, wherever he was, would have smiled and raised his head to praise the Lord if he had witnessed Stefan's home made bomb in action. Stefan was wrong about there being four thugs to deal with. There were only three. The fourth member of Berswiski's band of cut-throats had spotted a strange looking object sitting just outside the gates to the factory and had gone over to see what it was. He was surprised to see that some fool had left an old but seemingly perfectly useable jerrycan by the gate. He had been in the process of unlocking the gate when he was blown off his feet by a tremendous explosion. The Egyptian died instantly and now lay some fifteen metres back from where the gate had once been, with a large, jagged piece of jerrycan protruding from his forehead.

His comrades in arms, however, were very much in attendance. The second guard, one who like his dead friend, had been charged with defending the main entrance, was crouched behind what was left of the Mercedes van. He had a MK47 machine gun at the ready, and was waiting for the wave of attacking Egyptian Military he felt certain were storming the building. When Stefan and Peggy came creeping through the gateway he opened fire. Stefan hurled himself sideways knocking Peggy to the ground as he did so. A rain of bullets shot over their heads and kicked up tiny clouds of dust just a metre from where they had fallen. They quickly crawled across the open courtyard and took refuge behind a large pile of lumber, which sat waiting to be used in the factory. Stefan loaded the spear gun and stood up, taking careful aim at the back of the Mercedes van where he believed the Egyptian thug was taking cover.

"Maybe this wasn't such a good idea," he said. "A spear gun is really no match for a machine gun". They were trapped unable to go back and unable to go forward. Another burst of machine gun fire ripped into the timber. The guard yelled something in Arabic which they guessed must be a demand for them to surrender. Stephan dove back down behind the lumber for cover.

"I saw this in a movie once", said Peggy stripping off her top "I hope you're a good shot with that thing honey, or this is going to be the shortest rescue mission on record."

It was a sad but true fact of life that most Egyptian men didn't see a lot of bare breasted young women in Alexandria. So when Peggy held out her t-shirt, and waved it in the universally recognized 'flag of surrender' manner and then walked out naked from the waist up, the Egyptian guard could not believe his luck. A few moments later, he had foolishly lowered his firearm and left the security of his hiding place to get a better look. A second after that he realized his luck had run out, and that he really should have stayed behind the van. The bolt from the spear gun hit him in the centre of his throat, pierced his larynx and wedged itself between the vertebrae of his neck, neatly severing his spinal cord. Stefan ran to the dead thug and picked up the MK47 machine gun. The odds had suddenly got a whole lot better.

Someone was interfering with Vladimir Berswiski's fun and he was not happy about it. No sooner had he driven the first nail through the hand of the annoyingly nosy Miss Richards, when some fool detonated a bomb in front of the factory.

"Fuck!" howled Berswiski, slamming the hammer down on the bench top. "What now?"

He ran across the room to where he had thrown his clothes, picked up a small calibre handgun and raced from the room.

"Watch her", he called to his sister. "If she tries anything, kill her."

Iris pushed herself up from the bench top and looked at her hand. The nail had gone right through, shattering a bone between the wrist and her index finger and embedding itself in the tabletop. It was a packing case nail, the type used to make boxes out of pine. It had a large flat head and a shaft which was barbed to stop it pulling out of the soft wood. Iris was not going anywhere. She recalled her first meeting with Berswiski, remembered the modified stun gun and the pain it had caused, and started to panic. She breathed deeply, trying desperately to calm down, pushing the terror that threatened to engulf her out of her mind. She knew that if she panicked now, all would be lost. There was only one chance. Iris had to make Svetlana Berswiski see sense, convince the woman to let her go.

"H-H-Help me", pleaded Iris, stammering from the combination of fear and pain. "Your brother is sick, Svetlana. Surely you can see that. Let me go free so we can find a doctor who can help Vladimir get better". For an answer Berswiski the sister stepped closer, reached out and began to caress Iris's naked breast. When Iris tried to pull away, Svetlana grabbed hold of her left hand and jerked it upwards. White-hot pain shot through Iris's hand as the barbs on the nail tore into her flesh. Iris writhed in agony and did not pull away when Svetlana resumed stroking her.

"I know my brother is sick Miss Richards," said the older woman "He's totally insane, but that won't matter soon. You see Vladimir also has cancer. His body is riddled with it. A few months ago, a lab technician accidentally let two sub critical masses of uranium 234 get too close to each other. Do you know what occurs when that happens sweetie?" Iris shook her head. "Well I'll tell you," continued Svetlana, "a nuclear reaction starts. Just like in a nuclear power plant. Millions of Rads of radiation are released. Far more than the light duty radiation suits the scientists wear can cope with. Now my poor sweet brother is dying, being eaten from the inside by the cancer that has infested his body. So we have decided to end it all here, with you and your friends and Edmond Grey and a few hundred thousand Egyptians". Iris's ears picked up on the words Edmond Grey.

"The Major is here in Alexandria?" she asked.

"Yes my pretty girl. His plane would have landed about forty minutes ago. Grey or that bitch Veronica Crystal worked out who I was, and they've been tracking the GPS in my cell phone all the way here. I've turned it off now, so they won't find us until it's too late for you, but they know that Vladimir and I are in Alexandria somewhere. They're close enough to enjoy the show."

Suddenly Svetlana Berswiski lunged forward and kissed Iris passionately on the mouth, her tongue searching for the young girl's. Iris hesitated for a split-second and then kissed her back. Passionately Ms Berswiski smiled to herself and let the young Australian girl take control. Iris gently pushed her backwards until she was pressed hard against the workbench. They kissed again, tongues darting, probing and searching. Iris pushed her knee between the elder woman's legs and ground her thigh into the old dyke's pubic bone. Svetlana was not surprised. It had happened before and she had no delusions about what was going on. The young girl was trying to befriend her. By attempting to ingratiate herself with the older woman, she was hoping to delay the inevitable. Let her, she thought. It won't make ant difference. Svetlana was enjoying the attention Iris was giving her. It was nice to have a beautiful young girl make love to you. But when Vladimir returned, that was when the real fun would begin. Iris groaned theatrically and kissed the old woman harder, making her arch her back across the bench top. Suddenly Iris pulled away and Svetlana opened her eyes. A split-second later Iris smashed the hammer into the side of the old bitch's head.

Berswiski the sister, was wrong. When Iris had pushed her back against the workbench, it was not some ploy to ingratiate herself with her. She was not trying to convince Svetlana to help her escape. The plan was to try to get hold of the hammer, the hammer Vladimir had foolishly left lying on the bench. Iris had not meant to kill the old hag, merely to knock her out, render her unconscious long enough to escape. But fear and adrenaline had made her stronger than she realized and now the evil old bag was dead. The bad news was that the hammer was the type used by engineers. It didn't have a claw for pulling out nails, just that useless round ball that was supposed to be used for peening over rivets or something.

Suddenly she heard the rat-a-tat of machine gun fire from outside. She hoped it was the police, but decided not to hang around to find out unless she absolutely had too. Hanging on the wall next to her was a pile of tools. One of these she recognized as a pair of bolt cutters, similar too, but a lot bigger than the ones Alan had used to cut the barb off the fish-hook that had embedded itself in Stefan's leg. They were too far away to reach, so Iris dropped her shoulder onto the workbench and pushed. The bench moved. Only a few millimetres, but it did move. Iris pushed again and the bench inched closer.

Unless one was prepared to paraglide onto the roof, smash through one of the skylights and abseil down to the ground, the only way in or out of the old, abandoned Ishmael and Sons factory was through one of two doors. The first door was at the front of the building, an enormous, silver roller door, large enough to admit even the biggest of furniture trucks. It was locked. The second at the side of the building was a small, green personnel door with the

Egyptian Arabic equivalent of the words 'Keep Out. Trespassers Will Be Prosecuted' written on the outside. It too was locked.

"Stand back", commanded Stefan, aiming the recently acquired AK47 at the door and pulling the trigger. There was a loud crack and miraculously a fist-sized hole appeared in the door where the lock had been. Stefan kicked the door open and ushered Peggy inside.

The interior of the factory was cavernous and apart from the loom from the city that glowed weakly through the skylights in the roof, it was pitch black. As their eyes slowly became accustomed to the gloom, they began to make out dozens of old packing crates stacked haphazardly around the warehouse. Piles of rubbish littered the floor and in the far corner stood a shipping container.

Suddenly someone grabbed Peggy's arm and clasped a hand over her mouth stifling her scream.

"I thought I asked you two to wait outside for the Police", hissed Alan.

"Shit" hissed Stefan, "you nearly gave me a heart attack."

"Sorry, but you shouldn't be here. It's too dangerous," answered Alan.

"Iris is our friend too Alan", stated Peggy. "Besides Stefan, has already taken out two of the Egyptian thugs and nicked a machine gun"

Stefan held up the AK47 for Alan to see. Alan nodded. Peggy had a valid point. He had no right to ask them to just sit outside while their friend was in danger. Especially as they had the bigger gun.

"Okay. Well as far as I can make out in this darkness, the factory seems to be split up into three sections. This one appears to be the dispatch area," began Alan. "Next there is a warehouse section. I was on my way there when you two started shooting holes in everything. When I first got inside I was sure I heard voices coming from the other end of the building. That must be..." Alan's voice stopped abruptly and Peggy felt her blood turn to ice. Someone was giggling quietly at the other end of the room. "COVER YOUR EYES", yelled Alan as he pulled 'Harvey's' flare gun from his belt and fired. The brilliant flare arced across the room and landed on a mound of rubbish near the wall. Within seconds the timber off cuts, old cleaning rags and half-empty tins of varnish caught fire, lighting up the warehouse.

One of the Egyptian guards leapt out from behind a packing case and grabbed Peggy by the hair, pulling her backwards. As the Egyptian dragged her towards him, Peggy spun around, dropped onto one knee and lashed out, punching her attacker in the nuts. The man went down like a ton of bricks and she finished him off with a blow to the head with a piece of packing case timber. Peggy had three brothers, all much taller than she and all of whom teased her mercilessly about her stature. That is until she learnt how to use it to her advantage.

Stefan did not fair as well. In the brief flash of light from the flare, he caught a glimpse of a bald, big nosed, scrawny, little man, scurrying across the warehouse towards the shipping container. The man was naked. It had to be Berswiski. Stefan swung the barrel of the machine gun towards him, pulling the trigger as he did so. The AK47 barked a dozen times and a line of bullet holes raced across the wall behind the Russian. As he dove for cover behind the shipping container, Berswiski raised his pistol and fired. It was only one shot but it found its mark, hitting Stefan in the thigh a few centimetres below the hip. Peggy screamed as her boyfriend fell to the floor.

Stefan grabbed his leg, rolling around on the floor in agony. He'd had no idea a bullet wound would cause so much pain. Peggy put her arms under his shoulders and dragged him behind a packing crate. She tore open the leg of his jeans and inspected the wound. The bullet had passed right though, missing the bone by mere millimetres. It was bleeding but not copiously and Stefan knew instantly that the bullet had missed any major blood vessels.

"I'm okay," he reassured Peggy "It's just a flesh wound." Then he called to Alan who had taken cover on the other side of the building. "Go after him Alan. Don't let that bastard get away. I'm not badly hurt."

By this time the mound of rubbish was well ablaze, lighting up the warehouse, so Alan had no trouble picking his way across the floor towards the shipping container. As he passed the fire, he stooped and picked up a piece of timber, wrapped an old, paint covered rag around it and set it aflame. Slowly he edged his way closer to Berswiski's hiding place, and when he was close enough, threw the torch over the top of the container. The torch started a second blaze and a few moments later Berswiski made a dash for it, firing his pistol wildly as he ran. This time the shots went wide and Alan raised the sawn-off shotgun to his shoulder and fired. The disadvantage with a shotgun, especially one which has had its barrel shortened, is that they are wildly inaccurate except at very close range. As Berswiski bolted through the door into the next section of the factory, part of the heavy wooden door jamb exploded in a cloud of wood chips but Berswiski escaped unharmed into the next room.

The doorway through which the mad Russian fled, led into a large hangar type area. It was in total darkness and Alan had the presence of mind to hang back long enough to ensure Berswiski was not waiting to ambush him just inside the door. He picked up the torch he had thrown over the shipping container and keeping himself away from the door, hurled it through the doorway. It skidded to a halt on the bare, concrete floor a few metres inside and continued to burn, throwing some light into the room. Alan cracked open his shotgun and replaced the spent cartridge. He dropped to the floor and peered around the doorway. When he had ascertained that the coast was clear, he crept into the room and took cover behind one of the concrete pillars supporting the roof.

Alan quickly made his way across the warehouse, running as fast and quietly as his sprained ankle would allow him. The torch lying in the middle of the room started to splutter and die and suddenly the factory was plunged into total darkness. Alan froze willing himself to somehow merge with the pillar he was hiding behind, trying to give his eyes time to adjust to the blackness that engulfed him. He strained his ears for any sound that might indicate Berswiski's whereabouts. But the only sound he heard was something scurrying along the wall. Tiny, rapid footsteps, probably a rat or a mouse that had been disturbed by the fracas. Everywhere he looked, ominous shadows seemed to swirl and ooze around the room. In the darkness, his eyes were starting to play tricks on him. He began to imagine he could see someone or something moving about just in front of him. The pounding in his ears from his heart and his laboured breath sounded as loud as a steam train in the deathly quiet of the factory. Alan forced himself to slow his breathing, straining his ears and eyes, trying desperately to find his quarry. Someone or something dislodged a packing case or a piece of timber from its stack and it smashed to the floor with a deafening crash. Alan swung around, the shotgun aiming in the direction of the noise, but there was no further sound. Slowly his eyes began to adjust to the darkness and he was able to make out some of the room's more obvious features. This section of the factory was similar to the dispatch area, except the room was largely empty save for a large truck that had been raised up on blocks. Its tyres and wheels had been removed and its engine lay on its side on the floor next to it. Alan edged closer and could make out that part of the vehicle's chassis had been cut away with an oxt-acetylene torch. In the dark he could just make out writing on the truck's side. Although he had no way of knowing for sure, the words looked Russian.

There were large metal tool cupboards all along one wall and on the opposite side of the room was a timber storage area which housed the long timber planks that had once been destined to become furniture. At the far end of the warehouse was another stack of packing crates. There seemed to be a faint light coming from behind the crates, perhaps from an open doorway or an internal window.

Suddenly Berswiski leapt out from behind one of the tool cupboards and fired his pistol. The bullet hit the stack of timber just a few centimetres from Alan's head. He dove to the ground and crawled as fast a he could towards the packing cases and safety.

But the third Egyptian guard was waiting for him. In the dim light from the doorway Alan could tell the Egyptian was a big man. As tall as Alan himself and even more powerfully built. His long, black, greasy hair was tied back in a ponytail and he sported a moustache that hung down each side of his mouth, drooping past his chin. His most obvious feature however was the jagged scar that ran from his forehead down his left cheek. Whatever horrible accident or malicious act had caused the scar had also damaged the Egyptian's left eye and its colourless, lifeless eyeball stared blindly from its damaged socket. In his hand the Egyptian held a large curved knife and as Alan tried to crawl past on hands and knees he slashed downward slicing the flesh behind Alan's shoulder and opening a gaping wound that went through to the bone. Alan rolled away from his attacker, kicking out with his left foot as he went. The kick deflected the Egyptian's next thrust and gave Alan enough time to clamber to his feet and swing the shotgun into action. The first shell exploded just as 'Scarface' threw himself to one side and the blast went wide. Alan took cover behind another concrete pillar and reloaded.

Suddenly there was a loud mechanical clunk followed by an electronic hum and as Alan peered into the gloom, bracing himself for either Berswiski or the Egyptian to attack again, he became vaguely aware that the overhead lights were beginning to glow weakly as they warmed up. Someone had found the main light switch. Scarface lunged again, but this time the Australian was prepared for him. As the big Egyptian slashed the blade towards Alan's face, he swung the shotgun across in front of him, deflecting the knife down and away from his body. He continued the motion, forcing his attacker's knife arm in a wide arc down towards the floor. Then he brought the shotgun upwards in a wide, anti clockwise curve. When the butt of the shotgun was level with the Egyptians face, Alan stabbed back as hard as he could with the gun, breaking the thugs nose, but the guard came at him again with a bellow, slashing and stabbing with his knife. Alan grabbed the Egyptians knife arm and pulled the attacker towards himself, guiding the attackers blow away and then lashing out with the barrel of the shotgun. He hissed in pain as the dislocated finger, still held rigid in its splint jarred as the gun smashed into the thug's head. The blow wasn't enough to phase the man for long, but it had done enough damage to make the Egyptian to falter for a second. Long enough for Alan to raise the shotgun, and at point-blank range, pull the trigger.

Only a few seconds had past, but already the powerful electric lights were lighting up the factory as if it were midday. As Alan watched the Egyptian guard slump to the floor dead, Berswiski hurled himself onto the big Aussie's back knocking him to the ground. Alan landed face down with the insane little Russian still clinging to him with all his madness-induced strength. Alan pushed himself up and reached behind his head, trying to drag the madman off him, but Berswiski had picked up a length of electrical cord and he wrapped the cable around Alan's neck and began to pull as hard as he could.

The garotte tightened, cutting off the air that Alan's lungs craved so badly. The Aussie flailed uselessly behind his head again, trying to grab hold of the electrical cord, but Berswiski pulled tighter. Suddenly the Russian threw himself forward and sunk his teeth into Alan's injured shoulder. Alan swung around trying desperately to shake the madman from his back but Berswiski held on like a leach, pulling even tighter on the cable around Alan's throat. Slowly the world went black and Alan felt his life slipping away.

Chapter 58

Vladimir Micael Berswiski did not die of the cancer that ravaged his body. Nor did he die in the fiery inferno of a nuclear blast. He died when a young and beautiful Australian girl, naked and bleeding from the terrible wounds he had inflicted upon her, crushed his skull with a blow from a pair of heavy-duty bolt cutters.

"LEAVE HIM ALONE YOU HORRIBLE LITTLE BASTARD", screamed Iris as she smashed the bolt cutters as hard as she could into the back of the evil Russian's head.

Alan coughed for a good three minutes before he'd regained his breath enough to sit up and embrace the woman he loved.

"I'm supposed to be the one saving you", he complained hoarsely and covered his girlfriend's face with kisses.

"We're not out of the woods yet honey", said Iris and a look of despair passed across her face. "That mad bastard has left a nuclear bomb in the next room and it's ticking".

"You're joking," said a girl's voice from behind them and Iris looked up to see Peggy standing there, the injured Stefan supporting himself on her shoulder.

"Sorry we're a bit late, but Stefan couldn't get the bleeding to stop. We have to get him to a doctor as soon as possible." She noticed that the other two were also badly injured, "You pair as well by the look of it".

Alan stood and whipped off his. T-shirt and gave it to Iris. It was huge on her, with one shoulder seam coming half-way down her arm and the hem stopping just above her knees. Instant cotton dress.

"Let's have a look at this bomb", suggested Stefan, his voice quavering from pain and exertion. He looked dreadful, deathly pale and obviously weak from loss of blood, but it would have been futile to try to get him to rest. The four made their way to the next room and Berswiski's nuclear warhead. The LCD timer on the control panel read 2:01 and as they watched it changed to 2:00.

"Oh for fuck's sake", swore Peggy "two fucking minutes! How do we stop this thing in two minutes?" No one had any idea.

"No. It must be two hours. If it was minutes, the zero's would be seconds. It's still showing 2:00. We need to call the Army," suggested Stefan. "They've got bomb disposal experts don't they?"

Iris raced over to the workbench next to the bomb, where she had been nailed just minutes before. She dragged Svetlana Berswiski's body out of the way, dove into the old bat's handbag, and pulled out her mobile phone.

"We need to call Interpol," she explained. "I don't know Major Grey's number but I'll bet Ms Berswiski here has it in her contacts list." She turned the phone on and waited for the software to load. "Fuck. She's got a PIN. I can't get it to switch on."

"Give it here!" commanded Peggy. "I'll put my SIM card in it. She may have the number saved in the phones memory, not just on her SIM."

While the diminutive blonde swapped the cards and powered up Svetlana's phone, Iris explained who Ms Jones or rather Berswiski was and how she came to be lying on the floor, naked and with a bloody hammer lying next to her.

"Houston we have lift off!" announced Peggy. "There's no listing here under Grey, but there's a number for a D. Randall. My guess is that would be your mate Dave."

She stabbed 'call' and handed the phone to Iris. Seconds later she was rapidly explaining their plight to the young Interpol man.

"So how did you get hold of Svetlana Berswiski's phone?" he asked.

Iris explained, adding "She told me you guys had discovered who she really was?"

"Sure. Veronica Crystal worked it out a few days ago. We've been tracking her movements via the GPS on her mobile phone. She led us to Alexandria and then we lost the signal. She must have known we were following her and intentionally turned off her phone once she was sure we were where she wanted us. If you give me the number of your SIM and activate the GPS, we can track you to your location and disarm the bomb... Or at least keep you company until it goes off."

They all hoped like hell he was joking. Iris handed the phone back to Peggy. Svetlana's phone was the same model as the one she had and she felt sure she knew how to activate the GPS. A few minutes later Randall confirmed they had the signal.

"Just sit tight for a while. We'll get some of the local guys there ASAP. The Major and I will be there in about half an hour." The phone went dead.

"Guy's!" It was Stefan, "I need to get to a hospital..." He collapsed onto the floor. Peggy yelled and rushed to his side. He was pale and his breathing was shallow and ragged. The leg of his jeans was covered in blood. The temporary dressing hadn't worked and Stefan was losing too much blood. He would die unless they could stop it. Alan rolled him onto his back, pulled down his jeans, and gently peeled back the rags that Peggy had used to staunch the bleeding. The bullet had gone right through his leg. The wounds, front and back, were oozing blood. Oozing was good, better than pumping out. It meant that Stefan was correct. The bullet had missed any major blood vessel. But Stefan was still loosing too much blood and he'd certainly die if they couldn't stop the flow quickly.

Alan whipped off his belt and wrapped it tightly around Stefan's leg above the wounds, making an effective tourniquet.

"Iris, see if you can find some packing tape. You know, that wide sticky tape stuff they use. Peggy, try to find some clean rags," ordered Alan. "Oh and keep your eyes open for a first aid kit. A box with a white or red cross on it hanging on the wall. Oh! also some super glue." The two girls rushed off.

By this time the warehouse lighting was at full power. Iris noticed that there was an office complex, built on a mezzanine floor at the rear of the production area. She raced up the stairs and into the first office, rubbing her hand up and down the wall just inside the doorway, searching for a light switch. She found it, fumbled for a few seconds and then the fluorescent tube lighting flickered and flashed and then settled to a brilliant, blazing, brightness. She scurried from office to office, searching desperately for packaging tape or a first-aid box. In the third office she found both. She also found three old sets of overalls hanging on a hook in the gent's toilets.

Peggy had already made it back with a pile of cleaning rags and a tube of superglue. What the hell was Alan going to do with that? thought Iris.

The big Aussie rolled Stefan on to his side and selected a crepe bandage from the first aid kit. The hole in Stefan's leg was big and ragged. The bullet had gone in easily enough but it had torn a sizeable chunk of flesh out as it exited. Alan cleaned the wound on the back of his crewman's leg carefully, then, to Iris and Peggy's horror, he squeezed out a big drop of superglue on the edge of the wound and pinched it closed with his fingers. Next he turned the Dutch man on his back and repeated the process on the bullet hole in the front. Finally he wrapped a wide strip of cloth around Stefan's leg and finished it off with turn after turn of packing tape. The bleeding had stopped totally.

"I saw that done in a movie once," he explained. "I don't know if it's toxic, but it's certainly stopped poor Stefan loosing any more blood. Anyway, my guess is it's not and it's better than letting him bleed to death."

Peggy rolled up two pairs of Iris's overalls and made a pillow for her boyfriends head. Then she dragged over a small wooden crate and used it to elevate Stefan's leg. He looked dreadful, perhaps even close to death, and Peggy was trying to keep calm. He needed her. Now was not the time to fall apart, she told herself. She had to be ready to react if something went wrong.

Something went wrong!

"Shit," This time it was Iris. "The timer on the bomb just clicked over to 1:00."

"What? How could that be? How long have we been here?"

Peggy looked at her watch. Six minutes or so. I checked the time when we thought we had only two minutes left."

Alan was kneeling next to Stefan checking his pulse. He jumped to his feet, rushed over and checked the timer himself.

"She's right. I don't think this is a timer at all. I think it's some type of computer interface. I reckon it's loading the program. Once it reaches zero, the count down begins... or it blows up."

"So how long have we got?"

Alan shrugged. "Haven't got a clue. Seconds, minutes, hours, your guess is as good as mine."

He rushed over to the work bench and retrieved some tools, a couple of screwdrivers and the hammer. Iris's murder weapon.

"Maybe we should try to disarm it. I have no idea how, but if we take this cover off the front of the timer, perhaps I can work out what to do."

"Are you mad?" screamed Peggy. You could set the thing off."

Alan shrugged sadly. "I'm sorry. I guess you're right. But maybe doing something is better than doing nothing. We have no idea of how long we have before this thing explodes. It could be a few seconds or even a few hours, but from what Iris has told us, I think it's going to be sooner rather than later. If it's going to go off anyway, we might as well try whatever we can. We'll either fix it or fuck it. One of those options means we're not going to be vaporized."

Neither Iris nor Peggy were convinced by Alan's doctrine of doing something is better than doing nothing, but Iris at least could see his point. Well sort of. Stefan was out for the count, so it was up to the three of them to decide.

Peggy picked up one of the screwdrivers and handed it to Alan. Seconds later he was kneeling in front of the bomb unscrewing the face plate.

Five minutes later the control device was disassembled. There were bits of wire leading in every direction. Some seemed to go to some sort of electronic component, but no one was absolutely sure which wire or which component was the one they needed to disable.

Alan shook his head. "I'm still in the dark here. But I'm going to take a guess and say I think we should keep going. Berswiski was too confident to figure someone would be able to stop him, so I reckon he wouldn't have bothered with any booby trap type set up. It should be just the one detonator set to go off for God knows when. We cut the wires and isolate the detonator from the bomb and we should be okay."

The two girls nodded. What did they have to lose. Alan picked up the pair of bolt cutters and slowly began to cut the wires. One by one.

Stefan groaned and tried to sit up. He had started to come around. Peggy rushed to his side and urged him to lay back down again.

"You'll be alright Darling," she told him. "Just lie still. Help is on its way." Then she sat on the floor next to him and cradled his head in her lap, gently stroking his hair and whispering words of love and encouragement.

"That's six," announced Alan, "about another eight or so to go. So far so good."

Soon there was only one wire left. It was sheathed in red plastic insulation and was about twice as thick as the other wires. Alan said he thought this was the main cable to the detonator. He surmised that such a wire would have to be a heavier gauge to handle the powerful DC current needed. He put the jaws of the bolt cutters over the wire and began to squeeze the handles together.

Suddenly, without warring, there was a loud crash from the roof of the factory and a small soft drink sized canister plopped onto the floor and started to belch clouds of thick black smoke.

"NOT AGAIN." yelled Iris, "PLEASE GOD, NOT AGAIN."

As she slipped slowly into unconsciousness, Iris held out her hand to the man she loved, she felt his fingers close gently around hers. She felt the world heave and spin and once again the blackness closed in.

Chapter 59

The wedding of Stefan Van Kesling to Miss Margaret Lee Winchester went off like clockwork. Well, except for the nanosecond of panic Stefan felt, before he realized that Peggy and Margaret were one and the same person. For a split-second he'd wondered if the celebrant was trying to hitch him to the wrong girl. The ceremony was both lavish and unique. After all, it's not every day a girl gets married while standing under the stars between the massive stone paws of Egypt's iconic Sphinx. Both the bride and groom were dressed in a blindingly white, traditional Egyptian costume. They exchanged simple yet heartfelt vows, white gold wedding rings and declared their love for each other by finishing their nuptials with a lingering, smouldering kiss.

Iris thought Alan made the most handsome best man who had ever drawn breath and did a sterling job herself in the role of maid of honour. She also followed to the letter, the well documented and traditional practice of blubbering like a baby throughout the entire proceedings.

The guest list at the wedding and the reception afterwards turned out to be quite substantial. Peggy's parents, George and Debra together with her brothers Nick and Paul had arrived a few days before. Stefan's dad, Lars left his busy medical practice for two days and flew down with Katja. Alex and Pamela were there, as was the enigmatic 'Major Edmond grey and his wife Marjorie. All the other guys from Interpol, including Mrs Crystal and her husband Andrew, plus the entire ensemble of St Raphael's orphanage were also invited. Naim looked splendid, dressed in a brilliant white suit, as he walked slowly down the aisle ahead of Peggy scattering flower petals. Finally, the Egyptian Foreign Minister, his wife and a quiet, silver haired woman with a walking cane whom the Major introduced as Ms Williams also attended. Iris felt certain she was most likely some big wig with Interpol.

The reception was held in a marquee erected a hundred metres or so from the famous, iconic, ancient Egyptian landmark. There was bottle after bottle of excellent wine, champagne flowed freely and there was a buffet with enough sumptuous and delectable food to feed a party twice the size of the assembled guests.

Music was provided by a talented string quartet and an army of waiters attended to the guests every whim. Best of all, the entire thing was paid for by an extremely grateful and equally generous Egyptian Government.

Iris gazed in amazement at the spectacle before her and pondered how much things had changed in the past four weeks. Her second foray into the wonderful world of CT18 nerve gas had not lasted as long as the first, but it was still an experience she wished she hadn't had to repeat. Once again there was the nausea and blinding, skull-splitting headaches, and once again she was subjected to the indignity of chucking up into a bucket. This time at least she had company. It appeared that the effect of CT18 was something you grew accustomed to, or maybe she didn't get such a large dose as the others. Whatever the reason Iris was awake hours before the rest of the group. When she felt well enough, the Major once again presented himself ready to apologize. But before he could say a word, Iris tore strips off him and told him in no uncertain terms, exactly how she felt about the way Interpol had handled itself.

"You didn't have to gas me and my friends you know", she berated the elderly agent. "All you had to do was look before you charged in, and you would have seen we already had the situation under control".

"Except for the little matter of a still armed nuclear warhead sitting right in front of you", countered Grey.

"Okay. You have a valid point there, but...." The Major held up his hand for silence and walked over to a television set that sat in the corner of the hospital room. He reached into his pocket, took out a disc and inserted it into the DVD player.

At first Iris could not make out what she was watching. The images bounced and jiggled, swaying from side to side, and never seemed to settle on anything she was able to identify. Then the picture stabilized and all became clear. She was watching images relayed back from one of Interpol's miniature cameras, one similar to the device Dave Randall had shown her in the café back in Athens. He'd said every operative used one during an assault or when in the field. The vision she was watching was taken by a man running across the roof of a building. The agent spoke into his communications unit relaying commands or reporting his position or something. Iris couldn't tell because the man spoke in Arabic and Edmond Grey did not offer to translate. The agent stopped near a skylight, its opaque cover illuminated by the light shining from inside the building. A gloved hand holding a large, flat bladed knife appeared on the screen and proceeded to prize off the cover of the skylight. Moments later Iris was looking down on herself, kneeling in front of Berswiski's nuclear warhead. She was wearing Alan's t-shirt and her left hand was wrapped in a blood soak rag. To her left was Alan, his shoulder sliced open by the Arab guard and his back drenched with blood. To her right was Stefan, his life slowly dripping away onto the concrete floor of the warehouse. Standing a metre or so to his right was the diminutive form of Peggy, uninjured and still clutching the AK47 as if her very life depended on it.

The Major pressed a button on the remote control and the image on the screen froze. "After we received your phone call on Svetlana Berswiski's cell phone", began Grey. "We contacted the local Interpol officers and informed them of the situation. Iris nodded her head to indicate she understood and the Major continued. "We told the men here in Alexandria that they were to use extreme caution. You'd told us that Berswiski was dead. But as yet we were still uncertain of the whereabouts of the arms dealer. The local guys were told to keep a very careful look out for him."

Edmond Grey indicated the picture on the television and went on.

"I assume that you've already guessed these pictures were taken by one of our men during the mission?" Iris once again nodded. "Quite so! We knew from evidence collected at other crime scenes that Berswiski had at least one female accomplice, may be even others ..." Iris's eyes went back to the image on the screen and for the first time she saw what the Egyptian agent must have seen. He had absolutely no way of knowing who the four people he was watching were. He would have almost certainly been given Berswiski's description, perhaps also that of Iris herself but not of Alan, Stefan or Peggy. He would know that the mad Russian had kidnapped an Australian girl and taken her to the old Ishmael and Son's factory. He would also know that Berswiski had a female accomplice. Peggy had been lucky enough to come through the whole thing without injury and she was standing next to them holding a machine gun. The image on the screen took on a whole new meaning. Now there were three badly injured 'Hostages' and a woman holding them captive with an AK47.

"Your man thought Peggy was Berswiski's accomplice!" interrupted Iris. "He thought she was Svetlana Berswiski".

Edmond Grey nodded. "Yes, that is to say, he knew she wasn't Svetlana Berswiski, Peggy is to young, but the Egyptian agent had wrongly assumed that Peggy was one of the bad guys."

Over the next few hours Iris and the Major chatted, taking it in turns to fill in the blanks whenever it was needed. Iris told of how she had been nailed to the workbench. She admitted to killing Svetlana in self-defence, and described in detail how she had used the bolt cutters to free herself. With only one hand, that part had been quite difficult. She'd placed the jaws of the bolt cutters over the head of the nail and pulled the handle towards her until one handle was pressing against her stomach and heaved on the other with all her strength. The nail went "plink" and the head flew off into the air. Of course she was still nailed to the table, but she was now able to rip her hand upwards, off the top of the severed nail. That hurt, heaps. Grey looked quite pale. It was also Iris who had found the light switch and turned on the lights inside the warehouse.

Disarming the bomb didn't prove to be the problem Iris and the others had envisaged. The timer on the bomb, the Major explained, wasn't a timer at all but a computerized control panel. It controlled the built in safety protocol which stopped the bomb being accidentally activated. There were five steps required for the bomb to be armed and each step required a security code to be entered before each arming sequence. There was also a delay between each step to allow the operator time to reconsider his options. Berswiski had entered the first four security codes, but as he wasn't around when the controller clicked over to allow the final instructions, -which was the detonation time, -the bomb was still waiting for that final instruction. The bomb was armed, but the detonation time had not yet been entered and because of this, it had reset to its default settings This meant that there was nearly an hour left before the bomb went past the point of no return and went bang. Following directions, by phone, from a bomb disposal expert with the appropriate knowledge in the US, Dave Randall had made the nuclear device safe.

Ironically the computerized controller had been designed and built by Berswiski himself back during the cold war. The Russians still denied that the bomb was theirs in the first place, but they took it away anyway. It was now on a Russian transporter on its way back to god knows where, to be decommissioned once again.

That was a month ago. Well twenty-six days to be precise. Iris's hand was healing nicely, as was Alan's shoulder. Poor Stefan had not faired so well. He'd lost a lot of blood and became gravely ill. In his weakened state the CT18 nerve gas had nearly killed him. He remained in a coma for three days. He now walked with a cane and according to his doctor probably would do so for a few months. Iris couldn't help feeling responsible in some way, but Stefan would not hear of it.

"Shit happens," he would say. "It is not your fault that some madman finds you irresistible and the people who love you have to come and rescue you. Berswiski was to blame and he's dead. We all came out alive, so 'all's well that ends well.'"

Of course that was not the end of it. There were endless interviews with a plethora of Government officials from a dozen 'involved countries'. Countless reports to sign and bits of evidence to verify, and then a number of audiences with high ranking Government big wigs who slowly, grudgingly came to accept that Iris and her friends were the good guys. Then there was a series of sessions with a trauma counsellor for the whole group. They helped immensely, but Iris still suffered with recurring nightmares.

The Major and the bean counters at Interpol HQ were not so slow in showing their gratitude however. The four shipmates were soon to learn that there was a sizeable reward for information leading to the capture, 'Dead or Alive' of the infamous Vladimir Micael

Berswiski. There was also another large chunk of money paid to them for the recovery of the nuclear warhead.

Iris Richards, Alan Tew and Mr and Mrs Stefan Van Kesling were now worth an almost obscene amount of money.

There was however a small detail that, even though everyone understood why, Iris and the others found hard to stomach. The Egyptian, Greek and Russian Governments together with the big wigs at Interpol, the CIA et al., decided it would be in the public interest, if the fact that a nuclear catastrophe in the centre of Alexandria had been narrowly averted, was kept a secret. Only a couple of dozen people would ever know what really happened.

Chapter 60

A lan Tew, skipper of the yacht 'Harvey Wharf Banger' took in the stays'l a couple of centimetres and watched as the luff of the sail quietly popped into the required shape. It was an old sail but it still had a couple of year's life left in it. Alan ran a loving hand over the polished timber coachwork and silently thanked the old girl for her friendship over the years, hoping as he did that there would be many more to come. He looked down at the water and saw with satisfaction the bow wave building slowly in front of them, rushing along the sides and then washing outwards before disappearing into the gloom. The Nile was wide at this point, so wide in fact that even during the day one would have been unable to see either bank. Still, a good lookout was needed, just in case they chanced upon a fishing dhow or something floating in the water. Iris wandered up to where he was standing at the rail, leaving the steering of the yacht in the capable hands of the electronic autopilot. She was dragging the enormous cushion that the couple used like a beanbag whenever they were on watch together.

"It's quiet with the others away" she whispered, falling into the old habit of talking quietly during the night watch. "It seems strange without them hanging around."

"They said they'd be back after the honeymoon", Alan reminded her. The young married couple had flown off to Australia earlier that day to meet all Peggy's other relatives and friends. They would stay about a month and then do the same thing in The Netherlands with Stefan's family. Stefan intended to continue his studies, but had delayed his return to university for another year. Surprisingly, Mr and Mrs Van Kesling senior had agreed, stating that they thought it was in his best interest if he took some time off to recover from his injuries. Besides, it wasn't as if he needed to rush out and earn some money, not after the huge reward.

Iris dropped the cushion onto the deck and plopped down, patting the space beside her for Alan.

"Iris, can I ask you a question?" asked the big Aussie when he was comfortable.

"Yes of course I'll marry you"

"How do you know that's what I was going to ask?" said Alan.

"Well", replied his new fiancée, "for the first time since the day we met, you've set the mains'l all wrong, so you obviously have something important on your mind. Was I wrong?"

"No."

"Well go on then ask me properly!" demanded Iris.

Alan rose from the cushion and then got down on one knee, extracting a small black felt covered box from his pocket as he did so.

"Iris Richards, will you marry me please?" For an answer Iris threw her arms around his neck and kissed him until they were both dizzy from lack of air.

"Yes, yes, yes" replied Iris as Alan placed the outrageously expensive diamond ring on her finger. Then they kissed again.

Later that evening, as they lounged together on the huge cushion watching the Nile slip silently by, it was Iris's turn to ask the questions.

"Alan, I love you madly, but is it alright if I keep my maiden name?"

Alan tried to look hurt, but even in the dark it was hard to hide the smile

"I thought you might prefer to keep the name Richards now that you mention it," commented Alan. The couple sat back and enjoyed the quiet for a few minutes but Alan couldn't resist for long. "Knock, Knock" he started.

"Oh no", groaned Iris, knowing something stupid was coming "Who's there?"

"Irish stew" replied Alan.

"Irish stew who?"

"Irish stew is the name of my new fiance," answered Alan laughing at his own joke. It was not one of his better ones. And that was saying something.

"Okay skipper." said Iris desperately trying to change the subject. "Where are you taking me for my honeymoon?"

"Well, I have it on very good authority that Sicily is just beautiful this time of year..."

Chapter 61

The 'arms dealer' was happy, very, very happy. The new arrangements were working admirably. The young woman who he'd engaged as an intermediary between himself and his clients seemed to be reliable. She was also both discreet and professional. She had to be, the 'arms dealer' knew where her young son went to school. She was a widow so there was no husband to ask awkward questions and as she was new to the large, impersonal American city she now called home. No one would notice any unexpected changes to her lifestyle that a sudden huge influx of cash might cause.

The 'arms dealer' smiled to himself at his good fortune. He had found a true gem. She had already arranged a meeting with a gentleman from the Italian Mafia who was in the market to purchase a considerable quantity of firearms. It seemed there was going to be a war between two rival factions of 'The Family' and Don Luigi was itching to get hold of all the weapons he could lay his hands on.

The 'arms dealer' smiled again. Those Sicilians, they were so hot headed.

The End

My other titles are:
A Murderous Addiction
Innocent Until Proven Deadly
Dead Tropical
Dark Murder
A Pain in the Arts
Alien Vermin
And the children's novel
Charlotte and the Morthe

Join me on Facebook
Kevin William Barry Author

Did you love *The Voyage*? Then you should read *Innocent Until Proven Deadly* by Kevin William Barry!

John Livingstone stood and slowly made his way to the kitchen. Detective Gary 'Schoolbags' Samson followed close behind. He grabbed the jug off the bench top, filled it with water and turned it on. "W-We were at a friends place, Maggie, playing cards. Her new boyfriend, Peter somebody. He was a real prick. So full of himself, Helen, that's my wife, couldn't stand him. Maggie's a bit desperate, but we both thought he was so awful we came home early. Good thing hey?" Mr. Livingstone was rambling. The adrenaline that had kept him going for the last half hour or so was wearing off and he was coming down. Coming down fast.He got himself a cup, then reached into the overhead cupboard for a jar of instant coffee. Gary noticed his hands were shaking. Suddenly the coffee jar slipped from his grasp, bounced off the bench top and smashed onto the floor, exploding into a thousand pieces and covering the floor with coffee powder. John began to shake uncontrollably, his breathing rapid and shallow. His legs gave way from under him and he slumped down onto the kitchen floor. His eyes filled then overflowed. "Oh Jesus", he wailed "Oh Jesus" over and over again. "How could anyone do that to my little girl Mr. Samson? He killed Steffy and then tried to do the same to my Becky, He raped her, cut her throat and left her to die"John let out a cry like a wounded animal. He hugged his knees to his chest and began to rock back and forth, bashing his head repeatedly against the cupboard door. Trying, perhaps, to distract himself from the unbearable pain he felt in his soul. Then John rolled over onto his side, curling up, covering his head with his arms, trying to block out the terrible thoughts that assaulted him. "He cut off her finger", he whispered, "raped her, slit her throat and then cut off her finger. Like some sort of trophy."Gary brushed away the broken glass fragments with his foot and joined the distraught man on the floor. He lifted the man into a sitting position and, leaning against the kitchen cupboard, placed his arm around John's shoulders. "It's alright John" he gently told him "I'm sure Rebecca will pull through, and I promise you, I will get the bastard who did this. I'll get him if it's the last thing I ever do".

Set in the cities and outback of Australia, 'Innocent Until Proven Deadly, tells of Detective Gary 'Schoolbags' Samson and his search for the soldier responsible for the rape and murder of three women.

About the Author

Kevin William Barry is the Australian author of numerous novels.
He lives on the Atherton Tableands, Far North Queensland
Australia with his wife Cathy